Any woman would find masterful, masculine and sexy Simon Hart and Chance Mackenzie a lot to handle, but to the virgins they were interested in, they were absolutely

Irresistible!

We're proud to present

SILHOUETTE SPOTLIGHT

a second chance to enjoy two bestselling novels by favourite authors every month —they're back by popular demand!

October 2005
Irresistible
Featuring
Beloved by Diana Palmer
A Game of Chance by Linda Howard

November 2005
Mistletoe Kisses
Featuring
Jingle Bell Baby by Kate Little
Code Name: Santa by Kayla Daniels

December 2005
Her Bodyguard
Featuring
Whitelaw's Wedding by Beverly Barton
The Renegade and the Heiress by Judith Duncan

Irresistible

DIANA PALMER
LINDA HOWARD

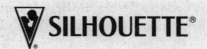

SILHOUETTE®

*Silhouette and Colophon are registered trademarks of
Harlequin Books S.A., used under licence.*

*Silhouette Books, Eton House, 18-24 Paradise Road,
Richmond, Surrey TW9 1SR*

IRRESISTIBLE © Harlequin Books S.A. 2005

The publisher acknowledges the copyright holders of the
individual works as follows:

Beloved © Diana Palmer 1999
A Game of Chance © Linda Hawington 2000

ISBN 0 373 60232 4

064-1005

*Printed and bound in Spain
by Litografia Rosés S.A., Barcelona*

Beloved
DIANA PALMER

DIANA PALMER

is a prolific writer who got her start as a newspaper reporter. As one of the top ten romance writers in America, she has a gift for telling the most sensual tales with charm and humour. Diana lives with her family in Cornelia, Georgia.

To Debbie and the staff at Books Galore,
in Watkinsville, GA
and to all my wonderful readers there
and in Athens.

Prologue

Simon Hart sat alone in the second row of the seats reserved for family. He wasn't really kin to John Beck, but the two had been best friends since college. John had been his only real friend. Now he was dead, and there *she* sat like a dark angel, her titian hair veiled in black, pretending to mourn the husband she'd cast off like a worn coat after only a month of marriage.

He crossed his long legs, shifting uncomfortably against the pew. He had an ache where his left arm ended just at the elbow. The sleeve was pinned, because he hated the prosthesis that disguised his handicap. He was handsome enough even with only one arm—he had thick, wavy black hair on a leonine head, with dark eyebrows and pale gray eyes. He was tall and well built, a dynamo of a man; former state attorney general of Texas and a nationally known trial lawyer, in addition to being one of the owners of the Hart

ranch properties, which were worth millions. He and
his brothers were as famous in cattle circles as Simon
was in legal circles. He was filthy rich and looked it.
But the money didn't make up for the loneliness. His
wife had died in the accident that took his arm. It had
happened just after Tira's marriage to John Beck.

Tira had nursed him in the hospital, and gossip had
run rampant. Simon was alluded to as the cause of the
divorce. Stupid idea, he thought angrily, because he
wouldn't have had Tira on a bun with catsup. Only a
week after the divorce, she was seen everywhere with
playboy Charles Percy, who was still her closest com-
panion. He was probably her lover, as well, Simon
thought with suppressed fury. He liked Percy no better
than he liked Tira. Strange that Percy hadn't come to
the funeral, but perhaps he did have some sense of
decency, however small.

Simon wondered if Tira realized how he really felt
about her. He had to be pleasant to her; anything else
would have invited comment. But secretly, he despised
her for what she'd done to John. Tira was cold inside—
selfish and cold and unfeeling. Otherwise, how could
she have turned John out after a month of marriage,
and then let him go to work on a dangerous oil rig in
the North Atlantic in an attempt to forget her? John
had died there this week, in a tragic accident, having
drowned in the freezing, churning waters before he
could be rescued. Simon couldn't help thinking that
John wanted to die. The letters he'd had from his friend
were full of his misery, his loneliness, his isolation
from love and happiness.

He glared in her direction, wondering how John's
father could bear to sit beside her like that, holding her
slender hand as if he felt as sorry for her as he felt for

himself at the loss of his son, his only child. Putting on a show for the public, he concluded irritably. He was pretending, to keep people from gossiping.

Simon stared at the closed casket and winced. It was like the end of an era for him. First he'd lost Melia, his wife, and his arm; now he'd lost John, too. He had wealth and success, but no one to share it with. He wondered if Tira felt any guilt for what she'd done to John. He couldn't imagine that she did. She was always flamboyant, vivacious, outgoing and mercurial. Simon had watched her without her knowing it, hating himself for what he felt when he looked at her. She was tall, beautiful, with long, glorious red-gold hair that went to her waist, pale green eyes and a figure right out of a fashion magazine. She could have been a model, but she was surprisingly shy for a pretty woman.

Simon had already been married when they met, and it had been at his prompting that John had taken Tira out for the first time. He'd thought they were compatible, both rich and pleasant people. It had seemed a marriage made in heaven; until the quick divorce. Simon would never have admitted that he threw Tira together with John to get her out of his own circle and out of the reach of temptation. He told himself that she was everything he despised in a woman, the sort of person he could never care for. It worked, sometimes. Except for the ache he felt every time he saw her; an ache that wasn't completely physical....

When the funeral service was over, Tira went out with John's father holding her elbow. The older man smiled sympathetically at Simon. Tira didn't look at him. She was really crying; he could see it even through the veil

Good, Simon thought with cold vengeance. *Good, I'm glad it's hurt you. You killed him, after all!*

He didn't look her way as he got into his black limousine and drove himself back to the office. He wasn't going to the graveside service. He'd had all of Tira's pathetic charade that he could stand. He wouldn't think about those tears in her tragic eyes, or the genuine sadness in her white face. He wouldn't think about her guilt or his own anger. It was better to put it all in the past and let it lie, forgotten. If he could. If he *could....*

One

The numbered lot of Hereford cattle at this San Antonio auction had been a real steal at the price, but Tira Beck had let it go without a murmur to the man beside her. She wouldn't ever have admitted that she didn't need to add to her substantial Montana cattle herd, which was managed by her foreman, since she lived in Texas. She'd only wanted to attend the auction because she knew Simon Hart was going to be there. Usually his four brothers in Jacobsville, Texas, handled cattle sales. But Simon, like Tira, lived in San Antonio where the auction was being held, so it seemed natural to let him make the bids.

He wasn't a rancher anymore. He was still tall and well built, with broad shoulders and a leonine head topped by thick black wavy hair. But the empty sleeve on his left side attested to the fact that his days of working cattle were pretty much over. It didn't affect his ability to make a living, at least. He was a former state attorney general and a nationally famous trial attorney who could pick and choose high-profile cases. He made a substantial wage. His voice was still his best asset, a deep velvety one that projected well in a courtroom. In addition to that was a dangerously deceptive manner that lulled witnesses into a false sense of security before he cut them to pieces on the stand. He had a verbal killer instinct, and he used it to good effect.

Tira, on the other hand, lived a hectic life doing charity work and was independently wealthy. She was a divorcée who had very little to do with men except on a platonic basis. There weren't many friends, either. Simon Hart and Charles Percy were the lot, and Charles was hopelessly in love with his brother's wife. She was the only person who knew that. Many people thought that she and Charles were lovers, which amused them both. She had her own secrets to keep. It suited her purposes to keep Simon in the dark about her emotional state.

"That was a hell of an anemic bid you made," Simon remarked as the next lot of cattle were led into the sale ring. "What's wrong with you today?"

"My heart's not in it," she replied. "I haven't had a lot to do with the Montana ranch since Dad died. I've given some thought to selling the property. I'll never live there again."

"You'll never sell. You have too many attachments to the ranch. Besides, you've got a good manager in place up there," he said pointedly.

She shrugged, pushing away a wisp of glorious hair that had escaped from the elegant French twist at her nape. "So I have."

"But you'd rather swan around San Antonio with Charles Percy," he murmured, his chiseled mouth twisting into a mocking smile.

She glanced at him with lovely green eyes and hid a carefully concealed hope that he might be jealous. But his expression gave no hint of his feelings. Neither did those pale gray eyes under thick black eyebrows. It was the same old story. The wreck eight years ago that had cost him his arm had also cost him his beloved wife, Melia. Despite their differences, no one had doubted his love for her. He hadn't been serious about a woman since her death, although he escorted his share of sophisticated women to local social events.

"What's the matter?" he asked when his sharp eyes caught her disappointment.

She shrugged in her elegant black pantsuit. "Oh, nothing. I just thought that you might like to stand up and threaten to kill Charles if he came near me again." She glanced at his shocked face and chuckled. "I'm kidding!" she chided.

His gaze cut into hers for a second and then they moved back to the sale ring. "You're in an odd mood today."

She sighed, returning her attention to the program in her beautifully manicured hands. "I've been in an odd mood for years. Not that I ever expect you to notice."

He closed his own program with a snap and glared down at her. "That's another thing that annoys me, those throwaway remarks you make. If you want to say something to me, just come out and say it."

Typically blunt, she thought. She looked straight at him and she made a gesture of utter futility with one hand. "Why bother?" she asked. Her eyes searched his and for the first time, a hint of the pain she felt was visible. She averted her gaze and stood up. "I've done all the bidding I came to do. I'll see you around, Simon."

She picked up her long black leather coat and folded it over her arm as she made her way out of the row and up the aisle to the exit. Eyes followed her, and not only because she was one of only a handful of women present. Tira was beautiful, although she never paid the least attention to her appearance except with a critical scrutiny. She wasn't vain.

Behind her, Simon sat scowling silently as she walked away. Her behavior piqued his curiousity. She was even more remote lately and hardly the same flamboyant, cheerful, friendly woman who'd been his secret solace since the accident that had cost Melia her life. His wife had been his whole heart, until that last night when she betrayed a secret that destroyed his pride and his love for her.

Fool that he was, he'd believed that Melia married him for love. In fact, she'd married him for money and kept a lover in the background. Her stark confession about her long-standing affair and the abortion of his child had shocked and wounded him. She'd even laughed at his consternation. Surely he didn't think she wanted a child? It would have ruined her figure and her social life. Besides, she'd added with calculating cruelty, she hadn't even been certain that it was Simon's, since she'd been with her lover during the same period of time.

The truth had cut like a knife into his pride. He'd taken his eyes off the road as they argued, and hit a patch of black ice on that winter evening. The car had gone off the road into a gulley and Melia, who had always refused to wear a seat belt because they were uncomfortable to her, had been thrown into the windshield headfirst. She'd died instantly. Simon had been luckier, but the airbag on his side of the car hadn't deployed, and the impact of the crash had driven the metal of the door right into his left arm. Amputation had been necessary to save his life.

He remembered that Tira had come to him in the hospital as soon as she'd heard about the wreck. She'd been in the process of divorcing John Beck, her husband, and her presence at Simon's side had started some malicious rumors about infidelity.

Tira never spoke of her brief marriage. She never spoke of John. Simon had already been married when they'd met for the first time, and it had been Simon who played matchmaker with John for her. John was his best friend and very wealthy, like Tira herself, and they seemed to have much in common. But the marriage had been over in less than a month.

He'd never questioned why, except that it seemed unlike Tira to throw in the towel so soon. Her lack of commitment to her marriage and her cavalier attitude about the divorce had made him uneasy. In fact, it had kept him from letting her come closer after he was widowed. She'd turned out to be shallow, and he wasn't risking his heart on a woman like that, even if she was a knockout to look at. As he knew firsthand, there was more to a marriage than having a beautiful wife.

John Beck, like Tira, had never said anything about the marriage. But John had avoided Simon ever since the divorce, and once when he'd had too much to drink at a party they'd both attended, he'd blurted out that Simon had destroyed his life, without explaining how.

The two men had been friends for several years until

John had married Tira. Not too long after the divorce,
John had moved out of Texas entirely and a year later
that tragic oil rig accident had claimed his life. Tira
had seemed devastated by John's death and for a time,
she went into seclusion. When she came back into society, she was a changed woman. The vivacious, happy
Tira of earlier days had become a dignified, elegant
matron who seemed to have lost her fighting spirit. She
went back to college and finished her degree in art. But
three years after graduation, she seemed to have done
little with her degree. Not that she skimped on charity
work or political fund-raising. She was a tireless
worker. Simon wondered sometimes if she didn't work
to keep from thinking.

Perhaps she blamed herself for John's death and
couldn't admit it. The loss of his former friend had hurt
Simon, too. He and Tira had become casual friends,
but nothing more, he made sure of it. Despite her at-
tractions, he wasn't getting caught by such a shallow
woman. But if their lukewarm friendship had been sat-
isfying once, in the past year, she'd become restless.
She was forever mentioning Charles Percy to him and
watching his reactions with strange, curious eyes. It
made him uncomfortable, like that crack she'd made
about kindling jealousy in him.

That remark hit him on the raw. Did she really think
he could ever want a woman of her sort, who could
discard a man she professed to love after only one
month of marriage and then parade around openly with
a philanderer like Charles Percy? He laughed coldly to
himself. That really would be the day. His heart was
safely encased in ice. Everyone thought he mourned
Melia—no one knew how badly she'd hurt him, or that
her memory disgusted him. It served as some protec-

tion against women like Tira. It kept him safe from any emotional involvement.

Unaware of Simon's hostile thoughts, Tira went to her silver Jaguar and climbed in behind the wheel. She paused there for a few minutes, with her head against the cold steering wheel. When was she ever going to learn that Simon didn't want her? It was like throwing herself at a stone wall, and it had to stop. Finally she admitted that nothing was going to change their shallow relationship. It was time she made a move to put herself out of Simon's orbit for good. Tearing her emotions to pieces wasn't going to help, and every time she saw him, she died a little more. All these years she'd waited and hoped and suffered, just to be around him occasionally. She'd lived too long on crumbs; she had to find some sort of life for herself without Simon, no matter how badly it hurt.

Her first step was to sell the Montana property. She put it on the market without a qualm, and her manager pooled his resources with a friend to buy it. With the ranch gone, she had no more reason to go to cattle auctions.

She moved out of her apartment that was only a couple of blocks from Simon's, too, and bought an elegant house on the outskirts of town on the Floresville Road. It was very Spanish, with graceful arches and black wrought-iron scrollwork on the fences that enclosed it. There was a cobblestone patio complete with a fountain and a nearby sitting area with a large goldfish pond and a waterfall cascading into it. The place was sheer magic. She thought she'd never seen anything quite so beautiful.

"It's the sort of house that needs a family," the real estate agent had remarked.

Tira hadn't said a word.

She remembered the conversation as she looked around the empty living room that had yet to be furnished. There would never be a family now. There would only be Tira, putting one foot in front of the other and living like a zombie in a world that no longer contained Simon, or hope.

It took her several weeks to have the house decorated and furnished. She chose every fabric, every color, every design herself. And when the house was finished, it echoed her own personality. Her real personality, that was, not the face she showed to the world.

No one who was acquainted with her would recognize her from the decor. The living room was done in soft white with a pastel blue, patterned wallpaper. The carpet was gray. The furniture was Victorian, rosewood chairs and a velvet-covered sofa. The other rooms were equally antique. The master bedroom boasted a four-poster bed in cherry wood, with huge ball legs and a headboard and footboard resplendent with hand-carved floral motifs. The curtains were Priscillas, the center panels of rose patterns with faint pink and blue coloring. The rest of the house followed the same subdued elegance of style and color. It denoted a person who was introverted, sensitive and old-fashioned. Which, under the flamboyant camouflage, Tira really was.

If there was a flaw, and it was a small one, it was the mouse who lived in the kitchen. Once the house was finished, and she'd moved in, she noticed him her first night in residence, sitting brazenly on a cabinet clutching a piece of cracker that she'd missed when she was cleaning up.

She bought traps and set them, hoping that the evil things would do their horrible work correctly and that she wouldn't be left nursing a wounded mouse. But the wily creature avoided the traps. She tried a cage and bait. That didn't work, either. Either the mouse was like those in that cartoon she'd loved, altered by some secret lab and made intelligent, or he was a figment of her imagination and she was going mad.

She laughed almost hysterically at the thought that Simon had finally, after all those years, driven her crazy.

Despite the mouse, she loved her new home. But even though she led a hectic life, there were still the lonely nights to get through. The walls began to close around her, despite the fact that she involved herself in charity work committees and was a tireless worker for political action fund-raisers. She worked long hours, and pushed herself unnecessarily hard. But she had no outside interests and too much money to work a daily job. What she needed was something interesting to do at home, to keep her mind occupied at night, when she was alone. But what?

It was a rainy Monday morning. She'd gone to the market for fresh vegetables and wasn't really watching where she was walking when she turned a corner and went right into the path of Corrigan Hart and his new wife, Dorothy.

"Good Lord," she gasped, catching her breath. "What are you two doing in San Antonio?"

Corrigan grinned. "Buying cattle," he said, drawing a radiant Dorothy closer. "Which reminds me, I didn't see you at the auction this time. I was standing in for Simon," he added. "For some reason, he's gone off sales lately."

"So have I, coincidentally," Tira remarked with a cool smile. It stung to think that Simon had given up those auctions that he loved so much to avoid her, but that was most certainly the reason. "I sold the Montana property."

Corrigan scowled. "But you loved the ranch. It was your last link with your father."

That was true, and it had made her sad for a time. She twisted the shopping basket in her hands. "I'd gotten into a rut," she said. "I wanted to change my life."

"So I noticed," Corrigan said quietly. "We went by your apartment to say hello. You weren't there."

"I moved." She colored a little at his probing glance. "I've bought a house across town."

Corrigan's eyes narrowed. "Someplace where you won't see Simon occasionally," he said gently.

The color in her cheeks intensified. "Where I won't see Simon at all, if you want the truth," she said bluntly. "I've given up all my connections with the past. There won't be any more accidental meetings with him. I've decided that I'm tired of eating my heart out for a man who doesn't want me. So I've stopped."

Corrigan looked surprised. Dorie eyed the other woman with quiet sympathy.

"In the long run, that's probably the best thing you could have done," Dorie said quietly. "You're still young and very pretty," she added with a smile. "And the world is full of men."

"Of course it is," Tira replied. She returned Dorie's smile. "I'm glad things worked out for you two, and

I'm very sorry I almost split you up,'' she added sincerely. ''Believe me, it was unintentional.''

''Tira, I know that,'' Dorie replied, remembering how a chance remark of Tira's in a local boutique had sent Dorie running scared from Corrigan. That was all in the past, now. ''Corrigan explained everything to me. I was uncertain of him then, that's all it really was. I'm not anymore.'' She hesitated. ''I'm sorry about you and Simon.''

Tira's face tautened. ''You can't make people love you,'' she said with a poignant sadness in her eyes. She shrugged fatalistically. ''He has a life that suits him. I'm trying to find one for myself.''

''Why don't you do a collection of sculptures and have a show?'' Corrigan suggested.

She chuckled. ''I haven't done sculpture in three years. Anyway, I'm not good enough for that.''

''You certainly are, and you've got an art degree. Use it.''

She considered that. After a minute, she smiled. ''Well, I do enjoy sculpting. I used to sell some of it occasionally.''

''See?'' Corrigan said. ''An idea presents itself.'' He paused. ''Of course, there's always a course in biscuit-making…?''

Knowing his other three brothers' absolute mania for that particular bread, she held up both hands. ''You can tell Leo and Cag and Rey that I have no plans to become a biscuit chef.''

''I'll pass the message along. But Dorie's dying for a replacement,'' he added with a grin at his wife. ''They'd chain her to the stove if I didn't intervene.'' He eyed Tira. ''They like you.''

''God forbid,'' she said with a mock shudder. ''For

years, people will be talking about how they arranged
your marriage.''

"They meant well," Dorie defended them.

"Baloney," Tira returned. "They had to have their
biscuits. Fatal error, Dorie, telling them you could
bake.''

"It worked out well, though, don't you think?" she
asked with a radiant smile at her husband.

"It did, indeed.''

Tira fielded a few more comments about her with-
drawal from the social scene, and then they were on
their way to the checkout stand. She deliberately held
back until they left, to avoid any more conversation.
They were a lovely couple, and she was fond of Corrigan, but he reminded her too much of Simon.

In the following weeks, she signed up for a refresher
sculpting course at her local community college, a
course for no credit since she already had a degree. In
no time, she was sculpting recognizable busts.

"You've got a gift for this," her instructor murmured as he walked around a fired head of her favorite
movie star. "There's money in this sort of thing, you
know. Big money.''

She almost groaned aloud. How could she tell this
dear man that she had too much money already? She
only smiled and thanked him for the compliment.

But he put her sculpture in a showing of his students'
work. It was seen by a local art gallery owner, who
tracked Tira down and offered her an exclusive showing. She tried to dissuade him, but the offer was all too
flattering to turn down. She agreed, with the priviso
that the proceeds would go to an outreach program

from the local hospital that worked in indigent neighborhoods.

After that, there was no stopping her. She spent hours at the task, building the strength in her hands and attuning her focus to more detailed pieces.

It wasn't until she finished one of Simon that she even realized she'd been sculpting him. She stared at it with contained fury and was just about to bring both fists down on top of it when the doorbell rang.

Irritated at the interruption, she tossed a cloth over the work in progress and went to answer it, wiping the clay from her hands on the way. Her hair was in a neat bun, to keep it from becoming clotted with clay, but her pink smock was liberally smeared with it. She looked a total mess, without makeup, even without shoes, wearing faded jeans and a knit top.

She opened the door without questioning who her visitor might be, and froze in place when Simon came into view on the porch. She noticed that he was wearing the prosthesis he hated so much, and she noted with interest that the hand at the end of it looked amazingly real.

She lifted her eyes to his, but her face wasn't welcoming. She didn't open the door to admit him. She didn't even smile.

"What do you want?" she asked.

He scowled. That was new. He'd visited Tira's apartment infrequently in the past, and he'd always been greeted with warmth and even delight. This was a cold reception indeed.

"I came to see how you were," he replied quietly. "You've been conspicuous by your absence around town lately."

"I sold the ranch," she said flatly.

He nodded. "Corrigan told me." He looked around at the front yard and the porch of the house. "This is nice. Did you really need a whole house?"

She ignored the question. "What do you want?" she asked again.

He noted her clay-smeared hands, and the smock she was wearing. "Laying bricks, are you?" he mused.

She didn't smile, as she might have once. "I'm sculpting."

"Yes, I remember that you took courses in college. You were quite good."

"I'm also quite busy," she said pointedly.

His eyebrow arched. "No invitation to have coffee?"

She hardened her resolve, despite the frantic beat of her heart. "I don't have time to entertain. I'm getting ready for an exhibit."

"At Bob Henderson's gallery," he said knowledgeably. "Yes, I know. I have part ownership in it." He held up his hand when she started to speak angrily. "I had no idea that he'd seen any of your work. I didn't suggest the showing. But I'd like to see what you've done. I do have a vested interest."

That put a new complexion on things. But she still didn't want him in her house. She'd never rid herself of the memory of him in it. Her reluctant expression told him that whatever she was feeling, it wasn't pleasure.

He sighed. "Tira, what's wrong?" he asked.

She stared at the cloth in her hands instead of at him. "Why does anything have to be wrong?"

"Are you kidding?" He drew in a heavy breath and wondered why he should suddenly feel guilty. "You've sold the ranch, moved house and given up any committees that would bring you into contact with me...."

She looked up in carefully arranged surprise. "Oh, heavens, it wasn't because of you," she lied convincingly. "I was in a rut, that's all. I decided that I needed to turn my life around. And I have."

His eyes glittered down at her. "Did turning it around include keeping me out of it?"

Her expression was unreadable. "I suppose it did. I was never able to get past my marriage. The memories were killing me, and you were a constant reminder."

His heavy eyebrows lifted. "Why should the memories bother you?" he asked with visible sarcasm. "You didn't give a damn about John. You divorced him a month after the wedding and never seemed to care if you saw him again or not. Barely a week later, you were keeping company with Charles Percy."

The bitterness in his voice opened her eyes to something she'd never seen. Why, he blamed her for John's death. She didn't seem to breathe as she looked up into those narrow, cold, accusing eyes. It had been three years since John's death and she'd never known that Simon felt this way.

Her hands on the cloth stilled. It was the last straw. She'd loved this big, formidable man since the first time she'd seen him. There had never been anyone else in her heart, despite the fact that she'd let him push her into marrying John. And now, years too late, she discovered the reason that Simon had never let her come close to him. It was the last reason she'd ever have guessed.

She let out a harsh breath. "Well," she said with forced lightness, "the things we learn about people we thought we knew!" She tucked the smeared cloth into a front pocket of her equally smeared smock. "So I killed John. Is that what you think, Simon?"

The frontal assault was unexpected. His guard was down and he didn't think before he spoke. "You played at marriage," he accused quietly. "He loved you, but you had nothing to give him. A month of marriage and you were having divorce papers served to him. You let him go without a word when he decided to work on oil rigs, despite the danger of it. You didn't even try to stop him. Funny, but I never realized what a shallow, cold woman you were until then. Everything you are is on the outside," he continued, blind to her white, drawn face. "Glorious hair, a pretty face, sparkling eyes, pretty figure...and nothing under it all. Not even a spark of compassion or love for anyone except yourself."

She wasn't breathing normally. Dear God, she thought, don't let me faint at his feet! She swallowed once, then twice, trying to absorb the horror of what he was saying to her.

"You never said a word," she said in a haunted tone. "In all these years."

"I didn't think it needed saying," he said simply. "We've been friends, of a sort. I hope we still are." He smiled, but it didn't reach his eyes. "As long as you realize that you'll never be allowed within striking distance of my heart. I'm not a masochist, even if John was."

Later, when she was alone, she was going to die. She knew it. But right now, pride spared her any further hurt.

She went past him, very calmly, and opened the front door, letting in a scent of dead leaves and cool October breeze. She didn't speak. She didn't look at him. She just stood there.

He walked past her, hesitating on the doorstep. His narrow eyes scanned what he could see of her face, and its whiteness shocked him. He wondered why she looked so torn up, when he was only speaking the truth.

Before he could say a thing, she closed the door, threw the dead bolt and put on the chain latch. She walked back toward her studio, vaguely aware that he was trying to call her back.

The next morning, the housekeeper she'd hired, Mrs. Lester, found her sprawled across her bed with a loaded pistol in her hands and an empty whiskey bottle lying on its side on the stained gray carpet. Mrs. Lester quickly looked in the bathroom and found an empty bottle that had contained tranquilizers. She jerked up the telephone and dialed the emergency services number with trembling hands. When the ambulance came screaming up to the front of the house, Tira still hadn't moved at all.

TWO

It took all of that day for Tira to come out of the stupor and discover where she was. It was a very nice hospital room, but she didn't remember how she'd gotten there. She was foggy and disoriented and very sick to her stomach.

Dr. Ron Gaines, an old family friend, came in the door ahead of a nurse in neat white slacks and a multicolored blouse with many pockets.

"Get her vitals," the doctor directed.

"Yes, sir."

While her temperature and blood pressure and pulse rate were taken, Dr. Gaines leaned against the wall quietly making notations on her chart. The nurse reported her findings, he charted them and he motioned her out of the room.

He moved to the bed and sat down in the chair beside Tira. "If anyone had asked me two weeks ago, I'd have said that you were the most levelheaded woman I knew. You've worked tirelessly for charities here, you've spearheaded fund drives... Good God, what's the matter with you?''

''I had a bad blow,'' she confessed in a subdued tone. ''It was unexpected and I did something stupid. I got drunk.''

''Don't hand me that! Your housekeeper found a loaded pistol in your hand.''

''Oh, that.'' She started to tell him about the mouse, the one she'd tried unsuccessfully to catch for weeks. Last night, with half a bottle of whiskey in her, shooting the varmint had seemed perfectly logical. But her dizzy mind was slow to focus. ''Well, you see—'' she began.

He sighed heavily and cut her off. ''Tira, if it wasn't a suicide attempt, I'm not a doctor. Tell me the truth.''

She blinked. ''I wouldn't try to kill myself!'' she said, outraged. She took a slow breath. ''I was just a little depressed, that's all. I found out yesterday that Simon holds me responsible for John's death.''

There was a long, shocked pause. ''He doesn't know why the marriage broke up?''

She shook her head.

''Why didn't you tell him, for God's sake?'' he exclaimed.

''It isn't the sort of thing you tell a man about his best friend. I never dreamed that he blamed me. We've been friends. He never wanted it to be anything except friendship, and I assumed it was because of the way he felt about Melia. Apparently I've been five kinds of an idiot.'' She looked up at him. ''Six, if you count last night,'' she added, flushing.

''I'm glad you agree that it was stupid.''

She frowned. "Did you pump my stomach?"

"Yes."

"No wonder I feel so empty," she said. "Why did you do that?" she asked. "I only had whiskey on an empty stomach!"

"Your housekeeper found an empty tranquilizer bottle in the bathroom," he said sternly.

"Oh, that," she murmured. "The bottle was empty. I never throw anything away. That prescription was years old. It's one Dr. James gave me to get me through final exams in college three years ago. I was a nervous wreck!" She gave him another unblinking stare. "But you listen here, I'm not suicidal. I'm the least suicidal person I know. But everybody has a breaking point and I reached mine. So I got drunk. I never touch alcohol. Maybe that's why it hit me so hard."

He took her hand in his and held it gently. While he was trying to find the words, the door suddenly swung open and a wild-eyed Simon Hart entered the room. He looked as if he'd been in an accident, his face was so white. He stared at Tira without speaking.

It wasn't his fault, really, but she hated him for what she'd done to herself. Her eyes told him so. There was no welcome in them, no affection, no coquettishness. She looked at him as if she wished she had a weapon in her hands.

"You get out of my room!" she raged at him, sitting straight up in bed.

The doctor's eyebrows shot straight up. Tira had never raised her voice to Simon before. Her face was flaming red, like her wealth of hair, and her green eyes were shooting bolts of lightning in Simon's direction.

"Tira," Simon began uncertainly.

"Get out!" she repeated, ashamed of being accused

of a suicide attempt in the first place. It was bad enough that she'd lost control of herself enough to get drunk. She glared at Simon as if he was the cause of it all—which he was. "Out!" she repeated, when he didn't move, gesturing wildly with her arm.

He wouldn't go, and she burst into tears of frustrated fury. Dr. Gaines got between Simon and Tira and hit the Call button. "Get in here, stat," he said into the intercom, following the order with instructions for a narcotic. He glanced toward Simon, standing frozen in the doorway. "Out," he said without preamble. "I'll speak to you in a few minutes."

Simon moved aside to let the skurrying nurse into the room with a hypodermic. He could hear Tira's sobs even through the door. He moved a little way down the hall, to where his brother Corrigan was standing.

It had been Corrigan whom the housekeeper called when she discovered Tira. And he'd called Simon and told him only that Tira had been taken to the hospital in a bad way. He had no knowledge of what had pushed Tira over the edge or he might have thought twice about telling his older brother at all.

"I heard her. What happened?" Corrigan asked, jerking his head toward the room.

"I don't know," Simon said huskily. He leaned back against the wall beside his brother. His empty sleeve drew curious glances from a passerby, but he ignored it. "She saw me and started yelling." He broke off. His eyes were filled with torment. "I've never seen her like this."

"Nobody has," Corrigan said flatly. "I never figured a woman like Tira for a suicide."

Simon gaped at him. "A *what?*"

"What would you call combining alcohol and tranquilizers?'' Corrigan demanded. ''Good God, Mrs. Lester said she had a loaded pistol in her hands!''

''A *pistol...?*'' Simon closed his eyes on a shudder and ran a hand over his drawn face. He couldn't bear to think about what might have happened. He was certain that he'd prompted her actions. He couldn't forget, even now, the look on her face when he'd almost flatly accused her of killing John. She hadn't said a word to defend herself. She'd gone quiet; dangerously quiet. He should never have left her alone. Worse, he should never have said anything to her. He'd thought her a strong, self-centered woman who wouldn't feel criticism. Now, almost too late, he knew better.

''I went to see her yesterday,'' Simon confessed in a haunted tone. ''She'd made some crazy remark at the last cattle auction about trying to make me jealous. She said she was only teasing, but it hit me the wrong way. I told her that she wasn't the sort of woman I could be jealous about. Then, yesterday, I told her how I felt about her careless attitude toward the divorce only a month after she married John, and letting him go off to get himself killed on an oil rig.'' His broad shoulders rose and fell defeatedly. ''I shouldn't have said it, but I was angry that she'd tried to make me jealous, as if she thought I might actually feel attracted to her.'' He sighed. ''I thought she was so hard that nothing I said would faze her.''

''And I thought I used to be blind,'' Corrigan said.

Simon glanced at him, scowling. ''What do you mean?''

Corrigan looked at his brother and tried to speak. Finally he just smiled faintly and turned away. ''Forget it.''

The door to Tira's room opened a minute later and

Dr. Gaines came out. He spotted the two men down the hall and joined them.

"Don't go back in there," he told Simon flatly. "She's too close to the edge already. She doesn't need you to push her the rest of the way."

"I didn't do a damned thing," Simon shot back, and now he looked dangerous, "except walk in the door!"

Dr. Gaines' lips thinned. He glanced at Corrigan, who only shrugged and shook his head.

"I'm going to try to get her to go to a friend of mine, a therapist. She could use some counseling," Gaines added.

"She's not a nut case," Simon said, affronted.

Dr. Gaines looked into that cold, unaware face and frowned. "You were state attorney general for four years," he said. "You're still a well-known trial lawyer, an intelligent man. How can you be this stupid?"

"Will someone just tell me what's going on?" Simon demanded.

Dr. Gaines looked at Corrigan, who held out a hand, palm-up, inviting the doctor to do the dirty work.

"She'll kill us both if she finds out we told him," Gaines remarked to Corrigan.

"It's better than letting her die."

"Amen." He looked at Simon, who was torn between puzzlement and fury. "Simon, she's been in love with you for years," Dr. Gaines said in a hushed, reluctant tone. "I tried to get her to give up the ranch and all that fund-raising mania years ago, because they were only a way for her to keep near you. She wore herself out at it, hoping against hope that if you were in close contact, you might begin to feel something for her, but I knew that wasn't going to happen. All I had to do was see you together to realize she didn't have a chance. Am I right?'' he asked Corrigan, who nodded.

Simon leaned back against the wall. He felt as if someone had put a knife right through him. He couldn't even speak.

''What you said to her was a kindness, although I don't imagine you see it that way now,'' Dr. Gaines continued doggedly. ''She had to be made to see that she couldn't go on living a lie, and the changes in her life recently are proof that she's realized how you feel about her. She'll accept it, in time, and get on with her life. It will be the very best thing for her. She's trying to be all things to all people, until she was worn to a nub. She's been headed for a nervous breakdown for weeks, the way she's pushed herself, with this one-woman art show added to the load she was already carrying. But she'll be all right.'' He put a sympathetic hand on Simon's good arm. ''It's not your fault. She's levelheaded about everything except you. But if you want to help her, for old time's sake, stay away from her. She's got enough on her plate right now.''

He nodded politely to Corrigan and went on down the hall.

Simon still hadn't moved, or spoken. He was pale and drawn, half crazy from the doctor's revelation.

Corrigan got on the other side of him and took his arm, drawing him along. ''We'll get a cup of coffee somewhere on the way back to your office,'' he told his older brother.

Simon allowed himself to be pulled out the door. He wasn't sure he remembered how to walk. He felt shattered.

Minutes later, he was sitting in a small café with his brother, drinking strong coffee.

"She tried to kill herself over me," Simon said finally.

"She missed. She won't try again. They'll make sure of it." He leaned forward. "Simon, she's been overextending for years, you know that. No one woman could have done as much as she has without risking her health, if not her sanity. If it hadn't been what you said to her, it would have been something else…maybe even this showing at the gallery that she was working night and day to get ready for."

Simon forced himself to breathe normally. He still couldn't quite believe it all. He sipped his coffee and stared into space.

"Did you know how she felt?" he asked Corrigan.

"She didn't tell me, if that's what you mean," his brother said. "But it was fairly obvious, the way she talked about you. I felt sorry for her. We all knew how much you loved Melia, that you've never let yourself get close to another woman since the wreck. Tira had to know that there was no hope in that direction."

The coffee in Simon's cup sloshed a little as he put it down. "It seems so clear now," he remarked absently. "She was always around, even when there didn't seem a reason for it. She worked on committees for organizations I belonged to, she did charity work for businesses where I was a trustee." He shook his head. "But I never noticed."

"I know."

He looked up. "John knew," he said suddenly.

Corrigan hesitated. Then he nodded.

Simon sucked in a harsh breath. "Good God, I broke up their marriage!"

"Maybe. I don't know. Tira never talks about John." His eyes narrowed thoughtfully. "But haven't you ever noticed that she and John's father are still friends? He doesn't blame her for his son's death. Shouldn't he, if it was all Tira's fault?"

Simon didn't want to think about it. He was sick to his stomach. "I pushed her at John," he recalled.

"I remember. They seemed to have a lot in common."

"They had me in common." Simon laughed bitterly. "She loved *me*..." He took a long sip of coffee and burned his mouth. The pain was welcome; it took his mind off his conscience.

"She can't ever know that we told you that," Corrigan said firmly, looking as formidable as his brother. "She's entitled to salvage a little of her pride. The newspapers got hold of the story, Simon. It's in the morning edition. The headline's really something—local socialite in suicide attempt. She's going to have hell living it down. I don't imagine they'll let her see a newspaper, but someone will tell her, just the same." His voice was harsh. "Some people love rubbing salt in wounds."

Simon rested his forehead against his one hand. He was so drained that he could barely function. It had been the worst day of his life; in some ways, worse than the wreck that had cost him everything.

For years, Tira's eyes had warmed at his approach, her mouth had smiled her welcome. She'd become radiant just because he was near her, and he hadn't known how she felt, with all those blatant signs.

Now, this morning, she'd looked at him with such hatred that he still felt sick from the violence of it. Her eyes had flashed fire, her face had burned with rage. He'd never seen her like that.

Corrigan searched his brother's worn face. "Don't take it so hard, Simon. None of this is your fault. She put too much pressure on herself and now she's paying the consequences. She'll be all right."

"She loved me," he said again, speaking the words harshly, as if he still couldn't believe them.

"You can't make people love you back," his brother replied. "Funny, Dorie and I saw her in the grocery store a few weeks ago, and she said that same thing. She had no illusions about the way you felt, regardless of how it looks."

Simon's eyes burned with anguish. "You don't know what I said to her, though. I accused her of killing John, of being so unconcerned about his happiness that she let him go into a dangerous job that he didn't have the experience to handle." His face twisted. "I said that she was shallow and cold and selfish, that I had nothing but contempt for her and that I'd never let a woman like her get close to me..." His eyes closed. "Dear God, how it must have hurt her to hear that from me."

Corrigan let out a savage breath. "Why didn't you just load the gun for her?"

"Didn't I?" the older man asked with tortured eyes.

Corrigan backed off. "Well, it's water under the bridge now. She's safely out of your life and she'll learn to get along on her own, with a little help. You can go back to your law practice and consider yourself off the endangered species list."

Simon didn't say another word. He stared into his coffee with sightless eyes until it grew cold.

* * *

Tira slept for the rest of the day. When she opened her eyes, the room was empty. There was a faint light from the wall and she felt pleasantly drowsy.

The night nurse came in, smiling, to check her vital signs. She was given another dose of medicine. Minutes later, without having dared remember the state she was in that morning, she went back to sleep.

When she woke up, a tall, blond, handsome man with dark eyes was sitting by the bed, looking quite devastating in white slacks and a red pullover knit shirt.

"Charles," she mumbled, and smiled. "How nice of you to come!"

"Who'll I talk to if you kill yourself, you idiot?" he muttered, glowering at her. "What a stupid thing to do."

She pushed herself up on an elbow, and pushed the mass of red-gold hair out of her eyes. She made a rough sound in her throat. "I wasn't trying to commit suicide!" she grumbled. "I got drunk and Mrs. Lester found an old empty prescription bottle and went ballistic." She shifted sleepily and yawned. "Well, I can't blame her, I guess. I still had the pistol in my hand and there was a hole in the wall…"

"Pistol!?"

"Calm down," she said, grimacing. "My head hurts. Yes, a pistol." She grinned at him a little sheepishly. "I was going to shoot the mouse."

His eyes widened. "Excuse me?"

"There's a mouse," she said. "I've set traps and put out bait, and he just keeps coming back into my kitchen. After a couple of drinks, I remembered a scene in *True Grit,* where John Wayne shot a rat, and when I got halfway through the whiskey bottle, it seemed perfectly logical that I should do that to my mouse."

She chuckled a little weakly. "You had to be there," she added helplessly.

"I suppose so." He searched her bloodshot eyes. "All those charity events, anybody calls and asks you to help, and you work day and night to organize things. You're everybody's helper. Now you're working on a collection of sculpture and still trying to keep up with your social obligations. I'm surprised you didn't fall out weeks ago. I tried to tell you. You know I did."

She nodded and sighed. "I know. I just didn't realize how hard I was working."

"You never do. You need to get married and have kids. That would keep you busy."

She lifted both eyebrows. "Are you offering to sacrifice yourself?"

He chuckled. "Maybe it would be the best thing for both of us," he said wistfully. "We're in love with people who don't want us. At least we like each other."

"Yes. But marriage should be more than that."

He shrugged. "Just a thought." He leaned over and patted her hand. "Get well. There's a society ball next week and you have to go with me. She's going to be there."

Tira knew who *she* was—his sister-in-law, the woman that Percy would have died to marry. She'd never noticed him, despite his blazing good looks, before she married his half brother. In fact, she seemed to actually dislike him, and Charles's half brother was twenty years her senior, a stiff-necked stuffed-shirt whom nobody in their circle had any use for. The marriage was a complete mystery.

"I don't have a dress."

"Buy one," he instructed.

She hesitated.

"I'll protect you from him," he said after a minute, having realized that Simon would most likely be in attendance. "I swear on my glorious red Mark VIII that I won't leave your side for an instant all evening."

She gave him a wary glance. His mania about that car was well-known. He wouldn't even entrust it to a car wash. He washed and waxed it lovingly, inch by inch, and called it "Big Red."

"Well, if you're willing to swear on your car," she agreed.

He grinned. "You can ride in it."

"I'm honored!"

"I brought you some flowers," he added. "One of the nurses volunteered to put them in a vase for you."

She gave him a cursory appraisal and smiled. "The way you look, I'm not surprised. Women fall over each other to get to you."

"Not the one I wanted," he said sadly. "And now it's too late."

She slid her hand into his and pressed it gently. "I'm sorry."

"So am I." He shrugged. "Isn't it a damned shame? I mean, look what they're missing!"

She knew he was talking about Simon and the woman Charles wanted, and she grinned in spite of herself. "It's their loss. I'd love to go to the ball with you. He'll let me out of here today. Like to take me home?"

"Sure!"

But when the doctor came into the room, he was reluctant to let her leave.

She was sitting on the side of the bed. She gave him

a long, wise look. "I wasn't lying," she said. "Suicide was the very last thing from my mind."

"With a loaded pistol, which had been fired."

She pursed her lips. "Didn't anyone notice where the shot landed? At a round hole in the baseboard?"

He frowned.

"The mouse!" she said. "I've been after him for weeks! Don't you watch old John Wayne movies? It was in *True Grit!*"

All at once, realization dawned in his eyes. "The rat writ."

"Exactly!"

He burst out laughing. "You were going to shoot the mouse?"

"I'm a good shot," she protested. "Well, when I'm sober. I won't miss him next time!"

"Get a trap."

"He's too wily," she protested. "I've tried traps and baits."

"Buy a cat."

"I'm allergic to fur," she confessed miserably.

"How about those electronic things you plug into the wall?"

She shook her head. "Tried it. He bit the electrical cord in half."

"Didn't it kill him?"

Her eyebrows arched. "No. Actually he seemed even healthier afterward. I'll bet he'd enjoy arsenic. Nope, I have to shoot him."

The doctor and Charles looked at each other. Then they both chuckled.

The doctor did see her alone later, for a few minutes while Charles was bringing the car around to the hospital entrance. "Just one more thing," he said gently.

"Regardless of what Simon said, you didn't kill John. Nobody, no woman, could have stopped what happened. He should never have married you in the first place."

"Simon kept throwing us together," she said. "He thought we made the perfect couple," she added bitterly.

"Simon never knew," he said. "I'm sure John didn't tell him, and you kept your own silence."

She averted her eyes. "John was the best friend Simon had in the world. If he'd wanted Simon to know, he'd have told him. That being the case, I never felt that I had the right." She looked at him. "I still don't. And you're not to tell him, either. He deserves to have a few unshattered illusions. His life hasn't been a bed of roses so far. He's missing an arm, and he's still mourning Melia."

"God knows why," Dr. Gaines added, because he'd known all about the elegant Mrs. Hart, things that even Tira didn't know.

"He loved her," she said simply. "There's no accounting for taste, is there?"

He smiled gently. "I guess not."

"You know, you really are a nice man, Dr. Gaines," she added.

He chuckled. "That's what my wife says all the time."

"She's right," she agreed.

"Don't you have family?"

She shook her head. "My father died of a heart attack, and my mother died even before he did. She had cancer. It was hard to watch, especially for Dad. He loved her too much."

"You can't love people too much."

She looked up at him with such sadness that her face seemed to radiate it. "Yes, you can," she said solemnly. "But I'm going to learn how to stop."

Charles pulled up at the curb and Dr. Gaines waved them off.

"Look at him," Charles said with a grin. "He's drooling! He wants my car." He stepped down on the accelerator. "Everybody wants my car. But it's mine. Mine!"

"Charles, you're getting obsessed with this automobile," she cautioned.

"I am not!" He glanced at her. "Careful, you'll get fingerprints on the window. And I do hope you wiped your shoes before you got in."

She didn't know whether to laugh or cry.

"I'm kidding!" he exclaimed.

She let out a sigh of relief. "And Dr. Gaines wanted *me* to have therapy," she murmured.

He threw her a glare. "I do not need therapy. Men love their cars. One guy even wrote a song about how much he loved his truck."

She glanced around the luxurious interior of the pretty car, leather coated with a wood-grained dash, and nodded. "Well, I could love Big Red," she had to confess. She leaned back against the padded headrest and closed her eyes.

He patted the dash. "Hear that, guy? You're getting to her!"

She opened one eye. "I'm calling the therapist the minute we get to my house."

He lifted both blond eyebrows. "Does he like cars?"

"I give up!"

* * *

When she arrived home, she was met at the door by a hovering, worried Mrs. Lester.

"It was an old, empty prescription bottle!" Tira told the kindly older woman. "And the pistol wasn't for me, it was for that mouse we can't catch in the kitchen!"

"The mouse?"

"Well, we can't trap him or drive him out, can we?" she queried.

The housekeeper blushed all the way to her white hairline and wrung her hands in the apron. "It was the way it looked…"

Tira went forward and hugged her. "You're a doll and I love you. But I was only drunk."

"You never drink," Mrs. Lester stated.

"I was driven to it," she replied.

Mrs. Lester looked at Charles. "By him?" she asked with a twinkle in her dark eyes. "You shouldn't let him hang around here so much, if he's driving you to drink."

"See?" he murmured, leaning down. "She wants my car, that's why she wants me to leave. She can't stand having to look at it day after day. She's obsessed with jealousy, eaten up with envy…"

"What's he talking about?" Mrs. Lester asked curiously.

"He thinks you want his car."

Mrs. Lester scoffed. "That long red fast flashy thing?" She sniffed. "Imagine me, riding around in something like that!"

Charles grinned. "Want to?" he asked, raising and lowering his eyebrows.

She chuckled. "You bet I do! But I'm much too old for sports cars, dear. Tira's just right."

"Yes, she is. And she needs coddling."

"I'll fatten her up and see that she gets her rest. I knew I should never have let her talk me into that vacation. The first time I leave her in a month, and look what happens! And the newspapers...!" She stopped so suddenly that she almost bit her tongue through.

Tira froze in place. "What newspapers?"

Mrs. Lester made a face and exchanged a helpless glance with Charles.

"You, uh, made the headlines," he said reluctantly.

She groaned. "Oh, for heaven's sake, there goes my one-woman show!"

"No, it doesn't," Charles replied. "I spoke to Bob this morning before I came after you. He said that the phone's rung off the hook all morning with queries about the show. He figures you'll make a fortune from the publicity."

"I don't need..."

"Yes, but the outreach program does," he reminded her. He grinned. "They'll be able to buy a new van!"

She smiled, but her heart wasn't in it. She didn't want to be notorious, whether or not she deserved to.

"Cheer up," he said. "It'll be old news tomorrow. Just don't answer the phone for a day or two. It will blow over as soon as some new tragedy catches the editorial eye."

"I guess you're right."

"Next Saturday," he reminded her. "I'll pick you up at six."

"Where will you be until then?" she asked, surprised, because he often came by for coffee in the afternoon.

"Memphis," he said with a sigh. "A business deal

that I have to conduct personally. I'll be out of town for a week. Bad timing, too."

"I'll be fine," she assured him. "Mrs. Lester's right here."

"I guess so. I do worry about you." He smiled sheepishly. "I don't have any family, either. You're sort of the only relative I have, even though you aren't."

"Same here."

He searched her eyes. "Two of a kind, aren't we? We loved not wisely, and too well."

"As you said, it's their loss," she said stubbornly. "Have a safe trip. Are you taking Big Red?"

He shook his head. "They won't let me take him on the plane," he said. "Walters is going to stand guard over him in the garage with a shotgun while I'm gone, though. Maybe he won't pine."

She burst out laughing. "I'm glad I have you for a friend," she said sincerely.

He took her hand and held it gently. "That works both ways. Take care. I'll phone you sometime during the week, just to make sure you're okay. If you need me..."

"I have your mobile number," she assured him. "But I'll be fine."

"See you next week, then."

"Thanks for the ride home," she said.

He shrugged and flashed her a white smile. "My pleasure."

She watched him drive away with sad eyes. She was going to have to live down the bad publicity without telling her side of the story. Well, what did it matter, she reasoned. It could, after all, have been worse.

Three

The week passed slowly until the charity ball on Saturday evening. It was to be a lavish one, hosted by the Carlisles, a founding family in the area and large supporters of the local hospital's charity work. Their huge brick mansion was just south of the perimeter of San Antonio, set in a grove of mesquite and pecan trees with its own duck pond and a huge formal garden. Tira had always loved coming to the house in the past for these gatherings, but she knew that Simon would be on the guest list. It was going to be hard facing him again after what had happened. It was going to be difficult appearing in public at all.

She did plan to go down with all flags flying, however, having poured her exquisite figure into a sleeveless, long black velvet evening gown with lace appliqués in entrancing places and a lace-up bodice that left little gaps from her diaphragm to her breasts. Her hair was in an elegant French twist with a diamond clip that matched her dangling earrings and delicate waterfall diamond necklace. She looked wealthy and sophisticated and Charles gave her a wicked grin when she came through to the living room with a black velvet and jewel wrap over one bare shoulder. It was November and the weather was unseasonably warm, so the wrap was just right.

Charles dressed up nicely, she thought, studying him. His tuxedo played up his extreme good looks and his fairness.

"Don't we make a pair?" he mused, glancing in the hall mirror at them. "Pity it isn't the right one."

"We'll both survive the evening," she assured him.

"Only if we drink hard enough," he said with graveyard humor. Then he noticed her expression and grimaced. "Sorry," he said genuinely.

"No need to apologize," she replied with a wry smile. "I did something stupid and had the misfortune to be found doing it. I'll survive all the gossip. But whatever you do, don't leave me alone with Simon, okay?"

"Count on it. What are friends for?"

She smiled at him. "To get us through rough times," she said, and was suddenly very grateful that she had a friend as good as Charles.

Charles chided her gently for her growing and obvious nervousness as he drove rapidly down the road that led to the Carlisle estate. "Don't worry so. You're old news," he reminded her. "There's the local political scandal to latch onto now."

"What political scandal?" she asked. "And how do you know about it when you've been out of town?"

"Because our lieutenant governor has been participating in a conference on the problems of inner cities in Memphis. I sat next to him on the flight home," he said smugly. Keeping his eyes on the road, he leaned toward her. "It seems that the attorney general intervened in a criminal case for a friend. The criminal he got paroled was serving time for armed robbery, but when he got out, he went right home and killed his ex-wife for testifying against him and is now back in prison. But the wheels of political change are going to roll over the governor's fair-haired boy."

"Oh, my goodness," she burst out. "But he was only doing a kindness. How could he know...?"

"He couldn't, and he isn't really to blame, but the opposition party is going to use it to crucify him. I understand his resignation is forthcoming momentarily."

"What a shame," Tira said honestly. "He's done a wonderful job. I met him at one of the charity benefits earlier this year and thought how lucky we were to have elected someone so capable to the position! Now, if he resigns, I guess the governor will have to temporarily appoint someone to finish his term."

"No doubt he will."

"Maybe he'll slide out of it. Lots of politicians do."

"Not this time, I'm afraid," Charles said. "He's made some bitter enemies since he took office. They'll love the opportunity to settle the score."

She recalled that Simon had antagonized plenty of people when he held the office of state attorney general. But it would have taken more than a scandal to unseat him. He had a clever habit of turning weapons against their wielders.

She closed her eyes and ground her teeth as she realized how pitiful she was about him, still. Everything reminded her of Simon. She hadn't wanted to come tonight, either, but the alternative was to stay home and let the whole city know what a coward she was. She had to hold her head up high and pretend that everything was fine, when her whole world was lying in shards around her feet.

She hadn't tried to kill herself, but one particularly lurid newspaper account said she had, and added that it had been over former attorney general Simon Hart, who'd rejected her. It was in a newspaper published by a relative of Jill Sinclair, a woman who'd been a rival of Tira's for Simon during the past few years. Tira had been even more humiliated at that particular story, but when she'd phoned the reporter who wrote it, he denied any knowledge of Jill Sinclair. Still, she was certain dear Jill had a hand in it.

Tira shuddered, realizing that Simon must have seen the story, too. He'd know what a fool she'd been over him, which was just one more humiliation. Living that down wasn't going to be easy. But she did have Charles beside her. And he had his own ordeal to face, because his sister-in-law would certainly be present.

A valet came to park the car for Charles, who was torn between escorting Tira inside or accompanying the elegantly dressed young man assigned to the car placement to make sure he didn't put a scratch on "Big Red."

"Go ahead," Tira said with amused resignation. "I'll wait on the steps for you."

"You're such a doll," he murmured and made a kissing motion toward her. "How many women in the world would understand a man's passion for his car?

Here, son, I'll just ride down with you to the parking lot.''

The valet seemed torn between shock and indignation.

''He's in love with it!'' Tira called to the young man. ''He can't help himself. Just humor him!''

The valet broke into a wide grin and climbed under the steering wheel.

It was unfortunate that while she was waiting on the wide porch for Charles to return, Simon and his date got out of his elegant Town Car at the steps and let the valet drive it off. He looked devastating, as usual. He was wearing the prosthesis, she noticed, and wondered at how much he seemed to use it these days. Just after the wreck, he wouldn't be caught dead wearing an artificial arm.

The woman with him was Jill Sinclair herself, a socialite, twice divorced and wealthy, with short black hair and dark eyes and a figure that drew plenty of interest. It would, Tira thought wickedly, considering that her red sequined dress must have been sprayed on and the paint ran out at midthigh. Advertising must pay, she mused, because Simon certainly seemed pleased as he smiled down at the small woman and held her elbow as they climbed up the steps.

He didn't see Tira until they were almost at the top. When he did, he seemed to jerk, as if the sight of her was unexpected.

She didn't let anything of her feelings show, despite the pain of seeing him now when her whole life had been laid bare in the press. She did her best not to let her embarrassment show, either. She smiled carelessly and nodded politely at the couple and deliberately turned away in the direction where Charles and the valet were just coming into view.

"Why, how brave she is," Jill Sinclair purred to Simon, just loud enough for Tira to hear her. "I'd never have had the nerve to face all these people after that humiliating story in the—Simon!"

Her voice died completely. Tira didn't look toward them. Her face was flaming and she knew her accelerated heartbeat was making her shake visibly. She and Jill had never liked each other, but the woman seemed to be looking for a way to hurt her. She was obviously exuding her power since she'd finally managed to get Simon to notice her and take her out. God knew, she'd been after him for years. Tira's fall from grace had obviously benefitted her.

Charles bounded up the steps and took Tira's arm. "Sorry about that," he said sheepishly.

"You love your car," she replied with a warm smile. "I understand."

"You're one in a million," he mused. His hand fell to grasp hers, and when she looked inside the open doors she knew why. His half brother was there, and so was his sister-in-law, looking unhappy.

"Gene," he called to his older half brother. "Nice to see you." He shook the other man's hand. Gene was tall and severe-looking with thinning gray hair. The woman beside him was tiny and blond and lovely, but she had the most tragic brown eyes Tira had ever seen.

"Hello, Nessa," Charles said to the woman, his face guarded, a polite smile on his lips.

"Hello, Charles, Tira," Nessa replied in her soft, sweet voice. "You both look very nice. Isn't this a good turnout?" she added nervously. "They'll make a lot of money at five hundred dollars a couple."

"Yes," Tira agreed with a broad smile. "The hospital outreach program will probably be able to afford two vans and the services of another nurse!"

"For indigents," Gene Marlowe said huffily, "who won't pay a penny of their own health care."

The other three people looked at him as if he'd gone mad. He glared at them, reddening. "I have to see Todd Groves about a contract we're pursuing. If you'll excuse me? Nessa, don't just stand there! Come along."

Nessa ground her teeth together as Gene took her arm roughly. Charles looked as if he might attack his own brother right there. Tira caught his hand and tugged.

"I'm starving," she told him quickly, exchanging speaking glances with a suddenly relieved Nessa. "Feed me!"

Charles hesitated for an instant, during which Gene dragged Nessa away toward a group of men.

"Damn him!" Charles bit off, his normally pleasant face contorted and threatening.

Tira shook his hand gently. "You're broadcasting," she murmured, bumping deliberately against his side to distract him. "Come on, before you cause her any more trouble than she's already got."

He let out a weary sigh. "Why did she marry him?" he groaned. *"Why?"*

"Whatever the reason doesn't matter much now. Let's go."

She pulled until he let her lead him to the long buffet table, where expensive nibbles and champagne were elegantly arranged.

"This is going to eat up all the profits," Tira murmured worriedly, noting the crystal flutes that were provided for the champagne, and the fact that caviar was furnished as well.

Charles leaned toward her. "It's grocery store caviar, and the champagne is the sort they deliver in big round metal tractor trucks…"

"Charles!" She couldn't repress a giggle at the insinuation, and just as she felt her face going red from glee, she looked up and saw Simon's pale eyes glittering at her from across the room. She averted her eyes to the table and didn't look in that direction again. His expression had been far different from the one he'd worn when he'd seen her in the hospital. Now it was indignant and outraged, as if he blamed her for the publicity that made him look guilty, too.

Charles did waltz divinely. Tira found herself on the floor with him time after time. People noticed her, and there were some obvious whispers, which probably concerned her "suicide attempt." She was uncomfortable at first, but then she realized that the opinion of most of these people didn't matter to her. She knew the truth about what had happened and so did Charles. If the others wanted to believe her to be so weak and helpless that she'd die rather than face up to her failures, let them.

"Doesn't it worry you, being seen with such a notorious woman?" she chided when they were standing again at the buffet table with more champagne.

"Notorious women are fascinating," he returned, and smiled. His eyes lifted to his half brother and Nessa and his jaw clenched. The two of them were going out the door and Nessa looked as if she were crying.

"You can't," she said, catching his arm when he looked as if he might follow them.

"She should leave him."

"She'll have to make that decision for herself."

He glanced down at her with worried eyes. "She isn't like you. She isn't independent and spirited. She's shy and gentle and people take advantage of her."

"And you want to protect her. I understand. But you can't, not tonight."

He made a rough sound in his throat. "Damn it!"

She leaned against him affectionately for an instant. "I'm sorry. I really am."

His arm slipped around her shoulders. "One day," he promised himself.

She nodded. "One day."

"Why, Charles, how handsome you look!" Jill Sinclair's high-pitched, grating voice turned them around. "Are you enjoying yourself?"

"I'm having a great time," Charles said through his teeth. "How about you?"

"Oh, Simon is just the most wonderful escort," she sighed and glanced at Tira with half-closed eyes. "We've been everywhere together lately. There are *so* many charity dos this time of year. And how are you, Tira? I was so sorry to hear about your near tragedy!" She was almost purring, enjoying Tira's stiff posture and cold face. She raised her voice, drawing attention from the couples hovering near the buffet table. "Isn't it a pity that the newspapers made such a big thing of your suicide attempt? I mean, the humiliation of having your feelings made public must be awful. And for the gossips to say that you wanted to die just because Simon couldn't love you back…why he was just shattered that you made him look like a coldhearted villain in the eyes of his friends. God knows, it isn't his fault that he doesn't love you!"

Tira was too shaken by the unexpected attack to reply. Charles wasn't.

"Why, you prissy little cat," Charles said with cold
venom, making Jill actually catch her breath in surprise
at the unexpected verbal jab. "Why don't you go
sharpen your claws on the curtains?"

He took Tira's arm and led her away. She was so
shocked and outraged that she couldn't even manage
words. She wanted to empty the punch bowl over the
woman, but that was hardly the sort of thing to do at
a benefit ball. Her proud spirit had all but been broken
by recent events. She was still licking her wounds.

Simon was talking to a man near the door that
Charles was urging her toward. He paused in midsent-
ence and looked at Tira's white face with curious concern.

Before he could speak, Charles did. "Never mind
adding your two cents worth. Your girlfriend said it all
for you."

Charles prodded her forward and Tira didn't look
Simon's way. She was barely able to see where she
was going at all. Until Jill's piece of mischief, she'd
actually thought she could get through the evening un-
scathed.

"That cat!" Charles muttered as they made their
way to the bottom of the steps.

"The world is full of them," she breathed. "And
how they love to claw you when you're down!"

None of the valets were anywhere in sight. Charles
grumbled. "I'll have to go fetch the car. Stay right
here. Will you be all right?"

"I'm fine, now that we're outside," she said.

He gave her a last, worried glance, and went around
the house to the parking area.

She drew her wrap closer, because the air was chilly. Once, she'd have made Jill pay dearly for her nasty comments, but not anymore. Now, her proud spirit was dulled and she'd actually walked away from a fight. It wasn't like her. Charles obviously knew that, or he wouldn't have rushed her out the door so quickly.

She heard footsteps behind her and her heart jumped, because she knew the very sound of Simon's feet. Her eyes closed as she wished him in China—anywhere but here!

"What did she say to you?" he asked shortly.

She wouldn't turn; she wouldn't look at him. She couldn't bear to look at him. The humiliation of having him know how she felt about him was so horrible that it suffocated her. All those years of hiding it from him, cocooning her love in secrecy. And now he knew, the whole world knew. And worst of all, she loved him still. Just being near him was agony.

"I said, what did she say to you?" he repeated, moving directly in front of her so that she had to look at him.

She lifted her eyes to his black tie and no further. Her voice was choked, and stiff with wounded pride. "Go and ask her."

There was a rough sigh and she saw his good hand go irritably into the pocket of his trousers. "This isn't like you," he said after a minute. "You don't run and you don't cry, regardless of what people say to you. You fight back. Why are you leaving?"

She lifted tired eyes to his and hated the sudden jolt of her heart at the sight of his beloved face. She clenched every muscle in her body to keep from sobbing out her rage and hurt. "I don't care what anyone thinks of me," she said huskily, "least of all your ma-

licious girlfriend. Yes, I've spent most of my life fighting, one way or another, but I'm tired. I'm tired of
everything."

Her lack of animation disturbed him, along with the
defeat in her voice, the cool poise. "You can't be worried about what the newspapers said," he said, his
voice deep and slow and oddly tender.

"Can't I? Why not? They believed every word."
She inclined her head toward the ballroom.

His features were unusually solemn. "I know you
better than they do."

She searched his pale eyes in the dim light from the
house. Her heart clenched. "You don't know me at all,
Simon," she said with painful realization. "You never
did."

He seemed to stiffen. "I thought I did. Until you
divorced John."

Her heart stilled at the reference. "And until he
died." Defeat was in every line of her elegant body.
"Yes, I know, I'm a murderess."

His face went taut. "I didn't say that!"

"You might as well have!" she shot back, raising
her voice, not caring if the whole world heard her. "If
Melia had died in a similar manner, I'd never have
believed you guilty of her death! I'd have known you
well enough to be certain that you had no part in anything that would cause another human being harm. But
then, I had a mad infatuation for you that I couldn't
cure." She saw his sudden stillness. "Don't pretend
that you didn't read all about it in the paper, Simon.
Yes, it's true, why shouldn't I admit it? I was obsessed
with you, desperate to be with you, in any way that I
could. It didn't even matter that you only tolerated me.
I could have lived on crumbs for the rest of my life—"

Her voice broke. She shifted on trembling legs and laughed with pure self-contempt. "What a fool I was! What a silly fool. I'm twenty-eight years old and I've only just realized how stupid I am!"

He frowned. "Tira…"

She moved back a step, her green eyes blazing with ruptured pride. "Jill told me what you said, that you blame me for making you look like a villain in public with my so-called suicide attempt, as well as for John's death. Well, go ahead, hate me! I don't give a damn anymore!" she spat, out of control and not caring. "I'm not even surprised to see you with Jill, Simon. She's as opinionated and narrow-minded as you are, and she knows how to put the knife in, too. I daresay you're a match made in heaven!"

His face clenched visibly. "And you don't care that I'm with another woman tonight, instead of with you?" he chided, hitting back as hard as he could, with a mocking smile on his lips.

Her face went absolutely white. But if it killed her, he'd never hear from her how she did care. She smiled deliberately. "No," she agreed softly. "Actually I don't. All this notoriety accomplished one good thing. It made me see how I'd wasted the past few miserable years mooning over you! You did me a favor when you told me what you really thought of me. I'm free of you at last, Simon," she lied with deliberation. "And I've never been quite so happy in all my life!"

And with that parting shot, she turned and walked slowly to the driveway where Charles was pulling up in front of the house, leaving Simon rigidly in place with an expression of shock that delighted her wounded pride.

After what she'd said, she didn't expect Simon to

follow her, and he didn't. When Charles had installed her in the passenger seat, she caught just a glimpse of Simon's straight back rapidly returning to the house. She even knew the posture. He was furious. Good! Let him be furious. She was not going to care. She wasn't!

"Take it easy," Charles said softly. "You'll burst something."

"I know how you felt earlier," she returned, leaning her hot forehead against the glass of the window. "Damn him! And damn her, too!"

"What did he say to you?"

"He wanted to know what she said, and then he gave me his opinion of my character again. But this time, he didn't know he'd hit me where it hurt. I made sure of it."

Charles let out a long breath. "Why can't we love to order?" he asked philosophically.

"I don't know. If you ever find out, you can tell me." She stared out the dark window at the flat landscape passing by. Her heart felt as if it might break all over again.

"He's an idiot."

"So is Jill. So is Gene. We're all idiots. Maybe we're certifiable and we can become a circus act."

They drove in silence until they reached her house. He turned off the engine and stared at her worriedly. She was pale and she looked so miserable that he hurt for her.

"Go inside and change your clothes and pack a suitcase," he said suddenly.

"What?"

"We'll fly down to Nassau for a long weekend. It's just Saturday. We'll take a three-day vacation. I have a friend who owns a villa there. He and his wife love company. We'll eat conch chowder and play at the casino and lay on the beach. How about it?''

She brightened. ''Could we?''

''We could. You need a break and so do I. Be a gambler.''

It sounded like fun. She hadn't been happy in such a long time. ''Okay,'' she said.

''Okay.'' He grinned. ''Maybe we'll cheer up in foreign parts. Don't take too long. I'll run home and change and make a few phone calls. I should be back within an hour.''

''Great!''

It was great. The brief holiday made Tira feel as if she had a new lease on life. Charles was wonderful, undemanding company, much more like a beloved brother than a boyfriend. They padded all over Nassau, down West Bay Street to the docks and out on the pier to look at the ships in port, and all the way to the shopping district and the vast straw markets. Nassau was the most exciting, cosmopolitan city in the world to Tira. She never tired of going there. Just now, it was a godsend. She hated the memory of Jill's taunting words and Simon's angry accusations. It was good to have a breathing space from them, and the publicity.

They stretched their stay to five days instead of three and returned to San Antonio refreshed and rested, although Charles had confessed that he did miss his car. He proved it by rushing home as soon as the limousine he'd hired to meet them at the airport delivered Tira at her house.

''I'll phone you in the morning. We might have a game of tennis Saturday, if you're up to it,'' he said.

''I will be. Thanks, Charles. Thanks so much!''

He chuckled. "I enjoyed it. So long."

She watched the limousine pull away and walked slowly up to her front door. She hated homecomings. She had nothing here but Mrs. Lester and an otherwise empty house, and her work. It was cold compensation.

Mrs. Lester greeted her with enthusiasm. "I'm so glad you're home!" she said. "The phone rang off the hook the day after you left and didn't stop until three days ago." She shook her head. "I can't imagine why those newspaper people wanted to drag the whole subject up again, but I guess the shooting downtown Tuesday afternoon gave them something new to go after."

"What shooting?"

"Well, that man the attorney general had paroled— you remember?—was in court to be arraigned and he went right over the table toward the judge and almost killed him. They managed to pull him away and he grabbed the bailiff's gun. They had to shoot him! It's been on all the television stations. They had the most awful photographs of it!"

Tira actually gasped. "For heaven's sake!"

"Mr. Hart was right in the middle of it, too. He had a case and was waiting for it to be called when the prisoner got loose."

"Simon? Was he…hurt?" Tira had to ask.

"No. He was the one who pulled the man off the judge. The man had that bailiff's gun leveled right at him, they said, when a deputy sheriff shot the man. It was a close call for Mr. Hart. A real close call. But you'd never think it worried him to hear him talk on television. He was as cold as ice."

She sat down on the edge of the sofa and thanked God for Simon's life. She wished that they were still friends, even distant ones, so that she could phone him and tell him so. But there was a wall between them now.

"Mr. Hart wondered why you hadn't gotten in touch with him, afterward," Mrs. Lester said, hesitating.

Tira glanced at her breathlessly. "He called?"

She nodded and then grimaced. "He wanted to know if you heard about the shooting and if you'd been concerned. I had to tell him that you were away, and didn't know a thing, and when he asked where, he got that out of me, too. I hope it was all right that I told him."

Simon would think she went on a lover's holiday with Charles. Well, why shouldn't he? He believed she was a murderess and a flighty, shallow flirt and suicidal. Let him think whatever else he liked. She couldn't be any worse in his eyes than she already was.

"Give a dog a bad name," she murmured.

"What?" Mrs. Lester asked.

She dragged her mind back to the subject at hand. "Yes, of course, it's perfectly all right that you told him, Mrs. Lester," Tira said quietly. "I had a wonderful time in Nassau."

"Did you good, I expect, and Mr. Percy is a nice man."

"A very nice man," Tira agreed. She got to her feet. "I'm tired. I think I'll lie down for a while, so don't fix anything to eat for another hour or so, will you?"

"Certainly, dear. You just rest. I'll have some coffee and sandwiches ready when you want them."

Would she ever want them? Tira wondered as she went slowly toward her bedroom. She was empty and cold and sick at heart. But that seemed to be her normal condition. At least for now.

Four

It was raining the day Tira began taking her sculptures to Bob Henderson's ''Illuminations'' art gallery for her showing. She was so gloomy she hardly felt the mist on her face. Christmas was only two weeks away and she was miserable and lonely. Only months before, she'd have phoned Simon and asked him to meet her for lunch in town, or she'd have shown up at some committee meeting or benefit conference at which he was present, just to feed her hungry heart on the sight of him. Now, she had nothing. Only Charles and his infrequent, undemanding company. Charles was a sweetheart, but it was like having a brother over for coffee.

She carried the last box carefully in the back door, which Lillian Day, the gallery's manager was holding open for her.

''That's the last of them, Lillian,'' Tira told her,

smiling as she surveyed the cluttered storage room. She shook her head. "I can't believe I did all those myself."

"It's a lot of work," Lillian agreed, smiling back. She bent to open one of the boxes and frowned slightly at what was inside. "Did you mean to include this?" she asked, indicating a bust of Simon that was painfully lifelike.

Tira's face closed up. "Yes, I meant to," she said curtly. "I don't want it."

Lillian wisely didn't say another word. "I'll place it with the others, then. The catalogs have been printed and they're perfect, I checked them myself. Everything's ready, including the caterer for the snack buffet and the media coverage. We're doing a Christmas motif for the buffet."

Media coverage. Tira ground her teeth. The last thing in the world she wanted to see now was a reporter.

Lillian, sensitive to moods, glanced at her reassuringly. "Don't worry. These were handpicked, by me," she added. "They won't ask any embarrassing questions, and anything they write for print will be about the show. Period."

Tira relaxed. "What would I do without you?" she asked, and meant it.

Lillian grinned. "Don't even think about trying. We're very glad to have your exhibit here."

Tira had worried about Simon's reaction to the showing, since he was a partner in Bob Henderson's gallery. They hadn't spoken since before his close call in the courtroom and she half expected him to cancel her exhibit. But he hadn't. Perhaps Mrs. Lester had been mistaken and he hadn't been angry that Tira hadn't phoned to check on him. Just because she hadn't called, it didn't mean that she hadn't worried. She'd had a few sleepless nights thinking about what could have happened to him. Despite her best efforts, her feelings for him hadn't changed. She was just as much in love with him now as she had been. She was only better at concealing it.

The night of the exhibit arrived. She was all nerves, and she was secretly glad that Charles would be by her side. Not that she expected Simon to show up, with the media present. He wouldn't want to give them any more ammunition to embarrass him with. But Charles would be a comfort to her.

Fate stepped in, however, to rob her of his presence. Charles phoned at the last minute, audibly upset, to tell her he couldn't go with her to the show.

"I'm more sorry than I can tell you, but Gene's had a heart attack," he said curtly.

"Oh, Charles, I'm so sorry!"

"No need to be. You know there's no love lost between us. But he's my half brother, just the same, and there's no one else to look after him. Nessa is in shock herself. I can't let her cope alone."

"How is he?"

"Stabilized, for the moment. I'm on my way to the hospital. Nessa's with him and he's giving her hell, as usual, even flat on his back," he said curtly.

"If there's anything I can do…"

"Thanks for your support. I'm sorry you have to go on your own. But it's unlikely that Simon will be there, you know," he added gently. "Just stick close to Lillian. She'll look out for you."

She smiled to herself. "I know she will. Let me know how it goes."

"Of course I will. See you."

He hung up. She stared at the phone blankly as she replaced the receiver. She looked good, she reasoned. Her black dress was a straight sheath, ankle-length, with spaghetti straps and a diamond necklace and earrings to set it off. It was a perfect foil for her pale, flawless complexion and her red-gold hair, done in a complicated topknot with tendrils just brushing her neck. From her austere get up, she looked more like a widow in mourning than a woman looking forward to Christmas, and she felt insecure and nervous. It would be the first time she'd appeared alone in public since the scandal and she was still uncomfortable around most people.

Well, she comforted herself as she went outside and climbed into her Jaguar, at least she didn't have to add Simon to her other complications tonight.

The gallery was packed full of interested customers, some of whom had probably only come for curiosity's sake. It wasn't hard to discern people who could afford the four-figure price tags on the sculptures from those who couldn't. Tira pretended not to notice. She took a flute of expensive champagne and downed half of it before she went with Lillian to mingle with the guests.

It didn't help that the first two people she saw were Simon and Jill.

"Oh, God," she ground out through her teeth, only too aware of the reporters and their sudden interest in him. "Why did he have to come?!"

Lillian took her arm gently. "Don't let him know that it bothers you. Smile, girl! We'll get through this."

"Do you think so?"

She plastered a cool smile to her lips as Simon pulled Jill along with him and came to a halt just in front of the two women.

"Nice crowd," he told Tira, his eyes slowly going over her exquisite figure in the close-fitting dress with unusual interest.

"A few art fans and a lot of rubberneckers, hadn't you noticed?" Tira said, sipping more champagne. Her fingers trembled a little and she held the flute with both hands, something Simon's keen eyes picked up on at once.

"Nice of you to come by," Lillian said quietly.

He glanced at her. "It would have been noticeable if I hadn't, considering that I own half the gallery." His attention turned back to Tira and his silvery eyes narrowed. "All alone? Where's your fair-haired shadow?"

She knew he meant Charles. She smiled lazily. "He couldn't make it."

"On the first night of your first exhibition?" he chided.

She drew in a sharp breath. "His half brother had a heart attack, if you must know," she said through her teeth. "He's at the hospital."

Simon's eyes flickered strangely. "And you have to be here, instead of at his side. Pity."

"He doesn't need comforting. Nessa does."

Jill, dressed in red again with a sprig of holly secured with a diamond clip in her black hair, moved closer to Simon. "We just stopped in for a peek at your work," she said, almost purring as she looked up at the tall man beside her. "We're on our way to the opera."

Tira averted her eyes. She loved opera. Many times

in the past, Simon had escorted her during the season. It hurt to remember how she'd looked forward to those chaste evenings with him.

"I don't suppose you go anymore?" Simon asked coldly.

She shrugged. "Don't have time," she said tightly.

"I noticed. You couldn't even be bothered to phone and check on me when that lunatic went wild in the courtroom."

Tira wouldn't look at him. "You can't hurt someone who's steel right through," she said.

"And you were out of the country when it happened."

She lifted her eyes to his hard face. "Yes. I was in Nassau with Charles, having a lovely time!"

His eyes seemed to blaze up at her.

Before the confrontation could escalate, Lillian diplomatically got between them. "Have you had time to look around?" she asked Simon.

"Oh, we've seen most everything," Jill answered for him. "Even the bust of Simon that Tira did. I was surprised that she was willing to sell it," she added in an innocent tone. "I wouldn't part with something so personal, Simon being such an old friend and all. But I guess under the circumstances, it was too painful a reminder of…things, wasn't it, dear?" she asked Tira.

Tira's hand automatically drew back, with the remainder of the champagne, but before she could toss it, Simon caught her wrist with his good hand.

"No catfights," he said through his teeth. "Jill, wait for me at the door, will you?"

"If you say so. My, she does look violent, doesn't she?" Jill chided, but she walked away quickly just the same.

"Get a grip on yourself!" Simon shot at Tira under his breath. "Don't you see the reporters staring at you?"

"I don't give a damn about the reporters," she flashed at him. "If she comes near me again, I swear I'll empty the punch bowl over her vicious little head!"

He let go of her wrist and something kindled in his pale eyes as he looked at her animated face. "That's more like you," he said in a deep, soft tone.

Tira flushed, aware that Lillian was quietly deserting her, stranding her with Simon.

"Why did you come?" she asked furiously.

"So the gossips wouldn't have a field day speculating about why I didn't," he explained. "It wouldn't have done either of us much good, considering what's been in print already."

She lifted her face, staring at him with cold eyes at the reference to things she only wanted to forget. "You've done your duty," she said. "You might as well go. And take the Wicked Witch of the West with you," she added spitefully.

"Jealous?" he asked in a sensuous tone.

Her face hardened. "I once asked you the same question. You can give yourself the same answer that you gave me. Like hell I'm jealous!"

He was watching her curiously, his eyes acutely alive in a strangely taciturn face. "You've lost weight," he remarked. "And you look more like a widow than a celebrity tonight. Why wear black?"

"I've decided that you were right. I should have mourned my husband. So now I'm in mourning," she said icily and with an arctic smile. "I expect to be in mourning for him until I die, and I'll never look at a man again. Doesn't that make you happy?"

He frowned slightly. "Tira..."

"Tira!"

The sound of a familiar voice turned them both around. Harry Beck, Tira's father-in-law, came forward, smiling, to embrace Tira. He turned to shake Simon's hand. "Great to see you both!" he said enthusiastically. "Dollface, you've outdone yourself," he told Tira, nodding toward two nearby sculptures. "I always knew you were talented, but this is sheer genius!"

Simon looked puzzled by Harry's honest enthusiasm for Tira's work, by his lack of hostility. She'd killed his only son, didn't he care?

"I'm glad to see you, Simon," Harry added with a smile. "It's been a long time."

"Simon was just leaving. Weren't you?" Tira added meaningfully.

"Someone's motioning to you," Harry noted, indicating Lillian frantically waving from across the room.

"It's Lillian. Will you excuse me?" Tira asked, smiling at Harry. "I won't be a minute." Simon, she ignored entirely.

The two men watched her go.

"I'm glad to see her looking so much better," Harry said on a sigh, shoving his hands into his pockets. "I've been worried since she went to the hospital."

"Do you really care what happens to her?" Simon asked curiously.

Harry was surprised. "Why wouldn't I be? She was my daughter-in-law. I've always been fond of her."

"She divorced John a month after they married and let him go off to work on a drill rig in the ocean," Simon returned. "He died there."

Harry stared at him blankly. ''But that wasn't her fault.''

''Wasn't it?''

''Why are you so bitter?'' Harry wanted to know. ''For God's sake, you can't think she didn't try to change him? He should have told her the truth before he married her, not let her find it out that way!''

Simon was puzzled. ''Find what out?''

Jill glared at Simon, but he made a motion for her to wait another minute and turned back to Harry. ''Find what out?'' he repeated curtly.

''That John was homosexual, of course,'' Harry said, puzzled.

The blood drained out of Simon's face. He stared down at the older man with dawning comprehension.

''She didn't tell you?'' Harry asked gently. He sighed and shook his head. ''That's like her, though. She wanted to preserve your illusions about John, even if it meant sacrificing your respect for her. She couldn't tell you, I guess. I can't blame her. If he'd only been able to accept what he was…but he couldn't. He tried so hard to be what he thought I wanted. And he never seemed to understand that I'd have loved him regardless of how he saw his place in the world.''

Simon turned away, his eyes finding Tira across the room. She wouldn't meet his gaze. She turned her back. He felt the pain right through his body.

''Dear God!'' he growled when he realized what he'd done.

''Don't look like that,'' Harry said gently. ''John made his own choice. It was nobody's fault. Maybe it was mine. I should have seen that he was distraught and done something.''

Simon let out a breath. He was sick right to his soul. What a fool he'd been.

"She should have told you," Harry was saying. "You're a grown man. You don't need to be protected from the truth. She was always like that, even with John, trying to protect him. She'd have gone on with the marriage if he hadn't insisted on a divorce."

"I thought…she got the divorce."

"He got it, in her name, and cited mental cruelty." He shrugged. "I don't think he considered how it might look to an outsider. It made things worse for him. He only did it to save her reputation. He thought it would hurt her publicly if he made it look like she was at fault." He glanced at Simon. "That was right after your wreck and she was trying to take care of you. He thought it might appear as if she was having an affair with you and he found out. It might have damaged both of you in the public eye."

His teeth clenched. "I never touched her."

"Neither did John," Harry murmured heavily. "He couldn't. He cried in my arms about it, just before he saw an attorney. He wanted to love her. He did, in his way. But it wasn't in a conventional way at all."

Simon pushed back a strand of dark, wavy hair that had fallen on his brow. He was sweating because the gallery was overheated.

"Are you all right?" Harry asked with concern.

"I'm fine." He wasn't. He'd never be all right again. He glanced toward Tira with anguish in every line of his face. But she wouldn't even look at him.

Jill, sensing some problem, came back to join him, sliding her hand into his arm. "Aren't you ready? We'll miss the curtain."

"I'm ready," he said. He looked down at her and

realized that here was one more strike against him. He was giving aid and comfort to Tira's worst enemy in the city. He'd done it deliberately, of course, to make her even more uncomfortable. But that was before he knew the whole truth. Now he felt guilty.

"Hello. I'm Jill Sinclair. Have we met?" she asked Harry, smiling.

"No, we haven't. I'm—"

"We have to go," Simon said abruptly. He didn't want to add any more weapons to Jill's already full arsenal by letting Harry tell her about John, too. "See you, Harry."

"Sure. Good night."

"Who was that?" Jill asked Simon as they went toward the door.

"An old friend. Just a minute. There's something I have to do."

"Simon…!"

"I won't be a minute," he promised, and caught one of the gallery's sales-people alone long enough to make a request. She seemed puzzled, but she agreed. He went back to Jill and escorted her out of the gallery, casting one last regretful look toward Tira, who was speaking to a group of socialites at the back of the gallery.

"Half the works are sold already," Jill murmured. "I guess she'll make a fortune."

"She's donating it all to charity," he replied absently.

"She can afford to. It will certainly help her image and, God knows, she needs that right now."

He glanced at her. "That isn't why."

She shrugged. "Whatever you say, darling. *Brrrr,* I'm cold! Christmas is week after next, too." She peered up at him. "I hope you got me something pretty."

"I wouldn't count on it. I probably won't be in town for Christmas," he said not quite truthfully.

She sighed. "Oh, well, I might go and spend the holidays with my aunt in Connecticut. I do love snow!"

She was welcome to all she could find of it, he thought. His heart already felt as if he were buried in snow and ice. He knew that Harry's revelation would keep him awake all night.

Tira watched Simon leave with Jill. She was glad he'd gone. Perhaps now she could enjoy her show.

Lillian was giving her strange looks and when Harry came to say goodbye, he looked rather odd, too.

"What's wrong?" she asked Harry.

He started to speak and thought better of it. Let Simon tell her what he wanted her to know. He was tired of talking about the past; it was too painful.

He smiled. "It's a great show, kiddo, you'll make a mint."

"Thanks, Harry. I had fun doing it. Keep in touch, won't you?"

He leaned forward and kissed her cheek. "You know I will. How's Charlie?"

"His brother-in-law had a heart attack. He's not doing well."

"I'm really sorry. Always liked Charlie. Still do."

"I'll tell him you asked about him," she promised.

He smiled at her. "You do that. Keep well."

"You, too."

By the end of the evening, Tira was calmer, despite the painful memory of her argument with Simon's and

Jill's catty remarks. She could just picture the two of them in Simon's lavish apartment, sprawled all over each other in an ardent tangle. It made her sick. Simon had never kissed her, never touched her in anything but an impersonal way. She'd lived like a religious recluse for part of her life and she had nothing to show for her reticence except a broken heart and shattered pride.

"What a great haul," Lillian enthused, breaking into her thoughts. "You sold three-forths of them. The rest we'll keep on display for a few weeks and see how they do."

"I'm delighted," Tira said, and meant it. "It's all going to benefit the outreach program at St. Mark's."

"They'll be very happy with it, I'm sure."

Tira was walking around the gallery with the manager. Most of the crowd had left and a few stragglers were making their way to the door. She noticed the bust of Simon had a Sold sign on it, and her heart jumped.

"Who bought it?" Tira asked curtly. "It wasn't Jill Sinclair, was it?"

"No," Lillian assured her. "I'm not sure who bought it, but I can check, if you like."

"No, that's not necessary," Tira said, clamping down hard on her curiosity. "I don't care who bought it. I only wanted it out of my sight. I don't care if I never see Simon Hart again!"

Lillian sighed worriedly, but she smiled when Tira glanced toward her and offered coffee.

Simon watched the late-night news broadcast from his easy chair, nursing a whiskey sour, his second in half an hour. He'd taken Jill home and adroitly avoided her coquettish invitation to stay the night. After what he'd learned from Harry Beck, he had to be by himself to think things out.

There was a brief mention of Tira's showing at the gallery and how much money had been raised for charity. He held his breath, but nothing was said about her suicide attempt. He only hoped the newspapers would be equally willing to put the matter aside.

He sipped his drink and remembered unwillingly all the horrible things he'd thought about and said to Tira over John. How she must have suffered through that mockery of a marriage, and how horrible if she'd loved John. She must have had her illusions shattered. She was the injured party. But Simon had taken John's side and punished her as if she was guilty for John's death. He'd deliberately put her out of his life, forbidding her to come close, even to touch him.

He closed his eyes in anguish. She would never let him near her again, no matter how he apologized. He'd said too much, done too much. She'd loved him, and he'd savaged her. And it had all been for nothing. She'd been innocent.

He finished his drink with dead eyes. Regrets seemed to pile up in the loneliness of the night. He glanced toward the Christmas tree his enthusiastic housekeeper had set up by the window, and dreaded the whole holiday season. He'd spend Christmas alone. Tira, at least, would have the despised Charles Percy for company.

He wondered why she didn't marry the damned man. They seemed to live in each others' pockets. He remembered that Charles had always been her champion, bolstering her up, protecting her. Charles had been her friend when Simon had turned his back on her, so how could he blame her for preferring the younger man?

He put his glass down and got to his feet. He felt every year of his age. He was almost forty and he had nothing to show for his own life. The child he might have had was gone, along with Melia, who'd never loved him. He'd lived on illusions of love for a long time, when the reality of love had ached for him and he'd turned his back.

If he'd let Tira love him...

He groaned aloud. He might as well put that hope to rest right now. She'd hate him forever and he had only himself to blame. Perhaps he deserved her hatred. God knew, he'd hurt her enough.

He went to bed, to lie awake all night with the memory of Tira's wounded eyes and drawn face to haunt him.

Five

Simon was not in a good mood the next morning when he went into work. Mrs. Mackey, his middle-aged secretary, stopped him at the door of his office with an urgent message to call the governor's office as soon as he came in. He knew what it was about and he groaned inwardly. He didn't want to be attorney general, but he knew for a fact that Wally was going to offer it to him. Wallace Bingley was a hard man to refuse, and he was a very popular governor as well as a friend. Both Simon and Tira had been actively involved in his gubernatorial campaign.

"All right, Mrs. Mack," he murmured, smiling as he used her nickname, "get him for me."

She grinned, because she knew, too, what was going on.

Minutes later, the call was put through to his office.

"Hi, Wally," Simon said. "What can I do for you?"

"You know the answer to that already," came the wry response. "Will you or won't you?"

"I'd like a week or so to think about it," Simon said seriously. "It's a part of my life I hadn't planned to take up again. I don't like living in a goldfish bowl and I hear it's open season on attorneys general in Texas."

Wallace chuckled. "You don't have as many political enemies as he does, and you're craftier, too. All right, think about it. Take the rest of the month. But two weeks is all you've got. After the holidays, his resignation takes effect, and I have to appoint someone."

"I promise to let you know by then," Simon assured him.

"Now, to better things. Are you coming to the Starks's Christmas party?"

"I'd have liked to, but my brothers are throwing a party down in Jacobsville and I more or less promised to show up."

"Speaking of the 'fearsome four,' how are they?"

"Desperate." Simon chuckled. "Corrigan phoned day before yesterday and announced that Dorie thinks she's pregnant. If she is, the boys are going to have to find a new victim to make biscuits for them."

"Why don't they hire a cook?"

"They can't keep one. You know why," Simon replied dryly.

"I guess I do. He hasn't changed."

"He never will," Simon agreed, referring to his brother Leopold, who was mischievous and sometimes outrageous in his treatment of housekeepers. Unlike the other two of the three remaining Hart bachelor brothers, Callaghan and Reynard, Leopold was a live wire.

"How's Tira?" Wallace asked unexpectedly. "I hear her showing was a huge success."

The mention of it was uncomfortable. It reminded him all too vividly of the mistakes he'd made with Tira. "I suppose she's fine," Simon said through his teeth.

"Er, well, sorry, I forgot. The publicity must have been hard on both of you. Not that anybody takes it seriously. It certainly won't hurt your political chances, if that's why you're hesitating to accept the position."

"It wasn't. I'll talk to you soon, Wally, and thanks for the offer."

"I hope you'll accept. I could use you."

"I'll let you know."

He said goodbye and hung up, glaring out the window as he recalled what he'd learned about Tira so unexpectedly. It hurt him to talk about her now. It would take a long time for her to forgive him, if she ever did.

If only there was some way that he could talk to her, persuade her to listen to him. He'd tried phoning from home early this very morning. As soon as she'd heard his voice, she'd hung up, and the answering machine had been turned on when he tried again. There was no point in leaving a message. She was determined to wipe him right out of her life, apparently. He felt so disheartened he didn't know what to try next.

And then he remembered Sherry Walker, a mutual friend of his and Tira's in the past who loved opera and had season tickets in the aisle right next to his, in the dress circle. He knew that Sherry had broken a leg skiing just recently and had said that she wasn't leaving the house until it healed completely. Perhaps, he told himself, there was a way to get Tira to talk to him after all.

* * *

The letdown after the showing made Tira miserable. She had nothing to do just now, with the holiday season in full swing, and she had no one to buy a present for except Mrs. Lester and Charles. She went from store to colorfully decorated store and watched mothers and fathers with their children and choked on her own pain. She wouldn't have children or the big family she'd always craved. She'd live and die alone.

As she stood at a toy store window, watching the electric train sets flashing around a display of papier mache mountains and small buildings, she wondered what it would be like to have children to buy those trains for.

A lone, salty tear ran down her cold-flushed cheek and even as she caught it on her knuckles, she felt a sudden pervasive warmth at her back.

Her heart jumped even before she looked up. She always knew when Simon was anywhere nearby. It was a sort of unwanted radar and just lately it was more painful than ever.

"Nice, aren't they?" he asked quietly. "When I was a boy, my father bought my brothers and me a set of 'O' scale Lionel trains. We used to sit and run them by the hour in the dark, with all the little buildings lighted, and imagine little people living there." He turned, resplendent in a charcoal gray cashmere overcoat over his navy blue suit. His white shirt was spotless, like the patterned navy-and-white tie he wore with it. He looked devastating. And he was still wearing the hated prosthesis.

"Isn't this a little out of your way?" she asked tautly.

"I like toy stores. Apparently so do you." He searched what he could see of her averted face. Her glorious hair was in a long braid today and she was wearing a green silk pantsuit several shades darker than her eyes under her long black leather coat.

"Toys are for children," she said coldly.

He frowned slightly. "Don't you like children?"

She clenched her teeth and stared at the train. "What would be the point?" she asked. "I won't have any. If you'll excuse me…"

He moved in front of her, blocking the way. "Doesn't Charles want a family?"

It was a pointed question, and probably taunting. Charles's brother was still in the hospital and no better, and from what Charles had been told, he might not get better. There was a lot of damage to Gene's heart. Charles would be taking care of Nessa, whom he loved, but Simon knew nothing about that.

"I've never asked Charles how he feels about children," she said carelessly.

"Shouldn't you? It's an issue that needs to be resolved before two people make a firm commitment to each other."

Was he deliberately trying to lacerate her feelings? She wouldn't put it past him now. "Simon, none of this is any of your business," she said in a choked tone. "Now will you please let me go?" she asked on a nervous laugh. "I have shopping to do."

His good hand reached out to lightly touch her shoulder, but she jerked back from him as if he had a communicable disease.

"Don't!" she said sharply. "Don't ever do that!"

He withdrew his hand, scowling down at her. She was white in the face and barely able to breathe from the look of her.

"Just…leave me alone, okay?" She choked, and

darted past him and into the thick of the holiday crowd on the sidewalk. She couldn't bear to let her weakness for him show. Every time he touched her, she felt vibrations all the way to her toes and she couldn't hide it. Fortunately she was away before he noticed that it wasn't revulsion that had torn her from his side. She was spared a little of her pride.

Simon watched her go with welling sadness. It could have been so different, he thought, if he'd been less judgmental, if he'd ever bothered to ask her side of her brief marriage. But he hadn't. He'd condemned her on the spot, and kept pushing her away for years. How could he expect to get back on any sort of friendly footing with her easily? It was going to take a long time, and from what he'd just seen, his was an uphill climb all the way. He went back to his office so dejected that Mrs. Mack asked if he needed some aspirin.

Tira brushed off the chance meeting with Simon as a coincidence and was cheered by an unexpected call from an old friend, who offered her a ticket to *Turandot,* her favorite opera, the next evening.

She accepted with pure pleasure. It would do her good to get out of the house and do something she enjoyed.

She put on a pretty black designer dress with diamanté straps and covered it with her flashy velvet wrap. She didn't look half bad for an old girl, she told her reflection in the mirror. But then, she had nobody to dress up for, so what did it matter?

She hired a cab to take her downtown because finding a parking space for the visiting opera performance would be a nightmare. She stepped out of the cab into a crowd of other music lovers and some of her painful loneliness drifted away in the excitement of the performance.

The seat she'd been given was in the dress circle. She remembered so many nights being here with Simon, but his reserved seat, thank God, was empty. If she'd thought there was a chance of his being here, she'd never have come. But she knew that Simon had taken Jill to see this performance already. It was unlikely that he'd want to sit through it again.

There was a drumroll. The theater went dark. The curtain started to rise. The orchestra began to play the overture. She relaxed with her small evening bag in her lap and smiled as she anticipated a joyful experience.

And then everything went suddenly wrong. There was a movement to her left and when she turned her head, there was Simon, dashing in dark evening clothes, sitting down right beside her.

He gave her a deliberately careless glance and a curt nod and then turned his attention back to the stage.

Tira's hands clenched on the evening bag. Simon's shoulder brushed against hers as he shifted in his seat and she felt the touch as if it were fire all the way down her body. It had never been so bad before. She'd walked with him, talked with him, shared seats at benefits and auctions and operas and plays with him, and even though his presence had been a bittersweet delight, it had never been so physically painful to her in the past. She wanted to turn and find his mouth with her lips, she wanted to press her body to his and feel his cheek against her own. The longing so was poignant that she shivered with it.

"Cold?" he whispered.

She clenched her jaw. "Not at all," she muttered, sliding further into her velvet wrap.

His good arm went, unobtrusively, over the back of her seat and rested there. She froze in place, barely daring to move, to breathe. It was just like the afternoon in front of the toy store. Did he know that it was torture for her to be close to him? Probably he did. He'd found a new way to get to her, to make her pay for all the terrible things he thought she'd done. She closed her eyes and groaned silently.

The opera, beautiful as it was, was forgotten. She was so miserable that she sat stiffly and heard none of it. All she could think about was how to escape.

She started to get up and Simon's big hand caught her shoulder a little too firmly.

"Stay where you are," he said gruffly.

She hesitated, but only for an instant. She was desperate to escape now. "I have to go to the necessary room, if you don't mind," she bit off near his ear.

"Oh."

He sighed heavily and moved his arm, turning to allow her to get past him. She apologized all the way down the row. Once she made it to the aisle, she felt safe. She didn't look back as she made her way gracefully and quickly to the back of the theater and into the lobby.

It was easy to dart out the door and hail a cab. This time of night, they were always a few of them cruising nearby. She climbed into the first one that stopped, gave him her address, and sat back with a relieved sigh. She'd done it. She was safe.

She went home more miserable than ever, changed into her nightgown and a silky white robe and let her hair down with a long sigh. She couldn't blame her friend, Sherry, for the fiasco. How could anyone have known that Simon would decide to see the opera a second time on this particular night? But it was a cruel blow of fate. Tira had looked forward to a performance that Simon's presence had ruined for her.

She made coffee, despite the late hour, and was sitting down in the living room to drink it when the doorbell rang.

It might be Charles, she decided. She hadn't heard from him today, and he could have stopped by to tell her about Gene. She went to the front door and opened it without thinking.

Simon was standing there with a furious expression on his face.

She tried to close the door, but one big well-shod foot was inside it before she could even move. He let himself in and closed the door behind him.

"Well, come in, then," she said curtly, her green eyes sparkling with bad temper as she pulled her robe closer around her.

He stared at her with open curiosity. He'd never seen her in night clothing before. The white robe emphasized her creamy skin, and the lace of her gown came barely high enough to cover the soft mounds of her breasts. With her red-gold hair loose in a glorious tangle around her shoulders, she was a picture to take a man's breath away.

"Why did you run?" he asked softly.

Her face colored gently. "I wasn't expecting you to be there," she said, and it came out almost as an accusation. "You've already seen the performance once."

"Yes, with Jill," he added deliberately, watching her face closely.

She averted her eyes. He looked so good in an eve-

ning jacket, she thought miserably. His dark, wavy hair
was faintly damp, as if the threatening clouds had let
some rain fall. His pale gray eyes were watchful, dis-
turbing. He'd never looked at her this way before, like
a predator with its prey. It made her nervous.

"Do you want some coffee?" she asked to break the
tense silence.

"If you don't put arsenic in it."

She glanced at him. "Don't tempt me."

She led him into the kitchen, got down a cup and
poured a cup of coffee for him. She didn't offer cream
and sugar, because she knew he took neither.

He turned a chair around and straddled it before he
picked up the cup and sipped the hot coffee, staring at
her disconcertingly over the rim.

With open curiosity, she glanced at the prosthesis
hand, which was resting on the back of the chair.

"Something wrong?" he asked.

She shrugged and picked up her own cup. "You
used to hate that." She indicated the artificial arm.

"I hate pity even more," he said flatly. "It looks
real enough to keep people from staring."

"Yes," she said. "It does look real."

He sipped coffee. "Even if it doesn't feel it," he
murmured dryly. He glanced up at her face and saw it
color from the faint insinuation in his deep voice.
"Amazing, that you can still blush, at your age," he
remarked.

It wouldn't have been if he knew how totally innocent she still was at her advanced age, but she wasn't
sharing her most closely guarded secret with the enemy. He thought she and Charles were lovers, and she
was content to let him. But that insinuation about why
he used the prosthesis was embarrassing and infuriat-

ing. She hated being jealous. She had to conceal it from him.

"I don't care how it feels, or to whom," she said stiffly. "In fact, I have no interest whatsoever in your personal life. Not anymore."

He drew in a long breath and let it out. "Yes, I know." He finished his coffee in two swallows. "I miss you," he said simply. "Nothing is the same."

Her heart jumped but she kept her eyes down so that he wouldn't see how much pleasure the statement gave her. "We were friends. I'm sure you have plenty of others. Including Jill."

His intake of breath was audible. "I didn't realize how much you and Jill disliked each other."

"What difference does it make?" She glanced at him with a mocking smile. "I'm not part of your life."

"You were," he returned solemnly. "I didn't realize how much a part of it you were, until it was too late."

"Some things are better left alone," she said evasively. "More coffee?"

He shook his head. "It keeps me awake. Wally called and offered me the attorney general's post," he said. "I've got two weeks to think about it."

"You were a good attorney general," she recalled. "You got a lot of excellent legislation through the general assembly."

He smiled faintly, studying his coffee cup. "I lived in a goldfish bowl. I didn't like it."

"You have to take the bad with the good."

He looked at her closely. "Tell me what happened the night they took you to the hospital."

She shrugged. "I got drunk and passed out."

"And the pistol?"

"The mouse." She nodded toward the refrigerator.

"He's under there, I can hear him. He can't be trapped and he's brazen. I got drunk and decided to take him out like John Wayne, with a six-shooter. I missed."

He chuckled softly. "I thought it was something like that. You're not suicidal."

"You're the only person who thinks so. Even Dr. Gaines didn't believe me. He wanted me to have therapy," she scoffed.

"The newspapers had a field day. I guess Jill helped feed the fire."

She glanced up, surprised. "You knew?"

"Not until she commented on it, when it was too late to do anything. For what it's worth," he added quietly, "I don't know many people who believed the accounts in her cousin's paper."

She leaned back in her chair and stared at him levelly. "That I did it for love of you?" she drawled with a poisonous smile. "You hurt my feelings when you accused me of killing my husband," she said flatly. "I was already overworked and depressed and I did something stupid. But I hope you don't believe that I sit around nights crying in my beer because of unrequited passion for you!"

Her tone hit him on the raw. He got slowly to his feet and his eyes narrowed as he stared down at her.

She felt at a distinct disadvantage. She'd only seen Simon lose his temper once. She'd never forgotten and she didn't want to repeat the experience.

"It's late," she said quickly. "I'd like to go to bed."

"Would you really?" His pale gaze slid over her body as he said it, his voice so sensuous that it made her bare toes curl up on the spotless linoleum floor.

She didn't trust that look. She started past him and found one of her hands suddenly trapped by his big one. He moved in, easing her hand up onto the silky fabric of his vest, inside it against the silky warmth of his body under the thin cotton shirt. She could feel the springy hair under it as well, and the hard beat of his heart as his breath whispered out at her temple, stirring her hair. She'd never been so close to him. It was as if her senses, numb for years, all came to life at once and exploded in a shattering rush of physical sensation. It frightened her and she pushed at his chest.

"Simon, let go!" she said huskily, all in a rush.

He didn't. He couldn't. The feel of her in his arms exceeded his wildest imaginings. She was soft and warm and she smelled of flowers. He drank in the scent and felt her begin to tremble. It went right to his head. His hand left hers and slid into her hair at her nape, clenching, so that she was helpless against him. He fought for control. He mustn't do this. It was too soon. Far too soon.

His breath came quickly. She could hear it, feel it. His cheek brushed against hers roughly, as if he wanted to feel the very texture of her skin there. He had a faint growth of beard and it rasped a little, but it was more sensual than uncomfortable.

Her heart raced as wildly as his. She wanted to draw back, to run, but that merciless hand wasn't unclenching. If anything, it had an even tighter grip on her long hair.

She wasn't protesting anymore. He felt her yield and his body clenched. His cheek drew slowly against hers. She felt his mouth at the corner of her own, felt his breath as his lips parted.

"Don't…" The little cry was all but inaudible.

"It's too late," he said roughly. "Years too late. God, Tira, turn your mouth against mine!"

She heard the soft, gruff command with a sense of total unreality. Her cold hands pressed against his shirtfront, but it was, as he said, already too late.

He moved his head just a fraction of an inch, and his hard, hot mouth moved completely onto hers, parting her lips as it explored, settled, demanded. There was a faint hesitation, almost of shock, as sensual electricity flashed between them. He felt her mouth tremble, tasted it, savored it, devoured it.

He groaned as his mouth began to part her lips insistently. Then his arm was around her, the one with the prosthesis holding her waist firmly while the good one lifted and traced patterns from her cheek down to her soft, pulsing throat. He could hear the tortured sound of his own breath echoed by her own.

She whimpered as she felt the full force of his mouth, felt the kiss she'd dreamed of for so many years suddenly becoming reality. He tasted of coffee. His lips were hard and demanding on her mouth, sensual, insistent. She didn't protest. She clung to him, savoring the most ecstatic few seconds of her life as if she never expected to feel anything so powerful again.

Her response puzzled him, because it wasn't that of an experienced woman. She permitted him to kiss her, clung to him closely, even seemed to enjoy his rough ardor; but she gave nothing back. It was almost as if she didn't know how...

He drew back slowly. His pale, fierce eyes looked down into hers with pure sensual arrogance and more than a little curiosity.

This was a Simon she'd never seen, never known, a sensual man with expert knowledge of women that was evident even in such a relatively chaste encounter. She was afraid of him because she had no defense against that kind of ardor, and fear made her push at his chest.

He put her away from him abruptly and his arms fell to his sides. She moved back, her eyes like saucers in a flushed, feverish face, until she was leaning against the counter.

Simon watched her hungrily, his eyes on the noticeable signs of her arousal in her body under the thin silk gown, in her swollen mouth and the faint redness on her cheek where his own had rubbed against it with his faint growth of beard. He'd never dreamed that he and Tira would kindle such fires together. In all their years of careless friendship, he'd never really approached her physically until tonight. He felt as if he were drowning in uncharted waters.

Tira went slowly to the back door and opened it, unnaturally calm. She still looked gloriously beautiful, even more so because she was emotionally aroused.

He took the hint, but he paused at the open door to stare down at her averted face. She was very flustered for a woman who had a lover. He found himself bristling with sudden and unexpected jealousy of the most important man in her life.

"Lucky Charles," he said gruffly. "Is that what he gets?"

Her eyes flashed at him. "You get out of here!" she managed to say through her tight throat. She pulled her robe tight against her throat. "Go. Just, please, go!"

He walked past her, hesitating on the doorstep, but she closed the door after him and locked it. She went back through the kitchen and down the hall to her bedroom before she dared let the tears flow. She was too shaken to try to delve into his motives for that hungry kiss. But she knew it had to be some new sort of re-

venge for his friend John. Well, it wouldn't work! He
was never going to hurt her again, she vowed. She only
wished she hadn't been stupid enough to let him touch
her in the first place.

Simon stood outside by his car in the misting rain,
letting the coolness push away the flaring heat of his
body. He shuddered as he leaned his forehead against
the cold roof of the car and thanked God he'd managed
to get out of there before he did something even more
stupid than he already had.

Tira had submitted. He could have had her. He was
barely able to draw back at all. What a revelation that
had been, that a woman he'd known for years should
be able to arouse such instant, sweeping passion in him.
Even Melia hadn't had such a profound effect on him,
in the days when he'd thought he loved her.

He hadn't meant to touch her. But her body, her
exquisite body, in that thin robe and gown had driven
him right over the edge. He still had the taste of her
soft, sweet lips on his mouth, he could still feel her
pressed completely to him. It was killing him!

He clenched his hand and forced himself to breathe
slowly until he began to relax. At least she hadn't seen
him helpless like this. If she knew how vulnerable he
was, she might feel like a little revenge. He couldn't
blame her, but his pride wouldn't stand it. She might
decide to seduce him and then keep him dangling. That
would be the cruelest blow of all, when he knew she
was Charles Percy's lover. He had sick visions of Tira
telling him everything Simon had done to her and
laughing about how easily she'd knocked him off balance. Charles was Tira's lover. Her lover. God, the
thought of it made him sick!

He could see why Charles couldn't keep away from her. It made him bitter to realize that he could probably have cut Charles out years ago if he hadn't been so blind and prejudiced. Tira could have been his. But instead, she was Charles's, and she could only hate Simon now for the treatment he'd dealt out to her. He couldn't imagine her still loving him, even if he had taunted her with it to salvage what was left of his pride.

He got into his car finally and drove away in a roar of fury. Damn her for making him lose his head, he thought, refusing to remember that he'd started the whole damned thing. And damn him for letting her do it!

Six

After consuming far more whiskey than he should have the night before, Simon awoke with vivid memories of Tira in his arms and groaned heavily. He'd blown it, all over again. He didn't know how he was going to smooth things over this time. Jill called and invited herself to lunch with him, fishing for clues to his unusual bad humor. He mumbled something about going to the opera and having an argument with Tira, but offered no details at all. She asked him if he'd expected Tira to be there, and he brushed off further questions, pleading work.

Jill was livid at the thought that Tira was cutting in on her territory, just when things were going so well. She phoned the house and was told by Mrs. Lester that Tira had gone shopping. The rest was easy....

Tira, still smoldering from the betrayal of her weak body the night before, treated herself to lunch at a small sandwich shop downtown. Fate seemed to be against her, she thought with cold resignation, when Jill Sinclair walked into the shop and made a beeline for her just as she was working on dessert and a second cup of coffee.

"Well, how are you doing?" Jill asked with an innocent smile. "Just sandwiches? Poor you! Simon's taking me to Chez Paul for crepes and cherries jubilee."

"Then why are you here?" Tira asked, not disposed to be friendly toward her worst enemy.

Jill's perfect eyebrows arched. "Why, I was shopping next door for a new diamond tennis bracelet and I spotted you in here," she lied. "I thought a word to the wise, you know," she added, glancing around with the wariness of a veteran intelligence agent before she leaned down to whisper, "Simon was very vexed to have found you sitting next to him at the opera last night. You really should be more careful about engineering these little 'accidental' meetings and chasing after him, dear. He's in a vicious mood today!"

"Good!" Tira said with barely controlled rage. She glared at the other woman. "Would you like to have coffee with me, Jill?" She asked, and drew back the hand that was holding the cup of lukewarm coffee. "Let me introduce you to Miss Cup!"

Jill barely stepped back in time as the coffee cup flew through the air and hit the floor inches in front of her. Her eyes were wide open, and her mouth joined it. She hadn't expected her worst enemy to fight back.

"My, my, aren't I the clumsy one!" Tira said sweetly. "I dropped Miss Cup and spilled my coffee!"

Jill swallowed, hard. "I'll just be off," she said quickly.

"Oh, look," Tira added, lifting the plastic coffeepot the waitress had left on her table with a whimsical smile. "Mr. Coffeepot's coming after Miss Cup!"

Jill actually ran. If Tira hadn't been so miserable, she might have laughed at the sight. As it was, she apologized profusely to the waitress about the spilled coffee and left a tip big enough to excuse the extra work she'd made for the woman.

But it didn't really cheer her up. She went back home and started sculpting a new piece for the gallery. It wasn't necessary work, but it gave her something to do so that she wouldn't spend the day remembering Simon's hard kisses or thinking about how good Jill would look buried up to her armpits in stinging nettles.

The next day she was asked to serve on a committee to oversee Christmas festivities for a local children's shelter. It was a committee that Simon chaired, and she refused politely, only to have him call her right back and ask why.

She was furious. "Don't you know?" she demanded. "You had Jill rub my nose in it for—how did she put this?—chasing you to the opera!"

There was a long pause. "I asked Sherry to give you the ticket to the opera, since she couldn't use it," he confessed, to her surprise. "If anyone was chasing, it was me."

She felt her heart stop. "What?"

"You heard me," he said curtly. There was another pause. "Work with me on the committee. You'll enjoy it."

She would. But she was reluctant to get closer to

him than a telephone receiver. "I don't know that I would," she said finally. "You're not yourself lately."

"I know that." He was feeling his way. "Can't we start again?"

She hesitated. "As what?" she asked bluntly.

"Co-workers. Friends. Whatever you like."

That was capitulation, of a sort, at least. Perhaps he was through trying to make her pay for John's untimely death. Whatever his reason, her life was empty without him, wasn't it? Surely friendship was better than nothing at all? She refused to think about how his kisses had felt.

"Is Jill on the committee?" she asked suddenly, wary of plots.

"No!"

That was definite enough. "All right, then," she said heavily. "I'll do it."

"Good! I'll pick you up for the meeting tomorrow night."

"No, you won't," she returned shortly. "I'll drive myself. Where is it?"

He told her. There was nothing in his voice to betray whether or not he was irritated by her stubborn refusal to ride with him. He was even more irritated by Jill's interference. He'd made a bad mistake there, taking out Tira's worst enemy. He'd been depressed and Jill was good company, but it would have to stop. Tira wasn't going to take kindly to having Jill antagonize her out of sheer rivalry.

Tira went to the meeting, finding several old friends serving on the committee. They worked for three hours on preparations for a party, complete with an elderly local man who had agreed to play Santa Claus for the children. Tira was to help serve and bring two cakes, having volunteered because she had no plans for Christmas Eve other than to lay a trap for that mouse in the kitchen. Another woman, a widow, also volunteered to help, and two of the men, including Simon.

He stopped her by her car after the meeting. "The boys are having a Christmas party Saturday night in Jacobsville. They'd like you to come."

"I don't…"

He put a big forefinger across her soft mouth, startling her. The intimacy was unfamiliar and worrisome.

"Charles can do without you for one Saturday night, can't he?" he asked curtly.

"I haven't seen Charles lately. His brother, Gene, is in the hospital," she said, having forgotten whether or not she'd mentioned it to him. "Nessa isn't coping well at all, and Charles can't leave her alone."

"Nessa?"

"Gene's wife." She wanted to tell him about Nessa and Charles, but it wasn't her secret and letting him think she and Charles were close was the only shield she had at the moment. She couldn't let her guard down. She still didn't quite trust him. His new attitude toward her was puzzling and she didn't understand why he'd changed.

"I see."

"You don't, but it doesn't matter. I want to go home. I'm cold."

He searched her quiet face. "I could offer an alternative," he said in a soft, velvety tone.

She looked up at him with cool disdain. "I don't do casual affairs, Simon," she said bluntly. "Just in case the thought had crossed your mind lately."

He looked as if he'd been slapped. His jaw tautened.

"Don't you? Then if your affair with Charles Percy isn't casual, why hasn't he married you?"

"I don't want to marry again," she said in a husky voice, averting her eyes. "Not ever."

He hesitated. He knew why she felt that way, that she'd been betrayed in the worst way. Her father-in-law had told him everything, but he was uncertain about whether or not to tell her that he knew.

She glanced at him warily. "Does Jill know that you're still grieving for your wife?" she asked, taking the fight right into the enemy camp. "Or is she just an occasional midnight snack?"

His eyebrows arched. "That's a hell of a comparison."

"Isn't it?" She smiled sweetly. "I'm going home."

"Come to Jacobsville with me."

"And into the jaws of death or kitchen slavery?" she taunted. "I know all about the biscuit mania. I'm not about to be captured by your loopy brothers."

"They won't come near you," he promised. "Corrigan's hired a new cook. She's redheaded and she can bake anything."

"She won't last two weeks before Leopold has her running for the border," she assured him.

It pleased him that she knew his brothers so well, that she took an interest in his family. She and Corrigan had been friends and occasionally had dated in the past, but there had been no spark between them. In fact, Charles Percy had always been in the way of any other man and Tira. Why hadn't he noticed that before?

"You've been going around with Charles ever since you left John," he recalled absently.

"Charles is my friend," she said.

"Friend," he scoffed, his eyes insulting. "Is that what it's called these days?"

"You should know," she returned. "What does Jill call it?"

His eyes narrowed angrily. "At least she's honest about what she wants from me," he replied. "And it isn't my money."

She shrugged. "To each his own."

He searched her face quietly. "You kissed me back the other night."

Her cheeks went ruddy and she looked away, clutching her purse. "I have to go."

He was right behind her. He didn't touch her, but she could feel the warm threat of him all down her spine, oddly comforting in the chilly December air.

"Stop running!"

Her eyes closed for an instant before she reached for the door handle. "We seemed to be friends once," she said in a husky tone. "But we weren't, not really. You only tolerated me. I'm amazed that I went through all those years so blind that I never saw the contempt you felt when you looked at me."

"Tira…"

She turned, holding up a hand. "I'm not accusing you. I just want you to know that I'm not carrying a torch for you or breaking my heart because you go around with Jill." Her eyes were lackluster and he realized with a start that she'd lost a lot of weight in the past few months. She looked fragile, breakable.

"What are you saying?" he asked.

"That I don't need you to pity me, Simon," she said with visible pride. "I don't really want a closer association with you, whatever Jill says or you think. I'm rearranging my life. I've started over. I don't want to go back to the way we were."

He felt those words like a knife. She meant them. It was in her whole expression.

"I see," he said quietly.

"No, you don't," she replied heavily. "You're sort of like a drug," she mused. "I was addicted to you and I've been cured, but even small doses are dangerous to my recovery."

His heart leaped. He caught her gaze and held it relentlessly. "What did you say?"

"You know what I mean," she returned. "I'm not going to let myself become addicted again. I have Charles and you have Jill. Let's go our separate ways and get on with our lives. I was serious about the pistol and the mouse, you know, it wasn't some face-saving excuse. I never meant to kill myself over you."

"Oh, hell, I knew that."

"Then why…"

"Yes?"

She turned her purse in her hands. "Why do you keep engineering situations where we'll be thrown together?" she asked. "It serves no purpose."

His hand came out of his pocket and lifted to touch, lightly, her upswept hair. She flinched and he dropped his hand with a long sigh.

"You can't forget, can you?" he asked slowly.

"I'm trying," she assured him. "But every time we're together, people speculate. The newspaper stories were pretty hard to live down, even for me. I don't really want to rekindle speculation."

"You never cared about gossip before."

"I was never publicly savaged before," she countered. "I've been made to look like some clinging, simpering nymph crying for a man who doesn't want her. My pride is in shreds!''

He was watching her narrowly. "How do you know that I don't want you, Tira?" he asked deliberately.

She stared at him without speaking, floored by the question.

"I'll pick you up at six on Saturday and drive you to Jacobsville," he said. "Wear something elegant. It's formal."

"I won't go," she said through her teeth.

"You'll go," he replied with chilling certainty.

He turned and walked to his own car with her glaring after him. Well, they'd just see about that! she told herself.

It was barely a week until Christmas. Tira had the party for the children to look forward to on Christmas Eve, to help her feel some Christmas spirit. She had an artificial tree that she set up in her living room every year. She'd have loved a real one, with its own dirt ball so that it could be set out in the yard after the holidays, but she was violently allergic to fir trees of any kind. The expensive artificial tree was very authentic-looking and once she decorated it, it could have fooled an expert at a distance.

She had a collection of faux gold-plated cherubs and elegant gold foil ribbons to use for decorations, along with gold and silver bead strands and fairy lights. For whimsy, there were a few mechanical ornaments scattered deep within the limbs, which could be activated by the touch of a finger. She had a red-and-white latch-hook rug that went around the base of the tree, and around that was a Lionel "O" scale train set—the one she'd seen in the window of the department store that day she'd come across Simon on the sidewalk. She'd gone back and bought the train, and now she enjoyed watching it run. It only lacked one or two little lighted buildings to go beside it. Those, she reasoned, she could add later.

She stood back and admired her handiwork. She was wearing a gold-and-white caftan that echoed the color scheme of the tree, especially with her hair loose. It was Saturday, but she wasn't going to the Hart party. In fact, when Simon rang the doorbell, he wasn't going to get into the house. She felt very smug about the ease with which she'd avoided him.

"Very nice," came a deep, amused voice from behind her.

She whirled and found Simon, in evening clothing, watching her from the doorway.

"How...how did you get in?" she gasped.

"Mrs. Lester kindly left the back door unlocked for me," he mused. "I told her that we were going out and that you'd probably forget. She's very obliging. A real romantic, Mrs. Lester."

"I'll fire her Monday the minute she gets back from her sister's!" she snarled.

"No, you won't. She's a treasure."

She swept back her hair. "I'm not going to Jacobsville!"

"You are," he said. "Either you get dressed, or I dress you."

"Ha!" She folded her arms across her chest and dared him to do his worst.

The prospect seemed to amuse him. He took her by the arm with his good hand and led her down the hall to her bedroom, opened the door, put her in and closed it behind them. He'd already been here, she could tell,

because a white strapless evening gown was laid out
on the bed, along with filmy underthings that matched
it.

"You...you invaded my bedroom!" she raged.

"Yes, I did. It was very educational. You don't dress
like a siren at all. Most of your wardrobe seems to
consist of cotton underthings and jeans and tank tops."
He glanced at her. "I like that caftan you're wearing,
but it's not quite appropriate for tonight's festivities."

"I'm not putting on that dress."

He chuckled softly. "You are. Sooner or later."

She started toward the door and found herself swept
up against him, held firmly by that damned prosthesis
that seemed to work every bit as well as the arm it had
replaced.

"I'm not going to hurt you," he promised softly.
"But you're going."

"I will...what are you...doing?"

She'd forgotten the front zip that kept the caftan on
her. He released it with a minimum of fuss and the
whole thing dropped to the floor, leaving her in her
bare feet and nude except for her serviceable white
briefs.

She gaped at him. He looked at her body with the
appreciation of an artist, noting the creamy soft rise of
her breasts with their tight rosy nipples and the supple
curve of her waist that flared to rounded hips and long,
elegant legs.

"Don't you...look at me!" she gasped, trying to
cover herself.

His eyes met hers quizzically. "Don't you want me
to?" he asked softly.

The question surprised her. She only stared at him,
watching his gaze fall again to her nudity and sweep

over it with pure delight. She shivered at the feel of his gaze.

"It's all right," he said gently, surprised by the way she was reacting. "I'm not even going to touch you. I promise."

She drew in a shaky breath, held close by one arm while his other hand traced along her flushed cheek and down to the corner of her tremulous mouth.

What an unexpected creature she was, he thought with some confusion. She was embarrassed, shy, even a little ashamed to stand here this way. She blushed like a girl. He knew that she couldn't be totally innocent, but her reaction was nothing like that of an experienced woman.

His fingers traced over her mouth and down the curve of her pulsating throat to her collarbone. They hesitated there and his gaze fell to her mouth.

The silence in the bedroom was like the silence in the eye of a hurricane. If she breathed the wrong way, it would break the spell, and he'd draw away. His fingers, even now, were hesitating at her collarbone and his mouth hovered above hers as if he couldn't quite decide what to do next.

She shivered, her own eyes lingering helplessly on the long, wide curve of his mouth.

He moved, just slightly, so that her body was completely against his, and he let her feel the slow burgeoning of his arousal. It shocked her. He saw the flush spread all over her high cheekbones.

"Tira," he said roughly, "tell me what you want."

"I don't…know," she whispered brokenly, searching his pale, glittering eyes. "I don't know!"

He felt her hips move, just a fraction, felt her body shift so that she was faintly arched toward him. "Don't you?'' he whispered back. ''Your body does. Shall I show you what it's asking me to do?''

She couldn't manage words, but he didn't seem to need them. With a faint smile, he lifted his hand and spread it against her rib cage, slowly, torturously sliding it up until it was resting just at the underside of her taut breast. She shivered and caught her breath, her eyes wide and hungry and still frightened.

''It won't hurt,'' he whispered, and his hand moved up and over her nipple, softly caressing.

She clutched his shoulders and hid her face against him in a torment of shattered sensations, moaning sharply at the intimate touch.

He hesitated. ''What's wrong?'' he asked gently. His face nuzzled against her cheek, forcing her head back so that he could see her shocked, helpless submission. He touched her again, easing his fingers together over the hard nipple as he tugged at it gently. The look on her face made his whole body go rigid.

Her head went back. Her eyes closed. She shivered, biting her lip to keep from weeping, the pleasure was so overwhelming.

If she was shaken, so was he. It was relatively chaste love play, but she was already reacting as if his body was intimately moving on hers. Her response was as unexpected as it was flattering.

''Come here,'' he said with rough urgency, tugging her to the bed. He pulled her down with him on the coverlet beside her gown and shifted so that she was beneath him. His rapid heartbeat was causing him to shake even before he found her mouth with his and began to caress her intimately.

''Simon,'' she sobbed. But she was pulling, not pushing. Her mouth opened for him, her body rose as he caressed it with his hand and then with his open mouth. He suckled her, groaning when she shivered and cried out from the pleasure. He was in so deep that he couldn't have pulled back to save his own life. He'd never known an exchange so heated, so erotic. He wanted to do things to and with her that he'd never dreamed of doing to a woman in his life.

His mouth eased back onto hers and gentled her as his hand moved under the elastic at her hips and descended slowly. Her legs parted for him. She gasped as he began to touch her, sobbed, wept, clutched him. She was ready for him, and he'd barely begun.

Even while his head spun with delight, he knew that it was wrong. It was all wrong. He'd been too long without a woman and this was too fiery, too consuming, for a first time with her. He was going in headfirst and she wouldn't enjoy it. But he couldn't stop himself.

"Tira," he groaned at her ear. "Sweetheart, not now. Not like this. For God's sake, help me…!"

His hand stilled, his mouth lay hot and hard against her throat while he lay against her, his big body faintly tremulous as he tried to overcome his urgent, aching need for her.

Seven

Tira barely heard him. Her body was shivering with new sensations, with exquisite glimpses of the pleasure he could offer her. She felt him go heavy in her arms and slowly, breath by breath, she began to realize where they were and what they were doing.

She caught her breath sharply, aware that her hands were still tangled in the thick, cool darkness of his wavy hair. She was almost completely nude and he'd touched her....

"Simon!" she exclaimed, aghast.

"Shhh." His mouth turned against her throat. His hand withdrew to her waist and his head lifted. He was breathing as raggedly as she was. The turbulence of his eyes surprised her, because his usual impeccable control was completely gone. He saw her expression and managed a smile. "Are you shocked that we could be like this, together?" he asked gently.

"Yes."

"So am I. But I don't want you like this, not in a fever so high that I can't think past relief," he said quietly. He moved away from her with obvious reluctance and took one last, sweeping glance at her yielded body before he sat up with his back to her and leaned forward to breathe.

She tugged the coverlet over her heated flesh and bit her swollen lips in an agony of shame and embarrassment. How in the world had *that* happened? If he hadn't stopped...!

He got to his feet, stretched hugely and then turned toward her. She lay with her glorious hair in a tangle around her white face, looking up at him almost fearfully.

"There's no need to look like that, Tira," he said softly, with eyes so tender that they confused her. He reached down and tugged the coverlet away, pulling her slowly to her feet. "The world won't end."

He reached for the strapless bra he'd taken from her bureau and using the prosthesis to anchor it, he looped it around her and held it in place.

"You'll have to fasten it," he said with a complete lack of self-consciousness. "I can't do operations that complex."

She obeyed him as if she were a puppet and he was pulling strings.

He held the half-slip and coaxed her to lean against him while she stepped into it. He pulled it up. He reached for the exquisite gown and deftly slid it over her head, watching while she tugged it into place. He turned her around and while she held up her hair, he zipped it into place.

He led her to the vanity and handed her a brush. She

sat down obediently and put her unruly hair back into some sort of order, belatedly using a faint pink lipstick and a little powder. He stood behind her the whole while, watching.

When she finished, he drew her up again and held her in front of him.

"How long have we known each other?" he asked solemnly.

"A long time. Years." She couldn't meet his probing gaze. She felt as if she had absolutely no will of her own. The sheer vulnerability was new and frightening. She took a deep breath. "We should go."

He tilted her remorseful eyes up to his. "Don't be ashamed of what we did together," he said quietly.

She winced. "You don't even like me…!"

He drew her close and rocked her against his tall body, his cheek pressed to her hair as he stroked the silken length of it. "Shhh." He kissed her hair and then her cheek, working his way up to her wet eyes. He kissed the tears away gently and then lifted his head and looked down into the drowned green depths. He couldn't remember ever feeling so tender with a woman. He remembered how her soft skin felt against his mouth and his breathing became labored. He stepped back a little, so that she wouldn't notice how easily she aroused him now.

She sniffed inelegantly and reached on the vanity for a tissue. "My nose will be as red as my eyes," she commented, trying to break the tension.

"As red as the highlights in your glorious hair," he murmured, touching it. He sighed. "I want you with me tonight," he said softly. "But if you really don't want to go, I won't force you."

She looked up, puzzled by his phrasing. "You said you would."

He frowned slightly. "I don't like making you cry," he said bluntly. "Until now, I didn't know that I could. It's uncomfortable."

"I've had a long week," she said evasively.

"We both have. Come with me. No strings. You'll have fun."

She hesitated, but only for a minute. "All right."

He reached down and curled her small hand into his big one. The contact was thrilling, exciting. She looked up into eyes that confused her.

"Don't think," he said. "Come along."

He pulled her along with him, out of the bedroom, out the door. It was new to have Simon act possessively about her, to be tender with her. It hurt terribly, in a way, because now she knew exactly what she'd missed in her life. Simon would be all she'd ever need, but she cared too much to settle for a casual affair. Regardless of what he thought of her marriage to John, and she had no reason to believe that he'd changed his mind about it, she did believe in marriage. She didn't want to be anyone's one-night stand; not even Simon's.

The long drive down to Jacobsville wasn't as harrowing as she'd expected it to be. Simon talked about politics and began asking pointed questions about an upcoming fund-raiser.

She wasn't comfortable with the new relationship between them, so when he asked if she might like to help with some projects for the governor if he took on the attorney general's job, she immediately suspected that he was using her helpless attraction to him to win her support.

She looked down at the small white beaded evening bag in her lap. "If I have time," she said, stalling.

He glanced at her as they passed through the gaily decorated downtown section of Jacobsville, dressed like a Christmas tree for the holidays with bright colored lights and tinsel.

"What else have you got to do lately?" he asked pointedly.

She stared at her bag. "I might do another exhibit."

He didn't ask again, but he looked thoughtful.

The Hart ranch was impressive, sprawling for miles, with the white fence that surrounded the house and immediate grounds draped with green garlands and artificial poinsettias.

"They haven't done that before," she commented as they went down the long paved driveway to the house.

"Oh, they've made a number of improvements since Dorie married Corrigan last Christmas and moved into their new house next door to this one," he explained.

"Reluctant improvements, if I know Callaghan."

He chuckled. "Cag doesn't go in much for frills."

"Is he still not eating pork?"

He gave her a wry glance. "Not yet."

It was a family joke that the eldest bachelor brother wouldn't touch any part of a pig since he'd seen the movie about the one that talked, a box office smash.

"I can't say that I blame him," she murmured. "I saw the movie three times myself."

He chuckled. It was a rare sound these days and she glanced at him with a longing that she quickly concealed when his eyes darted toward her.

He pulled up in front of the sprawling ranch house and got out, noting that Tira did the same without wait-

ing for him to open her door. Her independent spirit
irritated him at times, but he respected her for it.

When she started up the steps ahead of him, he
caught her hand and kept it in his as they reached the
porch, where Corrigan and Dorie greeted them with
warm hugs and smiles. Tira smiled automatically, so
aware of Simon's big hand in hers that she was almost
floating.

"You're just in time," Corrigan said. "Leopold
spiked the punch and didn't tell Tess, and she got the
wrong side of Evan Tremayne's tongue. She's in the
kitchen giving Leo hell and swearing that he'll never
get another biscuit."

"He must be in tears by now," Simon mused.

"He's on his knees, in fact, groveling." Corrigan
grinned. "It suits him."

They went inside, where they met Evan and his wife,
Anna, who was obviously and joyfully pregnant with
their first child, and the Ballenger brothers, Calhoun
and Justin, with their wives Abby and Shelby, all
headed toward the front door together. They were all
founding families in the area, with tremendous wealth
and power locally. Tira knew of them, but it was the
first time she'd met them face-to-face. It didn't surprise
her that the brothers had such contacts. They made
friends despite their sometimes reclusive tendencies.
All the same, the party looked as if it had only just
started, and it puzzled her that these people were leaving so soon. They didn't seem angry, but with those
bland expressions, it was sometimes hard to tell if they
were.

Tira looked around for Cag and Rey and just spotted
them going through the swinging door of the kitchen.
In the open doorway she caught a glimpse of Leopold

on his knees in a prayerful stance with a thin young redhead standing over him looking outraged.

Tira chuckled. Simon, having seen the same thing, laughed out loud.

"This is too good to miss. Come on." He nodded at other people he knew as they wove their way through the crowd and reached the kitchen.

Stealthily Simon pushed open the door. The sight that met their eyes was pitiful. Leopold was still on his knees, with Cag verbally flaying him while Rey looked on approvingly.

They glanced toward the door when Simon and Tira entered. Leopold actually blushed as he scrambled to his feet.

Tess grimaced as she spotted Simon, one of the only two brothers who actively intimidated her. "I don't care what they say, I'm quitting!" she told him despite her nervousness. "He—" she pointed at Leopold "—poured two bottles of vodka in my special tropical punch, and Evan Tremayne didn't realize it was spiked until he'd had his second glass and fell over a chair." She blushed. "He said terrible things to me! And he—" she pointed at Leopold again "—thought it was funny!"

"Evan Tremayne falling over a chair would make most people in Jacobsville giggle," Tira stated, "knowing how he hates alcohol."

"It gets worse," Tess continued, brushing back a short strand of red hair, her blue eyes flashing. "Evan thought the punch was so good that he gave a glass of it to Justin Ballenger."

"Oh, God," Simon groaned. "Two of the most fanatical teetotalers in the county."

"Justin got a guitar and started singing some Spanish song. Shelby dragged the guitar out of his hands just in time,'' Tess explained. She put her face in her hands. ''That was when Evan realized the punch was spiked and he said I should be strung up over the barn by my apron strings for doing such a nasty thing to your guests.''

''I'll speak to Evan.''

''Not now, you won't,'' Tira mentioned. ''We just met the Tremaynes going out the front door, along with both Ballenger brothers and their wives.''

''Oh, God!'' Leo groaned again.

''I'll phone him and apologize,'' Rey promised. ''I'll call them all and apologize. You can't leave!''

''Yes, I can. I quit.'' Tess had taken off her apron and thrown it at Leopold. ''You'd better learn how to bake biscuits, is all I can say. They—'' she pointed toward Cag and Rey ''—will probably kill you when I leave, and I'm glad! I hope they throw you out in the corral and let the crows eat you! That would get rid of two evils, because the crows will die of food poisoning for sure!''

She stormed through the door and Leopold groaned out loud. Cag's quiet eyes followed her and his face tautened curiously.

''Leo, how could you?'' Rey asked, aghast.

''It wasn't two bottles of vodka,'' he protested. ''It was one. And I meant to give it to Tess, just to irritate her, but I got sidetracked and Evan and Justin...well, you know.'' He brightened. ''At least Calhoun didn't get a taste of it!'' he added, as if that made things all right. Calhoun, once a playboy, was as bad as his brother about liquor since his marriage.

''He left, just the same. But you've got problems

closer to home. You'd better go after her," Simon pointed out.

"And fast!" Rey said through his teeth, black eyes flashing.

"Like a twister," Cag added with narrowed eyes. "If she leaves, you're going to get branded along with that stock I had shipped in today."

"I'm going, I'm going!" Leopold rushed out the back door after their housekeeper.

"Isn't she a little young for a housekeeper?" Simon asked his brothers. "She barely looks nineteen."

"She's twenty-two," Cag said. "Her dad was working for us when he dropped dead of a heart attack. There's no family and she can cook." His powerful shoulders lifted and fell. "It seemed an ideal solution. If we could just keep Leo away from her, things would be fine."

"Why does he have to torment the housekeepers all the time?" Rey asked miserably.

"He'll settle down one day," Cag murmured. He looked distracted, and he was glaring toward the back door. "He'd better not upset her again. In fact, I think I'll make sure he doesn't."

He nodded to the others and went after Leo and Tess.

"He's sweet on her," Rey said when the door closed behind him. "Not that he'll admit it. He thinks she's too young, and she's scared to death of him. She finds every sort of excuse to get out of the kitchen if he's the first one down in the mornings. It's sort of comical, in a way. I don't guess she knows that she could bring him to his knees with a smile."

"She's very young," Tira commented.

Rey glanced at her. "Yes, she is. Just what Cag needs, too, something to nurture. He's always bringing home stray kittens and puppies…just like her.'' He pointed to a small kitten curled up in a little bed in the corner of the kitchen. ''She rescued the kitten from the highway. Cag bought the bed for it. They're a match made in heaven, but Leo's going to ruin everything. I think he's sweet on her, too, and trying to cut Cag out before she notices how much time he spends watching her.''

''This is not our problem,'' Simon assured his brother. ''But I'd send Leo off to cooking school if I were you. No woman is ever going to be stupid enough to marry him and if he learns to make biscuits, you can do without housekeepers.''

''He made scrambled eggs one morning when Tess had to go to the eye doctor early to pick up her contacts,'' Rey said. ''The dogs wouldn't even touch them!'' He glared at Tira and Simon and shrugged. ''Come on. We've still got a few guests who haven't gone home. I'll introduce you to them.''

He led them into the other room and stopped suddenly, turning to look at them. ''Wait a minute. Corrigan said you weren't speaking to each other after that newspaper stupidity.''

Simon still had Tira's slender hand tight in his. ''A slight misunderstanding. We made up. Didn't we?'' he asked, looking down at Tira with an expression that made her face turn red.

Rey made a sound under his breath and quickly changed the subject.

Corrigan and Dorie joined them at the punch bowl, which had been refilled and dealcoholized. Dorie looked almost as pregnant as Anna Tremayne had, and she was radiant. Not even the thin scar on her delicate cheek could detract from her beauty.

"We'd almost given up hope," she murmured, laughing up at her adoring husband. "And then, wham!"

"We're over the moon," Corrigan said. The limp left over from his accident of years ago was much less noticeable now, he didn't even require a cane.

"I'm going to be an uncle," Simon murmured. "I might like that. I saw a terrific set of "O" scale electric trains in a San Antonio toy store a few days ago. Kids love trains."

"That's right, boys and girls alike," Tira murmured, not mentioning that she'd bought that train set for herself.

"Did you know that two of our local doctors, who are married to each other, have several layouts of them?" Corrigan murmured. "The doctors Coltrain. They invited kids from the local orphanage over for Christmas this year and have them set up and running. It's something of a local legend."

"I like trains," Simon said. "Remember that set Dad bought us?" he asked Corrigan.

"Yeah." The brothers shared a memory, not altogether a good one judging from their expression.

"This isn't spiked, anymore?" Tira asked, changing the subject as she stared at the punch bowl.

"I swear," Corrigan said, smiling affectionately at her. "Help yourself."

She did, filling one for Simon as well, and talk went to general subjects rather than personal ones.

The local live cowboy band played a slow, lazy tune and Simon pulled Tira onto the dance floor, wrapping her up tight in his arms.

The one with the prosthesis was a little uncomfortable and she moved imperceptibly.

"Too tight?" Simon asked softly, and let up on the pressure. "Sorry. I'm used to the damned thing, but I still can't quite judge how much pressure to use."

"It's all right. It didn't hurt."

He lifted his head and looked down into her eyes. "You're the only woman who's ever seen me without it," he mused. "In the hospital, when it was a stump—"

"You may have lost part of your arm, but you're alive," she interrupted. "If you hadn't been found for another hour, nothing would have saved you. As it was, you'd lost almost too much blood."

"You stayed with me," he recalled. "You made me fight. You made me live. I didn't want to."

She averted her eyes. "I know how much Melia meant to you, Simon. You don't have to remind me."

Secrets, he thought. There were so many secrets that he kept, that she didn't know about. Perhaps it kept the distance between them. It was time to shorten it.

"Melia had an abortion."

She didn't grasp what he was saying at first, and the lovely green eyes she lifted to his were curious. "What?"

"I made her pregnant and she ended it, and never told me," he said shortly. "She didn't want to ruin her figure. Of course, she wasn't positive that the baby was mine. It could have been by one of her other lovers."

She'd stopped dancing to stare up at him uncomprehendingly.

"She told me, the night of the accident," he continued. "That's why I lost control of the car in a curve, in the rain, and I remember thinking in the split second before it crashed that I didn't care to live with all my illusions dead."

"Illusions?" she echoed.

"That my marriage was perfect," he said. "That my beloved wife loved me equally, that she wanted my children and a lifetime with only me." He laughed coldly. "I married a cheap, selfish woman whose only concern was living in luxury and notching her bedpost. It excited her that she had men and I didn't know. She had them in my bed." His voice choked with anger, and he looked over her head. His arm had unconsciously tightened around Tira, and this time she didn't protest. She was shocked by what he was telling her. She'd thought, everyone had thought, that he'd buried his heart in Melia's grave and had mourned her for years.

"The child was what hurt the most," he said stiffly. "I believed her when she said she thought she was sterile. It was a lie. Everything she said was a lie, and I was too besotted to realize it. She made a fool of me."

"I'm so sorry for all the pain you've been through." Her eyes filled with tears. "It must have been awful."

He looked down at her, his eyes narrow and probing. "You were married to John when it happened. You came to the hospital every day. You held my hand, my good hand, and talked to me, forced me to get up, to try. I always felt that you left John because of me, and it made me feel guilty. I thought I'd broken up your marriage."

She dropped her gaze to his strong neck. "No," she said tersely. "You didn't break it up."

He curled her fingers into his and brought them to his chest, holding them there warmly. "Were you in love with him, at first?"

"I was attracted to him, very fond of him," she confessed softly. "And I wanted, badly, to make our marriage work." She shivered a little and he drew her closer. Her eyes closed. "I thought...I wasn't woman enough."

His indrawn breath was audible. He knew the truth about her marriage now, but he hesitated to bring up a painful subject again when things were going so well for them. His lips moved down to her eyes and kissed the eyelids with breathless tenderness.

"Don't cry," he said curtly. "You're more than woman enough. Come closer, and I'll prove it to you, right here."

"Simon..."

His arm slid down, unobtrusively, and drew her hips firmly against his. He shuddered as the touch of her body produced an immediate, violent effect.

She gasped, but he wouldn't let her step back.

"Do you feel how much I want you?" he whispered in her ear. "I've barely touched you and I'm capable."

"You're a man..."

"It doesn't, it never has, happened that fast with anyone else," he said through his teeth. "I want you so badly that it hurts like hell. Yes, Tira, you're woman enough for any man. I'm sorry that your husband didn't... No, that's a lie." He lifted his head and looked into her shocked eyes. "I'm glad he couldn't have you."

The words went right over her head because she was so shocked at what he was saying. She stared at him in evident confusion and embarrassment, her eyes darting around to see if anyone was watching. Nobody was.

"It doesn't show. There's no reason to be so tense." His arm moved back up to her waist and loosened a little.

She drew in steadying breaths, but she felt weak. Her head went to his chest and she made a plaintive little sound against it.

His fingers contracted around hers. "We opened Pandora's box together in your bedroom, on your bed," he whispered at her ear. "We want each other, Tira."

She swallowed. "I can't."

"Why not?"

She hesitated, but only for an instant. "I don't have affairs, Simon."

"Of course you do, darling," he drawled with barely concealed jealousy. "What else do you have with Charles Percy?"

Eight

Tira stopped dancing. She wasn't sure why she was upset, because Simon had made no bones about thinking she was sleeping with Charles. Apparently when he'd made light love to her earlier, he'd thought her responses were those of an experienced woman. She wondered what he'd think if he knew the truth, that she'd waited for him all these years, that she wanted no other man.

"Go ahead," he invited, a strange light in his eyes. "Deny it."

She let her gaze fall to his wide, firm mouth. "Think what you like," she invited. "You will anyway. And I'll remind you, Simon, that you have no right to question me about Charles."

"No right? After what you let me do to you?"

She flushed and her teeth clenched. "One weak moment…"

"Weak, the devil," he muttered quietly. "You were starving to death. Doesn't he make love to you anymore?"

"Simon, please don't," she pleaded. "Not tonight."

The hand holding hers contracted. "Were you thinking of him, then?"

"Heavens, no!" she burst out, aghast.

He searched her eyes for a long moment, until he saw her cheeks flush. His hand relaxed.

"I wasn't the only one who was starving," she murmured, a little embarrassed.

He coaxed her cheek onto his chest. "No, you weren't," he agreed. He closed his eyes as they moved to the music.

She was surprised that he could admit his own hunger. They were moving into a totally new relationship. She didn't know what to make of it, and she didn't quite trust him, either. But what she was feeling was so delicious that she couldn't fight it. She let her body go lax against him and breathed in the spicy scent of his cologne. Her hand moved gently against his shirt, feeling hair and hard, warm muscle under it. He stiffened and it delighted her that he could react so strongly to such an innocent caress.

"You'd better not," he whispered at her ear.

Her hand stilled. "Are you...hairy all over?" she whispered back.

He stiffened even more. "In places."

Her cheek moved against his chest and she sighed. "I'm sleepy," she murmured, closing her eyes as they moved lazily to the music.

"Want to go home?"

"We haven't been here very long."

"It doesn't matter. I've had a hard week, too." He

let her move away. "Come on. We'll make our excuses and leave."

They found Corrigan and asked him to tell the others Merry Christmas for them.

"They're still trying to talk Tess out of leaving," he murmured dryly. "I hope they can. The smell of baking biscuits makes Dorie sick right now," he said, glancing down at his wife lovingly. "So they'll have to go without if they can't change her mind."

"I wish them luck," Simon said. "We enjoyed the party. Next year, maybe I'll throw one and you can all come up to San Antonio for it."

"I'll hold you to that," Corrigan replied. He glanced from one of them to the other. "Have you two given up combat?"

"For the moment," Tira agreed with a wan smile.

"For good," Simon added.

"We'll see about that," Tira returned, her eyes flashing at him even through her fatigue.

They said their goodbyes and Simon drove them back to San Antonio. But instead of taking her home, he took her to his apartment.

She wondered why she didn't protest, which she certainly should have. She was too curious about why he'd come here.

"No questions?" he asked when they stepped out of the elevator on the penthouse floor.

"I suppose you'll tell me when you're ready," she replied, but with a faintly wary gaze.

"No need to worry," he said as he unlocked his door. "You won't get seduced unless you want to."

She blushed again and hated her own naivete. She followed him inside.

She'd never seen his apartment before. This was one

invitation she'd always hoped for and never got. Simon's private life was so private that even his brothers knew little of it.

The apartment was huge and furnished in browns and creams and oranges. He had large oil paintings, mostly of landscapes, on the walls, and the furniture had a vaguely Mediterranean look to it. It was heavy and old, and beautifully polished.

She ran her hand over the rosewood back of the green velvet-covered sofa that graced the living room. "This is beautiful," she commented.

"I hoped you might think so."

There was a long pause, during which she became more and more uncomfortable. She glanced at Simon and found him watching her with quiet, unblinking silvery eyes.

"You're making me nervous," she laughed unsteadily.

"Why?"

She shrugged in the folds of her velvet wrap. "I'm not sure."

He moved toward her with a walk that was as blatant as if he'd been whispering seductive comments to her. He took the cloak from her shoulders and the evening bag from her hands, tossing both onto the sofa. His jacket followed it. He took her hands and lifted them to his tie.

She hesitated. His fingers pressed her hands closer.

With breath that was coming hard and fast into her throat, she unfastened the silk tie and tossed it onto the sofa. He guided her fingers back to the top buttons of his shirt.

The silence in the apartment was tense, like the set of Simon's handsome, lean face. He stood quietly before her, letting her unfasten the shirt. But when she started to push it away, he shook his head.

"Looking at the prosthesis doesn't bother me," she said huskily.

"Humor me."

He drew her close and, pressing her fingers into the thick hair that covered his broad, muscular chest, he bent to her mouth.

His lips were tender and slow. He kissed her with something akin to reverence, brushing her nose with his as he made light contacts that provoked a new and sweeping longing for more.

Her fingers contracted in the hair on his chest and she went on tiptoe to coax his mouth harder against her own.

She felt his good hand on the zipper that held up her gown. She didn't protest as he slid it down and let the dress fall to the floor. She didn't protest, either, when he undid the catches to her longline bra with just the fingers of one hand. That, too, fell away and his gaze dropped hungrily to her pretty, taut breasts.

She stepped out of her shoes and he took her hand, pulling her along with him to his bedroom. It was decorated in the same earth tones as the living room. The bed was king-size, overlaid with a cream-and-brown striped quilted bedspread and a matching dust ruffle.

He reached behind him and closed the door, locking it as well.

She looked into his eyes with mingled hunger and apprehension. She knew exactly what he was going to do. She wanted to tell him how inexperienced she was, but she couldn't quite get the words out.

He led her to the bed and eased her down onto it. His hand went to his belt. He let his slacks fall to the floor and, clad only in black silk boxer shorts, he sat down on the bed and removed his shoes and socks.

"Your shirt," she whispered.

He eased down beside her, levering himself just above her at an angle. "I don't think I can do this without the prosthesis," he said quietly. "But I'd rather you didn't see it. Do you mind?"

She shook her head. He was devastating at close range. She loved the look of him, the feel of his hand on her face, her throat, then suddenly whispering over her taut breasts.

She arched under even that light pressure and her hands clenched as she looked up at him.

"Are you going to let me take you?" he asked in a soft, blunt tone.

She bit her lower lip worriedly. "Simon, I'm not sure—"

"Yes, you are," he interrupted. "You want me every bit as badly as I want you."

She still hesitated, but then she spoke. "Yes, I do." that was all she said—she couldn't tell him her secret yet.

He touched the hard tip of her breast and watched her shiver. "You beautiful creature," he said half under his breath. "I only hope I can do you justice."

While she was searching for the right words to make her confession, his head bent and his mouth suddenly opened right on her breast.

She caught his head, her nails biting into his scalp.

He lifted himself just enough to see her worried eyes. "I'm only going to suckle you," he said with soft surprise, wondering what sort of lover Charles Percy must have been to make her so afraid. "I won't hurt you."

He bent again, and this time she didn't protest. She couldn't. It was so sweet that it made her head spin to feel his hot, hard, moist mouth closing over the tight nipple. She moaned under her breath and writhed with pleasure. He nibbled her for a long time, moving slowly from one breast to the other while his hand traced erotic patterns on her belly and the insides of her thighs.

She barely noticed when he removed her briefs and then his own. His practiced caresses overwhelmed her. She was so enthralled by them that she ached to know him completely.

A long, feverish few minutes later, he moved between her long legs and his mouth pushed hard against her lips as his hips eased down against hers and he penetrated her.

The sensation was shocking, frightening. She drifted from a euphoric tension to harsh pain. Her nails bit into his broad shoulders and she called his name. But he was in over his head, all too quickly. He groaned harshly and pushed harder, crying out as he felt her envelope him.

"Oh…!" she sobbed, pushing against his chest.

He stilled for an instant, shuddering, and lifted tortured eyes to hers. "I'm hurting you?" he whispered shakenly. "Dear God…no, sweetheart!…don't move like that…!"

She shifted her hips in an effort to avoid the pain, and her sharp movements took him right over the edge.

His face tautened. He pushed, hard, his body totally out of control. "Oh, God, Tira, I'm so sorry…!" he said through his teeth, his eyes closed, his body suddenly urgent on hers.

He whispered it constantly until he completed his

possession of her, and seconds later, he arched and shuddered and cried out in a hoarse groan as completion left him exhausted and shivering on her damp body.

She felt him relax heavily onto her damp skin, so that she could barely breathe for the weight. She wept silently at the reality of intimacy. It wasn't glorious fireworks of ecstasy at all. It was just a painful way to give a man pleasure. She hated him. She hated herself more for giving in.

"Please," she choked. "Let me go."

There was a pause. He drew in a long breath. "Not on your life," he said huskily.

He lifted his head and stared into her eyes with an expression on his lean face that she couldn't begin to understand.

"Charles Percy," he said deliberately, "is definitely not your lover."

She swallowed and her face flamed. "I...I never said he was, not really," she stammered.

He supported himself on the prosthesis and looked down at what he could see of her damp, shivering body. He touched her delicately on her stomach and then trailed his hand down to her thighs. There was a smear of blood on them that seemed to capture his attention for a moment.

"Simon, it hurts," she whispered, embarrassed.

His eyes went back to hers. "I know," he replied gently. His hand moved gently between her long legs to where their bodies were still completely joined, and she caught his wrist, gasping.

"Shhh," he whispered. Ignoring her protests, he began to touch her.

Shocked at the sudden burst of unexpected pleasure,

her wide eyes went homing to his. Her mouth opened as the breath came careening out of her. She caught his shoulders again, digging her nails in. This was…it was… Her eyes closed and she moaned harshly and shivered.

"That's it," he whispered, easing his mouth down onto hers as she shivered and shivered again. "This isn't going to hurt. Open your mouth. I want you to know me completely, in every way there is." His hips moved slowly, and he felt her whole body jump as his sensual caresses began to kindle a frightening sweet tension in her. "I'm going to teach you to feel pleasure."

She gripped his shoulders and held on, her eyes closed as his mouth worked its way even deeper into her own. She moved her legs around his muscular thighs to help him, to bring him into even closer contact, and gasped when she felt his invasion of her grow even more powerful, more insistent. The pain was still there, but it didn't matter anymore, because there was such pleasure overlaying it. She wanted him!

She heard her own voice sobbing, pleading with him, as the frenzy of pleasure grew to unbearable proportions. She was beyond pride, beyond protest. He was giving her pleasure of a sort she'd never dreamed existed. She belonged to him, was part of him, owned by him.

His movements grew urgent, deep. He whispered something into her open mouth but she couldn't hear him anymore. She was focused on some dark, sweet goal, every muscle straining toward it, her heartbeat pulsing in time with it, her tense body lifting to meet his as she pleaded for it.

His hips shifted all at once in a violent, hard rhythm

that brought the ecstasy rushing over her like a wave of white-hot sensation. She cried out endlessly as it swept her away, her body pressing to his in a convulsive arch as the pleasure went on and on and on and she couldn't get close enough…!

This time, she didn't feel the weight of him as he collapsed onto her exhausted body. She held him tightly, pulsing in the soft aftermath, her legs trembling as they curled around his. She could hear his ragged breathing as she heard her own.

A long time later, he lifted his head and looked down into her wide eyes. He smiled at the faint shock in them. "Yes," he whispered. "It was good, wasn't it?"

She made an embarrassed sound and hid her face against him.

He smiled against her hair. "I thought it would never stop," he whispered huskily, brushing damp strands of hair away from her lips, her eyes as he turned her toward him. "I've never been fulfilled so completely in all my life."

She searched his eyes, seeing such tenderness in them that she felt warm all over. She reached up and touched his damp face with pure wonder, from his thick eyebrows to his wide, firm mouth and his stubborn chin. She couldn't even speak.

"You must be the only twenty-eight-year-old virgin in Texas," he murmured, and he wasn't joking. His eyes were solemn. "Did you save it for me, all these years?"

She didn't want to admit that. He probably guessed that she had, but only a little pride remained in her arsenal.

She sighed quietly. "I never knew a man that I wanted enough," she confessed, averting a direct answer. She dropped her gaze to his broad, bare chest where the thick hair was damp with sweat. "I suppose you've lost count of all the women you've had in the past few years."

His finger traced her soft mouth. "I haven't had a woman since Melia died. I dated Jill, but we were never intimate."

Her surprise was all too evident as she met his rueful gaze. "What?"

His powerful shoulders rose and fell. "A one-armed man isn't a lover many women would choose. I've been sensitive about it, and perhaps a little standoffish when it came to invitations." He searched her eyes. "I've always been comfortable with you. I knew that if I fumbled, you wouldn't laugh at me."

"Never that," she agreed quietly. She looked at the way they were laying and flushed.

"Now you know," he murmured with a warm smile.

"Yes. Now I know."

"I'm sorry I had to hurt you." Regret was in his eyes as well as his tone. He traced her eyebrows. "It had been too long and I lost control. I couldn't pull away."

"I understood."

"You were tight," he said bluntly. "And very much a virgin. I apologize wholeheartedly for every nasty insinuation I've ever made about you."

She was uncomfortable. Was he apologizing for making love to her?

He tilted her face back up to his and kissed her tenderly. "I won't say I'm sorry," he whispered into her mouth. "You can't imagine how it felt, to know I was the first with you."

She frowned worriedly.

He lifted his head and saw her expression. "What's wrong?" he asked.

"You didn't use anything," she said.

"No. I assumed that you were on the pill," he replied. "That went along with the assumption that you were sleeping with Charles and you'd never gotten pregnant."

The very word made her flush even more. "Well, I'm not," she faltered.

An expression crossed his face that she couldn't understand. He looked down at her body pressed so closely, so intimately to his, and curiously, his big hand smoothed over her flat belly in a strangely protective caress.

"If I made you pregnant..."

He didn't have to finish the sentence. She always seemed to know what he was thinking. She reached up and put her cool fingers against his wide mouth.

"You know me," she whispered, anticipating the question he was afraid to ask.

He sighed and let the worry flow out of him. He bent to her mouth and traced it with his lips. "It would complicate things."

She only smiled. "Yes."

His mouth pressed down hard on hers all at once and his hips moved suggestively.

She cried out.

He stilled instantly, because it wasn't a cry of pleasure. "This is uncomfortable for you now," he said speculatively.

"It is," she confessed reluctantly. "I'm sorry."

"No, I'm sorry that I hurt you." He lifted his weight away and met her eyes. "It may be uncomfortable when I withdraw. I'll be as slow as I can."

The blunt remark made her cheeks go hot, but she watched him lift away from her with frank curiosity and a little awe.

"Oh, my," she whispered when he rolled over onto his back.

"Yes, isn't it shocking?" he whispered and pulled her gently against his side. "And now you know why it was so uncomfortable, don't you?" he teased softly.

She laid her cheek on his broad shoulder. "I have seen the occasional centerfold," she murmured, embarrassed. "Although I have to admit that they weren't in your class!"

He chuckled and took a deep, slow breath. "Your body will adjust to me."

That sounded as if he didn't mean tonight to be an isolated incident, and she frowned, because it worried her. She didn't want to be his mistress. Did he think that she'd agreed to some casual sexual relationship because she'd given in to his ardor?

His hand smoothed over her long, graceful fingers. "When you heal a little, I'll teach you how to give it back," he murmured sleepily. "That was the first thing I noticed when I kissed you," he added. "You didn't fight me, but you didn't respond, either."

She sighed. "I didn't know how," she said honestly. Her wide eyes stared across his chest to the big, dark bureau against the wall. Her nails scraped through the thick hair on his chest and she felt him move sinuously, as if he enjoyed it.

His hand pressed hers closer and he stretched, shivering a little in the aftermath. "I'd forgotten how good it could be," he murmured. He tugged on a damp strand of red-gold hair. "I'm not taking you home."

She stiffened. "But I..."

"But, nothing. You're mine. I'm not letting you go."

That sounded possessive. Perhaps it was a sexual thing that men felt afterward. She knew so little about intimacy and how men reacted to it.

As if he sensed her concern, he eased her over onto her side so that he could see her face. It disturbed him to see her expression.

"This was a mistake," he said at once when he saw her eyes. "Probably my biggest in a long line of them." His big hand pressed hard against her stomach. "But we're going to make it right. If you've got my baby in here, there's no way you're raising it alone. We'll get married as soon as I can get a license."

She was even more shocked by that statement than if he'd asked her to live in sin with him.

She took a breath and hesitated.

His eyes held hers firmly. "Do you want my baby?"

The way he said it made delicious chills run down her spine. There was all the tenderness in the world in the soft question, and tears stung her eyes.

"Oh, yes," she whispered.

He looked at her until her breathing changed, his eyes solemn and possessive as they trailed down to her submissive body and her soft, pretty breasts. He touched them delicately.

"Then we won't use anything," he murmured, lifting his eyes back to hers.

Her lips parted. There were so many questions spinning around in her mind that she couldn't grasp one to single out.

His fingers went up to her lips and traced them very slowly. "Why did you give yourself to me?" he asked.

She stared at him worriedly. "I thought you knew."

"I hope I do." He looked worried now. "I really didn't have any intention of seducing you, in case you wondered. I was going to kiss you. Maybe a little more than just that," he added with a rueful smile. "But you came in here with me like a lamb," he said, as if it awed him that she'd yielded so easily. "You never protested once, until I hurt you." He grimaced and brought her hand to his mouth, kissing the palm hungrily. "I never thought it would hurt you so much!" he said, as if the memory itself was painful. "You cried and started moving, and I lost my head completely. I couldn't even stop…"

"But, it's…it's normal for it to be a little uncomfortable the first time," she said quickly, putting her fingers against his hard mouth. "Simon, some girls are just a little unlucky. I suppose I was one of them. It's all right."

He met her eyes. His were still turbulent. "I wouldn't have hurt you for the world," he whispered huskily. "I wanted you to feel what I was feeling. I wanted you to feel as if the sun had exploded inside you." His fingers tangled softly in her hair. "It was…never like that," he added in quiet wonder as he searched her eyes. "I never knew it could be." He bent and touched his mouth to hers with breathless tenderness. "Dear God, I wanted to cherish you, and I couldn't keep my head long enough! It should have been tender between us, as tender as I feel inside when I touch you. But it had been years, and I was like an animal. I thought you were experienced…!"

She drew his face down to hers and kissed his eyelids closed. Her lips touched softly all over his face, his cheeks, his nose, his hard mouth. She kissed him as if he needed comforting.

"You wanted me," she whispered against his ear as she held him to her. "I wanted you, too. It didn't hurt the second time."

His arms slid under her and he shivered. "It won't ever hurt again. I swear it."

Her legs curled into his and she smiled dreamily. He might not love her, but he felt something much more than physical desire for her. That long, stumbling speech had convinced her of one thing, at least. She would marry him. There was enough to build on.

"Simon?" she whispered.

"Hmmm?"

"I'll marry you."

His mouth turned against her warm throat. "Of course you will," he whispered tenderly.

She closed her eyes and linked her arms around him, her fingers encountering the leather strap of the prosthesis. "Why don't you take it off?" she murmured sleepily.

He lifted his head and frowned. "Tira…"

She sat up, proudly nude, and drew him up with her so that she could push the shirt away. She watched his teeth clench as she undid the straps and eased the artificial appliance away, along with the sleeve that covered the rest of his missing arm.

She drew it softly to her breasts and held it there, watching the expression that bloomed on his lean, hard face at the gesture.

"Yes, you still have feeling in it, don't you?" she murmured with the first glint of humor she'd felt in a long time as she saw the desire kindle in his pale eyes.

"There, and other places," he said tautly. "And you're walking wounded. Don't torture me."

"Okay." She pushed him back down and curled up against him with absolute trust.

She looked like a fairy lying there next to him, as natural as rain or sun with his torn body. He looked at her with open curiosity.

"Doesn't it bother you, really?" he asked.

She nuzzled closer. "Simon, would it bother you if I was missing an arm?" she asked unexpectedly.

He thought about that for a minute. "No."

"Then that answers your question." She smiled. "I'm sleepy."

He laughed softly. "So am I."

He reached up and turned off the lamp, drowsily pulling the covers over them.

She stiffened and he held her closer.

"What is it?" he asked quickly.

"Simon, do you have a housekeeper?"

"Sure. She comes in on Tuesdays and Thursdays." His mouth brushed her forehead. "It's Saturday night," he reminded her. "And we're engaged."

"Okay."

His arm gathered her even closer. "We'll get the license first thing Monday morning and we'll be married Thursday. Who do you want to stand up with us?"

"I suppose it will have to be your brothers," she groaned.

He grinned. "Just thank your lucky stars you didn't refuse to marry me. Remember what happened to Dorie?"

She did. She closed her eyes. "I'm thankful." She drank in the spicy scent of him. "Simon, are you sure?"

"I'm sure." He drew her closer. "And so are you. Go to sleep."

Nine

They got up and showered and then made breakfast together. Tira was still shy with him, after what they'd done, and he seemed to find it enchanting. He watched her fry bacon and scramble eggs while he made coffee. She was wearing one of his shirts and he was wearing only a pair of slacks.

"We'll make an economical couple," he mused. "I like the way you look in my shirts. We'll have to try a few more on you."

"I like the way you look without your shirt," she murmured, casting soft glances at him.

He wasn't wearing the prosthesis and he frowned, as if he wasn't certain whether she was teasing.

She took up the eggs, slid them onto the plate with the bacon, turned the burner off and went to him.

"You're still Simon," she said simply. "It never mattered to me. It never will, except that I'm sorry it had to happen to you.'' She touched his chest with soft, tender hands. ''I like looking at you,'' she told him honestly. ''I wasn't teasing.''

He looked at her in the morning light with eyes that puzzled her. He touched the glory of her long hair tenderly. ''This is all wrong,'' he said quietly. ''I should have taken you out, bought you roses and candy, called you at two in the morning just to talk. Then I should have bought a ring and asked you, very correctly, to marry me. I spoiled everything because I couldn't wait to get you into bed with me.''

She was surprised that it worried him so much. She studied his hard face. ''It's all right.''

He drew in a harsh breath and bent to kiss her forehead tenderly. ''I'm sorry, just the same.''

She smiled and snuggled close to him. ''I love you.''

The words hit him right in the stomach. He drew in his breath as if he felt them. His hand tightened on her shoulder until it bruised. Inevitably he thought of all the wasted years when he'd kept her at a distance, treated her with contempt, ignored her.

''Hey.'' She laughed, wiggling.

He let go belatedly. His expression disturbed her. He didn't look like a happy prospective bridegroom. The eyes that met hers were oddly tortured.

He put her away from him with a forced smile that wouldn't have fooled a total stranger, much less Tira.

''Let's have breakfast.''

''Of course.''

They ate in silence, hardly speaking. He had a second cup of coffee and then excused himself while she put the breakfast things into the dishwasher.

She assumed that he was dressing and wanted her to do the same. She went back into the bedroom and quickly donned the clothing he'd removed the night before, having retrieved half of it from the living room. She didn't understand what was wrong with him, unless he really had lost his head and was now regretting everything including the marriage proposal. She knew from gossip that men often said things they didn't mean to make a woman go to bed with them. She must have been an easy mark, at that, so obviously in love with him that he knew she wouldn't resist him.

Last night it had seemed right and beautiful. This morning it seemed sordid and she felt cheap. Looking at herself in his mirror, she saw the new maturity in her face and eyes and mourned the hopeful young woman who'd come home with him.

He paused in the doorway, watching her. He was fully dressed, right down to the prosthesis.

"I'll take you home," he said quietly.

She turned, without looking at him. "That would be best."

He drove her there in a silence as profound as the one they'd shared over breakfast. When he pulled into her driveway, she held up a hand when he started to cut off the engine.

"You don't need to walk me to the door," she said formally. "I'll...see you."

She scrambled out of the car and slammed the door behind her, all but running for her front door.

The key wouldn't go in the first time, and she could hardly see the lock anyway for the tears.

She didn't realize that Simon had followed her until she felt his hand at her back, easing her inside the house.

"No, please..." she sobbed.

He pulled her into his arms and held her, rocked her, his lips in her hair.

"Sweetheart, don't," he whispered, his deep voice anguished. "It's all right! Don't cry!"

Which only made the tears fall faster. She cried until she was almost sick from crying, and when she finally lifted her head from his chest and saw his grim expression, it was all she could manage not to start again.

"I wish I could carry you," he murmured angrily, catching her by the hand to pull her toward the living room. "It used to give me a distinct advantage at times like these to have two good arms."

He sat down on the sofa and pulled her down into his lap, easing her into the elbow that was part prosthesis so that he could mop up her tears with his handkerchief.

"I don't even have to ask what you're thinking," he muttered irritably as he dried her eyes and nose. "I saw it all in my mirror. Good God, don't you think I'm sorry, too?"

"I know you are," she choked. "It's all right. You don't have to feel guilty. I could have said no."

He stilled. "Guilty about what?"

"Seducing me!"

"I didn't."

Her eyes opened wide and she gaped at him. "You did!"

"You never once said you didn't want to," he reminded her. "In fact, I distinctly remember asking if you did."

She flushed. "Well?"

"I don't feel guilty about *that*," he said curtly.

Her eyebrows lifted. "Then what are you sorry about?"

"That you had to come home in your evening gown feeling like a woman I bought for the night," he replied irritably. He touched her disheveled hair. "You didn't even have a brush or makeup with you."

She searched his face curiously. He was constantly surprising her these days.

He touched her unvarnished lips with a wry finger. "Now you're home," he said. "Go put on some jeans and a shirt and we'll go to Jacobsville and ride horses and have a picnic."

She lost her train of thought somewhere. "You want to take me riding?"

He let his gaze slide down her body and back up and his lips drew up into a sardonic smile. "On second thought, I guess that isn't a very good idea."

She realized belatedly what he was saying and flushed. "Simon!"

"Well, why dance around it? You're sore, aren't you?" he asked bluntly.

She averted her eyes. "Yes."

"We'll have the picnic, but we'll go in a truck when we get to the ranch."

She lifted her face back to his and searched his pale eyes. He looked older today, but more relaxed and approachable than she'd ever seen him. There were faint streaks of silver at his temples now, and silver threads mixed in with the jet black of his hair. She reached up and touched them.

"I'm almost forty," he said.

She bit her lower lip, thinking how many years had passed when they could have been like this, younger and looking forward to children, to a life together.

He drew her face to his chest and smoothed over her hair. She was so very fragile, so breakable now. He'd seen her as a flamboyant, independent, spirited woman who was stubborn and hot-tempered. And here she lay in his arms as if she were a child, trusting and gentle and so sweet that she made his heart ache.

He nuzzled his cheek against hers so that he could find her soft mouth, and he kissed it until a groan of anguish forced its way out of his throat. Oh, God, he thought, the years he'd wasted!

She heard the groan and drew back to look at him.

He was breathing roughly. His eyes, turbulent and fierce, lanced down into hers. He started to speak, just as the doorbell rang.

They both jumped at the unexpected loudness of it.

"That's probably Mrs. Lester," she said worriedly.

"On a Sunday? I thought she spent weekends with her sister?"

She did. Tira climbed out of his arms with warning bells going off in her head. She had a sick feeling that when she opened that door, her whole life was going to change.

And it did.

Charles Percy stood there with both hands in his pockets, looking ten years older and sick at heart.

"Charles!" she exclaimed, speechless.

His eyes ran over her clothing and his eyebrows arched. "Isn't it early for evening gowns?" He scowled. "Surely you aren't just getting home?"

"As a matter of fact, she is," Simon said from the doorway of the living room, and he looked more dangerous than Tira had ever seen him.

He approached Charles with unblinking irritation. "Isn't it early for you to be calling?" he asked pointedly.

"I have to talk to Tira," Charles said, obviously not understanding the situation at all. "It's urgent."

Simon leaned against the doorjamb and waved a hand in invitation.

Charles glared at him. "Alone," he emphasized. His scowl deepened. "And what are you doing here, anyway?" he added, having been so occupied with Gene and Nessa that he still thought Simon and Tira were feuding. "After what you and your vicious girlfriend said to her at the charity ball, I'm amazed she'll even speak to you."

Jill had gone right out of Tira's mind in the past twenty-four hours. Now she looked at Simon and remembered the other woman vividly, and a look of horror overtook her features.

Simon saw his life coming apart in those wide green eyes. Tira hadn't remembered Jill until now, thank God, but she was going to remember a lot more, thanks to Charles here. He glared at the man as if he'd have liked to punch him.

"Jill is part of the past," he said emphatically.

"Is she, really?" Charles asked haughtily. "That's funny. She's been hinting to all and sundry that you're about to pop the question."

Tira's face drained of color. She couldn't even look at Simon.

Simon called him a name that made her flush and caused Charles to stiffen his spine.

Charles opened the door wide. "I think this would be a good time to let Tira collect herself. Don't you?"

Simon didn't budge. "Tira, do you want me to leave?" he asked bluntly.

She still couldn't lift her eyes. "It might be best."

What a ghostly, thin little voice. The old Tira would

have laid about him with a baseball bat. But he'd weakened her, and now she thought he'd betrayed her. Jill had lied. If Tira loved him, why couldn't she see that? Why was she so ready to believe Charles?

Unless... He glared at the other man. Did she love Charles? Had she given in to a purely physical desire the night before and now she was ashamed and using Jill as an excuse?

"Please go, Simon," Tira said when he hesitated. She couldn't bear the thought that he'd seduced her on a whim and everything he'd said since was a lie. But how could Jill make up something as serious as an engagement? She put a hand to her head. She couldn't think straight!

Simon shot a cold glare at Tira and another one at Charles. He didn't say a single word as he stalked out the door to his car.

Tira served coffee in the living room, having changed into jeans and a sweater. She didn't dare think about what had happened or she'd go mad. Simon and Jill. Simon and Jill...

"What happened?" Charles asked curtly.

"One minute we were engaged and the next minute he was gone," she said, trying to make light of it.

"Engaged?"

She nodded, refusing to meet his eyes.

He put the evening gown and Simon's fury together and groaned. "Oh, no. Please tell me I didn't put my foot in it again?"

She shrugged. "If Jill says he's proposed to her, I don't know what to think. I guess I've been an idiot."

"I shouldn't have come. I shouldn't have opened my mouth." He put his face in his hands. "I'm so sorry."

"Why did you come?" she asked suddenly.

He drew his hands over his face, down to his chin. "Gene died this morning," he said gruffly. "I've just left Nessa with a nurse and made the arrangements at the funeral home. I came by to ask if you could stay with her tonight. She doesn't want to be alone, and for obvious reasons, I can't stay in my own house with her right now."

"You want me to stay with her in your house?" she asked.

He nodded. "Can you?"

"Charles, of course I can," she said, putting aside her own broken relationship for the moment. Charles's need was far greater. "I'll just pack a few things."

"I'll drive you over," he said. "You won't need your car until tomorrow. I'll bring you home then."

"Nessa can come with me," she said. "Mrs. Lester and I will take good care of her."

"That would be nice. But tonight, she doesn't need to be moved. She's sedated, and sleeping right now."

"Okay."

"Tira, do you want me to call Simon and explain, before we go?" he asked worriedly.

"No," she said. "It can wait."

Charles was the one in trouble right now. She refused to think about her own situation. She packed a bag, left a note for Mrs. Lester and locked the door behind them.

The next morning Mrs. Lester found only a hastily scribbled note saying that Tira had gone home with Charles—and not why. So when Simon called the next morning, she told him with obvious reluctance that apparently Tira had gone to spend the night at Charles's house and hadn't returned.

"I suppose it was his turn," he said with bridled fury, thanked her and hung up. He packed a bag without taking time to think things through and caught the next flight to Austin to see the governor about the job he'd been offered.

Gene's funeral was held on the Wednesday, and from the way Nessa clung to Charles, Tira knew that at least somebody's life was eventually going to work out. Having heard from Mrs. Lester that Simon had phoned and gone away furious having thought she spent the night with Charles, she had no hope at all for her own future.

She spent the next few days helping Nessa clear away Gene's things and get her life in some sort of order. Charles was more than willing to do what he could. By the time Christmas Eve rolled around, Tira was all by herself and so miserable that she felt like doing nothing but cry.

Nevertheless, she perked herself up, dressed in a neat red pantsuit and went to the orphans' Christmas party that she'd promised to attend.

She carried two cakes that she and Mrs. Lester had baked, along with all the paraphernalia that went with festive eats. Other people on the committee brought punch and cookies and candy, and there were plenty of gaily wrapped presents.

Tira hadn't expected to see Simon, and she didn't. But Jill, of all people, showed up with an armload of presents.

"Why, how lovely to see you, Tira," Jill exclaimed. She didn't get too close—she probably remembered the cup of coffee.

"Lovely to see you, too, Jill," Tira said with a noxious smile. "Do join the fun."

"Oh, I can't stay," she said quickly. "I'm filling in for Simon. Poor dear, he's got a raging headache and he couldn't make it."

"Simon doesn't have headaches," Tira said curtly, averting her eyes. "He gives them."

"I thought you knew he frequently gets them when he flies," Jill murmured condescendingly. "I've nursed him through several. Anyway, he just got back from Austin. He's accepted the appointment as attorney general, by the way." She sighed dramatically. "I'm to go with him to the governor's New Year's Ball! And I've got just the dress to wear, too!"

Tira wanted to go off and be sick. Her life had become a nightmare.

"Must run, dear," Jill said quickly. "I have to get home to Simon. Hope the party's a great success. See you!"

She was gone in the flash of an eye. Tira put on the best act she'd ever given for the orphans, handing out cake and presents with a smile that felt glued-on. The media showed up to film the event for the eleven o'clock news, as a human interest story, and Tira managed to keep her back to the cameras. She didn't want Simon to gloat if he saw how she really looked.

After the party, she wrapped herself in her leather coat, went home and threw up for half an hour. The nausea was new. She never got sick. There could only be one reason for it, and it wasn't anything she'd eaten. Two weeks into her only pregnancy with Tira, her mother had said, the nausea had been immediately apparent long before the doctors could tell she was pregnant.

Tira went to bed and cried herself to sleep. She did want the child, that was no lie, but she was so mad at Simon that she could have shot him. Poor little baby, to have such a lying pig for a father!

Just as she opened her eyes, there was a scratching sound and she looked up in time to see the unwelcome mouse, who'd been delightfully absent for two weeks, return like a bad penny. He scurried down the hall and she cursed under her breath. Well, now she had a mission again. She was going to get that mouse. Then she was going to get Simon!

She fixed herself a small milk shake for Christmas dinner and carried it to her studio. She wasn't even dressed festively. She was wearing jeans and a sweater and socks, with her hair brushed but not styled and no makeup on. She felt lousy and the milk shake was the only thing she could look at without throwing up.

Charles and Nessa had offered to let her spend Christmas with them, but she declined. The last thing she felt like was company.

She wandered through the studio looking at her latest creations. She sat down at her sculpting table and stared at the lump of clay under the wet cloth that she'd only started that morning. She wasn't really in the mood to work, least of all on Christmas Day, but she didn't feel like doing anything else, either.

Why, oh, why, had she gone to Simon's apartment? Why hadn't she insisted that he take her home? In fact, why hadn't she left him strictly alone after John died? She couldn't blame anyone for the mess her life was in. She'd brought it on herself by chasing after a man who didn't want her. Well, he did now—but only in one way. And after he married Jill…

She placed a protective hand over her stomach and sighed. She had the baby. She knew that she was pregnant. She'd have the tests, but they really weren't necessary. Already she could feel the life inside her instinctively, and she wondered if the baby would look like her or like Simon.

There was a loud tap at the back door. She frowned. Most people rang the doorbell. It wasn't likely to be Charles and Nessa, and it was completely out of the question that it could be Simon. Perhaps a lost traveler?

She got up, milk shake in hand, and went to the back door, slipping the chain before she opened it.

Simon stared down at her with quiet, unreadable eyes. He had dark circles under his eyes and new lines in his face. "It's Christmas," he said. "Do I get to come in?"

He was wearing a suit and tie. He looked elegant, hardly a match for her today.

She shrugged. "Suit yourself," she said tautly. She looked pointedly past him to see if he was alone.

His jaw tautened. "Did you expect me to bring someone?"

"I thought Jill might be with you," she said.

He actually flinched.

She let out a long breath. "Sorry. Your private life is none of my business," she said as she closed the door.

When she turned around, it was to find his hand clenched hard at his side.

"Speaking of private lives, where's Charles?" he asked icily.

She stared at him blankly. "With Nessa, of course."

He scowled. "What's he still doing with her?"

"Gene died and Nessa needs Charles now more than

ever.'' She frowned when he looked stunned. ''Charles has been in love with Nessa for years. Gene tricked her into marrying him, hoping to inherit her father's real estate company. It went broke and he made Nessa his scapegoat. She wouldn't leave him because she knew he had a bad heart, and Charles almost went mad. Now that Gene's gone, they'll marry as soon as they can.''

He looked puzzled. ''You went home with him...''

''I went to his house to stay with Nessa, the night after Gene had died,'' she said flatly. ''Charles said that it wouldn't look right for her to be there alone, and she wouldn't stay at her own house.''

He averted his eyes. He couldn't look at her. Once again, it seemed, he'd gotten the whole thing upside down and made a mess of it.

''Why are you here?'' she asked with some of her old hauteur. ''In case you were wondering, I'm not going to shoot myself,'' she added sarcastically. ''I'm through pining for you.''

He shoved his hand into his pocket and glanced toward her, noticing her sock-clad feet and the milk shake in her hand. ''What's that?'' he asked suddenly.

''Lunch,'' she returned curtly.

His face changed. His eyes lifted to hers and he didn't miss her paleness or the way she quickly avoided meeting his searching gaze.

''No turkey and dressing?''

She shifted. ''No appetite,'' she returned.

He lifted an eyebrow and his eyes began to twinkle as they dropped eloquently to her stomach. ''Really?''

She threw the milk shake at him. He ducked, but it hit the kitchen cabinet in its plastic container and she groaned at the mess she was going to have to clean up later. Right now, though, it didn't matter.

"I hate you!" she raged. "You seduced me and then you ran like the yellow dog you are! You let Jill nurse you through headaches and spend Christmas Eve with you, and I hope you do marry her, you deserve each other, you...you...!"

She was sobbing by now, totally out of control, with tears streaming down her red face.

He drew her close to him and rocked her warmly, his hand smoothing her wild hair while she cried. "There, there," he whispered at her ear. "The first few months are hard, but it will get better. I'll buy you dill pickles and feed you ice cream and make dry toast and tea for you when you wake up in the morning feeling queasy."

She stilled against him. "W...what?"

"My baby, you're almost certainly pregnant," he whispered huskily, holding her closer. "From the look of things, very, very pregnant, and I feel like dancing on the lawn!"

Ten

She looked up at him with confusion, torn between breaking his neck and kissing him.

"Wh…what makes you think I'm pregnant?" she asked haughtily.

He smiled lazily. "The milk shake."

She shifted. "It's barely been two weeks."

"Two long, lonely weeks," he said heavily. He touched her hair, her face, as if he'd ached for her as badly as she had for him. "I can't seem to stop putting my foot in my mouth."

She lowered her eyes to his tie. It was a nice tie, she thought absently, touching its silky red surface. "You had company."

He tilted her face up to his eyes. "Jill likes to hurt you, doesn't she?" he asked quietly. "Why are you so willing to believe everything she says? I've never had any inclination to marry her, in the past or now. And as for her nursing me through a headache, you, of all people, should know I don't get them, ever."

"She said...!"

"I came home from Austin miserable and alone and I got drunk for the first time since the wreck," he said flatly. "She got in past the doorman at the hotel and announced that she'd come to nurse me. I had her shown to the front door."

Her eyebrows arched. That wasn't what Jill had said.

His eyes searched over her wan face. "And you don't believe me, do you?" he asked with resignation. "I can't blame you. I've done nothing but make mistakes with you, from the very beginning. I've lived my whole life keeping to myself, keeping people at bay. I loved Melia, in my way, but even she was never allowed as close as you got. Especially," he added huskily, "in bed."

"I don't understand."

His fingers traced her full lower lip. "I never completely lost control with her," he said softly. "The first time with you, I went right over the edge. I hurt you because I couldn't hold anything back." He smiled gently. "You didn't realize, did you?"

"I don't know much about...that."

"So I discovered." His jaw tautened as he looked at her. "Married but untouched."

Something niggled at the back of her mind, something he'd said about John. She couldn't remember it.

He bent and brushed his mouth gently over her forehead. "We have to get married," he whispered. "I want to bring our baby into the world under my name."

"Simon..."

He drew her close and his lips slid gently over her half-open mouth. She could feel his heartbeat go wild the minute he touched her. His big body actually trembled.

She looked up at him with quiet curiosity, seeing the raging desire he wasn't bothering to conceal blazing in his eyes, and her whole body stilled.

"That's right," he murmured. "Take a good look. I've managed to hide it from you for years, but there's no need now."

"You wanted me, before?" she asked.

"I wanted you the first time I saw you," he said huskily. His lean hand moved from her neck down to the hard peak of her breast visible under the sweater, and he brushed over it with his fingers, watching her shiver. "You were the most gloriously beautiful creature I'd ever seen. But I was married and I imagined that it was nothing more than the sort of lust a man occasionally feels for a totally inappropriate sort of woman."

"You thought I was cheap."

"No. I thought you were experienced," he said, and there was regret in his eyes. "I threw you at John to save myself, without having the first idea what I was about to subject you to. I'm sorry, if it matters. I never used to think of myself as the sort of man to run from trouble, but I spent years running from you."

She lowered her gaze to his tie again. Her heart was racing. He'd never spoken to her this way in the past. She felt his hand in her hair, tangling in it as if he loved its very feel, and her eyes closed at the tenderness in the caress.

"I don't want to be vulnerable," he said through his teeth. "Not like this."

She let out a long sigh. She understood what he meant. "Neither did I, all those years ago," she said heavily. "Charles was kind to me. He knew how I felt about you, and he provided me with the same sort of camouflage I gave him for Nessa's sake. Everyone thought we were lovers."

"I suppose you know I thought you were experienced when I took you to bed?"

She nodded.

"Even when you cried out, the first time, I thought it was pleasure, not pain. I'll never forget how I felt when I realized how wrong I'd been about you." His hand tightened on her soft body unconsciously. "I know how bad it was. Are you...all right?"

"Yes."

He drew her forehead against him and held it there while he fought for the right words to heal some of the damage he'd done. His eyes closed as he bent over her. It was like coming home. He'd never known a feeling like it.

She sighed and slid her arms under his and around him, giving him her weight.

He actually shivered.

She lifted her head and looked up, curious. His face was tight, his eyes brilliant with feeling. She didn't need a crystal ball to understand why. His very vulnerability knocked down all the barriers. She knew how proud he was, how he hated having her see him this way. But it was part of loving, a part he had yet to learn.

She took his hand in hers. "Come on," she said softly. "I can fix what's wrong with you."

"How do you know what's wrong with me?" he taunted.

She tugged at his hand. "Don't be silly."

She pulled him along with her out of the kitchen to

her bedroom and closed the door behind her. She was a little apprehensive. Despite the pleasure he'd given her, the memory of the pain was still very vivid.

He took a slow breath. "I'll always have to be careful with you," he said, as if he read the thoughts in her eyes. "I'm overendowed and you're pretty innocent, in spite of what we did together."

She blinked. "You...are?"

He scowled. "You said you'd seen centerfolds."

She colored wildly. "Not...of men...like that!"

"Well, well." He chuckled softly and moved closer to her. "I feel like a walking anatomy lab."

"Do you, really?" She drew his hand under her sweater and up to soft, warm skin, and shivered when he touched her. Her heart was in the eyes she lifted to his. "It won't hurt...?"

He drew her close and kissed her worried eyes shut. "No," he whispered tenderly. "I promise it won't!"

She let him undress her, still hesitant and shy with him, but obviously willing.

When she was down to her briefs, she began undressing him, to his amusement.

"This is new," he mused. "I've had to do it myself for a number of years."

She looked up, hesitating. "All that time," she said. "Didn't you want anyone?"

"I wanted you," he replied solemnly. "Sometimes, I wanted you desperately."

"You never even hinted...!"

"You know why," he said, as if it shamed him to remember. "I should have been shot."

She lowered her eyes to the bare, broad chest she'd uncovered. "That would have been a waste," she said with a husky note in her voice. Her fingers spread over the thick hair that covered him, and he groaned softly. She put her mouth against his breastbone. "I've missed you," she whispered, and her voice broke.

"I've missed you!"

He bent to her mouth and kissed her slowly, tenderly, while between them, they got the rest of the obstacles out of the way.

When she reached for the strap of the prosthesis, his fingers stayed her.

"We'll have to find out sometime if you can do without it," she said gently. Her eyes searched his. "You can always put it back on, if you have to."

He sighed heavily. "All right."

He let her take it off, the uncertainty plain in his dark face. It made him vulnerable somehow, and he felt vulnerable enough with his hunger for her blatantly clear.

She stretched out on the pale pink sheets and watched him come down to her with wide, curious eyes.

Amazingly he was able to balance, if a little heavily at first. But she helped him, her body stabilizing his as they kissed and touched in the most tender exchange of caresses they'd ever shared for long, achingly sweet minutes until the urgency began to break through.

It was tender even as he eased down against her and she felt him probing at her most secret place. She tensed, expecting pain, but it was easy now, if a little uncomfortable just at first.

He turned her face to his and made her watch his eyes as they moved together slowly. He pressed soft, quiet kisses against her mouth as the lazy tempo of his hips brought them into stark intimacy.

She gasped and pushed upward as the pleasure shot through her, but he shook his head, calming her.

"Wh...why?" she gasped.

"Because I want it to be intense," he whispered unsteadily, nuzzling her face with his as he fought for enough breath to speak. His teeth clenched as he felt the first deep bites of pleasure rippling through him. "I want it to take a long time. I want to...touch you...as deeply inside...as it's humanly possible!"

She felt him in every pore, every cell. Her fingers clenched behind his strong neck because he was even more potent now than he'd been their first time together. Her teeth worried her lower lip as she looked up at him, torn between pleasure and apprehension.

"Don't be afraid," he whispered brokenly. "Don't be afraid of me."

"It wasn't like this...before," she sobbed. Her eyes closed on a wave of pleasure so sharp that it stiffened her from head to toe. "Dear...God...Simon!"

"Baby," he choked at her ear. His body moved tenderly, even in its great urgency, from side to side, intensifying the pleasure, bringing her to the brink of some unbelievably deep chasm. She was going to fall...to fall...

She barely heard her own voice shattering into a thousand pieces as she reached up to him in an arc, sobbing, wanting more of him, more, ever more!

"Oh, God, don't...I'll hurt you!" he bit off as she pulled him down sharply to her.

"Never," she breathed. "Never! Oh, Simon...!"

She sobbed as the convulsions took her. It had never been this sweeping. Her eyes opened in the middle of the spasms and met his, and she saw in them the same helpless loss of control, the ecstasy that made a tight, agonized caricature of his face. It faded into a black oblivion as the pleasure became unbearable and she lost consciousness for a space of seconds.

"Tira? *Tira!*"

His hand was trembling as it touched her face, her neck where the pulse hammered.

"Oh, God, honey, open your eyes and look at me! Are you all right?"

She felt her eyelids part slowly. His face was above hers, worried, tormented, his eyes glittering with fear.

She smiled lazily. "Hello," she whispered, so exhausted that she could barely manage words. She moved and felt him deep in her body and moaned with pleasure.

"Good God, I thought I'd killed you!" he breathed, relaxing on her. He was heavy, and she loved his weight. She held him close, nuzzling her face into his cool, damp throat. "You fainted!"

"I couldn't help it," she murmured. "Oh, it was so good. So good, so good!"

He rolled over onto his back, carrying her with him. He shivered, too, as the movements kindled little skirls of pleasure.

She curled her legs into his and closed her eyes. "I love you," she whispered sleepily.

He drew in a shaky breath. "I noticed."

She kissed his neck lazily and sighed. "Simon, I think I really am pregnant."

"So do I."

She moved against him sinuously. "Are you sorry?"

"I'm overjoyed."

That sounded genuine, and reassuring.

"I'm sleepy."

He stretched under her. He'd used more muscles than he realized he had. "So am I."

It was the last thing she heard for a long time. When she woke again, she was under the sheet with her hair spread over the pillow. Simon was wearing everything but his jacket, and he was sitting on the edge of the bed just looking at her.

She opened her eyes and stared up at him. She'd never seen that expression on his face before. It wasn't one she could understand.

"Is something wrong?" she asked.

His hand went to her flat stomach over the sheet. "You don't think we hurt the baby?"

She smiled sleepily. "No. We didn't hurt the baby."

He wasn't quite convinced. "The way we loved this time…"

"Oh, that sounds nice," she murmured, smiling up at him with quiet, dreamy eyes.

His hand moved to hers and entangled with it. "What? That we loved?"

She nodded.

He drew their clasped hands to his broad thigh and studied them. "I've been thinking."

"What about?"

"It shouldn't be a quick ceremony in a justice of the peace's office," he said. He shrugged. "It should be in a church, with you in white satin."

"White? But…"

He lifted his eyes. They glittered at her. "White."

She swallowed. "Okay."

He relaxed a little. "I don't want people talking about you, as if we'd done something to be ashamed of—even though we have."

Her eyes opened wide. "What?"

"I used to go to church. I haven't forgotten how things are supposed to be done. We jumped the gun, twice, and I'm not very proud of it. But considering the circumstances, and this," he added gently, touching her belly with a curious little smile, "I think we're not quite beyond redemption."

"Of course we're not," she said softly. "God is a lot more understanding than most people are."

"And it isn't as if we aren't going to get married and give our baby a settled home and parents who love him," he continued. "So with all that in mind, I've put the wheels in motion."

"Wheels?"

He cleared his throat. "I phoned my brothers."

She sat straight up in bed with eyes like an owl's. "*Them?* You didn't! Simon, you couldn't!"

"There, there," he soothed her, "it won't be so bad. They're old hands at weddings. Look what a wonderful one they arranged for Corrigan. You went. So did I. It was great."

"They arranged Corrigan's wedding without any encouragement from Dorie at all! They kidnapped her and wrapped her in ribbons and carried her home to Corrigan for Christmas, for heaven's sake! I know all about those hooligans, and I can arrange my own wedding!" she burst out.

Just as she said that, the back door—the one they'd forgotten to lock—opened and they heard footsteps along with voices in the corridor.

The bedroom door flew open, and there they were, all of them except Corrigan. They stopped dead at the sight that met their eyes.

Cag glared at Simon. "You cad!" he snarled. "No

wonder you needed us to arrange a wedding! How could you do that to a nice girl like her?"

"Disgraceful," Leopold added, with a rakish grin. "Doesn't she look pretty like that?"

"Don't leer at your future sister-in-law," Rey muttered, hitting him with his Stetson. He put half a hand over his eyes. "Simon, we'd better do this quick."

"All we need is a dress size," Leopold said.

"I am not giving you my dress size, you hooligans!" Tira raged, embarrassed.

"Better get it one size larger, she's pregnant," Simon offered.

"Oh, thank you very much!" Tira exclaimed, horrified.

"You're welcome." He grinned, unrepentant.

"Pregnant?" three voices echoed.

The insults were even worse now, and Leopold began flogging Simon with that huge white Stetson.

"Oh, Lord!" Tira groaned, hiding her head in the hands propped on her upbent knees.

"It's a size ten," Rey called from the closet, where he'd been inspecting Tira's dresses. "We'd better make it a twelve. Lots of lace, too. We can get the same minister that married Corrigan and Dorie. And it had better be no later than three weeks," he added with a black glare at Simon. "Considering her condition!"

"It isn't a condition," Simon informed him curtly, "it's a baby!"

"And we thought they weren't speaking." Leopold grinned.

"We don't know yet that it's a baby," Tira said with a glare.

"She was having a milk shake for Christmas dinner," Simon told them.

"We saw it. Goes well with the cabinets, I thought,"
Rey commented.

"Don't worry, the mouse will eat it," Tira muttered.

"Mouse?" Cag asked.

"He can't be trapped or run out or baited," she
sighed. "I've had three exterminators in. They've all
given up. The mouse is still here."

"I'll bring Herman over," Cag said.

The others looked at him wide-eyed. "No!" they
chorused.

"About the service," Simon diverted them, "we
need to invite the governor and his staff—Wally said
he'd give her away," he added, glancing at Tira.

"The governor is going to give me away? Our governor? The governor of our state?" Tira asked, aghast.

"Well, we've only got one." He grimaced. "Forgot
to tell you, didn't I? I've accepted the attorney general
slot. I hope you won't mind living in Austin."

"Austin."

She looked confused. Simon glanced at his brothers
and waved his hand toward them. "Get busy, we
haven't got a lot of time," he said. "And don't forget
the media. It never hurts any political party to have
coverage of a sentimental event."

"There he goes again, being a politician," Cag muttered.

"Well, he is, isn't he?" Rey chuckled. "Okay, boys,
let's go. We've got a busy day ahead of us tomorrow.
See you."

Cag hesitated as they went out the door. "This
wasn't done properly," he told his brother. "Shame on
you."

Simon actually blushed. "One day," he told the
other man, "you'll understand."

"Don't count on it."

Cag closed the door, leaving two quiet people behind.

"He's never been in love," Simon murmured, staring at his feet. "He doesn't have a clue what it's like to want someone so bad that it makes you sick."

She stared at him curiously. "Is that how it was for you, today?"

"Today, and the first time," he said, turning his face to her. He searched her eyes quietly. "But in case you've been wondering, I'm not marrying you for sex."

"Oh."

He glowered. "Or for the baby. I want him very much, but I would have married you if there wasn't going to be one."

She was really confused now. Did this mean what it sounded like? No, it had to have something to do with politics. It certainly wouldn't hurt his standing in the political arena to have a pregnant, pretty, capable wife beside him, especially when there was controversy.

That was when the reality of their situation hit her. She was going to marry a public official, not a local attorney. He was going to be appointed attorney general to fill the present unexpired term, but he'd have to run for the office the following year. They'd live in a goldfish bowl.

She stared at him with horror in every single line of her face as the implications hit her like a ton of bricks. She sat straight up in bed, with the sheet clutched to her breasts, and stared at Simon horrified. He didn't know about John. Despite the enlightened times, some revelations could be extremely damaging, and not only to her and, consequently, Simon. There was John's father, a successful businessman. How in the world would it affect him to have the whole state know that John had been gay?

The fear was a living, breathing thing. Simon had no idea about all this. He hadn't spoken of John or what he thought now that he knew Tira wasn't a murderess, but the truth could hurt him badly. It might hurt the governor as well; the whole political party, in fact.

She bit her lip almost through and lowered her eyes to the bed. "Simon, I can't marry you," she whispered in a ghostly tone.

"You what?"

"You heard me. I can't marry you. I'm sorry."

He moved closer, and tilted her face up to his quiet eyes. "Why not?"

"Because..." She hesitated. She didn't want to ever have to tell him the truth about his best friend. "Because I don't want to live in a goldfish bowl," she lied.

He knew her now. He knew her right down to her soul. He sighed and smiled at her warmly. "You mean, you don't want to marry me because you're afraid the truth about John will come to light and hurt me when I run for office next year."

Eleven

She was so astonished that she couldn't even speak. "You...know?" she whispered.

He nodded. "I've known since that night at the gallery, when I spoke to your ex-father-in-law," he replied quietly. "He told me everything." His face hardened. "That was when I knew what I'd done to you, and to myself. That was when I hit rock bottom."

"But you never said a word..." Things came flying back into her mind. "Yes, you did," she contradicted herself. "You said that you were glad John couldn't have me...you knew then!"

He nodded. "It must have been sheer hell for you."

"I was fond of him," she said. "I would have tried to be a good wife. But I married him because I couldn't have you and it didn't really matter anymore." Her eyes were sad as they met his. "You loved Melia."

"I thought I did," he replied. "I loved an illusion,

a woman who only existed in my imagination. The reality was horrible.'' He reached out and touched her belly lightly, and she knew he was remembering.

Her fingers covered his. ''You don't even have to ask how I feel about the baby, do you?''

He chuckled. ''I never would have. You love kids.'' He grimaced. ''I hated missing the Christmas Eve party. I watched you on television. I even knew why you kept your back to the camera. It was eloquent.''

''Jill has been a pain,'' she muttered.

''Not only for you,'' he agreed. He sighed softly. ''Tira, I hope you know that there hasn't been anyone else.''

''It would have been hard to miss today,'' she said, and flushed a little.

He drew her across him and into the crook of his arm, studying her pretty face. ''It doesn't bother you at all that I'm crippled, does it?''

''Crippled?'' she asked, as if the thought had never occurred to her.

That surprise was genuine. He leaned closer. ''Sweetheart, I'm missing half my left arm,'' he said pointedly.

''Are you, really?'' She drew his head down to hers and kissed him warmly on his hard mouth. ''You didn't need the prosthesis, either, did you?''

He chuckled against her lips. ''Apparently not.'' His eyes shone warmly into hers. ''How can you still love me after all I've put you through?'' he asked solemnly.

She let the sheet fall away from her high, pretty breasts and laid back against his arm to let him look. ''Because you make love so nicely?''

He shook his head. ''No, that's not it.'' He touched

her breasts, enjoying their immediate reaction. "Habit, perhaps. God knows, I don't deserve you."

She searched his face quietly. "I never knew you were vulnerable at all," she said, "that you could be tender, that you could laugh without being cynical. I never knew you at all."

"I didn't know you, either." He bent and kissed her softly. "What a lot of secrets we kept from each other."

She snuggled close. "What about John?" she asked worriedly. "If it comes out, it can hurt you and the party, it could even hurt John's father."

"You worry entirely too much," he said. "So what if it does? It's ancient history. I expect to be an exemplary attorney general—again—and what sort of pond scum would attack a beautiful pregnant woman?"

"I won't always be pregnant."

He lifted his head and gave her a wicked look. "No?"

She hit his chest. "I don't want to be the mother of a football team!"

"You'd love it," he returned, smiling at the radiance of her face. He chuckled. "I can see you already, letting them tackle you in mud puddles."

"They can tackle you. I'll carry the ball."

He glanced ruefully at the arm that was supporting her. "You might have to."

She touched his shoulder gently. "Does it really worry you so much?"

"It used to," he said honestly. "Until the first time you let me make love to you." He drew in a long breath. "You can't imagine how afraid I was to let you see the prosthesis. Then I was afraid to take it off,

because I thought I might not be able to function as a
man without using it for balance."

"We'd have found a way," she said simply. "People do."

He frowned slightly. "You make everything so
easy."

She lifted her fingers and smoothed away the frown.
"Not everything. You don't feel trapped?"

He caught her hand and pulled the soft palm to his
lips, kissing it with breathless tenderness. "I feel as if
I've got the world in my arms," he returned huskily.

She smiled. "So do I."

He looked as if he wanted to say something more,
but he brought her close and wrapped her up against
him instead.

The arrangements were complicated. Instead of a
wedding, they seemed to be planning a political coup
as well. The governor sent his private secretary and the
brothers ended up in a furious fight with her over control of the event. It almost came to blows before Simon
stepped in and reminded them that they couldn't plan
the wedding without assistance. They informed him
haughtily that they'd done it before. He threw up his
hand and left them to it.

Tira had coffee with him in her living room in the
midst of wedding invitations that she was hand signing.
There must have been five hundred.

"I'm being buried," she said pointedly, gesturing
toward the overflowing coffee table. "And that mouse
is getting to me," she added. "I found *him* under one
of the envelopes earlier!"

"Cag will take care of him while we're on our honeymoon. We can stay here until we find a house in Austin in a neighborhood you like.''

"One you like, too," she said.

"If you like it, so will I."

It bothered her that he was letting her make all these decisions. She knew she was being cosseted, but she wasn't sure why.

"The brothers haven't been by today."

"They're in a meeting with Miss Chase, slugging it out," he replied. "When I left, she was reaching for a vase."

"Oh, dear."

"She's a tough little bird. She's not going to let them turn our wedding into a circus."

"They have fairly good taste," she admitted.

"They called Nashville to see how many country music stars they could hire to appear at the reception."

"Oh, good Lord!" she burst out.

"That isn't what Miss Chase said. She really needs to watch her language," he murmured. "Rey was turning red in the face when I ran for my life."

"You don't run."

"Only on occasion. Rey has the worst temper of the lot."

"I'd put five dollars on Miss Chase," she giggled.

He watched her lift the cup to her lips. "Should you be drinking coffee?"

"It's decaf, darling," she teased.

The endearment caught him off guard. His breath caught in his throat.

The reaction surprised her, because he usually seemed so unassailable. She wasn't quite sure of herself even now. "If you don't like it, I won't..." she began.

"Oh, I like it," he said huskily. "I'm not used to endearments, that's all."

"Yes, I know. You don't use them often."

"Only when I make love to you," he returned.

She lowered her eyes. He hadn't done that since the day they got engaged, when the brothers had burst into their lives again. She'd wondered why, but she was too shy to ask him.

"Hey," he said softly, coaxing her eyes up. "It isn't lack of interest. It's a lack of privacy."

She smiled wanly. "I wondered." She shrugged. "You haven't been around much."

"I've been trying to put together an office staff before I'm sworn in the first of January," he reminded her. "It's been a rush job."

"Of course. I know how much pressure you're under. If you'd like, we could postpone the wedding," she offered.

"Do you really want to be married in a maternity dress?" he teased.

Her reply was unexpected. She started crying.

He got up and pulled her up, wrapping her close. "It's nerves," he whispered. "They'll pass."

She didn't stop. The tears were worse.

"Tira?"

"I started," she sobbed.

"What?"

She looked up at him. Her eyes were swimming and red. "I'm not pregnant." She sounded as if the world had ended.

He pulled out a handkerchief and dried the tears. "I'm sorry," he whispered, and looked it. "I really am."

She took the handkerchief and made a better job of

her face, pressing her cheek against his chest. "I didn't know how to tell you. But now you know. So if you don't want to go through with it…"

He stiffened. His head lifted and he looked at her as if he thought she was possessed. "Why wouldn't I want to go through with it?" he burst out.

"Well, I'm not pregnant, Simon," she repeated.

He let out the breath he was holding. "I told you I wasn't marrying you because of the baby. But you weren't completely convinced, were you?"

She looked sheepish. "I had my doubts."

He searched her wet eyes slowly. He held her cheek in his big, warm hand and traced her mouth with his thumb. "I'm sorry that you aren't pregnant. I want a baby very much with you. But I'm marrying you because I love you. I thought you knew."

Her heart jumped into her throat. "You never said."

"Some words come harder than others for me," he replied. He drew in a long breath. "I thought, I hoped, you'd know by the way we were in bed together. I couldn't have been so out of control the first time or so tender the next if I hadn't loved you to distraction."

"I don't know much about intimacy."

"You'll learn a lot more pretty soon," he murmured dryly. He frowned quizzically. "You were going to marry me, thinking I only wanted you for the baby?"

"I love you," she said simply. "I thought, when the baby came, you might learn to love me." Her face dissolved again into tears. "And then…then I knew there wasn't going to be a baby."

He kissed her tenderly, sipping the tears from her wet eyes, smiling. "There will be," he whispered. "One day, I promise you, there will be. Right now, I only want to marry you and live with you and love you. The rest will fall into place all by itself.''

She looked into his eyes and felt the glory of it all the way to her soul. ''I love you,'' she sobbed. ''More than my life.''

''That,'' he whispered as he bent to her mouth, ''is exactly the way I feel about you!''

The wedding, despite the warring camps of its organizers, came off perfectly. It was a media event, at the ranch in Jacobsville, with all the leading families of the town in attendance and Tira glorious in a trailing white gown as she walked down the red carpet to the rose arbor where Simon and all his brothers and the minister waited. Dorie Hart was her matron of honor and the other Hart boys were best men.

The service was brief but eloquent, and when Simon placed the ring on her finger and then lifted her veil and kissed her, it was with such tenderness that she couldn't even manage to speak afterward. They went back down the aisle in a shower of rice and rose petals, laughing all the way.

The reception didn't have singers from Nashville. Instead the whole Jacobsville Symphony Orchestra turned out to play, and the food was flown in from San Antonio. It was a gala event and there were plenty of people present to enjoy it.

Tira hid a yawn and smiled apologetically at her new husband. ''Sorry! I'm so tired and sleepy I can hardly stand up. I don't know what's wrong with me!''

''A nice Jamaican honeymoon is going to cure you of wanting sleep at all,'' he promised in a slow, deep drawl. ''You are the most beautiful bride who ever walked down an aisle, and I'm the luckiest man alive.''

She reached a hand up to his cheek and smiled lovingly at him. "I'm the luckiest woman."

He kissed her palm. "I wish we were ten years younger, Tira," he said with genuine regret. "I've wasted all that time."

"It wasn't wasted. It only made what we have so much better," she assured him.

"I hope we have fifty years," he said, and meant it.

They flew out late that night for their Caribbean destination. Cag, who hadn't forgotten the mouse, asked for the key to Tira's house and assured her that the mouse would be a memory when they returned. She had a prick of conscience, because in a way the mouse had brought her and Simon together. But it was for the best, she told herself. They couldn't go on living with a mouse! Although she did wonder what plan Cag had in mind that hadn't already been tried.

The Jamaican hotel where they stayed was right on the beach at Montego Bay, but they spent little time on the sand. Simon was ardent and inexhaustible, having kept his distance until the wedding.

He lay beside her, barely breathing after a marathon of passion that had left them both drenched in sweat and too tired to move.

"You need to take more vitamins," he teased, watching her yawn yet again. "You aren't keeping up with me."

She chuckled and rolled against him with a loving sigh. "It's the wedding and all the preparations," she whispered. "I'm just worn-out. Not that worn-out, though," she added, kissing his bare shoulder softly. "I love you, Simon."

He pulled her close. "I love you, Mrs. Hart. Very, very much."

She trailed her fingers across his broad, hair-roughened chest and wanted to say something else, but she fell asleep in the middle of it.

A short, blissful week later, they arrived back at her house with colorful T-shirts and wonderful memories.

"I could use some coffee," Simon said. "Want me to make it?"

"I'll do it, if you'll take the cases into the bedroom," she replied, heading for the kitchen.

She opened the cupboard to get out the coffee and came face-to-face with the biggest snake she'd ever seen in her life.

Simon heard a noise in the kitchen, put down the suitcases and went to see what had happened.

His heart jumped into his throat when he immediately connected the open cupboard, the huge snake and his new wife lying unconscious on the floor.

He bent, lifting her against his chest. "Tira, sweetheart, are you all right?" he asked softly, smoothing back her hair. "Can you hear me?"

She moved. Her eyelids fluttered and she opened her eyes, saw Simon, and immediately remembered why she was on the floor.

"Simon, there's a…a…*sssssssnake!*"

"Herman."

She stared at him. "There's a snake in the cupboard," she repeated.

"Herman," he repeated. "It's Cag's albino python."

"It's in *our* cupboard," she stated.

"Yes, I know. He brought it over to catch the mouse. Herman's a great mouser," he added. "Hell of a barrier to Cag's social life, but a really good mousetrap. We won't have a mouse now. Looks healthy, doesn't he?'' he added, nodding toward the cupboard.

While they were staring at the huge snake, the back door suddenly opened and Cag came in with a gunnysack. He saw Tira and Simon on the floor and groaned.

"Oh, God, I'm too late!" he said heartily. "I'm sorry, Tira, I let the time slip away from me. I forgot all about Herman until I remembered the date, and you'd already left the airport when I tried to catch you." He sighed worriedly. "I haven't killed you, have I?"

"Not at all," Tira assured him with grim humor. "I've been tired a lot lately, too. I guess I'm getting fragile in my old age."

Simon helped her to her feet, but he was watching her with a curious intensity. She made coffee while Cag got his scaly friend into a bag and assured her that she'd have no more mouse problems. Tira offered him coffee, but he declined, saying that he had to get Herman home before the big python got irritable. He was shedding, which was always a bad time to handle him.

"Any time would be a bad time for me," Tira told her husband when their guest had gone.

"You fainted," he said.

"Yes, I know. I was frightened."

"You've been overly tired and sleeping a lot, and I notice that you don't eat breakfast anymore." He caught her hand and pulled her down onto his lap. "You were sure you weren't pregnant. I'm sure you are. I want you to see a doctor."

"But I started," she tried to explain.

"I want you to see a doctor."

She nuzzled her face into his throat. "Okay," she said, and kissed him. "But I'm not getting my hopes up. It's probably just some female dysfunction."

The telephone rang in Simon's office, where he was winding up his partnership before getting ready to move into the state government office that had been provided for him.

"Hello," he murmured, only half listening.

"Mr. Hart, your wife's here," his secretary murmured with unusual dryness.

"Okay, Mrs. Mack, send her in."

"I, uh, think you should come out, sir."

"What? Oh. Very well."

His mind was still on the brief he'd been preparing, so when he opened the door he wasn't expecting the surprise he got.

Tira was standing there in a very becoming maternity dress, and had an ear-to-ear smile on her face.

"It's weeks too early, but I don't care. The doctor says I'm pregnant and I'm wearing it," she told him.

He went forward in a daze and scooped her close, bending over her with eyes that were suspiciously bright. "I knew it," he whispered huskily. "I knew!"

"I wish I had!" she exclaimed, hugging him hard. "All that wailing and gnashing of teeth, and for nothing!"

He chuckled. "What a nice surprise!"

"I thought so. Will you take me to lunch?" she added. "I want dill pickles and strawberry ice cream."

"Yuuuck!" Mrs. Mack said theatrically.

"Never you mind, Mrs. Mack, I'll take her home and feed her," Simon said placatingly. He glanced at his wife with a beaming smile. "We'll have Mrs. Les-

ter fix us something. I want to enjoy looking at you in
that outfit while we eat.''

She held his hand out the door and felt as if she had
the world.

Later, after they arrived home, Mrs. Lester seated
them at the dining-room table and brought in a nice
lunch of cold cuts and omelets with decaffeinated coffee for Tira. She was smiling, too, because she was
going with them to Austin.

"A baby and a husband who loves me, a terrific
cook and housekeeper, and a mouseless house to leave
behind," Tira said. "What more could a woman ask?"

"Mouseless?" Mrs. Lester asked.

"Yes, don't you remember?" Tira asked gleefully.
"Cag got rid of the mouse while we were on our honeymoon and you were at your sister's."

Mrs. Lester nodded. "Got rid of the mouse. Mmm-
hmm." She went and opened the kitchen door and invited them to look at the cabinet. They peered in the
door and there he was, the mouse, sitting on the counter
with a cracker in his paws, blatantly nibbling away.

"I don't believe it!" Tira burst out.

It got worse. Mrs. Lester went into the kitchen, held
out her hand, and the mouse climbed into it.

"He's domesticated," she said proudly. "I came in
here the other morning and he was sitting on the cabinet. He didn't even try to run, so I held out my hand
and he climbed into it. I had a suspicion, so I put him
in a box and took him to the vet. The vet says that he
isn't a wild mouse at all, he's somebody's pet mouse
that got left behind and had to fend for himself. Obviously he belonged to the previous owners of this
house. So I thought, if you don't mind, of course," she

added kindly, "I'd keep him. He can come with us to Austin."

Tira looked at Simon and burst out laughing. The mouse, who had no interest whatsoever in human conversation, continued to nibble his cracker contentedly, safe in the hands of his new owner.

* * * * *

Look out for Diana Palmer's next book,
Carrera's Bride, *coming out in December, only*
from Silhouette Special Edition.

A Game of Chance
LINDA HOWARD

Dear Reader,

When I wrote *Mackenzie's Mountain*, one of the supporting characters was Wolf's son Joe. I fell in love with Joe, and so did everyone else. I have never received so many letters asking for a character to have his own book as I did about Joe—until Chance Mackenzie came along.

Chance was one of those characters I didn't plan. All of a sudden he was just there, without warning. He was instantly fascinating, his past mysterious and unknown, his appeal so strong he inspired literally hundreds of readers to write asking for his full story, sometimes even suggesting plot lines if I didn't have one of my own! Thank you for your suggestions, but Chance's story was in my head from the beginning.

A Game of Chance will probably be the last of the Mackenzie books. I say 'probably' because all the Mackenzie offspring are still children in my mind, and they may well stay children. I can't let them grow up without Wolf and Mary dying of old age, and I can't bear that.

There were no books on Mike and Josh, the other Mackenzie sons. Somehow I already had them settled in my mind, so their stories didn't spark for me. I wish they had.

Few readers have caught it, but all of the Mackenzie books since *Mackenzie's Mountain* have been set slightly in the future. I haven't made drastic changes, just little details here and there, to have fun and keep the time line straight. So if you catch something that doesn't seem quite right…it may be twenty years in the future!

I hope you enjoy Chance's story as much as I did!

Sincerely,

Linda Howard

For the readers

The Beginning

Coming back to Wyoming—coming home—always evoked in Chance Mackenzie such an intense mixture of emotions that he could never decide which was strongest, the pleasure or the acute discomfort. He was, by nature and nurture—not that there had been any nurturing in the first fourteen or so years of his life—a man who was more comfortable alone. If he was alone, then he could operate without having to worry about anyone but himself, and, conversely, there was no one to make him uncomfortable with concern about his own well-being. The type of work he had chosen only reinforced his own inclinations, because covert operations and anti-terrorist activities predicated he be both secretive and wary, trusting no one, letting no one close to him.

And yet... And yet, there was his family. Sprawling, brawling, ferociously overachieving, refusing to let him withdraw, not that he was at all certain he could even if they would allow it. It was always jolting, alarming, to step back into that all-enveloping embrace, to be teased and questioned—*teased,* him, whom some of the most deadly people on earth justifiably feared—hugged and kissed, fussed over and yelled at and…loved, just as if he were like everyone else. He knew he wasn't; the knowledge was always there, in the back of his mind, that he was *not* like them. But he was drawn back, again and again, by something deep inside hungering for the very things that so alarmed him. Love was scary; he had learned early and hard how little he could depend on anyone but himself.

The fact that he had survived at all was a testament to his toughness and intelligence. He didn't know how old he was, or where he had been born, what he was named as a child, or if he even had a name—nothing. He had no memory of a mother, a father, anyone who had taken care of him. A lot of people simply didn't remember their childhoods, but Chance couldn't comfort himself with that possibility, that there had been someone who had loved him and taken care of him, because he remembered too damn many other details.

He remembered stealing food when he was so small he had to stand on tiptoe to reach apples in a bin in a small-town supermarket. He had been around so many kids now that, by comparing what he remembered to the sizes they were at certain ages, he could estimate he had been no more than three years old at the time, perhaps not even that.

He remembered sleeping in ditches when it was warm, hiding in barns, stores, sheds, whatever was handy, when it was cold or raining. He remembered stealing clothes to wear, sometimes by the simple means of catching a boy playing alone in a yard, overpowering him and taking the clothes off his back. Chance had always been much stronger physically than other boys his size, because of the sheer physical difficulty of staying alive—and he had known how to fight, for the same reason.

He remembered a dog taking up with him once, a black-and-white mutt that tagged along and curled up next to him to sleep, and Chance remembered being grateful for the warmth. He also remembered that when he reached for a piece of steak he had stolen from the scraps in back of a restaurant, the dog bit him and stole the steak. Chance still had two scars on his left hand from the dog's teeth. The dog had gotten the meat, and Chance had gone one more day without food. He didn't blame the dog; it had been hungry, too. But Chance ran it off after that, because stealing enough food to keep himself alive was difficult enough, without having to steal for the dog, too. Besides, he had learned that when it came to survival, it was every dog for himself.

He might have been five years old when he learned that particular lesson, but he had learned it well.

Of course, learning how to survive in both rural and urban areas, in all conditions, was what made him so good at his job now, so he supposed his early childhood had its benefits. Even considering that, though, he wouldn't wish his childhood on a dog, not even the damn mutt that had bitten him.

His real life had begun the day Mary Mackenzie found him lying beside a road, deathly ill with a severe case of flu that had turned into pneumonia. He didn't remember much of the next few days—he had been too ill—but he had known he was in a hospital, and he had been wild with fear, because that meant he had fallen into the hands of the system, and he was now, in effect, a prisoner. He was obviously a minor, without identification, and the circumstances would warrant the child welfare services being notified. He had spent his entire life avoiding just such an event, and he had tried to make plans to escape, but his thoughts were vague, hard to get ordered, and his body was too weak to respond to his demands.

But through it all he could remember being soothed by an angel with soft blue-gray eyes and light, silvery brown hair, cool hands and a loving voice. There had also been a big, dark man, a half-breed, who calmly and repeatedly addressed his deepest fear. "We won't let them take you," the big man had said whenever Chance briefly surfaced from his fever-induced stupor.

He didn't trust them, didn't believe the big half-breed's reassurances. Chance had figured out that he himself was part American Indian, but big deal, that didn't mean he could trust these people any more than he could trust that damn thieving, ungrateful mutt. But he was too sick, too weak, to escape or even struggle, and while he was so helpless Mary Mackenzie had somehow hog-tied him with devotion, and he had never managed to break free.

He hated being touched; if someone was close enough to touch him, then they were close enough to attack him. He couldn't fight off the nurses and doctors who poked and prodded and moved him around as if he were nothing more than a mindless piece of meat. He had endured it, gritting his teeth, struggling with both his own panic and the almost overpowering urge to fight, because he knew if he fought them he would be restrained. He had to stay free, so he could run when he recovered enough to move under his own power.

But *she* had been there for what seemed like the entire time, though logically he knew she had to have left the hospital sometimes. When he burned with fever, she washed his face with a cold cloth and fed him slivers of ice. She brushed his hair, stroked his forehead when his head ached so bad he thought his skull would crack; and took over bathing him when she saw how alarmed he became when the nurses did it. Somehow he could bear it better when she bathed him, though even in his illness he had been puzzled by his own reaction.

She touched him constantly, anticipating his needs so that his pillows were fluffed before he was aware of any discomfort, the heat adjusted before he became too hot or too cold, his legs and back massaged when the fever made him ache from head to toe. He was swamped by maternal fussing, enveloped by it. It terrified him, but Mary took advantage of his weakened state and ruthlessly overwhelmed him with her mothering, as if she were determined to pack enough loving care into those few days to make up for a lifetime of nothing.

Sometime during those fever-fogged days, he began to like the feel of her cool hand on his forehead, to listen for that sweet voice even when he couldn't drag his heavy eyelids open, and the sound of it reassured him on some deep, primitive level. Once he dreamed, he didn't know what, but he woke in a panic to find her arms around him, his head pillowed on her narrow shoulder as if he were a baby, her hand gently stroking his hair while she murmured reassuringly to him—and he drifted back to sleep feeling comforted and somehow...safe.

He was always startled, even now, by how small she was. Someone so relentlessly iron-willed should have been seven feet tall and weighed three hundred pounds; at least then it would have made sense that she could bulldoze the hospital staff, even the doctors, into doing what she wanted. She had estimated his age at fourteen,

but even then he was over a full head taller than the
dainty woman who took over his life, but in this case
size didn't matter; he was as helpless against her as was
the hospital staff.

There was nothing at all he could do to fight off his
growing addiction to Mary Mackenzie's mothering, even
though he knew he was developing a weakness, a vulnerability, that terrified him. He had never before cared
for anyone or anything, instinctively knowing that to do
so would expose his emotional underbelly. But knowledge and wariness couldn't protect him now; by the time
he was well enough to leave the hospital, he loved the
woman who had decided she was going to be his mother,
loved her with all the blind helplessness of a small child.

When he left the hospital it had been with Mary and
the big man, Wolf. Because he couldn't bear to leave
her just yet, he braced himself to endure her family. Just
for a little while, he had promised himself, just until he
was stronger.

They had taken him to Mackenzie's Mountain, into
their home, their arms, their hearts. A nameless boy had
died that day beside the road, and Chance Mackenzie
had been born in his place. When Chance had chosen a
birthday—at his new sister Maris's insistence—he chose
the day Mary found him, rather than the perhaps more
logical date that his adoption was final.

He had never had anything, but after that day he had
been flooded with…everything. He had always been
hungry, but now there was food. He had been starved,
too, for learning, and now there were books everywhere,
because Mary was a teacher down to her fragile bones,
and she had force-fed him knowledge as fast as he could
gulp it down. He was accustomed to bedding down
wherever and whenever he could, but now he had his

own room, his own bed, a routine. He had clothes, new ones, bought specifically for him. No one else had ever worn them, and he hadn't had to steal them.

But most of all, he had always been alone, and abruptly he was surrounded by family. Now he had a mother and a father, *four* brothers, a little sister, a sister-in-law, an infant nephew, and all of them treated him as if he had been there from the beginning. He could still barely tolerate being touched, but the Mackenzie family touched *a lot*. Mary—Mom—was constantly hugging him, tousling his hair, kissing him good-night, fussing over him. Maris, his new sister, pestered the living hell out of him just the way she did her other brothers, then would throw her skinny arms around his waist and fiercely hug him, saying, "I'm so glad you're ours!"

He was always taken aback on those occasions, and would dart a wary glance at Wolf, the big man who was the head of the Mackenzie pack and who was now Chance's dad, too. What did he think, seeing his innocent little daughter hug someone like Chance? Wolf Mackenzie was no innocent; if he didn't know exactly what experiences had molded Chance, he still recognized the dangerous vein in the half-wild boy. Chance always wondered if those knowing eyes could see clear through him, see the blood on his hands, find in his mind the memory of the man he had killed when he was about ten.

Yes, the big half-breed had known very well the type of wild animal he had taken into his family and called son, had known and, like Mary, had loved him, anyway.

His early years had taught Chance how risky life was, taught him not to trust anyone, taught him that love would only make him vulnerable and that vulnerability could cost him his life. He had known all that, and still

he hadn't been able to stop himself from loving the
Mackenzies. It never stopped scaring him, this weakness
in his armor, and yet when he was in the family bosom
was the only time he was completely relaxed, because
he knew he was safe with them. He couldn't stay away,
couldn't distance himself now that he was a man who
was more than capable of taking care of himself, because
their love for him, and his for them, fed his soul.

He had stopped even trying to limit their access to his
heart and instead turned his considerable talents to doing
everything he could to make their world, their lives, as
safe as possible. They kept making it tougher for him;
the Mackenzies constantly assaulted him with expan-
sions: his brothers married, giving him sisters-in-law to
love, because his brothers loved them and they were part
of the family now. Then there were the babies. When he
first came into the family there was only John, Joe and
Caroline's first son, newly born. But nephew had followed nephew, and somehow Chance, along with everyone else in the Mackenzie family, found himself rocking
infants, changing diapers, holding bottles, letting a dimpled little hand clutch one of his fingers while tottering
first steps were made…and each one of those dimpled
hands had clutched his heart, too. He had no defense
against them. There were twelve nephews now, and one
niece against whom he was particularly helpless, much
to everyone else's amusement.

Going home was always nerve-racking, and yet he
yearned for his family. He was afraid for them, afraid
for himself, because he didn't know if he could live now
without the warmth the Mackenzies folded about him.
His mind told him he would be better off if he gradually
severed the ties and isolated himself from both the pleasure and the potential for pain, but his heart always led
him home again.

Chapter 1

Chance loved motorcycles. The big beast between his legs throbbed with power as he roared along the narrow winding road, the wind in his hair, leaning his body into the curves with the beast so they were one, animal and machine. No other motorcycle in the world sounded like a Harley, with that deep, coughing rumble that vibrated through his entire body. Riding a motorcycle always gave him a hard-on, and his own visceral reaction to the speed and power never failed to amuse him.

Danger was sexy. Every warrior knew it, though it wasn't something people were going to read about in their Sunday newspaper magazines. His brother Josh freely admitted that landing a fighter on a carrier deck had always turned him on. "It falls just short of orgasm," was the way Josh put it. Joe, who could fly any jet built, refrained from commenting but always smiled a slow, knowing smile.

As for both Zane and himself, Chance knew there

were times when each had emerged from certain tense situations, usually involving bullets, wanting nothing more than to have a woman beneath him. Chance's sexual need was ferocious at those times; his body was flooded with adrenaline and testosterone, he was *alive,* and he desperately needed a woman's soft body in which he could bury himself and release all the tension. Unfortunately, that need always had to wait: wait until he was in a secure position, maybe even in a different country entirely; wait until there was an available, willing woman at hand; and, most of all, wait until he had settled down enough that he could be relatively civilized in the sack.

But for now, there was only the Harley and himself, the rush of sweet mountain air on his face, and the inner mixture of joy and fear of going home. If Mom saw him riding the Harley without a helmet she would tear a strip off his hide, which was why he had the helmet with him, securely fastened behind the seat. He would put it on before sedately riding up the mountain to visit them. Dad wouldn't be fooled, but neither would he say anything, because Wolf Mackenzie knew what it was to fly high and wild.

He crested a ridge, and Zane's house came into view in the broad valley below. The house was large, with five bedrooms and four baths, but not ostentatious; Zane had instinctively built the house so it wouldn't attract undue attention. It didn't look as large as it was, because some of the rooms were underground. He had also built it to be as secure as possible, positioning it so he had an unrestricted view in all directions, but using natural formations of the land to block land access by all but the one road. The doors were steel, with state-of-the-art locks; the windows were shatterproof, and had cost a small fortune. Strategic walls had interior armor, and an emergency generator was installed in the basement. The basement also concealed another means of escape, if escape became necessary. Motion sensors were installed around the house, and as Chance wheeled the motorcycle into the driveway, he knew his arrival had already been signaled.

Zane didn't keep his family locked in a prison, but the security provisions were there if needed. Given their jobs, prudence demanded caution, and Zane had always prepared for emergencies, always had a backup plan.

Chance cut off the motor and sat for a minute, letting his senses return to normal while he ran a hand through his windswept hair. Then he kicked the stand down and leaned the Harley onto it, and dismounted much the way he would a horse. Taking a thin file from the storage compartment, he went up on the wide, shady porch.

It was a warm summer day, mid-August, and the sky was a cloudless clear blue. Horses grazed contentedly in the pasture, though a few of the more curious had come to the fence to watch with huge, liquid dark eyes as the noisy machine roared into the driveway. Bees buzzed around Barrie's flowers, and birds sang continuously in the trees. Wyoming. Home. It wasn't far away, Mackenzie's Mountain, with the sprawling house on the mountaintop where he had been given...life and everything else in this world that was important to him.

"The door's open." Zane's low, calm voice issued from the intercom beside the door. "I'm in the office."

Chance opened the door and went inside, his booted feet silent as he walked down the hall to Zane's office. With small clicks, the door locks automatically engaged behind him. The house was quiet, meaning Barrie and the kids weren't at home; if Nick was anywhere in the house she would have run squealing to him, hurling herself into his arms, chattering nonstop in her mangled English while holding his face clasped between both her little hands, making certain his attention didn't wander from her—as if he would dare look away. Nick was like a tiny package of unstable explosives; it was best to keep a weather eye on her.

The door to Zane's office was unexpectedly closed. Chance paused a moment, then opened it without knocking.

Zane was behind the desk, computer on, windows open to the warm, fresh air. He gave his brother one of his rare, warm smiles. "Watch where you step," he advised. "Munchkins on deck."

Automatically Chance looked down, checking out the floor, but he didn't see either of the twins. "Where?"

Zane leaned back in his chair a little, looking around for his offspring. Spotting them, he said, "Under the desk. When they heard me let you in, they hid."

Chance raised his eyebrows. To his knowledge, the ten-month-old twins weren't in the habit of hiding from anyone or anything. He looked more carefully and saw four plump, dimpled baby hands peeping from under the cover of Zane's desk. "They aren't very good at it," he observed. "I can see their hands."

"Give them a break, they're new at this stuff. They've only started doing it this week. They're playing Attack."

"Attack?" Fighting the urge to laugh, Chance said, "What am I supposed to do?"

"Just stand there. They'll burst from cover as fast as they can crawl and grab you by the ankles."

"Any biting involved?"

"Not yet."

"Okay. What are they going to do with me once they have me captured?"

"They haven't gotten to that part yet. For now, they just pull themselves up and stand there giggling." Zane scratched his jaw, considering. "Maybe they'll sit on your feet to hold you down, but for the most part they like standing too much to settle for sitting."

The attack erupted. Even with Zane's warning, Chance was a little surprised. They were remarkably quiet, for babies. He had to admire their precision; they launched themselves from under the desk at a rapid crawl, plump little legs pumping, and with identical triumphant crows attached themselves to his ankles. Dimpled hands clutched his jeans. The one on the left plopped down on his foot for a second, then thought better of the tactic and twisted around to begin hauling himself to an upright position. Baby arms wrapped around his knees, and the two little conquerors squealed with delight, their bubbling chuckles eliciting laughter from both men.

"Cool," Chance said admiringly. "Predator babies." He tossed the file onto Zane's desk and leaned down to scoop the little warriors into his arms, settling each diapered bottom on a muscular forearm. Cameron and Zack grinned at him, six tiny white baby teeth shining in each identical dimpled face, and immediately they began patting his face with their fat little hands, pulling his ears, delving into his shirt pockets. It was like being attacked by two squirming, remarkably heavy marshmallows.

"Good God," he said in astonishment. "They weigh a ton." He hadn't expected them to have grown so much in the two months since he had seen them.

"They're almost as big as Nick. She still outweighs

them, but I swear they feel heavier." The twins were sturdy and strongly built, the little boys already showing the size of the Mackenzie males, while Nick was as dainty as her grandmother Mary.

"Where are Barrie and Nick?" Chance asked, missing his pretty sister-in-law and exuberant, cheerfully diabolic niece.

"We had a shoe crisis. Don't ask."

"How do you have a shoe crisis?" Chance asked, unable to resist. He sat down in a big, comfortable chair across from Zane's desk, setting the babies more comfortably in his lap. They lost interest in pulling his ears and began babbling to each other, reaching out, entwining their arms and legs as if they sought the closeness they had known while forming in the womb. Chance unconsciously stroked them, enjoying the softness of their skin, the feel of squirming babies in his arms. All the Mackenzie babies grew up accustomed to being constantly, lovingly touched by the entire extended family.

Zane laced his hands behind his head, his big, powerful body relaxed. "First you have a three-year-old who loves her shiny, black, patent leather Sunday shoes. Then you make the severe tactical error of letting her watch *The Wizard of Oz.*" His stern mouth twitched, and his pale eyes glittered with amusement.

Chance's agile mind immediately made the connection, and his acquaintance with the three-year-old in question allowed him to make a logical assumption: Nick had decided she had to have a pair of red shoes. "What did she use to try to dye them?"

Zane sighed. "Lipstick, what else?" Each and every young Mackenzie had had an incident with lipstick. It was a family tradition, one John had started when, at the age of two, he had used his mother's favorite lipstick to recolor the impressive rows of fruit salad on Joe's dress uniform. Caroline had been impressively outraged, because the shade had been discontinued and finding a new tube had been much more difficult than replacing the small colored bars that represented medals Joe had earned and services he had performed.

"You couldn't just wipe it off?" The twins had discovered his belt buckle and zipper, and Chance moved the busy little hands that were trying to undress him. They began squirming to get down, and he leaned over to set them on the floor.

"Close the door," Zane instructed, "or they'll escape."

Leaning back, Chance stretched out a long arm and closed the door, just in time. The two diaper-clad escape artists had almost reached it. Deprived of freedom, they plopped down on their padded bottoms and considered the situation, then launched themselves in crawling patrol of the perimeters of the room.

"I *could* have wiped it off," Zane continued, his tone bland, "if I had known about it. Unfortunately, Nick cleaned the shoes herself. She put them in the dishwasher."

Chance threw back his head with a shout of laughter.

"Barrie bought her a new pair of shoes yesterday. Well, you know how Nick's always been so definite about what she wants to wear. She took one look at the shoes, said they were ugly, *even though they were just like the ones she ruined,* and refused to even try them on."

"To be accurate," Chance corrected, "what she said was that they were 'ugwy.'"

Zane conceded the point. "She's getting better with

her *L*s, though. She practices, saying the really important words, like lollipop, over and over to herself.''

"Can she say 'Chance' yet, instead of 'Dance'?'' Chance asked, because Nick stubbornly refused to even acknowledge she couldn't say his name. She insisted everyone else was saying it wrong.

Zane's expression was totally deadpan. "Not a chance.''

Chance groaned at the pun, wishing he hadn't asked. "I gather Barrie has taken my little darling shopping, so she can pick out her own shoes.''

"Exactly.'' Zane glanced over to check on his roaming offspring. As if they had been waiting for his parental notice, first Cam and then Zack plopped down on their butts and gave brief warning cries, all the while watching their father expectantly.

"Feeding time,'' Zane said, swiveling his chair around so he could fetch two bottles from a small cooler behind the desk. He handed one to Chance. "Grab a kid.''

"You're prepared, as always,'' Chance commented as he went over to the twins and leaned down to lift one in his arms. Holding the baby up, he peered briefly at the scowling little face to make sure he had the one he thought he had. It was Zack, all right. Chance couldn't say exactly how he knew which twin was which, how anyone in the family knew, because the babies were so identical their pediatrician had suggested putting ID anklets on them. But they each had such definite personalities, which were reflected in their expressions, that no one in the family ever confused one twin for the other.

"I have to be prepared. Barrie weaned them last month, and they don't take kindly to having to wait for dinner.''

Zack's round blue eyes were fiercely focused on the bottle in Chance's hand. "Why did she wean them so early?" Chance asked as he resumed his seat and settled the baby in the crook of his left arm. "She nursed Nick until she was a year old."

"You'll see," Zane said dryly, settling Cam on his lap.

As soon as Chance brought the bottle within reach of Zack's fat little hands the baby made a grab for it, guiding it to his rapacious, open mouth. He clamped down ferociously on the nipple. Evidently deciding to let his uncle hold the bottle, he nevertheless made certain the situation was stabilized by clutching Chance's wrist with both hands, and wrapping both chubby legs around Chance's forearm. Then he began to growl as he sucked, pausing only to swallow.

An identical growling noise came from Zane's lap. Chance looked over to see his brother's arm captured in the same manner as the two little savages held on to their meals.

Milk bubbled around Zack's rosebud mouth, and Chance blinked as six tiny white teeth gnawed on the plastic nipple.

"Hell, no wonder she weaned you!"

Zack didn't pause in his gnawing, sucking and growling, but he did flick an absurdly arrogant glance at his uncle before returning his full attention to filling his little belly.

Zane was laughing softly, and he lifted Cam enough that he could nuzzle one of the chubby legs so determinedly wrapped around his arm. Cam paused to scowl at the interruption, then changed his mind and instead favored his father with a dimpled, milky smile. The next second the smile was gone and he attacked the bottle again.

Zack's fuzzy black hair was as soft as silk against Chance's arm. Babies were a pure tactile pleasure, he thought, though he hadn't been of that opinion the first time he'd held one. The baby in question had been John, screaming his head off from the misery of teething.

Chance hadn't been with the Mackenzies long, only a few months, and he had still been extremely wary of all these people. He had managed—barely—to control his instinct to attack whenever someone touched him, but he still jumped like a startled wild animal. Joe and Caroline came to visit, and from the expressions on their faces when they entered the house, it had been a very long trip. Even Joe, normally so controlled and unflappable, was frustrated by his futile efforts to calm his son, and Caroline had been completely frazzled by a situation she couldn't handle with her usual impeccable logic. Her blond hair had been mussed, and her green eyes expressed an amazing mixture of concern and outrage.

As she had walked by Chance, she suddenly wheeled and deposited the screaming baby in his arms. Startled, alarmed, he tried to jerk back, but before he knew it he was in sole possession of the wiggling, howling little human. "Here," she said with relief and utmost confidence. "You get him calmed down."

Chance had panicked. It was a wonder he hadn't dropped the baby. He'd never held one before, and he didn't know what to do with it. Another part of him was astounded that Caroline would entrust her adored child to *him,* the mongrel stray Mary—Mom—had brought home with her. Why couldn't these people see what he was? Why couldn't they figure out he had lived wild in a kill-or-be-killed world, and that they would be safer if they kept their distance from him?

Instead, no one seemed to think it unusual or alarming that he was holding the baby, even though in his panic he held John almost at arm's length, clutched between his two strong young hands.

But blessed quiet fell in the house. John was startled out of his screaming. He stared interestedly at this new person and kicked his legs. Automatically Chance changed his grip on the baby, settling him in the cradle of one arm as he had seen the others do. The kid was drooling. A tiny bib was fastened around his neck, and Chance used it to wipe away most of the slobber. John saw this opportunity and grabbed Chance by the thumb, immediately carrying the digit to his mouth and chomping down. Chance had jumped at the force of the hard little gums, with two tiny, sharp teeth already breaking the surface. He grimaced at the pain, but hung in there, letting John use his thumb as a teething ring until Mom rescued him by bringing a cold wet washcloth for the baby to chew.

Chance had expected then to be relieved of baby duty, because Mom usually couldn't wait to get her hands on her grandson. But that day everyone had seemed content to leave John in his hands, even the kid himself, and after a while Chance calmed down enough to start walking around and pointing out things of interest to his little pal, all of which John obediently studied while gnawing on the relief-giving washcloth.

That had been his indoctrination to the ways of babies, and from that day on he had been a sucker for the parade of nephews his virile brothers and fertile sisters-in-law had produced on a regular basis. He seemed to be getting even worse, because with Zane's three he was total mush.

"By the way, Maris is pregnant."

Chance's head jerked up, and a wide grin lit his tanned face. His baby sister had been married nine whole months and had been fretting because she hadn't immediately gotten pregnant.

"When is it due?" He always ruthlessly arranged things so he could be home when a new Mackenzie arrived. Technically, this one would be a MacNeil, but that was a minor point.

"March. She says she'll be crazy before then, because Mac won't let her out of his sight."

Chance chuckled. Other than her father and brothers, Mac was the only man Maris had ever met whom she couldn't intimidate, which was one of the reasons she loved him so much. If Mac had decided he was going to ride herd on Maris during her pregnancy, she had little hope of escaping on one of those long, hard rides she so loved.

Zane nodded toward the file on his desk. "You going to tell me about it?"

Chance knew Zane was asking about more than the contents of the file. He was asking why it hadn't been transmitted by computer, instead of Chance personally bringing a hard copy. Zane knew his brother's schedule; he was the only person, other than Chance himself, who did, so he knew Chance was currently supposed to be in France. He was also asking why he hadn't been notified of Chance's change in itinerary, why his brother hadn't made a simple phone call to let him know he was coming.

"I didn't want to risk even a hint of this leaking out."

Zane's eyebrows rose. "We have security problems?"

"Nothing that I know of," Chance said. "It's what I don't know about that worries me. But, like I said, no one else can hear even a whisper of this. It's between us."

"Now you've made me curious." Zane's cool blue eyes gleamed with interest.

"Crispin Hauer has a daughter."

Zane didn't straighten from his relaxed position, but his expression hardened. Crispin Hauer had been number one on their target list for years, but the terrorist was as elusive as he was vicious. They had yet to find any way to get close to him, any vulnerability they could exploit or bait they could use to lure him into a trap. There was a record of a marriage in London some thirty-five years ago, but Hauer's wife, formerly Pamela Vickery, had disappeared, and no trace of her had ever been found. Chance, along with everyone else, had assumed the woman died soon after the marriage, either by Hauer's hand or by his enemies'.

"Who is she?" Zane asked. "*Where* is she?"

"Her name is Sonia Miller, and she's here, in America."

"I know that name," Zane said, his gaze sharpening.

Chance nodded. "Specifically, she's the courier who was supposedly robbed of her package last week in Chicago."

Zane didn't miss the "supposedly," but then, he never missed anything. "You think it was a setup?"

"I think it's a damn good possibility. I found the link when I checked into her background."

"Hauer would have known she'd be investigated after losing a package, especially one containing aerospace documents. Why take the risk?"

"He might not have thought we would find anything.

She was adopted. Hal and Eleanor Miller are listed as her parents, and they're clean as a whistle. I wouldn't have known she was adopted if I hadn't tried to pull up her birth certificate on the computer. Guess what—Hal and Eleanor never had any children. Little Sonia Miller didn't have a birth certificate. So I did some digging and found the adoption file—''

Zane's eyebrows rose. Open adoptions had caused so many problems that the trend had veered sharply back to closed files, which, coupled with electronic privacy laws and safeguards, had made it damn difficult to even locate those closed files, much less get into them. ''Did you leave any fingerprints?''

''Nothing that will lead back to us. I went through a couple of relays, then hacked into the Internal Revenue and accessed the file from their system.''

Zane grinned. If anyone did notice the electronic snooping, it likely wouldn't even be mentioned; no one messed with the tax people.

Zack had finished his bottle; his ferocious grip on it slackened, and his head lolled against Chance's arm as he briefly struggled against sleep. Automatically Chance lifted the baby to his shoulder and began patting his back. ''Ms. Miller has been employed as a courier for a little over five years. She has an apartment in Chicago, but her neighbors say she's seldom there. I have to think this is a long-term setup, that she's been working with her father from the beginning.''

Zane nodded. They had to assume the worst, because it was their job to do so. Only by anticipating the worst could they be prepared to handle it.

''Do you have anything in mind?'' he asked, taking the bottle from Cam's slackened grip and gently lifting the sleeping baby to his own shoulder.

"Getting next to her. Getting her to trust me."

"She's not going to be the trusting sort."

"I have a plan," Chance said, and grinned, because that was usually Zane's line.

Zane grinned in return, then paused as a small security console in the wall dinged a soft alarm. He glanced at the security monitor. "Brace yourself," he advised. "Barrie and Nick are home."

Seconds later the front door opened and a shriek filled the house. "Unca *Dance*! UncaDanceUncaDance-Unca*Dance!*" The chant was punctuated by the sound of tiny feet running and jumping down the hall as Nick's celebration of his visit came closer. Chance leaned back in his chair and opened the office door a bare second before Nick barreled through it, her entire little body quivering with joy and eagerness.

She hurled herself at him, and he managed to catch her with his free arm, dragging her onto his lap. She paused to bestow a big-sisterly kiss and a pat on the back of Zack's head—never mind that he was almost as big as she was—then turned all her fierce attention to Chance.

"Are you staying dis time?" she demanded, even as she lifted her face for him to kiss. He did, nuzzling her soft cheek and neck and making her giggle, inhaling the faint sweet scent of baby that still clung to her.

"Just for a few days," he said, to her disappointment. She was old enough now to notice his long and frequent absences, and whenever she saw him she tried to convince him to stay.

She scowled; then, being Nick, she decided to move on to more important matters. Her face brightened. "Den can I wide your moborcycle?"

Alarm flared through him. "No," he said firmly.

"You can't ride it, sit on it, lean on it, or put any of your toys on it *unless I'm with you*." With Nick, it was best to close all the loopholes. She seldom disobeyed a direct order, but she was a genius at finding cracks to slip through. Another possibility occurred to him. "You can't put Cam or Zack on it, either." He doubted she could lift either of them, but he wasn't taking any risks.

"Thank you," Barrie said dryly, entering the office in time to catch his addendum. She leaned down to kiss him on the cheek, at the same time lifting Zack from his arms so he could protect himself from Nick's feet. All the Mackenzie males, at one time or another, had fallen victim to a tiny foot in the crotch.

"Mission accomplished?" Zane asked, leaning back in his chair and smiling at his wife with that lazy look in his pale eyes that said he liked what he was seeing.

"Not without some drama and convincing, but, yes, mission accomplished." She pushed a feather lock of red hair out of her eyes. As always, she looked stylish, though she was wearing nothing dressier than beige slacks and a white sleeveless blouse that set off her slim, lightly tanned arms. You could take the girl out of the finishing school, Chance thought admiringly, but you could never take the finishing school out of the girl, and Barrie had gone to the most exclusive one in the world.

Nick was still focused on negotiating riding rights on the motorcycle. She caught his face between her hands and leaned down so her nose practically touched his, insuring his complete attention. He nearly laughed aloud at the fierce intent in her expression. "I wet you wide my twicycle," she said, evidently deciding to cajole instead of demand.

"Somehow I missed that," Zane murmured in amusement, while Barrie laughed softly.

"You *offered* to let me ride your tricycle," Chance corrected. "But I'm too big to ride a tricycle, and you're too little to ride a motorcycle."

"Den when *can* I wide it?" She made her blue eyes wide and winsome.

"When you get your driver's license."

That stymied her. She had no idea what a driver's license was, or how to get it. She stuck a finger in her mouth while she pondered this situation, and Chance tried to divert her interest. "Hey! Aren't those new shoes you're wearing?"

Like magic, her face brightened again. She wriggled around so he could hold one foot up so close to his face she almost kicked him in the nose. "Dey're so *pwetty*," she crooned in delight.

He caught the little foot in his big hand, admiring the shine of the black patent leather. "Wow, that's so shiny I can see my face in it." He pretended to inspect his teeth, which set her to giggling.

Zane rose to his feet. "We'll put the boys down for their naps while you have her occupied."

Keeping Nick occupied wasn't a problem; she was never at a loss for something to say or do. He curled one silky black strand of her hair around his finger while she chattered about her new shoes, Grampa's new horses, and what Daddy had said when he hit his thumb with a hammer. She cheerfully repeated exactly what Daddy had said, making Chance choke.

"But I'm not 'posed to say dat," she said, giving him a solemn look. "Dat's a weally, weally bad word."

"Yeah," he said, his voice strained. "It is."

"I'm not 'posed to say 'damn,' or 'hell,' or 'ass,' or—"

"Then you shouldn't be saying them now." He managed to inject a note of firmness in his tone, though it was a struggle to keep from laughing.

She looked perplexed. ''Den how can I tell you what dey are?''

''Does Daddy know what the bad words are?''

The little head nodded emphatically. ''He knows dem *all*.''

''I'll ask him to tell me, so I'll know which words not to say.''

''Otay.'' She sighed. ''But don't hit him too hard.''

''Hit him?''

''Dat's de only time he says *dat* word, when he hits his dumb wid de hammer. He said so.''

Chance managed to turn his laugh into a cough. Zane was an ex-SEAL; his language was as salty as the sea he was so at home in, and Chance had heard ''dat word,'' and worse, many times from his brother. But Mom had also instilled strict courtesy in all her children, so their language was circumspect in front of women and children. Zane must not have known Nick was anywhere near him when he hit his thumb, or no amount of pain could have made him say that in her hearing. Chance only hoped she forgot it before she started kindergarten.

''Aunt Mawis is goin' to have a baby,'' Nick said, scrambling up to stand in his lap, her feet braced on his thighs. Chance put both hands around her to steady her, though his aid probably wasn't needed; Nick had the balance of an acrobat.

''I know. Your daddy told me.''

Nick scowled at not being the first to impart the news. ''She's goin' to foal in de spwing,'' she announced.

He couldn't hold back the laughter this time. He gathered the little darling close to him and stood, whirling her around and making her shriek with laughter as she clung to his neck. He laughed until his eyes were wet. God, he loved this child, who in the three short years of her life had taught them all to be on their toes at all times, because there was no telling what she was going to do or say. It took the entire Mackenzie family to ride herd on her.

Suddenly she heaved a sigh. "When's de spwing? Is it a wong, wong time away?"

"Very long," he said gravely. Seven months was an eternity to a three-year-old.

"Will I be old?"

He put on a sympathetic face and nodded. "You'll be four."

She looked both horrified and resigned. "Four," she said mournfully. "Whodadunkit?"

When he stopped laughing this time, he wiped his eyes and asked, "Who taught you to say *whoda-thunkit?*"

"John," she said promptly.

"Did he teach you anything else?"

She nodded.

"What? Can you remember it?"

She nodded.

"Will you tell me what they are?"

She rolled her eyes up and studied the ceiling for a moment, then gave him a narrow-eyed look. "Will you wet me wide your moborcycle?"

Damn, she was bargaining! He trembled with fear at the thought of what she would be like when she was sixteen. "No," he said firmly. "If you got hurt, your mommy and daddy would cry, Grampa and Gamma would cry, *I* would cry, Aunt Maris would cry, Mac would cry, Unca Mike would cry—"

She looked impressed at this litany of crying and interrupted before he could name everyone in the family. "I can wide a horse, Unca Dance, so why can't I wide your moborcycle?"

God, she was relentless. Where in the hell were Zane and Barrie? They'd had plenty of time to put the twins down for their naps. If he knew Zane, his brother was taking advantage of having a baby-sitter for Nick to get in some sexy time with his wife; Zane was always prepared to use a fluid situation to his advantage.

It was another ten minutes before Zane strolled back into the office, his eyes slightly heavy-lidded and his hard face subtly relaxed. Chance scowled at his brother. He'd spent the ten minutes trying to talk Nick into telling him what John had taught her, but she wasn't budging from her initial negotiation. "It's about time," he groused.

"Hey, I hurried," Zane protested mildly.

"Yeah, right."

"As much as possible," he added, smiling. He smoothed his big hand over his daughter's shining black hair. "Have you kept Uncle Chance entertained?"

She nodded. "I told him de weally, weally bad word you said when you hit your dumb."

Zane looked pained, then stern. "How did you tell him when you aren't supposed to say the word?"

She stuck her finger in her mouth and began studying the ceiling again.

"Nick." Zane plucked her from Chance's arms. "Did you say the word?"

Her lower lip stuck out a little, but she nodded, owning up to her transgression.

"Then you can't have a bedtime story tonight. You promised you wouldn't say it."

"I'm sowwy," she said, winding her arms around his neck and laying her head on his shoulder.

Gently he rubbed his hand up and down her back. "I know you are, sweetheart, but you have to keep your promises." He set her on her feet. "Go find Mommy."

When she was gone, out of curiosity Chance asked, "Why didn't you tell her that she couldn't watch television, instead of taking away the bedtime story?"

"We don't want to make television attractive by using it as a treat or a privilege. Why? Are you taking notes on being a parent?"

Appalled, Chance said, "Not in this lifetime."

"Yeah? Fate has a way of jumping up and biting you on the ass when you least expect it."

"Well, my ass is currently bite-free, and I intend to keep it that way." He nodded at the file on Zane's desk. "We have some planning to do."

Chapter 2

This whole assignment was a tribute to Murphy's Law, Sunny Miller thought in disgust as she sat in the Salt Lake City airport, waiting for her flight to be called—if it were called at all, which she was beginning to doubt. This was her fifth airport of the day, and she was still almost a thousand miles from her destination, which was Seattle. She was *supposed* to have been on a direct flight from Atlanta to Seattle, but that flight had been canceled due to mechanical problems and the passengers routed on to other flights, none of which were direct.

From Atlanta she had gone to Cincinnati, from Cincinnati to Chicago, from Chicago to Denver, and from Denver to Salt Lake City. At least she was moving west instead of backtracking, and the flight from Salt Lake City, assuming it ever started boarding, was supposed to actually land in Seattle.

The way her day had gone, she expected it to crash instead.

She was tired, she had been fed nothing but peanuts all day, and she was afraid to go get anything to eat in case her flight was called and the plane got loaded and in the air in record time, leaving her behind. When Murphy was in control, anything was possible. She made a mental note to find this Murphy guy and punch him in the nose.

Her normal good humor restored by the whimsy, she resettled herself in the plastic seat and took out the paperback book she had been reading. She was tired, she was hungry, but she wasn't going to let the stress get to her. If there was one thing she was good at, it was making the best of a situation. Some trips were smooth as silk, and some were a pain in the rear; so long as the good and the bad were balanced, she could cope.

Out of ingrained habit, she kept the strap of her soft leather briefcase looped around her neck, held across her body so it couldn't easily be jerked out of her grasp. Some couriers might handcuff the briefcase or satchel to their wrists, but her company was of the opinion that handcuffs drew unwanted attention; it was better to blend in with the horde of business travelers than to stand out. Handcuffs practically shouted "Important stuff inside!"

After what had happened in Chicago the month before, Sunny was doubly wary and also kept one hand on the briefcase. She had no idea what was in it, but that didn't matter; her job was to get the contents from point A to point B. When the briefcase had been jerked off her shoulder by a green-haired punk in Chicago last month, she had been both humiliated and furious. She was *always* careful, but evidently not careful enough, and now she had a big blotch on her record.

On a very basic level, she was alarmed that she had

been caught off guard. She had been taught from the cradle to be both prepared and cautious, to be alert to what was going on around her; if a green-haired punk could get the best of her, then she was neither as prepared nor alert as she had thought. When one slip could mean the difference between life and death, there was no room for error.

Just remembering the incident made her uneasy. She returned the book to her carry-on bag, preferring to keep her attention on the people around her.

Her stomach growled. She had food in her carry-on, but that was for emergencies, and this didn't qualify. She watched the gate, where the two airline reps were patiently answering questions from impatient passengers. From the dissatisfied expressions on the passengers' faces as they returned to their seats, the news wasn't good; logically, she should have enough time to find something to eat.

She glanced at her watch: one-forty-five p.m., local time. She had to have the contents of the briefcase in Seattle by nine p.m. Pacific time tonight, which should have been a breeze, but the way things were going, she was losing faith the assignment could be completed on time. She hated the idea of calling the office to report another failure, even one that wasn't her fault. If the airline didn't get on the ball soon, though, she would have to do something. The customer needed to know if the packet wasn't going to arrive as scheduled.

If the news on the flight delay hadn't improved by the time she returned from eating, she would see about transferring to another airline, though she had already considered that option and none of the possibilities looked encouraging; she was in flight-connection hell. If she couldn't work out something, she would have to make that phone call.

Taking a firm grip on the briefcase with one hand and her carry-on bag with the other, she set off down the concourse in search of food that didn't come from a vending machine. Arriving passengers were pouring out of a gate to her left, and she moved farther to the right to avoid the crush. The maneuver didn't work; someone jostled her left shoulder, and she instinctively looked around to see who it was.

No one was there. A split-second reaction, honed by years of looking over her shoulder, saved her. She automatically tightened her grip on the briefcase just as she felt a tug on the strap, and the leather fell limply from her shoulder.

Damn it, not again!

She ducked and spun, swinging her heavy carry-on bag at her assailant. She caught a glimpse of feral dark eyes and a mean, unshaven face; then her attention locked on his hands. The knife he had used to slice the briefcase strap was in one hand, and he already had his other hand on the briefcase, trying to jerk it away from her. The carry-on bag hit him on the shoulder, staggering him, but he didn't release his grip.

Sunny didn't even think of screaming, or of being scared; she was too angry for either reaction, and both would have splintered her concentration. Instead, she wound up for another swing, aiming the bag for the hand holding the knife.

Around her she heard raised voices, full of confused alarm as people tried to dodge around the disturbance, and jostled others instead. Few, if any, of them would have any idea what the ruckus was about. Vision was hampered; things were happening too fast. She couldn't rely on anyone coming to help, so she ignored the noise, all her attention centered on the cretin whose dirty hand clutched her briefcase.

Whap! She hit him again, but still he held on to the knife.

"Bitch," he snarled, his knife-hand darting toward her.

She jumped back, and her fingers slipped on the leather. Triumphantly he jerked it away from her. Sunny grabbed for the dangling strap and caught it, but the knife made a silver flash as he sliced downward, separating the strap from the briefcase. The abrupt release of tension sent her staggering back.

The cretin whirled and ran. Catching her balance, Sunny shouted, "Stop him!" and ran in pursuit. Her long skirt had a slit up the left side that let her reach full stride, but the cretin not only had a head start, he had longer legs. Her carry-on bag banged against her legs, further hampering her, but she didn't dare leave it behind. Doggedly she kept running, even though she knew it was useless. Despair knotted her stomach. Her only prayer was that someone in the crowd would play hero and stop him.

Her prayer was abruptly answered.

Up ahead, a tall man standing with his back to the concourse turned and glanced almost negligently in the direction of the ruckus. The cretin was almost abreast of him. Sunny drew breath to yell out another "Stop him," even though she knew the cretin would be past before the man could react. She never got the words out of her mouth.

The tall man took in with one glance what was happening, and in a movement as smooth and graceful as a ballet pirouette, he shifted, pivoted and lashed out with one booted foot. The kick landed squarely on the cretin's right knee, taking his leg out from under him. He cartwheeled once and landed flat on his back, his arms flung over his head. The briefcase skidded across the concourse before bouncing against the wall, then back into the path of a stream of passengers. One man hopped over the briefcase, while others stepped around it.

Sunny immediately swerved in that direction, snatching up the briefcase before any other quick-fingered thief could grab it, but she kept one eye on the action.

In another of those quick, graceful movements, the tall man bent and flipped the cretin onto his stomach, then wrenched both arms up high behind his back and held them with one big hand.

"Owww!" the cretin howled. "You bastard, you're breaking my arms!"

The name-calling got his arms roughly levered even higher. He howled again, this time wordlessly and at a much higher pitch.

"Watch your language," said his captor.

Sunny skidded to a halt beside him. "Be careful," she said breathlessly. "He had a knife."

"I saw it. It landed over there when he fell." The man didn't look up but jerked his chin to the left. As he spoke he efficiently stripped the cretin's belt from its loop and wound the leather in a simple but effective snare around his captive's wrists. "Pick it up before someone grabs it and disappears. Use two fingers, and touch only the blade."

He seemed to know what he was doing, so Sunny obeyed without question. She took a tissue out of her skirt pocket and gingerly picked up the knife as he had directed, being careful not to smear any fingerprints on the handle.

"What do I do with it?"

"Hold it until Security gets here." He angled his dark head toward the nearest airline employee, a transportation escort who was hovering nervously as if unsure what to do. "Security *has* been called, hasn't it?"

"Yes, sir," said the escort, his eyes round with excitement.

Sunny squatted beside her rescuer. "Thank you," she said. She indicated the briefcase, with the two dangling pieces of its strap. "He cut the strap and grabbed it away from me."

"Any time," he said, turning his head to smile at her and giving her her first good look at him.

Her first look was almost her last. Her stomach fluttered. Her heart leaped. Her lungs seized. *Wow,* she thought, and tried to take a deep breath without being obvious about it.

He was probably the best-looking man she had ever seen, without being pretty in any sense of the word. *Drop-dead handsome* was the phrase that came to mind. Slightly dazed, she took in the details: black hair, a little too long and a little too shaggy, brushing the collar at the back of his battered brown leather jacket; smooth, honey-tanned skin; eyes of such a clear, light brown that they looked golden, framed by thick black lashes. As if that wasn't enough, he had also been blessed with a thin, straight nose, high cheekbones, and such clearly delineated, well-shaped lips that she had the wild impulse to simply lean forward and kiss him.

She already knew he was tall, and now she had the time to notice the broad shoulders, flat belly and lean hips. Mother Nature had been in a *really* good mood when he was made. He should have been too perfect and pretty to be real, but there was a toughness in his expression that was purely masculine, and a thin, crescent-shaped scar on his left cheekbone only added to the impression. Looking down, she saw another scar slashing across the back of his right hand, a raised line that was white against his tanned skin.

The scars in no way detracted from his attractiveness; the evidence of rough living only accentuated it, stating unequivocally that this was a *man.*

She was so bemused that it took her several seconds to realize he was watching her with mingled amusement and interest. She felt her cheeks heat in embarrassment at being caught giving him a blatant once-over. Okay, twice-over.

But she didn't have time to waste in admiration, so she forced her attention back to more pressing concerns. The cretin was grunting and making noises designed to show he was in agony, but she doubted he was in any great pain, despite his bound hands and the way her hero had a knee pressed into the small of his back. She had the briefcase back, but the cretin still presented her with a dilemma: It was her civic duty to stay and press charges against him, but if her flight left any time soon, she might very well miss it while she was answering questions and filling out forms.

"Jerk," she muttered at him. "If I miss my flight…"

"When is it?" asked her hero.

"I don't know. It's been delayed, but they could begin boarding at any time. I'll check at the gate and be right back."

He nodded with approval. "I'll hold your friend here and deal with Security until you get back."

"I'll only be a minute," she said, and walked swiftly back to her gate. The counter was now jammed with angry or upset travelers, their mood far more agitated than when she had left just a few moments before. Swiftly she glanced at the board, where CANCELED had been posted in place of the DELAYED sign.

"Damn," she said, under her breath. "Damn, damn, damn." There went her last hope for getting to Seattle in time to complete her assignment, unless there was another miracle waiting for her. Two miracles in one day was probably too much to ask for, though.

She needed to call in, she thought wearily, but first she could deal with the cretin and airport security. She retraced her steps and found that the little drama was now mobile; the cretin was on his feet, being frog-marched under the control of two airport policemen into an office where they would be out of the view of curious passersby.

Her hero was waiting for her, and when he spotted her, he said something to the security guys, then began walking to meet her.

Her heart gave a little flutter of purely feminine appreciation. My, he was good to look at. His clothes were nothing special: a black T-shirt under the old leather jacket, faded jeans and scuffed boots, but he wore them with a confidence and grace that said he was utterly comfortable. Sunny allowed herself a moment of regret that she would never see him again after this little contretemps was handled, but then she pushed it away. She couldn't take the chance of letting anything develop into a relationship—assuming there was anything there to develop—with him or anyone else. She never even let anything start, because it wouldn't be fair to the guy, and she didn't need the emotional wear and tear, either. Maybe one day she would be able to settle down, date, eventually find someone to love and marry and maybe have kids, but not now. It was too dangerous.

When he reached her, he took her arm with old-fashioned courtesy. "Everything okay with your flight?"

"In a way. It's been canceled," she said ruefully. "I have to be in Seattle tonight, but I don't think I'm going to make it. Every flight I've had today has either been delayed or rerouted, and now there's no other flight that would get me there in time."

"Charter a plane," he said as they walked toward the office where the cretin had been taken.

She chuckled. "I don't know if my boss will spring for that kind of money, but it's an idea. I have to call in, anyway, when we're finished here."

"If it makes any difference to him, I'm available right now. I was supposed to meet a customer on that last flight in from Dallas, but he wasn't on the plane, and he hasn't contacted me, so I'm free."

"You're a charter pilot?" She couldn't believe it. It—*he*—was too good to be true. Maybe she did qualify for two miracles in one day after all.

He looked down at her and smiled, making a tiny dimple dance in his cheek. God, he had a dimple, too! Talk about overkill! He held out his hand. "Chance McCall—pilot, thief-catcher, jack-of-all-trades—at your service, ma'am."

She laughed and shook his hand, noticing that he was careful not to grip her fingers too hard. Considering the strength she could feel in that tough hand, she was grateful for his restraint. Some men weren't as considerate. "Sunny Miller, tardy courier and target of thieves. It's nice to meet you, Mr. McCall."

"Chance," he said easily. "Let's get this little problem taken care of, then you can call your boss and see if he thinks a charter flight is just what the doctor ordered."

He opened the door of the unmarked office for her, and she stepped inside to find the two security officers, a woman dressed in a severe gray suit and the cretin, who had been handcuffed to his chair. The cretin glared at her when she came in, as if all this were her fault instead of his.

"You lyin' bitch—" the cretin began.

Chance McCall reached out and gripped the cretin's shoulder. "Maybe you didn't get the message before," he said in that easy way of his that in no way disguised the iron behind it, "but I don't care for your language. Clean it up." He didn't issue a threat, just an order— and his grip on the cretin's shoulder didn't look gentle.

The cretin flinched and gave him an uneasy look, perhaps remembering how effortlessly this man had manhandled him before. Then he looked at the two airport policemen, as if expecting them to step in. The two men crossed their arms and grinned. Deprived of allies, the cretin opted for silence.

The gray-suited woman looked as if she wanted to protest the rough treatment of her prisoner, but she evidently decided to get on with the business at hand. "I'm Margaret Fayne, director of airport security. I assume you're going to file charges?"

"Yes," Sunny said.

"Good," Ms. Fayne said in approval. "I'll need statements from both of you."

"Any idea how long this will take?" Chance asked. "Ms. Miller and I are pressed for time."

"We'll try to hurry things along," Ms. Fayne assured him.

Whether Ms. Fayne was super-efficient or yet another small miracle took place, the paperwork was completed in what Sunny considered to be record time. Not much more than half an hour passed before the cretin was taken away in handcuffs, all the paperwork was prepared and signed, and Sunny and Chance McCall were free to go, having done their civic duty.

He waited beside her while she called the office and explained the situation. The supervisor, Wayne Beesham, wasn't happy, but bowed to reality.

"What's this pilot's name again?" he asked.

"Chance McCall."

"Hold on, let me check him out."

Sunny waited. Their computers held a vast database of information on both commercial airlines and private charters. There were some unsavory characters in the charter business, dealing more in drugs than in passengers, and a courier company couldn't afford to be careless.

"Where's his home base?"

Sunny repeated the question to Chance.

"Phoenix," he said, and once again she relayed the information.

"Okay, got it. He looks okay. How much is his fee?" Sunny asked.

Mr. Beesham grunted at the reply. "That's a bit high."

"He's here, and he's ready to go."

"What kind of plane is it? I don't want to pay this price for a crop-duster that still won't get you there in time."

Sunny sighed. "Why don't I just put him on the line? It'll save time." She handed the receiver to Chance. "He wants to know about your plane."

Chance took the receiver. "McCall." He listened a moment. "It's a Cessna Skylane. The range is about eight hundred miles at seventy-five percent power, six hours flying time. I'll have to refuel, so I'd rather it be around the midway point, say at Roberts Field in Redmond, Oregon. I can radio ahead and have everything rolling so we won't spend much time on the ground.'' He glanced at his wristwatch. ''With the hour we gain when we cross into the Pacific time zone, she can make it—barely.''

He listened for another moment, then handed the receiver back to Sunny. ''What's the verdict?'' she asked.

''I'm authorizing it. For God's sake, get going.''

She hung up and grinned at Chance, her blood pumping at the challenge. ''It's a go! How long will it take to get airborne?''

''If you let me carry that bag, and we run...fifteen minutes.''

Sunny never let the bag out of her possession. She hated to repay his courtesy with a refusal, but caution was so ingrained in her that she couldn't bring herself to take the risk. ''It isn't heavy,'' she lied, tightening her grip on it. ''You lead, I'll follow.''

One dark eyebrow went up at her reply, but he didn't argue, just led the way through the busy concourse. The private planes were in a different area of the airport, away from the commercial traffic. After several turns and a flight of stairs, they left the terminal and walked across the concrete, the hot afternoon sun beating down on their heads and making her squint. Chance slipped on a pair of sunglasses, then shrugged out of the jacket and carried it in his left hand.

Sunny allowed herself a moment of appreciation at the way his broad shoulders and muscled back filled out the black T-shirt he wore. She might not indulge, but she could certainly admire. If only things were different—but they weren't, she thought, reining in her thoughts. She had to deal with reality, not wishful thinking.

He stopped beside a single-engine airplane, white with gray-and-red striping. After storing her bag and briefcase and securing them with a net, he helped her into the co-pilot's seat. Sunny buckled herself in and looked around with interest. She'd never been in a private plane before, or flown in anything this small. It was surprisingly comfortable. The seats were gray leather, and behind her was a bench seat with individual backs. Carpet covered the metal floor.

There were two sun visors, just like in a car. Amused, she flipped down the one in front of her and laughed aloud when she saw the small mirror attached to it.

Chance walked around the plane, checking details one last time before climbing into the seat to her left and buckling himself in. He put on a set of headphones and began flipping switches while he talked to the air traffic control tower. The engine coughed, then caught, and the propeller on the nose began to spin, slowly at first, then gaining speed until it was an almost invisible blur.

He pointed to another set of headphones, and Sunny put them on. "It's easier to talk using the headphones," came his voice in her ear, "but be quiet until we get airborne."

"Yes, sir," she said, amused, and he flashed a quick grin at her.

They were airborne within minutes, faster than she had ever experienced on a commercial carrier. Being in the small plane gave her a sense of speed that she had never before felt, and when the wheels left the ground the lift was incredible, as if she had sprouted wings and jumped into the air. The ground quickly fell away below, and the vast, glistening blue lake spread out before her, with the jagged mountains straight ahead.

"Wow," she breathed, and brought one hand up to shield her eyes from the sun.

"There's an extra pair of sunglasses in the glove box," he said, indicating the compartment in front of her. She opened it and dug out a pair of inexpensive but stylish Foster Grants with dark red frames. They were obviously some woman's sunglasses, and abruptly she wondered if he was married. He would have a girlfriend, of course; not only was he very nice to look at, he seemed to be a nice person. It was a combination that was hard to find and impossible to beat.

"Your wife's?" she asked as she put on the glasses and breathed a sigh of relief as the uncomfortable glare disappeared.

"No, a passenger left them in the plane."

Well, that hadn't told her anything. She decided to be blunt, even while she wondered why she was bothering, since she would never see him again after they arrived in Seattle. "Are you married?"

Again she got that quick grin. "Nope." He glanced at her, and though she couldn't see his eyes through the dark glasses, she got the impression his gaze was intense. "Are you?"

"No."

"Good," he said.

Chapter 3

Chance watched her from behind the dark lenses of his sunglasses, gauging her reaction to his verbal opening. The plan was working better than he'd hoped; she was attracted to him and hadn't been trying very hard to hide it. All he had to do was take advantage of that attraction and win her trust, which normally might take some doing, but what he had planned would throw her into a situation that wasn't *normal* in any sense of the word. Her life and safety would depend on him.

To his faint surprise, she faced forward and pretended she hadn't heard him. Wryly, he wondered if he'd misread her and she wasn't attracted to him after all. No, she had been watching him pretty blatantly, and in his experience, a woman didn't stare at a man unless she found him attractive.

What was *really* surprising was how attractive he found *her*. He hadn't expected that, but sexual chemistry was an unruly demon that operated outside logic. He had known she was pretty, with brilliant gray eyes and golden-blond hair that swung smoothly to her shoulders, from the photographs in the file he had assembled on her. He just hadn't realized how damn *fetching* she was.

He slanted another glance at her, this time one of pure male assessment. She was of average height, maybe, though a little more slender than he liked, almost delicate. Almost. The muscles of her bare arms, revealed by a white sleeveless blouse, were well-toned and lightly tanned, as if she worked out. A good agent always stayed in good physical condition, so he had to expect her to be stronger than she looked. Her delicate appearance probably took a lot of people off guard.

She sure as hell had taken Wilkins off guard. Chance had to smother a smile. While Sunny had gone back to her gate to check on the status of her flight, which Chance had arranged to be cancelled, Wilkins had told him how she had swung her carry-on bag at him, one-armed, and that the damn thing had to weigh a ton, because it had almost knocked him off his feet.

By now, Wilkins and the other three, "Ms. Fayne" and the two security "policemen," would have vanished from the airport. The real airport security had been briefed to stay out of the way, and everything had worked like a charm, though Wilkins had groused at being taken down so roughly. "First that little witch damn near breaks my arm with that bag, then you try to break my back," he'd growled, while they all laughed at him.

Just what was in that bag, anyway? She had held on to it as if it contained the crown jewels, not letting him carry it even when she was right there with him, and only reluctantly letting him take it to stow in the luggage compartment behind them. He'd been surprised at how heavy it was, too heavy to contain the single change of clothes required by an overnight trip, even with a vast array of makeup and a hairdryer thrown in for good measure. The bag had to weigh a good fifty pounds, maybe more. Well, he would find out soon enough what was in it.

"What were you going to do with that guy if you'd caught him?" he asked in a lazy tone, partly to keep her talking, establishing a link between them, and partly because he was curious. She had been chasing after Wilkins with a fiercely determined expression on her face, so determined that, if Wilkins were still running, she would probably still be chasing him.

"I don't know," she said darkly. "I just knew I couldn't let it happen again."

"Again?" Damn, was she going to tell him about Chicago?

"Last month, a green-haired cretin snatched my briefcase in the airport in Chicago." She slapped the arm of the seat. "That's the first time anything like that has ever happened on one of my jobs, then to have it happen again just a month later—I'd have been fired. Heck, *I* would fire me, if I were the boss."

"You didn't catch the guy in Chicago?"

"No. I was in Baggage Claims, and he just grabbed the briefcase, zipped out the door and was gone."

"What about security? They didn't try to catch him?"

She peered at him over the top of the oversize sunglasses. "You're kidding, right?"

He laughed. "I guess I am."

"Losing another briefcase would have been a catastrophe, at least to me, and it wouldn't have done the company any good, either."

"Do you ever know what's in the briefcases?"

"No, and I don't want to. It doesn't matter. Someone could be sending a pound of salami to their dying uncle Fred, or it could be a billion dollars worth of diamonds—not that I think anyone would ever ship diamonds by a courier service, but you get the idea."

"What happened when you lost the briefcase in Chicago?"

"My company was out a lot of money—rather, the insurance company was. The customer will probably never use us again, or recommend us."

"What happened to you? Any disciplinary action?" He knew there hadn't been.

"No. In a way, I would have felt better if they had at least fined me."

Damn, she was good, he thought in admiration—either that, or she was telling the truth and hadn't had anything to do with the incident in Chicago last month. It was possible, he supposed, but irrelevant. Whether or not she'd had anything to do with losing that briefcase, he was grateful it had happened, because otherwise she would never have come to his notice, and he wouldn't have this lead on Crispin Hauer.

But he didn't think she was innocent; he thought she was in this up to her pretty neck. She was better than he had expected, an actress worthy of an Oscar—so good he might have believed she didn't know anything about her father, if it wasn't for the mystery bag and her deceptive strength. He was trained to put together seemingly insignificant details and come up with a coherent picture, and experience had made him doubly cynical. Few people were as honest as they wanted you to believe, and the people who put on the best show were often the ones with the most to hide. He should know— he was an expert at hiding the black secrets of his soul.

He wondered briefly what it said about him that he was willing to sleep with her as part of his plan to gain her trust, but maybe it was better not to think about it. Someone had to be willing to work in the muck, to do things from which ordinary people would shrink, just to protect those ordinary people. Sex was…just sex. Part of the job. He could even divorce his emotions to the point that he actually looked forward to the task.

Task? Who was he kidding? He couldn't wait to slide into her. She intrigued him, with her toned, tight body and the twinkle that so often lit her clear gray eyes, as if she was often amused at both herself and the world around her. He was fascinated by her eyes, by the white striations that made her eyes look almost faceted, like the palest of blue diamonds. Most people thought of gray eyes as a pale blue, but when he was close to her, he could see that they were, very definitely, brilliantly gray. But most of all he was intrigued by her expression, which was so open and good-humored she could almost trademark the term ''Miss Congeniality.'' How could she look like that, as sweet as apple pie, when she was working hand in glove with the most-wanted terrorist in his files?

Part of him, the biggest part, despised her for what she was. The animal core of him, however, was excited by the dangerous edge of the game he was playing, by the challenge of getting her into bed with him and convincing her to trust him. When he was inside her, he wouldn't be thinking about the hundreds of innocent people her father had killed, only about the linking of their bodies. He wouldn't let himself think of anything else, lest he give himself away with some nuance of expression that women were so good at reading. No, he would make love to her as if he had found his soul mate, because that was the only way he could be certain of fooling her.

But he was good at that, at making a woman feel as if he desired her more than anything else in the world. He knew just how to make her aware of him, how to push hard without panicking her—which brought him back to the fact that she had totally ignored his first opening. He smiled slightly to himself. Did she really think that would work?

"Will you have dinner with me tonight?"

She actually jumped, as if she had been lost in her thoughts. "What?"

"Dinner. Tonight. After you deliver your package."

"Oh. But—I'm supposed to deliver it at nine. It'll be late, and—"

"And you'll be alone, and I'll be alone, and you have to eat. I promise not to bite. I may lick, but I won't bite."

She surprised him by bursting into laughter.

Of all the reactions he had anticipated, laughter wasn't one of them. Still, her laugh was so free and genuine, her head tilted back against the seat, that he found himself smiling in response.

"'I may lick, but I won't bite.' That was good. I'll have to remember it," she said, chuckling.

After a moment, when she said nothing else, he realized that she was ignoring him again. He shook his head. "Does that work with most men?"

"Does what work?"

"Ignoring them when they ask you out. Do they slink away with their tails tucked between their legs?"

"Not that I've ever noticed." She grinned. "You make me sound like a femme fatale, breaking hearts left and right."

"You probably are. We guys are tough, though. We can be bleeding to death on the inside and we'll put up such a good front that no one ever knows." He smiled at her. "Have dinner with me."

"You're persistent, aren't you?"

"You still haven't answered me."

"All right—no. There, I've answered you."

"Wrong answer. Try again." More gently, he said, "I know you're tired, and with the time difference, nine o'clock is really midnight to you. It's just a meal, Sunny, not an evening of dancing. That can wait until our second date."

She laughed again. "Persistent *and* confident." She paused, made a wry little face. "The answer is still no. I don't date."

This time he was more than surprised, he was stunned. Of all the things he had expected to come out of her mouth, that particular statement had never crossed his mind. Damn, had he so badly miscalculated? "At all? Or just men?"

"At all." She gestured helplessly. "See, this is why I tried to ignore you, because I didn't want to go into an explanation that you wouldn't accept, anyway. No, I'm not gay, I like men very much, but I don't date. End of explanation."

His relief was so intense, he felt a little dizzy. "If you like men, why don't you date?"

"See?" she demanded on a frustrated rush of air. "You didn't accept it. You immediately started asking questions."

"Damn it, did you think I'd just let it drop? There's something between us, Sunny. I know it, and you know it. Or are you going to ignore that, too?"

"That's exactly what I'm going to do."

He wondered if she realized what she had just admitted. "Were you raped?"

"No!" she half shouted, goaded out of control. "I just...don't...date."

She was well on her way to losing her temper, he thought, amused. He grinned. "You're pretty when you're mad."

She sputtered, then began laughing. "How am I supposed to stay mad when you say things like that?"

"You aren't. That's the whole idea."

"Well, it worked. What it didn't do was change my mind. I'm sorry," she said gently, sobering. "It's just...I have my reasons. Let it drop. Please."

"Okay." He paused. "For now."

She gave an exaggerated groan that had him smiling again. "Why don't you try to take a nap?" he suggested. "You have to be tired, and we still have a long flight ahead of us."

"That's a good idea. You can't badger me if I'm asleep."

With that wry shot, she leaned her head back against the seat. Chance reached behind her seat and produced a folded blanket. "Here. Use this as a pillow, or you'll get a stiff neck."

"Thanks." She took off the headset and tucked the blanket between her head and shoulder, then shifted around in her seat to get more comfortable.

Chance let silence fall, occasionally glancing at her to see if she really fell asleep. About fifteen minutes later, her breathing deepened and evened out into a slow rhythm. He waited a few minutes longer, then eased the plane into a more westerly direction, straight into the setting sun.

Chapter 4

"Sunny." The voice was insistent, a little difficult to hear, and accompanied by a hand on her shoulder, shaking her. "Sunny, wake up."

She stirred and opened her eyes, stretching a little to relieve the kinks in her back and shoulders. "Are we there?"

Chance indicated the headset in her lap, and she slipped it on. "We have a problem," he said quietly.

The bottom dropped out of her stomach, and her heartbeat skittered. No other words, she thought, could be quite as terrifying when one was in an airplane. She took a deep breath, trying to control the surge of panic. "What's wrong?" Her voice was surprisingly steady. She looked around, trying to spot the problem in the cluster of dials in the cockpit, though she had no idea what any of them meant. Then she looked out of the window at the rugged landscape below them, painted in stark reds and blacks as the setting sun threw shadows over jagged rock. "Where are we?"

"Southeastern Oregon."

The engine coughed and sputtered. Her heart felt as if it did, too. As soon as she heard the break in the rhythm, she became aware that the steady background whine of the motor had been interrupted several times while she slept. Her subconscious had registered the change in sound but not put it in any context. Now the context was all too clear.

"I think it's the fuel pump," he added, in answer to her first question.

Calm. She had to stay calm. She pulled in a deep breath, though her lungs felt as if they had shrunk in size. "What do we do?"

He smiled grimly. "Find a place to set it down before it falls down."

"I'll take setting over falling any day." She looked out the side window, studying the ground below. Jagged mountain ridges, enormous boulders and sharp-cut arroyos slicing through the earth were all she could see. "Uh-oh."

"Yea. I've been looking for a place to land for the past half hour."

This was not good, not good at all. In the balance of good and bad, this weighed heavily on the bad side.

The engine sputtered again. The whole frame of the aircraft shook. So did her voice, when she said, "Have you radioed a Mayday?"

Again that grim smile. "We're in the middle of a great big empty area, between navigational beacons. I've tried a couple of times to raise someone, but there haven't been any answers."

The scale tipped even more out of balance. "I knew

it,'' she muttered. ''The way today has gone, I *knew* I'd crash if I got on another plane.''

The grouchiness in her voice made him chuckle, despite the urgency of their situation. He reached over and gently squeezed the back of her neck, startling her with his touch, his big hand warm and hard on her sensitive nape. ''We haven't crashed yet, and I'm going to try damn hard to make sure we don't. The landing may be rough, though.''

She wasn't used to being touched. She had accustomed herself to doing without the physical contact that it was human nature to crave, to keep people at a certain distance. Chance McCall had touched her more in one afternoon than she had been touched in the past five years. The shock of pleasure almost distracted her from their situation—almost. She looked down at the unforgiving landscape again. ''How rough does a landing have to get before it qualifies as a crash?''

''If we walk away from it, then it was a landing.'' He put his hand back on the controls, and she silently mourned that lost connection.

The vast mountain range spread out around them as far as she could see in any direction. Their chances of walking away from this weren't good. How long would it be before their bodies were found, if ever? Sunny clenched her hands, thinking of Margreta. Her sister, not knowing what had happened, would assume the worst— and dying in an airplane crash was *not* the worst. In her grief, she might well abandon her refuge and do something stupid that would get her killed, too.

She watched Chance's strong hands, so deft and sure on the controls. His clear, classic profile was limned against the pearl and vermillion sky, the sort of sunset one saw only in the western states, and likely the last sunset she would ever see. He would be the last person she ever saw, or touched, and she was suddenly, bitterly angry that she had never been able to live the life most women took for granted, that she hadn't been free to accept his offer of dinner and spend the trip in a glow of anticipation, free to flirt with him and maybe see the glow of desire in his golden-brown eyes.

She had been denied a lot, but most of all she had been denied opportunity, and she would never, never forgive her father for that.

The engine sputtered, caught, sputtered again. This time the reassuring rhythm didn't return. The bottom dropped out of her stomach. God, oh God, they were going to crash. Her nails dug into her palms as she fought to contain her panic. She had never before felt so small and helpless, so fragile, with soft flesh and slender bones that couldn't withstand such battering force. She was going to die, and she had yet to live.

The plane jerked and shuddered, bucking under the stress of spasmodic power. It pitched to the right, throwing Sunny against the door so hard her right arm went numb.

"That's it," Chance said between gritted teeth, his knuckles white as he fought to control the pitching aircraft. He brought the wings level again. "I have to take it down now, while I have a little control. Look for the best place."

Best place? There *was* no best place. They needed somewhere that was relatively flat and relatively clear; the last location she had seen that fit that description had been in Utah.

He raised the right wingtip, tilting the plane so he had a better side view.

"See anything?" Sunny asked, her voice shaking just a little.

"Nothing. Damn."

"Damn is the wrong word. Pilots are supposed to say something else just before they crash." Humor wasn't much of a weapon with which to face death, but it was how she had always gotten herself through the hard times.

Unbelievably, he grinned. "But I haven't crashed yet, sweetheart. Have a little faith. I promise I'll say the right word if I don't find a good-looking spot pretty soon."

"If you don't find a good-looking spot, I'll say it for you," she promised fervently.

They crossed a jagged, boulder-strewn ridge, and a long, narrow black pit yawned beneath them like a doorway to hell. "There!" Chance said, nosing the plane down.

"What? Where?" She sat erect, desperate hope flaring inside her, but all she could see was that black pit.

"The canyon. That's our best bet."

The black pit was a canyon? Weren't canyons supposed to be big? That looked like an arroyo. How on earth would the plane ever fit inside it? And what difference did it make, when this was their only chance? Her heart lodged itself in her throat, and she gripped the edge of the seat as Chance eased the pitching aircraft lower and lower.

The engine stopped.

For a moment all she heard was the awful silence, more deafening than any roar.

Then she became aware of the air rushing past the metal skin of the plane, air that no longer supported them. She heard her own heart beating, fast and heavy, heard the whisper of her breath. She heard everything except what she most wanted to hear, the sweet sound of an airplane engine.

Chance didn't say anything. He concentrated fiercely on keeping the plane level, riding the air currents down, down, aiming for that long, narrow slit in the earth. The plane spiraled like a leaf, coming so close to the jagged mountainside on the left that she could see the pits in the dark red rock.

Sunny bit her lip until blood welled in her mouth, fighting back the terror and panic that threatened to erupt in screams. She couldn't distract him now, no matter what. She wanted to close her eyes, but resolutely kept them open. If she died now, she didn't want to do it in craven fear. She couldn't help the fear, but she didn't have to be craven. She would watch death come at her, watch Chance as he fought to bring them down safely and cheat the grim horseman.

They slipped below the sunshine, into the black shadows, deeper and deeper. It was colder in the shadows, a chill that immediately seeped through the windows into her bones. She couldn't see a thing. Quickly she snatched off the sunglasses and saw that Chance had done the same. His eyes were narrowed, his expression hard and intent as he studied the terrain below.

The ground was rushing at them now, a ground that was pocked and scored with rivulets, and dotted with boulders. It was flat enough, but not a nice, clear landing spot at all. She braced her feet against the floor, her body rigid as if she could force the airplane to stay aloft.

"Hold on." His voice was cool. "I'm going to try to make it to the stream bed. The sand will help slow us down before we hit one of those rocks."

A stream bed? He was evidently much better at reading the ground than she was. She tried to see a ribbon of water, but finally realized the stream was dry; the bed was that thin, twisting line that looked about as wide as the average car.

She started to say "Good luck," but it didn't seem appropriate. Neither did "It was nice knowing you." In the end, all she could manage was "Okay."

It happened fast. Suddenly they were no longer skimming above the earth. The ground was *there,* and they hit it hard, so hard she pitched forward against the seat belt, then snapped back. They went briefly airborne again as the wheels bounced, then hit again even harder. She heard metal screeching in protest; then her head banged against the side window, and for a chaotic moment she didn't see or hear anything, just felt the tossing and bouncing of the plane. She was boneless, unable to hold on, flopping like a shirt in a clothes dryer.

Then there came the hardest bounce of all, jarring her teeth. The plane spun sideways in a sickening motion, then lurched to a stop. Time and reality splintered, broke apart, and for a long moment nothing made any sense; she had no grasp on where she was or what had happened.

She heard a voice, and the world jolted back into place.

"Sunny? Sunny, are you all right?" Chance was asking urgently.

She tried to gather her senses, tried to answer him. Dazed, battered, she realized that the force of the landing had turned her inside the confines of the seat belt, and she was facing the side window, her back to Chance. She felt his hands on her, heard his low swearing as he unclipped the seat belt and eased her back against his chest, supporting her with his body.

She swallowed, and managed to find her voice. "I'm

okay.'' The words weren't much more than a croak, but if she could talk at all that meant she was alive. They were both alive. Joyful disbelief swelled in her chest. He had actually managed to land the plane!

''We have to get out. There may be a fuel leak.'' Even as he spoke, he shoved open the door and jumped out, dragging her with him as if she was a sack of flour. She felt rather sacklike, her limbs limp and trembling.

A fuel leak. The engine had been dead when they landed, but there was still the battery, and wiring that could short out and spark. If a spark got to any fuel, the plane and everything in it would go up in a fireball.

Everything in it. The words rattled in her brain, like marbles in a can, and with dawning horror she realized what that meant. Her bag was still in the plane.

''Wait!'' she shrieked, panic sending a renewed surge of adrenaline through her system, restoring the bones to her legs, the strength to her muscles. She twisted in his grasp, grabbing the door handle and hanging on. ''My bag!''

''Damn it, Sunny!'' he roared, trying to break her grip on the handle. ''Forget the damn bag!''

''No!''

She jerked away from him and began to climb back into the plane. With a smothered curse he grabbed her around the waist and bodily lifted her away from the plane. ''I'll get the damn bag! Go on—get out of here! Run!''

She was appalled that he would risk his life retrieving her bag, while sending her to safety. ''I'll get it,'' she said fiercely, grabbing him by the belt and tugging. ''*You* run!''

For a split second he literally froze, staring at her in shock. Then he gave his head a little shake, reached in for the bag and effortlessly hefted it out. Wordlessly Sunny tried to take it, but he only gave her an incendiary look and she didn't have time to argue. Carrying the bag in his left hand and gripping her upper arm with his right, he towed her at a run away from the plane. Her shoes sank into the soft grit, and sand and scrub brush bit at her ankles, but she scrambled to stay upright and keep pace with him.

They were a good fifty yards away before he judged it safe. He dropped the bag and turned on her like a panther pouncing on fresh meat, gripping her upper arms with both hands as if he wanted to shake her. "What the hell are you thinking?" he began in a tone of barely leashed violence, then cut himself off, staring at her face. His expression altered, his golden-brown eyes darkening.

"You're bleeding," he said harshly. He grabbed his handkerchief out of his pocket and pressed it to her chin. Despite the roughness of his tone, his touch was incredibly gentle. "You said you weren't hurt."

"I'm not." She raised her trembling hand and took the handkerchief, dabbing it at her chin and mouth. There wasn't much blood, and the bleeding seemed to have stopped. "I bit my lip," she confessed. "Before you landed, I mean. To keep from screaming."

He stared down at her with an expression like flint. "Why didn't you just scream?"

"I didn't want to distract you." The trembling was growing worse by the second; she tried to hold herself steady, but every limb shook as if her bones had turned to gelatin.

He tilted up her face, staring down at her for a moment in the deepening twilight. He breathed a low, savage curse, then slowly leaned down and pressed his lips to her mouth. Despite the violence she sensed in him, the kiss was light, gentle, more of a salute than a kiss. She caught her breath, beguiled by the softness of his lips, the warm smell of his skin, the hint of his taste. She fisted her hands in his T-shirt, clinging to his strength, trying to sink into his warmth.

He lifted his head. "That's for being so brave," he murmured. "I couldn't have asked for a better partner in a plane crash."

"Landing," she corrected shakily. "It was a landing."

That earned her another soft kiss, this time on the temple. She made a strangled sound and leaned into him, a different sort of trembling beginning to take hold of her. He framed her face with his hands, his thumbs gently stroking the corners of her mouth as he studied her. She felt her lips tremble a little, but then, all of her was shaking. He touched the small sore spot her teeth had made in her lower lip; then he was kissing her again, and this time there was nothing gentle about it.

This kiss rocked her to her foundation. It was hungry, rough, deep. There were reasons why she shouldn't respond to him, but she couldn't think what they were. Instead, she gripped his wrists and went on tiptoe to slant her parted lips against his, opening her mouth for the thrust of his tongue. He tasted like man, and sex, a potent mixture that went to her head faster than hundred-proof whiskey. Heat bloomed in her loins and breasts, a desperate, needy heat that brought a low moan from her throat.

He wrapped one arm around her and pulled her against him, molding her to him from knee to breast while his kisses became even deeper, even harder. She locked her arms around his neck and arched into him, wanting the feel of his hard-muscled body against her with an urgency that swept away reason. Instinctively she pushed her hips against his, and the hard length of his erection bulged into the notch of her thighs. This time she cried out in want, in need, in a desire that burned through every cell of her body. His hand closed roughly around her breast, kneading, rubbing her nipple through the layers of blouse and bra, both easing and intensifying the ache that made them swell toward his touch.

Suddenly he jerked his head back. "I don't believe this," he muttered. Reaching up, he prised her arms from around his neck and set her away from him. He looked even more savage than he had a moment before, the veins standing out in his neck. "Stay here," he barked. "Don't move an inch. I have to check the plane."

He left her standing there in the sand, in the growing twilight, suddenly cold all the way down to the bone. Deprived of his warmth, his strength, her legs slowly collapsed, and she sank to the ground.

Chance swore to himself, steadily and with blistering heat, as he checked the plane for fuel leaks and other damage. He had deliberately made the landing rougher than necessary, and the plane had a reinforced landing gear as well as extra protection for the fuel lines and tank, but a smart pilot didn't take anything for granted. He had to check the plane, had to stay in character.

He didn't want to stay in character. He wanted to back her against one of those big boulders and lift her skirt. Damn! What was wrong with him? In the past fifteen years he'd held a lot of beautiful, deadly women in his arms, and even though he let his body respond, his mind had always remained cool. Sunny Miller wasn't the most beautiful, not by a long shot; she was more gamine than goddess, with bright eyes that invited laughter rather than seduction. So why was he so hot to get into her pants?

"Why" didn't matter, he angrily reminded himself. Okay, so his attraction to her was unexpected; it was an advantage, something to be used. He wouldn't have to fake anything, which meant there was even less chance of her sensing anything off-kilter.

Danger heightened the emotions, destroying inhibitions. They had lived through a life-threatening situation together, they were alone, and there was a definite physical attraction between them. He had arranged the first two circumstances; the third was a bonus. It was a textbook situation; studies in human nature had shown that, if a man and a woman were thrown together in a dangerous situation and they had only each other to rely on, they quickly formed both sexual and emotional bonds. Chance had the advantage, in that he knew the plane hadn't been in any danger of crashing, and that they weren't in a life-and-death situation. Sunny would think they were stranded, while he knew better. Whenever he signaled Zane, they would promptly be "rescued," but he wouldn't send that signal until Sunny took him into her confidence about her father.

Everything was under control. They weren't even in Oregon, as he'd told her. They were in Nevada, in a narrow box canyon he and Zane had scouted out and selected because it was possible to land a plane in it, and, unless one had the equipment to scale vertical rock walls, impossible to escape. They weren't close to any commercial flight pattern, he had disabled the transponder so no search plane would pick up a signal, and they were far off their route. They wouldn't be found.

Sunny was totally under his control; she just didn't know it.

The growing dusk made it impossible to see very much, and it was obvious that if the plane was going to explode in flames, it would already have done so. Chance strode back to where Sunny was sitting on the ground, her knees pulled up and her arms wrapped around her legs, and that damn bag close by her side. She scrambled to her feet as he approached. "All clear?"

"All clear. No fuel leaks."

"That's good." She managed a smile. "It wouldn't do us any good for you to fix the fuel pump if there wasn't any fuel left."

"Sunny...if it's a clogged line, I can fix it. If the fuel pump has gone out, I can't."

He decided to let her know right away that they might not be flying out of here in the morning.

She absorbed that in silence, rubbing her bare arms to ward off the chill of the desert air. The temperature dropped like a rock when the sun went down, which was one of the reasons he had chosen this site. They would have to share their body heat at night to survive.

He leaned down and hefted the bag, marveling anew at its weight, then took her arm to walk with her back to the plane. "I hope you have a coat in this damn bag, since you thought it was important enough to risk your life getting it," he growled.

"A sweater," she said absently, looking up at the crystal clear sky with its dusting of stars. The black walls of the canyon loomed on either side of them, making it obvious they were in a hole in the earth. A big hole, but still a hole. She shook herself, as if dragging her thoughts back to the problem at hand. "We'll be all right," she said. "I have some food, and—"

"Food? You're carrying food in here?" He indicated the bag.

"Just some emergency stuff."

Of all the things he'd expected, food was at the bottom of the list. Hell, food wasn't even *on* the list. Why would a woman on an overnight trip put food in her suitcase?

They reached the plane, and he set the bag down in the dirt. "Let me get some things, and we'll find a place to camp for the night. Can you get anything else in there, or is it full?"

"It's full," she said positively, but then, he hadn't expected her to open it so easily.

He shrugged and dragged out his own small duffel, packed with the things a man could be expected to take on a charter flight: toiletries, a change of clothes. The duffel was unimportant, but it wouldn't look right if he left it behind.

"Why can't we camp here?" she asked.

"This is a stream bed. It's dry now, but if it rains anywhere in the mountains, we could be caught in the runoff."

As he spoke, he got a flashlight out of the dash, the blanket from the back, and a pistol from the pocket in the pilot's side door. He stuck the pistol in his belt, and draped the blanket around her shoulders. "I have some water," he said, taking out a plastic gallon milk jug that he'd refilled with water. "We'll be all right tonight." Water had been the toughest thing to locate. He and Zane had found several box canyons in which he could have landed the plane, but this was the only one with water. The source wasn't much, just a thin trickle running out of the rock at the far end of the canyon, but it was enough. He would "find" the water tomorrow.

He handed her the flashlight and picked up both bags.

"Lead the way," he instructed, and indicated the direction he wanted. The floor of the canyon sloped upward on one side; the stream bed was the only smooth ground. The going was rough, and Sunny carefully picked her way over rocks and gullies. She was conscientious about shining the light so he could see where he was going, since he was hampered by both bags.

Damn, he wished she had complained at least a little, or gotten upset. He wished she wasn't so easy to like. Most people would have been half-hysterical, or asking endless questions about their chances of being rescued if he couldn't get the plane repaired. Not Sunny. She coped, just as she had coped at the airport, with a minimum of fuss. Without *any* fuss, actually; she had bitten the blood out of her lip to keep from distracting him while he was bringing the plane down.

The canyon was so narrow it didn't take them long to reach the vertical wall. Chance chose a fairly flat section of sandy gray dirt, with a pile of huge boulders that formed a rough semi-circle. "This will give us some protection from the wind tonight."

"What about snakes?" she asked, eyeing the boulders.

"Possible," he said, as he set down the bags. Had he found a weakness he could use to bring her closer to him? "Are you afraid of them?"

"Only the human kind." She looked around as if taking stock of their situation, then kind of braced her shoulders. It was a minute movement, one he wouldn't have noticed if he hadn't been studying her so keenly. With an almost cheerful note she said, "Let's get this camp set up so we can eat. I'm hungry."

She squatted beside her bag and spun the combination dial of the rather substantial lock on her bag. With a quiet *snick* the lock opened, and she unzipped the bag.

Chance was a bit taken aback at finding out what was in the bag this easily, but he squatted beside her. "What do you have? Candy bars?"

She chuckled. "Nothing so tasty."

He took the flashlight from her and shone it into the bag as she began taking out items. The bag was as neatly packed as a salesman's sample case, and she hadn't been lying about not having any room in there for anything else. She placed a sealed plastic bag on the ground between them. "Here we go. Nutrition bars." She slanted a look at him. "They taste like you'd expect a nutrition bar to taste, but they're concentrated. One bar a day will give us all we need to stay alive. I have a dozen of them."

The next item was a tiny cell phone. She stared at it, frozen, for a moment, then looked up at him with fragile hope in her eyes as she turned it on. Chance knew there wasn't a signal here, but he let her go through the motions, something inside him aching at the disappointment he knew she would feel.

Her shoulders slumped. "Nothing," she said, and turned the phone off. Without another word she returned to her unpacking.

A white plastic box with a familiar red cross on the top came out next. "First aid kit," she murmured, reaching back into the bag. "Water purification tablets. A couple of bottles of water, ditto orange juice. Light sticks. Matches." She listed each item as she set it on the ground. "Hairspray, deodorant, toothpaste, pre-moistened towelettes, hairbrush, curling iron, blow dryer, two space blankets—" she paused as she reached the bottom of the bag and began hauling on something bigger than any of the other items. "—and a tent."

Chapter 5

A tent. Chance stared down at it, recognizing the type. This was survivalist stuff, what people stored in underground shelters in case of war or natural disaster—or what someone who expected to spend a lot of time in the wilderness would pack.

"It's small," she said apologetically. "Really just a one-man tent, but I had to get something light enough for me to carry. There will be enough room for both of us to sleep in it, though, if you don't mind being a little crowded."

Why would she carry a *tent* on board a plane, when she expected to spend one night in Seattle—in a hotel— then fly back to Atlanta? Why would anyone carry that heavy a bag around when she could have checked it? The answer was that she hadn't wanted it out of her possession, but he still wanted an explanation of why she was carrying it at all.

Something didn't add up here.

*   *   *

His silence was unnerving. Sunny looked down at her
incongruous pile of possessions and automatically emp-
tied out the bag, removing her sweater and slipping it
on, sitting down to pull on a pair of socks, then stuffing
her change of clothes and her grooming items back into
the bag. Her mind was racing. There was something
about his expression that made a chill go down her spine,
a hardness that she hadn't glimpsed before. Belatedly,
she remembered how easily he had caught the cretin in
the airport, the deadly grace and speed with which he
moved. This was no ordinary charter pilot, and she was
marooned with him.

She had been attracted to him from the first moment
she saw him, but she couldn't afford to let that blind her
to the danger of letting down her guard. She was accustomed to living with danger, but this was a different sort
of danger, and she had no idea what form it could, or
would, take. Chance could simply be one of those men
who packed more punch than others, a man very capable
of taking care of himself.

Or he could be in her father's pay.

The thought chilled her even more, the cold going
down to her bones before common sense reasserted itself. No, there was no way her father could have arranged for everything that had happened today, no way
he could have known she would be in the Salt Lake City
airport. Being there had been pure bad luck, the result
of a fouled-up flight schedule. *She* hadn't known she
would be in Salt Lake City. If her father had been involved, he would have tried to grab her in either Atlanta
or Seattle. All the zig-zagging across the country she had
done today had made it impossible for her father to be
involved.

As her mind cleared of that silent panic, she remembered how Chance had dragged her bodily from the plane, the way he had draped the blanket around her, even the courtesy with which he had treated her in the airport. He was a strong man, accustomed to being in the lead and taking the risks. *Military training,* she thought with a sudden flash of clarity, and wondered how she had missed it before. Her life, and Margreta's, depended on how well she could read people, how prepared she was, how alert. With Chance, she had been so taken off guard by the strength of her attraction to him, and the shock of finding that interest returned, that she hadn't been thinking.

"What's this about?" he asked quietly, squatting down beside her and indicating the tent. "And don't tell me you were going to camp out in the hotel lobby."

She couldn't help it. The thought of setting up the tent in a hotel lobby was so ludicrous that she chuckled. Seeing the funny side of things was what had kept her sane all these years.

One big hand closed gently on the nape of her neck. "Sunny," he said warningly. "Tell me."

She shook her head, still smiling. "We're stranded here tonight, but essentially we're strangers. After we get out of here we'll never see each other again, so there's no point in spilling our guts to each other. You keep your secrets, and I'll keep mine."

The flashlight beam sharpened the angles of his face. He exhaled a long, exasperated breath. "Okay—for now. I don't know why it matters, anyway. Unless I can get the plane fixed, we're going to be here a long time, and the reason why you have the tent will be irrelevant."

She searched his face, trying to read his impassive expression. "That isn't reassuring."

"It's the truth."

"When we don't show up in Seattle, someone will search for us. The Civil Air Patrol, someone. Doesn't your plane have one of those beacon things?"

"We're in a canyon."

He didn't have to say more than that. Any signal would be blocked by the canyon walls, except for directly overhead. They were in a deep, narrow slit in the earth, the narrowness of the canyon limiting even more their chances of anyone picking up the signal.

"Well, darn," she said forcefully.

This time he was the one who laughed, and he shook his head as he released her neck and stood up. "Is that the worst you can say?"

"We're alive. That outcome is so good considering what *could* have happened that, in comparison, being stranded here only rates a 'darn.' You may be able to fix the plane." She shrugged. "No point in wasting the really nasty words until we know more."

He leaned down and helped her to her feet. "If I can't get us going again, I'll help you with those words. For now, let's get this tent set up before the temperature drops even more."

"What about a fire?"

"I'll look for firewood tomorrow—*if* we need it. We can get by tonight without a fire, and I don't want to waste the flashlight batteries. If we're here for any length of time, we'll need the flashlight."

"I have the lightsticks."

"We'll save those, too. Just in case."

Working together, they set up the tent. She could have done it herself; it was made for one person to handle, and she had practiced until she knew she could do it with a minimum of fuss, but with two people the job took only moments. Brushing away the rocks so they would have a smooth surface beneath the tent floor took longer, but even so, they weren't going to have a comfortable bed for the night.

When they were finished, she eyed the tent with misgivings. It was long enough for Chance, but... She visually measured the width of his shoulders, then the width of the tent. She was either going to have to sleep on her side all night long—or on top of him.

The heat that shot through her told her which option her body preferred. Her heart beat a little faster in anticipation of their enforced intimacy during the coming night, of lying against his strong, warm body, maybe even sleeping in his arms.

To his credit, he didn't make any insinuating remarks, even though when he looked at the tent he must have drawn the same conclusion as she had. Instead, he bent down to pick up the bag of nutrition bars and said smugly, "I knew you'd have dinner with me tonight."

She began laughing again, charmed by both his tact and his sense of humor, and fell a little in love with him right then.

She should have been alarmed, but she wasn't. Yes, letting herself care for him made her emotionally vulnerable, but they had lived through a terrifying experience together, and she *needed* an emotional anchor right now. So far she hadn't found a single thing about the man that she didn't like, not even that hint of danger she kept sensing. In this situation, a man with an edge to him was an asset, not a hindrance.

She allowed herself to luxuriate in this unaccustomed feeling as they each ate a nutrition bar—which was edible, but definitely not tasty—and drank some water. Then they packed everything except the two space blankets back in the bag, to protect their supplies from snakes and insects and other scavengers. They didn't have to worry about bears, not in this desertlike part of the country, but coyotes were possible. Her bag was supposedly indestructible; if any coyotes showed up, she supposed she would find out if the claim about the bag was true, because there wasn't room in the tent for both them and the bag.

Chance checked the luminous dial of his watch. "It's still early, but we should get in the tent to save our body heat, and not burn up calories trying to stay warm out here. I'll spread this blanket down, and we'll use your two blankets for cover."

For the first time, she realized he was in his T-shirt. "Shouldn't you get your jacket from the plane?"

"It's too bulky to wear in the tent. Besides, I don't feel the cold as much as you do. I'll be fine without it." He sat down and pulled off his boots, tossed them inside the tent, then crawled in with the blanket. Sunny slipped off her own shoes, glad she had the socks to keep her feet warm.

"Okay, come on in," Chance said. "Feet first."

She gave him her shoes, then sat down and worked herself feetfirst into the tent. He was lying on his side, which gave her room to maneuver, but it was still a chore keeping her skirt down and trying not to bunch up the blanket as she wiggled into place. Chance zipped the tent flaps shut, then pulled his pistol out of his waistband and placed it beside his head. Sunny eyed the big black automatic; she wasn't an expert on pistols, but she knew it was one of the heavier calibers, either a .45 or a 9mm. She had tried them, but the bigger pistols were too heavy for her to handle with ease, so she had opted for a smaller caliber.

He had already unfolded the space blankets and had them ready to pull in place. She could already feel his body heat in the small space, so she didn't need a blanket yet, but as the night grew colder, they would need all the covering they could get.

They both moved around, trying to get comfortable. Because he was so big, Sunny tried to give him as much room as possible. She turned on her side and curled her arm under her head, but they still bumped and brushed against each other.

"Ready?" he asked.

"Ready."

He turned off the flashlight. The darkness was complete, like being deep in a cave. "Thank God I'm not claustrophobic," she said, taking a deep breath. His scent filled her lungs, warm and…different, not musky, exactly, but earthy, and very much the way a man should smell.

"Just think of it as being safe," he murmured. "Darkness can feel secure."

She did feel safe, she realized. For the first time in her memory, she was certain no one except the man beside her knew where she was. She didn't have to check locks, scout out an alternate exit, or sleep so lightly she sometimes felt as if she hadn't slept at all. She didn't have to worry about being followed, or her phone being tapped, or any of the other things that could happen. She did worry about Margreta, but she had to think positively. Tomorrow Chance would find the problem was a clogged fuel line, he would get it cleared, and they would finish their trip. She would be too late to deliver the package in Seattle, but considering they had landed safely instead of crashing, she didn't really care about the package. The day's outcome could have been so much worse that she was profoundly grateful they were all in one piece and relatively comfortable—"relatively" being the key word, she thought, as she tried to find a better position. The ground was as hard as a rock. For all she knew the ground *was* a rock, covered by a thin layer of dirt.

She was suddenly exhausted. The events of the day—the long flight and fouled-up connections, the lack of food, the stress of being mugged, then the almost unbearable tension of those last minutes in the plane—finally took their toll on her. She yawned and unconsciously tried yet again to find a comfortable position, turning over to pillow her head on her other arm. Her elbow collided with something very solid, and he grunted.

"I'm sorry," she mumbled. She squirmed a little more, inadvertently bumping him with her knee. "This is so crowded I may have to sleep on top."

She heard the words and in shock realized that she had actually said them aloud. She opened her mouth to apologize again.

"Or I could be the one on top."

His words stopped her apology cold. Her breath tangled in her lungs and didn't escape. His deep voice seemed to echo in the darkness, that single sentence reverberating through her consciousness. She was suddenly, acutely, aware of every inch of him, of the sensual promise in his tone. The kiss—the kiss she could write off as reaction; danger was supposed to be an aphrodisiac, and evidently that was true. But this wasn't reaction; this was desire, warm and curious, seeking.

"Is that a 'no' I'm hearing?"

Her lungs started working again, and she sucked in a breath. "I haven't said anything."

"That's my point." He sounded faintly amused. "I guess I'm not going to get lucky tonight."

Feeling more certain of herself with his teasing, she said dryly, "I guess not. You've already used up your quota of luck for the day."

"I'll try again tomorrow."

She stifled a laugh.

"Does that snicker mean I haven't scared you?"

She should be scared, she thought, or at least wary. She had no idea why she wasn't. The fact was, she felt tempted. Very tempted. "No, I'm not scared."

"Good." He yawned. "Then why don't you pull off that sweater and let me use it as a pillow, and you can use my shoulder. We'll both be more comfortable."

Common sense said he was right. Common sense also said she was asking for trouble if she slept in his arms. She trusted him to behave, but she wasn't that certain of herself. He was sexy, with a capital SEX. He made her laugh. He was strong and capable, with a faintly wicked edge to him. He was even a little dangerous. What more could a woman want?

That was perhaps the most dangerous thing about him, that he made her want him. She had easily resisted other men, walking away without a backward look or a second thought. Chance made her long for all the things she had denied herself, made her aware of how lonely and alone she was.

"Are you sure you can trust me to behave?" she asked, only half joking. "I didn't mean to say that about being on top. I was half-asleep, and it just slipped out."

"I think I can handle you if you get fresh. For one thing, you'll be sound asleep as soon as you stop talking."

She yawned. "I know. I'm crashing hard, if you'll pardon the terminology."

"We didn't crash, we landed. Come on, let's get that sweater off, then you can sleep."

There wasn't room to fully sit up, so he helped her struggle out of the garment. He rolled it up and tucked it under his head, then gently, as if worried he might frighten her, drew her against his right side. His right arm curled around her, and she nestled close, settling her head in the hollow of his shoulder.

The position was surprisingly comfortable, and comforting. She draped her right arm across his chest, because there didn't seem to be any other place to put it. Well, there were other places, but none that seemed as safe. Besides, she liked feeling his heartbeat under her hand. The strong, even thumping satisfied some primitive instinct in her, the desire not to be alone in the night.

"Comfortable?" he asked in a low, soothing tone.

"Um-hmm."

With his left arm he snagged one of the space blankets and pulled it up to cover her to the shoulders, keeping the chill from her bare arms. Cocooned in warmth and darkness, she gave in to the sheer pleasure of lying so close to him. Sleepy desire hummed just below the surface, warming her, softening her. Her breasts, crushed against his side, tightened in delight, and her nipples felt achy, telling her they had hardened. Could he feel them? she wondered. She wanted to rub herself against him like a cat, intensifying the sensation, but she lay very still and concentrated on the rhythm of his heartbeat.

He had touched her breasts when he kissed her. She wanted to feel that again, feel his hard hand on her bare flesh. She wanted him, wanted his touch and his taste and the feel of him inside her. The force of her physical yearning was so strong that she actually ached from the emptiness.

If we don't get out of here tomorrow, she thought in faint despair just before she went to sleep, I'll be under him before the sun goes down again.

Sunny was accustomed to waking immediately when anything disturbed her; once, a car had backfired out in the street and she had grabbed the pistol from under the pillow and rolled off the bed before the noise had completely faded. She had learned how to nap on demand, because she never knew when she might have to run for her life. She could count on one hand the number of nights since she had stopped being a child that she had slept through undisturbed.

But she woke in Chance's arms aware that she had slept all night long, that not only had lying next to him not disturbed her, in a very basic way his presence had been reassuring. She was safe here, safe and warm and unutterably relaxed. His hand was stroking slowly down her back, and that was what had awakened her.

Her skirt had ridden up during the night, of course, and was twisted at midthigh. Their legs were tangled together, her right leg thrown over his; his jeans were old and soft, but the denim was still slightly rough against the inside of her thigh. She wasn't lying completely on top of him, but it was a near thing. Her head lay pillowed on his chest instead of his shoulder, with the steady thumping of his heart under her ear.

The slow motion of his hand continued. "Good morning," he said, his deep voice raspy from sleep.

"Good morning." She didn't want to get up, she realized, though she knew she should. It was after dawn; the morning light seeped through the brown fabric of the tent, washing them with a dull gold color. Chance should get started on the fuel pump, so they could get airborne and in radio contact with someone as soon as possible, to let the FAA know they hadn't crashed. She knew what she should do, but instead she continued to lie there, content with the moment.

He touched her hair, lifting one strand and watching it drift back down. "I could get used to this," he murmured.

"You've slept with women before."

"I haven't slept with *you* before."

She wanted to ask how she was different, but she was better off not knowing. Nothing could come of this fast-deepening attraction, because she couldn't let it. She had to believe that he could repair the plane, that in a matter of hours they would be separating and she would never see him again. That was the only thing that gave her the strength, finally, to pull away from him and straighten her clothes, push her hair out of her face and unzip the tent.

The chill morning air rushed into their small cocoon. "Wow," she said, ignoring his comment. "Some hot coffee would be good, wouldn't it? I don't suppose you have a jar of instant in the plane?"

"You mean you don't have coffee packed in that survival bag of yours?" Taking his cue from her, he didn't push her to continue their provocative conversation.

"Nope, just water." She crawled out of the tent, and he handed her shoes and sweater out through the opening. Quickly she slipped them on, glad she had brought a heavy cardigan instead of a summer-weight one.

Chance's boots came out next, then him. He sat on the ground and pulled on his boots. "Damn, it's cold. I'm going to get my jacket from the plane. I'll take care of business there, and you go on the other side of these boulders. There shouldn't be any snakes stirring around this early, but keep an eye out.''

Sunny dug some tissues out of her skirt pocket and set off around the boulders. Ten minutes later, nature's call having been answered, she washed her face and hands with one of the pre-moistened towelettes, then brushed her teeth and hair. Feeling much more human and able to handle the world, she took a moment to look around at their life-saving little canyon.

It was truly a slit in the earth, no more than fifty yards wide where he had landed the plane. About a quarter of a mile farther down it widened some, but the going was much rougher. The stream bed was literally the only place they could have safely landed. Just beyond the widest point, the canyon made a dog leg to the left, so she had no idea how long it was. The canyon floor was littered with rocks big and small, and a variety of scrub brush. Deep grooves were cut into the ground where rain had sluiced down the steep canyon walls and arrowed toward the stream.

All the different shades of red were represented in the dirt and rock, from rust to vermillion to a sandy pink. The scrub brush wasn't a lush green; the color was dry, as if it had been bleached by the sun. Some of it was silvery, a bright contrast against the monochromatic tones of the earth.

They seemed to be the only two living things there. She didn't hear any birds chirping, or insects rustling. There had to be small wildlife such as lizards and snakes, she knew, which meant there had to be something for them to eat, but at the moment the immense solitude was almost overwhelming.

Looking at the plane, she saw that Chance was already

poking around in its innards. Shoving her cold hands into the sweater pockets, she walked down to him.

"Don't you want to eat something?"

"I'd rather save the food until I see what the problem is." He gave her a crooked grin. "No offense, but I don't want to eat another one of those nutrition bars unless I absolutely have to."

"And if you can fly us out of here, you figure you can hold out until we get to an airport."

"Bingo."

She grinned as she changed positions so she could see what he was doing. "I didn't eat one, either," she confessed.

He was checking the fuel lines, his face set in that intent expression men got when they were doing anything mechanical. Sunny felt useless; she could have helped if he was working on a car, but she didn't know anything about airplanes. "Is there anything I can do to help?" she finally asked.

"No, it's just a matter of taking off the fuel lines and checking them for clogs."

She waited a few more minutes, but the process looked tedious rather than interesting, and she began getting restless. "I think I'll walk around, explore a bit."

"Stay within yelling distance," he said absently.

The morning, though still cool, was getting warmer by the minute as the sun heated the dry desert air. She walked carefully, watching where she placed each step, because a sprained ankle could mean the difference between life and death if she had to run for it. Someday, she thought, a sprain would be an inconvenience, nothing more. One day she would be free.

She looked up at the clear blue sky and inhaled the clean, crisp air. She had worked hard to retain her enjoyment of life, the way she had learned to rely on a sense of humor to keep her sane. Margreta didn't handle things nearly as well, but she already had to deal with a heart condition that, while it could be controlled with medication, nevertheless meant that she had to take certain precautions. If she were ever found, Margreta lacked Sunny's ability to just drop out of sight. She had to have her medication refilled, which meant she had to occasionally see her doctor so he could write a new prescription. If she had to find a new doctor, that would mean being retested, which would mean a lot more money.

Which meant that Sunny never saw her sister. It was safer if they weren't together, in case anyone was looking for sisters. She didn't even have Margreta's phone number. Margreta called Sunny's cell phone once a week at a set time, always from a different pay phone. That way, if Sunny was captured, she had no information her captors could get by any means, not even drugs.

She had four days until Margreta called, Sunny thought. If she didn't answer the phone, or if Margreta didn't call, then each had to assume the other had been caught. If Sunny didn't answer the phone, Margreta would bolt from her safe hiding place, because with the phone records her location could be narrowed down to the correct city. Sunny couldn't bear to think what would happen then; Margreta, in her grief and rage, might well throw caution to the wind in favor of revenge.

Four days. The problem *had* to be a clogged fuel line. It just had to be.

Chapter 6

Mindful of Chance's warning, Sunny didn't wander far. In truth, there wasn't much to look at, just grit and rocks and scraggly bushes, and those vertical rock walls. The desert had a wild, lonely beauty, but she was more appreciative when she wasn't stranded in it. When rain filled the stream this sheltered place probably bloomed with color, but how often did it rain here? Once a year?

As the day warmed, the reptiles began to stir. She saw a brown lizard dart into a crevice as she approached. A bird she didn't recognize swooped down for a tasty insect, then flew back off to freedom. The steep canyon walls didn't mean anything to a bird, while the hundred feet or so were unscalable to her.

She began to get hungry, and a glance at her watch told her she had been meandering through the canyon for over an hour. What was taking Chance so long? If there was a clog in the lines he should have found it by now.

She began retracing her steps to the plane. She could see Chance still poking around the engine, which meant he probably hadn't found anything. A chilly finger of fear prodded her, and she pushed it away. She refused to anticipate trouble. She would deal with things as they happened, and if Chance couldn't repair the plane, then they would have to find some other way out of the canyon. She hadn't explored far; perhaps the other end was open, and they could simply walk out. She didn't know how far they were from a town, but she was willing to make the effort. Anything was better than sitting and doing nothing.

As she approached, Chance lifted his hand to show he saw her, then turned back to the engine. Sunny let her gaze linger, admiring the way his T-shirt clung to the muscles of his back and shoulders. The fit of his jeans wasn't bad, either, she thought, eyeing his butt and long legs.

Something moved in the sand near his feet.

She thought she would faint. Her vision dimmed and narrowed until all she saw was the snake, perilously close to his left boot. Her heart leaped, pounding against her ribcage so hard she felt the thuds.

She had no sensation or knowledge of moving; time took on the viscosity of syrup. All she knew was that the snake was getting bigger and bigger, closer and closer. Chance looked around at her and stepped back from the plane, almost on the coiling length. The snake's head drew back and her hand closed on a coil, surprisingly warm and smooth, and she threw the awful thing as far as she could. It was briefly outlined against the stark rock, then sailed beyond a bush and dropped from sight.

"Are you all right? Did it bite you? Are you hurt?"

She couldn't stop babbling as she went down on her knees and began patting his legs, looking for droplets of blood, a small tear in his jeans, anything that would show if he had been bitten.

"I'm all right. I'm all right. Sunny! It didn't bite me." His voice overrode hers, and he hauled her to her feet, shaking her a little to get her attention. "Look at me!" The force of his tone snagged her gaze with his and he said more quietly, "I'm okay."

"Are you sure?" She couldn't seem to stop touching him, patting his chest, stroking his face, though logically she knew there was no way the snake could have bitten him up there. Neither could she stop trembling. "I hate snakes," she said in a shaking voice. "They terrify me. I saw it—it was right under your feet. You almost *stepped* on it."

"Shh," he murmured, pulling her against him and rocking her slowly back and forth. "It's all right. Nothing happened."

She clutched his shirt and buried her head against his chest. His smell, already so familiar and now with the faint odor of grease added, was comforting. His heartbeat was steady, as if he hadn't almost been snakebitten. *He* was steady, rock solid, his body supporting hers.

"Oh my God," she whispered. "That was awful." She raised her head and stared at him, an appalled expression on her face. "Yuk! I *touched* it!" She snatched her hand away from him and held it at arm's length. "Let me go, I have to wash my hand. Now!"

He released her, and she bolted up the slope to the tent, where the towelettes were. Grabbing one, she scrubbed furiously at her palm and fingers.

Chance was laughing softly as he came up behind her.

"What's the matter? Snakes don't have cooties. Besides, yesterday you said you weren't afraid of them."

"I lied. And I don't care what they have, I don't want one anywhere near me." Satisfied that no snake germs lingered on her hand, she blew out a long, calming breath.

"Instead of swooping down like a hawk," he said mildly, "why didn't you just yell out a warning?"

She gave him a blank look. "I couldn't." Yelling had never entered her mind. She had been taught her entire life not to yell in moments of tension or danger, because to do so would give away her position. Normal people could scream and yell, but she had never been allowed to be normal.

He put one finger under her chin, lifting her face to the sun. He studied her for a long moment, something dark moving in his eyes; then he tugged her to him and bent his head.

His mouth was fierce and hungry, his tongue probing. She sank weakly against him, clinging to his shoulders and kissing him in return just as fiercely, with just as much hunger. More. She felt as if she had always hungered, and never been fed. She drank life itself from his mouth, and sought more.

His hands were all over her, on her breasts, her bottom, lifting her into the hard bulge of his loins. The knowledge that he wanted her filled her with a deep need to know more, to feel everything she had always denied herself. She didn't know if she could have brought herself to pull away, but he was the one who broke the kiss, lifting his head and standing there with his eyes closed and a grim expression on his face.

"Chance?" she asked hesitantly.

He growled a lurid word under his breath. Then he

opened his eyes and glared down at her. "I can't believe
I'm stopping this a second time," he said with a raw,
furious frustration. "Just for the record, I'm *not* that noble. Damn it all to hell and back—" He broke off,
breathing hard. "It isn't a clogged fuel line. It must be
the pump. We have other things we need to do. We can't
afford to waste any daylight."

Margreta. Sunny bit her lip to hold back a moan of
dismay. She stared up at him, the knowledge of the danger of their situation lying like a stark shadow between
them.

She wasn't licked yet. She had four days. "Can we
walk out?"

"In the desert? In August?" He looked up at the rim
of the canyon. "Assuming we can even get out of here,
we'd have to walk at night and try to find shelter during
the day. By afternoon, the temperature will be over a
hundred."

The temperature was probably already well into the
seventies, she thought; she was dying of heat inside her
heavy sweater, or maybe that was just frustrated lust,
since she hadn't noticed how hot it was until now. She
peeled off the sweater and dropped it on top of her bag.
"What do we need to do?"

His eyes gleamed golden with admiration, and he
squeezed her waist. "I'll reconnoiter. We can't get out
on this end of the canyon, but maybe there's a way farther down."

"What do you want me to do?"

"Look for sticks, leaves, anything that will burn.
Gather as much as you can in a pile."

He set off in the direction she had gone earlier, and
she went in the opposite direction. The scrub brush grew
heavier at that end of the canyon, and she would find

more wood there. She didn't like to think about how limited the supply would be, or that they might be here for a long, long time. If they couldn't get out of the canyon, they would eventually use up their meager resources and die.

He hated lying to her. Chance's expression was grim as he stalked along the canyon floor. He had lied to terrorists, hoodlums and heads of state alike without a twinge of conscience, but it was getting harder and harder to lie to Sunny. He fiercely protected a hard core of honesty deep inside, the part of him that he shared only with his family, but Sunny was getting to him. She wasn't what he had expected. More and more he was beginning to suspect she wasn't working with her father. She was too...*gallant* was the word that sprang to mind. Terrorists weren't gallant. In his opinion, they were either mad or amoral. Sunny was neither.

He was more shaken by the episode with the snake than he had let her realize. Not by the snake itself—he had on boots, and since he hadn't heard rattles he suspected the snake hadn't been poisonous—but by her reaction. He would never forget the way she had looked, rushing in like an avenging angel, her face paper-white and utterly focused. By her own admission she was terrified of snakes, yet she hadn't hesitated. What kind of courage had it taken for her to pick up the snake with her bare hand?

Then there was the way she had patted him, looking for a bite. Except with certain people, or during sex, he had to struggle to tolerate being touched. He had learned how to accept affection in his family, because Mom and Maris would *not* leave him alone. He unabashedly loved playing with all his nephews—and niece—but his family had been the only exception. Until now. Until Sunny. He not only hadn't minded, he had, for a moment, allowed himself the pure luxury of enjoying the feel of her hands on his legs, his chest. And that didn't even begin to compare to how much he had enjoyed sleeping with her, feeling those sweet curves all along his side. His hand clenched as he remembered the feel of her breast in his palm, the wonderful resilience that was both soft and firm. He ached to feel her bare skin, to taste her. He wanted to strip her naked and pull her beneath him for a long hard ride, and he wanted to do it in broad daylight so he could watch her brilliant eyes glaze with pleasure.

If she wasn't who she was he would take her to the south of France, maybe, or a Caribbean island, any place where they could lie naked on the beach and make love in the sunshine, or in a shaded room with fingers of sunlight slipping through closed blinds. Instead, he had to keep lying to her, because whether or not she was working with her father didn't change the fact that she was the key to locating him.

He couldn't change the plan now. He couldn't suddenly "repair" the plane. He thanked God she didn't know anything about planes, because otherwise she would never have fallen for the fuel pump excuse; a Skylane had a backup fuel pump, for just such an emergency. No, he had to play out the game as he had planned it, because the goal was too damned important to abandon, and he couldn't take the risk that she was involved up to her pretty ears, after all.

He and Zane had walked a fine line in planning this out. The situation had to be survivable but grim, so nothing would arouse her suspicion. There was food to be had, but not easily. There was water, but not a lot. He hadn't brought any provisions that might make her wonder why he had them, meaning he had limited himself to the blanket, the water and the pistol, plus the expected items in the plane, such as flares. Hell, she was a lot more prepared than he was, and that made him wary. She wasn't exactly forthcoming about her reason for toting a damn tent around, either. The lady had secrets of her own.

He reached the far end of the canyon and checked to make certain nothing had changed since he and Zane had been here. No unexpected landslide had caved in a wall, allowing a way out. The thin trickle of water still ran down the rock. He saw rabbit tracks, birds, things they could eat. Shooting them would be the easy way, though; he would have to build some traps, to save his ammunition for emergencies.

Everything was just as he had left it. The plan was working. The physical attraction between them was strong; she wouldn't resist him much longer, maybe not at all. She certainly hadn't done anything to call a halt earlier. And after he was her lover—well, women were easily beguiled by sexual pleasure, the bonds of the flesh. He knew the power of sex, knew how to use it to make her trust him. He wished he could trust *her*—this would be a lot easier if he could—but he knew too much about the human soul's capability of evil, and that a pretty face didn't necessarily mean a pretty person was behind it.

When he judged enough time had passed for him to completely reconnoiter the canyon, he walked back. She was still gathering sticks, he saw, going back and forth between the bushes and the growing pile next to the tent. She looked up when he got closer, hope blazing in her expression.

He shook his head. "It's a box canyon. There's no way out," he said flatly. "The good news is, there's water at the far end."

She swallowed. Her eyes were huge with distress, almost eclipsing her face. "We can't climb out, either?"

"It's sheer rock." He put his hands on his hips, looking around. "We need to move closer to the water, for convenience. There's an overhang that will give us shade from the sun, and the ground underneath is sandier, so it'll be more comfortable."

Or as comfortable as they could get, sleeping in that small tent.

Wordlessly she nodded and began folding the tent. She did it briskly, without wasted movement, but he saw she was fighting for control. He stroked her upper arm, feeling her smooth, pliant skin, warm and slightly moist from her exertion. "We'll be okay," he reassured her. "We just have to hold out until someone sees our smoke and comes to investigate."

"We're in the middle of nowhere," she said shakily. "You said so yourself. And I only have four days until—"

"Until what?" he asked, when she stopped.

"Nothing. It doesn't matter." She stared blindly at the sky, at the clear blue expanse that was turning whiter as the hot sun climbed upward.

Four days until what? he wondered. What was going to happen? Was she supposed to do something? Was a terrorist attack planned? Would it go forward without her?

The dogleg of the canyon was about half a mile long, and the angle gave it more shade than where they had landed. They worked steadily, moving their camp, with

Chance hauling the heaviest stuff. Sunny tried to keep her mind blank, to not think about Margreta, to focus totally on the task at hand.

It was noon, the white sun directly overhead. The heat was searing, the shade beneath the overhang so welcome she sighed with relief when they gained its shelter. The overhang was larger than she had expected, about twelve feet wide and deep enough, maybe eight feet, that the sunshine would never penetrate its depths. The rock sloped to a height of about four feet at the back, but the opening was high enough that Chance could stand up without bumping his head.

"I'll wait until it's cooler to get the rest," he said. "I don't know about you, but I'm starving. Let's have half of one of your nutrition bars now, and I'll try to get a rabbit for dinner."

She rallied enough to give him a look of mock dismay. "You'd eat Peter Cottontail?"

"I'd eat the Easter Bunny right now, if I could catch him."

He was trying to make her laugh. She appreciated his effort, but she couldn't quite shake off the depression that had seized her when her last hope of getting out of here quickly had evaporated.

She had lost her appetite, but she dug out one of the nutrition bars and halved it, though she hid the fact that Chance's "half" was bigger than hers. He was bigger; he needed more. They ate their spartan little meal standing up, staring out at the bleached tones of the canyon. "Drink all the water you want," he urged. "The heat dehydrates you even in the shade."

Obediently she drank a bottle of water; she needed it to get the nutrition bar down. Each bite felt as if it was getting bigger and bigger in her mouth, making it difficult to swallow. She resorted to taking only nibbles, and got it down that way.

After they ate, Chance made a small circle of rocks, piled in some sticks and leaves, both fresh and dead, and built a fire. Soon a thin column of smoke was floating out of the canyon. It took him no more than five minutes to accomplish, but when he came back under the overhang his shirt was damp with sweat.

She handed him a bottle of water, and he drank deeply, at the same time reaching out a strong arm and hooking it around her waist. He drew her close and pressed a light kiss to her forehead, nothing more, just held her comfortingly. She put her arms around him and clung, desperately needing his strength right now. She hadn't had anyone to lean on in a long time; she had always had to be the strong one. She had tried so hard to stay on top of things, to plan for every conceivable glitch, but she hadn't thought to plan for this, and now she had no idea what to do.

"I have to think of something," she said aloud.

"Shh. All we have to do is stay alive. That's the most important thing."

He was right, of course. She couldn't do anything about Margreta now. This damn canyon had saved their lives yesterday, but it had become a prison from which she couldn't escape. She had to play the hand with the cards that had been dealt to her and not let depression sap her strength. She had to hope Margreta wouldn't do anything foolish, just go to ground somewhere. How she would ever find her again she didn't know, but she could deal with that if she just knew her sister was alive and safe somewhere.

"Do you have family who will worry?" he asked.

God, that went to the bone! She shook her head. She

had family, but Margreta wouldn't worry; she would simply assume the worst.

"What about you?" she asked, realizing she had fallen halfway in love with the man and didn't know a thing about him.

He shook his head. "C'mon, let's sit down." With nothing to use for a seat, they simply sat on the ground. "I'll take two of the seats out of the plane this afternoon, so we'll be more comfortable," he said. "In answer to your question, no, I don't have anyone. My folks are dead, and I don't have any brothers or sisters. There's an uncle somewhere, on my dad's side, and my mom had some cousins, but we never kept in touch."

"That's sad. Family should stay together." *If they could,* she added silently. "Where did you grow up?"

"All over. Dad wasn't exactly known for his ability to keep a job. What about your folks?"

She was silent for a moment, then sighed. "I was adopted. They were good people. I still miss them." She drew a design in the dirt with her finger. "When we didn't show up in Seattle last night, would someone have notified the FAA?"

"They're probably already searching. The problem is, first they'll search the area I should have been over when I filed my flight plan."

"We were off course?" she asked faintly. It just kept getting worse and worse.

"We went off course looking for a place to land. But if anyone is searching this area, eventually he'll see our smoke. We just have to keep the fire going during the day."

"How long will they look? Before they call off the search?"

He was silent, his golden eyes narrowed as he

searched the sky. "They'll look as long as they think we might be alive."

"But if they think we've crashed—"

"Eventually they'll stop looking," he said softly. "It might be a week, a little longer, but they'll stop."

"So if no one finds us within, say, ten days—" She couldn't go on.

"We don't give up. There's always the possibility a private plane will fly over."

He didn't say that the possibility was slight, but he didn't have to. She had seen for herself the kind of terrain they'd flown over, and she knew how narrow and easily missed this canyon was.

She drew up her knees and wrapped her arms around her legs, staring wistfully at the languid curls of gray smoke. "I used to wish I could go someplace where no one could find me. I didn't realize there wouldn't be room service."

He chuckled as he leaned back on one elbow and stretched out his long legs. "Nothing gets you down for long, does it?"

"I try not to let it. Our situation isn't great, but we're alive. We have food, water and shelter. Things could be worse."

"We also have entertainment. I have a deck of cards in the plane. We can play poker."

"Do you cheat?"

"Don't need to," he drawled.

"Well, I do, so I'm giving you fair warning."

"Warning taken. You know what happens to cheaters, don't you?"

"They win?"

"Not if they get caught."

"If they're any good, they don't get caught."

He twirled a finger in her hair and lightly tugged. "Yeah, but if they get caught they're in big trouble. You can take that as my warning."

"I'll be careful," she promised. A yawn took her by surprise. "How can I be sleepy? I got plenty of sleep last night."

"It's the heat. Why don't you take a nap? I'll watch the fire."

"Why aren't you sleepy?"

He shrugged. "I'm used to it."

She really was sleepy, and there was nothing else to do. She didn't feel like setting up the tent, so she dragged her bag into position behind her and leaned back on it. Silently Chance tossed her sweater into her lap. Following his example, she rolled up the sweater and stuffed it under her head. She dozed within minutes. It wasn't a restful sleep, being one of those light naps in which she was aware of the heat, of Chance moving around, of her worry about Margreta. Her muscles felt heavy and limp, though, and completely waking up was just too much trouble.

The problem with afternoon naps was that one woke feeling both groggy and grungy. Her clothes were sticking to her, which wasn't surprising considering the heat. When she finally yawned and sat up, she saw that the sun was beginning to take on a red glow as it sank, and though the temperature was still high, the heat had lost its searing edge.

Chance was sitting cross-legged, his long, tanned fingers deftly weaving sticks and string into a cage. There was something about the way he looked there in the shadow of the overhang, his attention totally focused on the trap he was building while the light reflected off the sand outside danced along his high cheekbones, that made recognition click in her brain. "You're part Native American, aren't you?"

"American Indian," he corrected absently. "Everyone born here is a native American, or so Dad always told me." He looked up and gave her a quick grin. "Of course, 'Indian' isn't very accurate, either. Most labels aren't. But, yeah, I'm a mixed breed."

"And ex-military." She didn't know why she said that. Maybe it was his deftness in building the trap. She wasn't foolish enough to attribute that to any so-called Native American skills, not in this day and age, but there was something in the way he worked that bespoke survival training.

He gave her a surprised glance. "How did you know?"

She shook her head. "Just a guess. The way you handled the pistol, as if you were very comfortable with it. What you're doing now. And you used the word 'reconnoiter.'"

"A lot of people are familiar with weapons, especially outdoorsmen, who would also know how to build traps."

"Done in by your vocabulary," she said, and smirked. "You said 'weapons' instead of just 'guns,' the way most people—even outdoorsmen—would have."

Again she was rewarded with that flashing grin. "Okay, so I've spent some time in a uniform."

"What branch?"

"Army. Rangers."

Well, that certainly explained the survival skills. She didn't know a lot about the Rangers, or any military group, but she did know they were an elite corps.

He set the finished trap aside and began work on another one. Sunny watched him for a moment, feeling useless. She would be more hindrance than help in building traps. She sighed as she brushed the dirt from her skirt. Darn, stranded only one day and here she was, smack in the middle of the old sexual stereotypes.

She surrendered with good grace. "Is there enough water for me to wash out our clothes? I've lived in these for two days, and that's long enough."

"There's enough water, just nothing to collect it in." He unfolded his legs and stood with easy grace. "I'll show you."

He led the way out of the overhang. She clambered over rocks in his wake, feeling the heat burn through the sides of her shoes and trying not to touch the rocks with her hands. When they reached more shade, the relief was almost tangible.

"Here." He indicated a thin trickle of water running down the face of the wall. The bushes were heavier here, because of the water, and the temperature felt a good twenty degrees cooler. Part of it was illusion, because of the contrast, but the extra greenery did have a cooling effect.

Sunny sighed as she looked at the trickle. Filling their water bottles would be a snap. Washing off would be easy. But washing clothes—well, that was a different proposition. There wasn't a pool in which she could soak them, not even a puddle. The water was soaked immediately into the dry, thirsty earth. The ground was damp, but not saturated.

The only thing she could do was fill a water bottle over and over, and rinse the dust out. "This will take forever," she groused.

An irritating masculine smirk was on his face as he peeled his T-shirt off over his head and handed it to her. "We aren't exactly pressed for time, are we?"

She almost thrust the shirt back at him and demanded he put it on, but not because of his comment. She wasn't a silly prude, she had seen naked chests more times than she could count, but she had never before seen *his* naked chest. He was smoothly, powerfully muscled, with pectorals that looked like flesh-covered steel and a hard, six-pack abdomen. A light patch of black hair stretched from one small brown nipple to the other. She wanted to touch him. Her hand actually ached for the feel of his skin, and she clenched her fingers hard on his shirt.

The smirk faded, his eyes darkening. He touched her face, curving his fingers under her chin and lifting it. His expression was hard with pure male desire. "You know what's going to happen between us, don't you?" His voice was low and rough.

"Yes." She could barely manage a whisper. Her throat had tightened, her body responding to his touch, his intent.

"Do you want it?"

So much she ached with it, she thought. She looked up into those golden-brown eyes and trembled from the enormity of the step she was taking.

"Yes," she said.

Chapter 7

She had lived her entire life without ever having lived at all, Sunny thought as she mechanically rinsed out his clothes and draped them over the hot rocks to dry. She and Chance might never get out of this canyon alive, and even if they did, it could take a long time. Weeks, perhaps months, or longer. Whatever Margreta did, she would long since have done it, and there wasn't a damn thing Sunny could do about the situation. For the first time in her life, she had to think only about herself and what *she* wanted. That was simple; what she wanted was Chance.

She had to face facts. She was good at it; she had been doing it her entire life. The fact that had been glaring her in the face was that they could very well die here in this little canyon. If they didn't survive, she didn't want to die still clinging to the reasons for not getting involved that, while good and valid in civilization, didn't mean spit here. She already *was* involved with him, in a battle for their very lives. She certainly didn't want to die without having known what it was like to be loved by him, to feel him inside her and hold him close, and to tell him that she loved him. She had a whole world of love dammed up inside her, drying up because she hadn't had anyone to whom she could give it, but now she had this opportunity, and she wasn't going to waste it.

A psych analyst would say this was just propinquity: the "any port in a storm" type of attraction, or the Adam and Eve syndrome. That might be part of it, for him. If she had to guess, Sunny would say that Chance was used to having sex whenever he wanted it. He had that look about him, a bone-deep sexual confidence that would draw women like flies. She was currently the only fly available.

But it wasn't just that. He had been attracted to her before, just as she had been to him. If they had made it to Seattle without trouble, she would have been strong enough to refuse his invitation and walk away from him. She would never have allowed herself to get to know him. Maybe they had met only twenty-four hours before, but those hours had been more intense than anything else she had ever known. She imagined it was as if they had gone into battle together; the danger they had faced, and were still facing, had forged a bond between them like soldiers in a war. She had learned things about him that it would have taken her weeks to learn in a normal situation, weeks that she would never have given herself.

Of all the things she had learned about him in those twenty-four hours, there wasn't one she didn't like. He was a man willing to step forward and take a risk, get involved, otherwise he wouldn't have stopped the cretin in the airport. He was calm in a crisis, self-sufficient and capable, and he was more considerate of her than anyone else she had ever known. On top of all that, he was so sexy he made her mouth water.

Most men, after hearing something like what she had told him, would have immediately gone for the sex. Chance hadn't. Instead, he had kissed her very sweetly and said, "I'll get the rest of the things from the plane, so I can change clothes and give you my dirty ones to wash."

"Gee, thanks," she had managed to say.

He had winked at her. "Any time."

He was a man who could put off his personal pleasure in order to take care of business. So here she was, scrubbing his underwear. Not the most romantic thing in the world to be doing, yet it was an intimate chore that strengthened the link forming between them. He was working to feed her; she was working to keep their clothes clean.

So far, Chance was everything that was steadfast and reliable. So why did she keep sensing that edge of danger in him? Was it something his army training had given him that was just *there* no matter what he was doing? She had never met anyone else who had been a ranger, so she had no means of comparison. She was just glad of that training, if it helped keep them alive.

After his clothes were as clean as she could get them, she hesitated barely a second before stripping out of her own, down to her skin. She couldn't tolerate her grimy clothes another minute. The hot desert air washed over her bare skin, a warm, fresh caress on the backs of her knees, the small of her back, that made her nipples pinch into erect little nubs. She had never before been outside in the nude, and she felt positively decadent.

What if Chance saw her? If he was overcome with

lust by the sight of her naked body, nothing would happen that hadn't been going to happen, anyway. Not that it was likely he would be overcome, she thought wryly, smiling to herself, her curves were a long way from voluptuous. Still, if a man was faced with a naked, available woman—it could happen.

She poured a bottle of water over herself, then scooped up a handful of sand and began scrubbing. Rinsing off the sand was a matter of refilling the bottle several times. When she was finished she felt considerably refreshed and her skin was baby smooth. Maybe the skin-care industry should stop grinding up shells and rock for body scrubs, she thought, and just go for the sand.

Naked and wet, she could feel a slight breeze stirring the hot air, cooling her until she was actually comfortable. She didn't have a towel, so she let herself dry naturally while she washed her own clothes, then quickly dressed in the beige jeans and green T-shirt that she always carried. They were earth colors, colors that blended in well with vegetation and would make her more difficult to see if she had to disappear into the countryside. She would have opted for actual camouflage-patterned clothing, if that wouldn't have made her more noticeable in public. Her bra was wet from its scrubbing, so she hadn't put it back on, and the soft cotton of the T-shirt clung to her breasts, clearly revealing their shape and their soft jiggle when she walked, and the small peaks of her nipples. She wondered if Chance would notice.

"Hey," he said from behind her, his voice low and soft.

Startled, she whirled to face him. It was as if she had conjured him from her thoughts. He stood motionless about ten yards away, his eyes narrowed, his expression focused. His whiskey-coloured gaze went straight to her breasts. Oh, he noticed all right.

Her nipples got even harder, as if he had touched them.

She swallowed, trying to control a ridiculous twinge of her nerves. After all, he had already touched her breasts, and she had given him permission to do more. ''How long have you been there?''

''A while.'' His eyelids were heavy, his voice a little rough. ''I kept waiting for you to turn around, but you never did. I enjoyed the view, anyway.''

Her breath hitched. ''Thank you.''

''You have the sweetest little ass I've ever seen.''

Liquid heat moved through her. ''You sweet talker, you,'' she said, not even half kidding. ''When do I get a peep show?''

''Any time, honey.'' His tone was dark with sensual promise. ''Any time.'' Then he smiled ruefully. ''Any time except now. We need to move these clothes so I can set the trap up here. Since this is where the water is, this is where the game will come. I'll set the traps now and try to catch something for supper, then wash up after I clean whatever we catch—if we catch anything at all.''

He wasn't exactly swept away with lust, but there was that reassuring steadfastness again, the ability to keep his priorities straight. In this situation, she didn't want Gonad the Barbarian; she wanted a man on whom she could depend to do the smart thing.

He began gathering the wet clothes off the rocks, and Sunny moved to help him. ''Let me guess,'' she said. ''The clothes still smell like humans.''

''There's that, plus they're something different. Wild

animals are skittish whenever something new invades their territory.''

As they walked back to the overhang she asked, ''How long does it normally take to catch something in a trap?''

He shrugged. ''There's no 'normal' to it. I've caught game before within ten minutes of putting out the trap. Sometimes it takes days.''

She wasn't exactly looking forward to eating Peter Cottontail, but neither did she want another nutrition bar. It would be nice if some big fat chicken had gotten lost in the desert and just happened to wander into their trap. She wouldn't mind eating a chicken. After a moment of wishful thinking she resigned herself to rabbit—if they were lucky, that is. They would have to eat whatever Chance could catch.

When they reached ''home,'' which the overhang had become, they spread their clothes out on another assortment of hot rocks. The first items she had washed were already almost dry; the dry heat of the desert was almost as efficient as an electric clothes dryer.

When they had finished, Chance collected his two handmade traps and examined them one last time. Sunny watched him, seeing the same intensity in his eyes and body that she had noticed before. ''You're enjoying this, aren't you?'' she asked, only mildly surprised. This was, after all, the ultimate in primitive guy stuff.

He didn't look at her, but a tiny smile twitched the corners of his mouth. ''I guess I'm not all that upset. We're alive. We have food, water and shelter. I'm alone with a woman I've wanted from the first minute I saw her.'' He produced a badly crushed Baby Ruth candy bar from his hip pocket and opened the wrapper, then pinched off small pieces of it and put them in the traps.

Sunny was instantly diverted. "You're using a candy bar as bait?" she demanded in outraged tones. "Give me that! You can use my nutrition bar in the traps."

He grinned and evaded her as she tried to swipe the remainder of the candy bar. "The nutrition bar wouldn't be a good bait. No self-respecting rabbit would touch it."

"How long have you been hiding that Baby Ruth?"

"I haven't been hiding it. I found it in the plane when I got the rest of the stuff. Besides, it's melted from being in the plane all day."

"Melted, schmelted," she scoffed. "That doesn't affect chocolate."

"Ah." He nodded, still grinning. "You're one of those."

"One of those *what?*"

"Chocoholics."

"I am not," she protested, lifting her chin at him. "I'm a sweetaholic."

"Then why didn't you pack something sweet in that damn survival bag of yours, instead of something that tastes like dried grass?"

She scowled at him. "Because the idea is to stay alive. If I had a stash of candy, I'd eat it all the first day, then I'd be in trouble."

The golden-brown gaze flicked at her, lashing like the tip of a whip. "When are you going to tell me why you packed survival gear for an overnight plane trip to Seattle?" He kept his tone light, but she felt the change of mood. He was dead serious about this, and she wondered why. What did it matter to him why she lugged that stuff everywhere she went? She could understand why he would be curious, but not insistent.

"I'm paranoid," she said, matching his tone in lightness. "I'm always certain there will be some sort of emergency, and I'm terrified of being unprepared."

His eyes went dark and flat. "Bull. Don't try to blow me off with lies."

Sunny might be good-natured almost to a fault, but she didn't back down. "I was actually trying to be polite and avoid telling you it's none of your business."

To her surprise, he relaxed. "That's more like it."

"What? Being rude?"

"Honest," he corrected. "If there are things you don't want to tell me, fine. I don't like it, but at least it was the truth. Considering our situation, we need to be able to totally rely on each other, and that demands trust. We have to be up front with each other, even when the truth isn't all sweetness and light."

She crossed her arms and narrowed her eyes, giving him an "I'm not buying this" look. "Even when you're just being nosy? I don't think so." She sniffed. "You're trying to psych me into spilling my guts."

"Is it working?"

"I felt a momentary twinge of guilt, but then logic kicked in."

She sensed he tried to fight it, but a smile crinkled his eyes, then moved down to curl the corners of that beautifully cut mouth. He shook his head. "You're going to cause me a lot of trouble," he said companionably as he picked up the traps and started back to their little water hole, if a trickle could be called a hole.

"Why's that?" she called to his back.

"Because I'm afraid I'm going to fall in love with you," he said over his shoulder as he walked around a jutting curve of the canyon wall and disappeared from sight.

Sunny's legs felt suddenly weak; her knees actually

wobbled, and she reached out to brace her hand on the wall. Had he really said that? Did he mean it? Would a man admit to something like that if he wasn't already emotionally involved?

Her heart was pounding as if she had been running. She could handle a lot of things most people never even thought of having to do, such as running for her life, but when it came to a romantic relationship she was a babe in the woods—or in the desert, to be accurate. She had never let a man get close enough to her to matter, because she had to be free to disappear without a moment's notice or regret. But this time she couldn't disappear; she couldn't go anywhere. This time she was in a lot more trouble than Chance was, because she was already in love—fully, falling-down-a-mine-shaft, terrifyingly in love.

The feeling was a stomach-tightening mixture of ecstasy and horror. The last thing she wanted to do was love him, but it was way too late to worry about that now. What had already begun had blossomed into full flower when he *didn't* make love to her after she had said he could. Something very basic and primal had recognized him then as her mate. He was everything she had ever wanted in a man, everything she had ever dreamed about in those half-formed thoughts she had never let fully surface into her consciousness, because she had always known that life wasn't for her.

But those circumstances held sway up in the world, not down here in this sunlit hole where they were the only two people alive. She felt raw inside, as if all her nerve endings and emotions had been stripped of their protective coverings, leaving her vulnerable to feelings she had always before been able to keep at bay. Those emotions kept sweeping over her in exhilarating waves, washing her into unknown territory. She wanted very much to protect herself, yet all the shields she had used over the years were suddenly useless.

Tonight they would become lovers, and one last protective wall would be irrevocably breached. Sex wasn't just sex to her; it was a commitment, a dedication of self, that would be part of her for the rest of her life.

She wasn't naive about what else making love with him could mean. She wasn't on any form of birth control, and while he might have a few condoms with him, they would quickly be used. The bell couldn't be unrung, and once they had made love they couldn't go back to a chaste relationship. What would she do if she got pregnant and they weren't rescued? She had to hold out hope that they wouldn't be down here forever, yet a small kernel of logic told her that it was possible they wouldn't be found. What would she do if she got pregnant even if they *were* rescued? A baby would be a major complication. How would she protect it? Somehow she couldn't see herself and Chance and a baby making a normal little all-American family; she would still be running, because that was the only way to be safe.

Keeping him at a distance, remaining platonic, was the only safe, sane thing to do. Unfortunately, she didn't seem to have a good grip on her sanity any longer. She felt as if those waves had carried her too far from shore for her to make it back now. For better or worse, all she could do was ride the current where it would take her.

Nevertheless, she tried. She tried to tell herself how stupidly irresponsible it was to risk getting pregnant under any circumstances, but particularly in *this* circumstance. Yes, women all over the world conceived and gave birth in primitive conditions, but for whatever reasons, cultural, economic or lack of brain power, they didn't have a choice. She did. All she had to do was say "no" and ignore all her feminine instincts shrieking "yes, yes."

When Chance returned she was still standing in the same spot she had been when he left, her expression stricken. He was instantly alert, reaching for the pistol tucked into his waistband at the small of his back. "What's wrong?"

"What if I get pregnant?" she asked baldly, indicating their surroundings with a sweep of her hand. "That would be stupid."

He looked surprised. "Aren't you on birth control?"

"No, and even if I was, I wouldn't have an unlimited supply of pills."

Chance rubbed his jaw, trying to think of a way around this one without tipping his hand. He knew they wouldn't be here for long, only until she gave him the information he needed on her father, but he couldn't tell her that. And why in the hell wasn't she on some form of birth control? All of the female agents he knew were on long-term birth control, and Sunny's circumstances weren't that different. "I have some condoms," he finally said.

She gave him a wry smile. "How many? And what will we do when they're gone?"

The last thing he wanted to do now was make her hostile. Deciding to gamble a little, to risk not being able to make love to her in exchange for keeping her trust, he put his arms around her and cradled her against his chest. She felt good in his arms, he thought, firm with muscle and yet soft in all the right places. He hadn't been able to stop thinking about the way she looked naked: her slender, graceful back and small waist, and the tight, heart-shaped—and heart-stopping—curve of her butt. Her legs were as slim and sleekly muscled as he had expected, and the thought of them wrapping around his waist brought him to full, instant arousal. He held her so close there was no way she could miss his condition, but he didn't thrust himself at her; let her think he was a gentleman. *He* knew better, but it was essential she didn't.

He kissed the top of her head and took that gamble. "We'll do whatever you want," he said gently. "I want you—you know that. I have about three dozen condoms—"

She jerked back, glaring at him. *"Three dozen?"* she asked, horrified. "You carry around three dozen condoms?"

There it was again, that urge to laugh. She could get to him faster than any other woman he knew. "I had just stocked up," he explained, keeping his tone mild.

"They have an expiration date, you know!"

He bit the inside of his jaw—hard. "Yeah, but they don't go bad as fast as milk. They're good for a couple of years."

She gave him a suspicious look. "How long will thirty-six condoms keep you supplied?"

He sighed. "Longer than you evidently think."

"Six months?"

He did some quick math. Six months, thirty-six condoms…he would have to have sex more than once a week. If he were in a monogamous relationship, that would be nothing, but for an unattached bachelor…

"Look," he said, letting frustration creep into both his voice and his expression, "with you, three dozen might last a week."

She looked startled, and he could see her doing some

quick math now. As she arrived at the answer and her eyes widened, he thrust his hand into her hair, cupping the back of her head and holding her still while he kissed her, ruthlessly using all his skill to arouse her. Her hands fluttered against his chest as if she wanted to push him away, but her hands wouldn't obey. He stroked his tongue into her mouth, slow and deep, feeling the answering touch of her tongue and the pressure of her lips. She tasted sweet, and the fresh smell of her was pure woman. He felt her nipples peak under the thin fabric of her T-shirt, and abruptly he had to touch them, feel them stabbing into his palm. He had his hand under her shirt almost before the thought formed. Her breasts were firm and round, her skin cool silk that warmed under his touch. Her nipples were hard little nubs that puckered even tighter when he touched them. She arched in his arms, her eyes closed, a low moan humming in her throat.

He had intended only to kiss her out of her sudden attack of responsibility. Instead, the pleasure of touching her went to his head like old whiskey, and suddenly he had to see her, taste her. With one swift motion he pulled her shirt up, baring her breasts, and tilted her back over his arm so the firm mounds were offered up to him in a sensual feast. He bent his dark head and closed his mouth over one tight, reddening nipple, rasping his tongue over it before pressing it against the roof of his mouth and sucking. He heard the sound she made this time, the cry of a sharply aroused woman, a wild, keening sound that went straight to his loins. He was dimly aware of her nails biting into his shoulders, but the pain was small, and nothing in comparison with the urgency that had seized him. Blood thundered in his ears, roared through his veins. He wanted her with a savage intensity that rode him with sharp spurs, urging him to take instead of seduce.

Grimly he reached for his strangely elusive self-control. Only the experience and training of his entire adulthood, spent in the trenches of a dirty, covert, ongoing war, gave him the strength to rein himself in. Reluctantly he eased his clamp on her nipple, giving the turgid little bud an apologetic lick. She quivered in his arms, whimpering, her golden hair spilling back as she hung helplessly in his grasp, and he almost lost it again.

Damn it all, he couldn't wait.

Swiftly he dipped down and snagged the blanket from the ground, then hooked his right arm under her knees and lifted her off her feet, carrying her out into the sunlight. The golden glow of the lowering sun kissed her skin with a subtle sheen, deepened the glitter of her hair. Her breasts were creamy, with the delicate blue tracery of her veins showing through the pale skin, and her small nipples were a sweet rosy color, shining wetly, standing out in hard peaks. "God, you're beautiful," he said in a low, rough voice.

He set her on her feet; she swayed, her lovely eyes dazed with need. He spread out the blanket and reached for her before that need began to cool. He wanted her scorching hot, so ready for him that she would fight him for completion.

He stripped the T-shirt off over her head, dropped it on the blanket, and hooked his fingers in the waistband of her jeans. A quick pop of the snap, a jerk on the tab of the zipper, and the jeans slid down her thighs.

Her hands gripped his forearms. "Chance?" She sounded strangely uncertain, a little hesitant. If she changed her mind now—

He kissed her, slow and deep, and thumbed her nipples. She made that little humming sound again, rising on her toes to press against him. He pushed her jeans down to her ankles, wrapped both arms around her and carried her down to the blanket.

She gasped, her head arching back. "Here? Now?"

"I can't wait." That was nothing more than the hard truth. He couldn't wait until dark, until they had politely crawled into the tent together as if they were following some script. He wanted her now, in the sunlight, naked and warm and totally spontaneous. He stripped her panties down and freed her ankles from the tangle of jeans and underwear.

It seemed she didn't want to wait, either. She tugged at his shirt, pushing it up. Impatiently he gripped the hem and wrenched the garment off over his head, then spread her legs and eased his weight down on her, settling into the notch of her open thighs.

She went very still, her eyes widening as she stared up at him. He fished in his pocket for the condom he'd put there earlier, then lifted himself enough to unfasten his jeans and shove them down. He donned the condom with an abrupt, practiced motion. When he came back down to her, she braced her hands against his shoulders as if she wanted to preserve some small distance between them. But any distance was too much; he grasped her hands in one of his and pulled them over her head, pinning them to the blanket and arching her breasts against him. With his free hand he reached between them and guided his hard length to the soft, wet entrance of her body.

Sunny quivered, helpless in his grasp. She had never before felt so vulnerable, or so alive. His passion wasn't controlled and gentle, the way she had expected; it was fierce and tumultuous, buffeting her with its force. He held her down, dwarfed her with his big muscular body, and she trembled as she waited for the hard thrust of penetration. She was ready for him, oh, so ready. She ached with need; she burned with it. She wanted to beg him to hurry, but she couldn't make her lungs work. He reached down, and she felt the brush of his knuckles between her legs, then the stiff, hot length of him pushing against her opening.

Everything in her seemed to tighten, coiling, focusing on that intimate intrusion. The soft flesh between her legs began to burn and sting as the blunt pressure stretched her. He pushed harder, and the pressure became pain. Wild frustration filled her. She wanted him *now,* inside her, easing the ache and tension, stroking her back into feverish pleasure.

He started to draw back, but she couldn't let him, couldn't bear losing what his touch had promised. She had denied herself so many things, but not this, not now. She locked her legs around his and lifted her hips, fiercely impaling herself, thrusting past the resistance of her body.

She couldn't hold back the thin cry that tore from her throat. Shock robbed her muscles of strength, and she went limp on the blanket.

Chance moved over her, his broad shoulders blotting out the sun. He was a dark, massive silhouette, his shape blurred by her tears. He murmured a soft reassurance even as he probed deeper, and deeper still, until his full length was inside her.

He released her hands to cradle her in both arms. Sunny clung to his shoulders, holding as tight as she could, because without his strength she thought she might fly apart. She hadn't realized this would hurt so much, that he would feel so thick and hot inside her, or go so deep. He was invading all of her, taking over her body and commanding its responses, even her breathing, her heartbeat, the flow of blood through her veins.

He moved gently at first, slowly, angling his body so he applied pressure where she needed it most. He did things to her with his hands, stroking her into a return of pleasure. He kissed her, leisurely exploring her with his tongue. He touched her nipples, sucked them, nibbled on the side of her neck. His tender attention gradually coaxed her into response, into an instinctive motion as her hips rose and fell in time with his thrusts. She still clung to his shoulders, but in need rather than desperation. An overwhelming heat swept over her, and she heard herself panting.

He pushed her legs farther apart and thrust deeper, harder, faster. Sensation exploded in her, abruptly convulsing her flesh. She writhed beneath him, unable to hold back the short, sharp cries that surged upward, past her constricted throat. The pounding rhythm wouldn't let the spasms abate; they kept shuddering through her until she was sobbing, fighting him, wanting release, wanting more, and finally—when his hard body stiffened and began shuddering—wanting nothing.

Chapter 8

A virgin. Sunny Miller had been a *virgin*. He tried to think, when he could think at all, what the possible ramifications were, but none of that seemed important right now. Of far more immediate urgency was how to comfort a woman whose first time had been on a blanket spread over the rough ground, in broad daylight, with a man who hadn't even taken off his boots.

He lay sprawled on his back beside her on the blanket. She had turned on her side away from him, curling in on herself while visible tremors shook her slender, naked body. Moving was an effort—*breathing* was an effort—as he pulled off the condom and tossed it away. He had climaxed so violently that he felt dazed. And if it affected him so strongly, with his experience, what was she thinking? Feeling? Had she anticipated the pain, or been shocked by it?

He knew she had climaxed. She had been as aroused as he; when he had started to pull back in stunned realization, she had hooked her legs around his and forced the entry herself. He had seen the shock in her eyes as he penetrated her, felt the reverberations in her flesh. And he had watched her face as he carefully aroused her, holding himself back with ruthless control until he felt the wild clenching of her loins. Then nothing had been able to hold him back, and he had exploded in his own gut-wrenching release.

For a woman of twenty-nine to remain a virgin, she had to have some strongly held reason for doing so. Sunny had willingly, but not lightly, surrendered her chastity to him. He felt humbled, and honored, and he was scared as hell. He hadn't been easy with her, either in the process or the culmination. At first glance the fact that she had climaxed might make everything all right with her, but he knew better. She didn't have the experience to handle the sensual violence her body and emotions had endured. She needed holding, and reassuring, until she stopped shaking and regained her equilibrium.

He put his hand on her arm and tugged her over onto her back. She didn't actively resist, but she was stiff, uncoordinated. She was pale, her eyes unusually brilliant, as if she fought tears. He cradled her head on his arm and leaned over her, giving her the attention and the contact he knew she needed. She glanced quickly up at him, then away, and a surge of color pinkened her cheeks.

He was charmed by the blush. Gently he smoothed his hand up her bare torso, stroking her belly, trailing his fingers over her breasts. The lower curves of her breasts bore the marks of his beard stubble. He soothed them with his tongue, taking care not to add more abrasions, and made a mental note to shave when he washed.

Something needed to be said, but he didn't know what. He had talked his way into strongholds, drug dens and government offices; he had an uncanny knack for making a lightning assessment of any given person and situation, and then saying exactly the right thing to get the reaction he wanted. But from the moment he had seen Sunny, lust had gotten in the way of his usual expertise. No amount of prep work could have prepared him for the impact of her sparkling eyes and bright smile, or told him he could be so disarmed by a sense of humor. "Sunny" was a very apt nickname for her.

Just now his sunshine was very quiet, almost stricken, as if she regretted their intimacy. And he couldn't bear it. He had lost count, over the years, of the women who had tried to cling to him after the sex act was finished and he slipped away, both physically and mentally, but he couldn't bear it that this one woman wasn't trying to hold him. For some reason, whether this was simply too much too soon or for some deeper reason, she was trying to hold her distance from him. She wasn't curling in his arms, sighing with repletion; she was retreating behind an invisible wall, the one that had been there from the beginning.

Everything in him rejected the idea. A primitive, possessive rage swept over him. She was his, and he would not let her go. His muscles tightened in a renewed surge of lust, and he mounted her, sliding into the tight, swollen clasp of her sheath. She inhaled sharply, the shock of his entry jarring her out of her malaise. She wedged her hands between them and sank her nails into his chest, but she didn't try to push him away. Her legs came up almost automatically, wrapping around his hips. He caught her thighs and adjusted them higher, around his waist. "Get used to it," he said, more harshly than he'd intended. "To me. To this. To us. Because I won't let you pull away from me."

Her lips trembled, but he had her full attention now. "Even for your own sake?" she whispered, distress leaching the blue undertones from her eyes and leaving them an empty gray.

He paused for a fraction of a second, wondering if she was referring to her father. "Especially for that," he replied, and set himself to the sweet task of arousing her. This time was totally for her; he wooed her with a skill that went beyond sexual experience. His extensive training in the martial arts had taught him how to cripple with a touch, kill with a single blow, but it had also taught him all the places on the human body that were exquisitely sensitive to pleasure. The backs of her knees and thighs, the delicate arches of her feet, the lower curve of her buttocks, all received their due attention. Slowly she came alive under him, a growing inner wetness easing his way. She began to move in time with his leisurely thrusts, rising up to meet him. He stroked the cluster of nerves in the small of her back and was rewarded by the reflexive arch that took him deeper into her.

She sighed, her lips parted, her eyes closed. Her cheeks glowed; her lips were puffy and red. He saw all the signs of her arousal and whispered encouragement. Her head tossed to the side, and her hardened nipples stabbed against his chest. Gently, so gently, he bit the tender curve where her neck met her shoulder.

She cried out and began climaxing, her peak catching him by surprise. So did his own. He hadn't meant to climax, but the delicate inner clench and release of her body sent pleasure roaring through him, bursting out of control.

He tried to stop, tried to withdraw; his body simply wouldn't obey. Instead, he thrust deep and shuddered wildly as his seed spurted from him into the hot, moist depths of her. He heard his own deep, rough cry; then both time and thought stopped, and all that was left of him sank down on her in a heavy sprawl.

Shadow had crept across the canyon floor when he wrapped her in the blanket and carried her back to the sheltering overhang. The surrounding rock blocked the sun during the day, but it also absorbed its heat so that at night, when the temperature dropped, it was noticeably warmer in their snug little niche than it was outside. Sunny yawned, drowsy with satisfaction, and rested her head on his shoulder. "I can walk," she said mildly, though she made no effort to slide her feet to the ground.

"Hey, I'm doing my macho act here," he protested. "Don't ruin it."

She tilted her head back to look at him. "You aren't acting, though, are you?"

"No," he admitted, and earned a chuckle from her.

Time had gotten away from him while they drifted in the sleepy aftermath of passion. The sun was so far down in the sky that only the upper rim of the canyon was lit, the reds and golds and purples of the rock catching fire in the sunset, while the sky had taken on a deep violet hue.

"I'm going to check the traps while there's still a few minutes of light left," he said as he deposited her on the ground. "Sit tight. I won't be long."

Sunny sat tight for about two seconds after he disappeared from view, then bounced to her feet. Quickly she washed and dressed, needing the protection of her clothing. She had the uneasy feeling that nothing was the same as it had been before Chance carried her out into the sunlight. She had been prepared for the lovemaking, but not for that overwhelming assault on her senses. She had hoped for pleasure, and instead found something so much more powerful that she couldn't control it.

And most of all, Chance had revealed himself for the marauder he was.

She had seen glimpses of it before, in moments when the force of his personality broke through his control. She should have realized then; one didn't bolt a steel gate on an empty room. His control had given her the rare, luxurious feeling of safety, and she had been so beguiled that she had ignored the power that gate held constrained, or what would happen if it ever broke loose. This afternoon, she had found out.

He had said he'd been in the Army Rangers. That should have told her everything she needed to know about the kind of man he was. She could only think she'd let the stress of the situation, and her worry about Margreta, blind her to his true nature.

A shiver rippled down her spine, a totally sensual reaction as she remembered the tumultuous hour—or hours—on the blanket. She had been helpless, totally blindsided by the force of her reaction. She had known from the beginning that she responded to him as she never had before to any man, but she still hadn't been prepared for such a complete upheaval of her senses. He wasn't the only one accustomed to control; her very life had depended on her control of any given situation, and with Chance, she had found that she couldn't control either him or herself.

She had never been more terrified in her life.

The way she had felt about him before was nothing compared to now. It wasn't just the sex, which had been so much more intense and harsh than she had ever imagined. No, it was the part of his character he had revealed, the part that he had tried to keep hidden, that called to her so strongly she knew only her own death would end the love she felt for him. Chance was one of a very special breed of men, a warrior. All the little pieces of him she had sensed were now settled into place, forming the picture of a man who would always have something wild and ruthless inside him, a man willing to put himself at risk, step into the line of fire, to protect what he loved. He was the complete antithesis of her father, whose life was devoted wholly to destruction.

Sunny hadn't had a choice in a lot of the sacrifices of her life. Their mother had given her and Margreta away in an effort to save them, but hadn't been able to completely sever herself from her daughters' lives. Instead, she had taught them all her hard-learned skills, taught them how to hide, to disappear—and, if necessary, how to fight. By necessity, Pamela Vickery Hauer had become an expert in her own brand of guerrilla warfare. Whenever she thought it safe she would visit, and the kindly Millers would go out of their way to give her time with her girls.

When Sunny was sixteen, Pamela's luck had finally run out. Their father's network was extensive, and he had many more resources at his disposal than his fugitive wife could command. Logically, it had been only a matter of time before he found her. And when she was finally run to ground, Pamela had killed herself rather than take the chance he would, by either torture or drugs, be able to wring their location from her.

That was Sunny's legacy, a life living in shadows, and a courageous mother who had killed herself in order to protect her children. No one had asked her if this was the life she wanted; it was the life she had, so she had made the best of it she could.

Nor had it been her choice to live apart from Margreta; that had been her sister's decision. Margreta was older; she had her own demons to fight, her own battles to wage, and she had never been as adept at the survival skills taught by their mother as Sunny had been. So Sunny had lost her sister, and when the Millers died, first Hal and then Eleanor, she had been totally alone. The calls on her cell phone from Margreta were the only contact she had, and she knew Margreta was content to leave it at that.

She didn't think she had the strength to give up Chance, too. That was why she was terrified to the point of panic, because her very presence endangered his life. Her only solace was that because he was the man he was, he was very tough and capable, more able to look after himself.

She took a deep breath, trying not to anticipate trouble. If and when they got out of this canyon, then she would decide what to do.

Because she was too nervous to sit still, she checked the clothes she had washed out and found they were already dry. She gathered them off the various rocks where they had spread them, and though the little chore had taken only minutes, by the time she walked back to the overhang there was barely enough light for her to see.

Chance hadn't taken the flashlight with him, she remembered. It was a moonless night; if he didn't get back within the next few minutes, he wouldn't be able to see.

The fire had been kept smoldering all day, to maximize the smoke and conserve their precious store of wood, but now she quickly added more sticks to bring up a good blaze, both for her own sake and so he would have the fire as a beacon. The flickering firelight penetrated the darkness of the overhang, sending patterns dancing against the rock wall. She searched through their belongings until she found the flashlight, to have it at hand in case she had to search for him.

Total blackness came suddenly, as if Mother Nature had dropped her petticoats over the land. Sunny stepped to the front of the overhang. "Chance!" she called, then paused to listen.

The night wasn't silent. There were rustlings, the whispers of the night things as they crept about their business. A faint breeze stirred the scrub brush, sounding like dry bones rattling together. She listened carefully, but didn't hear an answering call.

"Chance!" She tried again, louder this time. Nothing. "Damn it," she muttered, and flashlight in hand set off for the deep end of the canyon where their life-giving water trickled out of a crack in the rock.

She walked carefully, checking where she put her feet. A second encounter with a snake was more than she could handle in one day. As she walked she periodically called his name, growing more irritated by the moment. Why didn't he answer her? Surely he could hear her by now; sound carried in the thin, dry air.

A hard arm caught her around the waist and swung her up against an equally hard body. She shrieked in alarm, the sound cut off by a warm, forceful mouth. Her head tilted back under the pressure, and she grabbed his shoulders for support. He took his time, teasing her with his tongue, kissing her until the tension left her body and she was moving fluidly against him.

When he lifted his head his breathing was a little ragged. Sunny felt obliged to complain about his treatment of her. "You scared me," she accused, though her voice sounded more sultry than sulky.

"You got what you deserved. I told you to sit tight." He kissed her again, as if he couldn't help himself.

"Is this part of the punishment?" she murmured when he came up for air.

"Yeah," he said, and she felt him smile against her temple.

"Do it some more."

He obliged, and she felt the magic fever begin burning again deep inside her. She ached all over from his previous lovemaking; she shouldn't feel even a glimmer of desire so soon, and yet she did. She wanted to feel all the power of his superbly conditioned body, take him inside her and hold him close, feel him shake as the pleasure overwhelmed him just as it did her.

Finally he tore his mouth from hers, but she could feel his heart pounding against her, feel the hard ridge in his jeans. "Have mercy," he muttered. "I won't have a chance to starve to death. I'm going to die of exhaustion."

Starving reminded her of the traps, because she was very hungry. "Did you catch a rabbit?" she asked, her tone full of hope.

"No rabbit, just a scrawny bird." He held up his free hand, and she saw that he held the plucked carcass of a bird that was quite a bit smaller than the average chicken.

"That isn't the Roadrunner, is it?"

"What's this thing you have with imaginary animals? No, it isn't a roadrunner. Try to be a little more grateful."

"Then what is it?"

"Bird," he said succinctly. "After I spit it and turn

it over the flames for a while, it'll be roasted bird. That's all that matters."

Her stomach growled. "Well, okay. As long as it isn't the Roadrunner. He's my favorite cartoon character. After Bullwinkle."

He began laughing. "When did you see those old cartoons? I didn't think they were on anywhere now."

"They're all on disk," she said. "I rented them from my local video store."

He took her arm, and they began walking back to camp, chatting and laughing about their favorite cartoons. They both agreed that the slick animated productions now couldn't match the older cartoons for sheer comedy, no matter how realistic the modern ones were. Sunny played the flashlight beam across their path as they walked, watching for snakes.

"By the way, why were you calling me?" Chance asked suddenly.

"It's dark, in case you didn't notice. You didn't carry the flashlight with you."

He made a soft, incredulous sound. "You were coming to *rescue* me?"

She felt a little embarrassed. Of course, a former ranger could find his way back to camp in the dark. "I wasn't thinking," she admitted.

"You were thinking too much," he corrected, and hugged her to his side.

They reached their little camp. The fire she had built up was still sending little tongues of flame licking around the remnants of the sticks. Chance laid the bird on a rock, swiftly fashioned a rough spit from the sticks, and sharpened the end of another stick with his pocket knife. He skewered the bird with that stick, and set it in the notches of the spit, then added some small sticks to the fire. Soon the bird was dripping sizzling juice into the flames, which leaped higher in response. The delicious smell of cooking meat made her mouth water.

She shoved a flat rock closer to the fire and sat down, watching him turn the bird. She was close enough to feel the heat on her arms; as chilly as the night was already, it was difficult to remember that just a few short hours ago the heat had been scorching. She had camped out only once before, but the circumstances had been nothing like this. For one thing, she had been alone.

The amber glow of the flames lit the hard angles of his face. He had washed up while he was gone, she saw; his hair was still a little damp. He had shaved, too. She smiled to herself.

He looked up and saw her watching him, and a wealth of knowledge, of sensual awareness, flashed between them. "Are you all right?" he asked softly.

"I'm fine." She had no idea how her face glowed as she wrapped her arms around her legs and rested her chin on her drawn-up knees.

"Are you bleeding?"

"Not now. And it was only a little, at first," she added hastily when his eyes narrowed in concern.

He returned his gaze to the bird, watching as he carefully turned it. "I wish I had known."

She wished he didn't know now. The reasons for her recently lost virginity weren't something she wanted to dissect. "Why?" she asked, injecting a light note into her tone. "Would you have been noble and stopped?"

"Hell, no," he said. "I'd have gone about it a little differently, is all."

Now, that was interesting. "What would have been different?"

"How rough I was. How long I took."

''You took long enough,'' she assured him, smiling. ''Both times.''

''I could have made it better for you.''

''How about for you?''

His dark gaze flashed upward, and he gave a rueful smile. ''Sweetheart, if it had been any better for me, my heart would have given out.''

''Ditto.''

He turned the bird again. ''I didn't wear a condom the second time.''

''I know.'' The evidence had been impossible to miss.

Their gazes met and locked again, and again they were linked by that silent communication. He might have made her pregnant. He knew it, and she knew it.

''How's the timing?''

She rocked her hand back and forth. ''Borderline.'' The odds were in their favor, she figured, but it wasn't a risk she wanted to take again.

''If we weren't stuck here—'' he began, then shrugged.

''What?''

''I wouldn't mind.''

Desire surged through her, and she almost jumped his bones right then. She got a tight grip on herself, literally, and fought to stay seated. Hormones were sneaky devils, she thought, ready to undermine her common sense just because he mentioned wanting to make her pregnant.

''Neither would I,'' she admitted, and watched to see if he had the same reaction. Color flared high on his carved cheekbones, and a muscle in his jaw flexed. His hand tightened on the spit until his knuckles were white. Yep, it went both ways, she thought, fascinated by his battle to remain where he was.

When he judged the bird was done, he took the skewer

off the spit and kicked another rock over to rest beside hers, then sat down on it. With his pocket knife he cut a strip of meat and held it out to her. "Careful, don't burn yourself," he warned as she reached eagerly for the meat.

She juggled the strip back and forth in her hands, blowing on it to cool it. When she could hold it, she took her first tentative bite. Her taste buds exploded with the taste of wood and smoke and roasted fowl. "Oh, that's good," she moaned, chewing slowly to get every ounce of flavor.

Chance cut off a strip for himself and took his first bite, looking as satisfied as she with their meal. They chewed in silence for a while. He was careful to divide the meat equally, until she was forced to stop eating way before she was satisfied. He was so much bigger than she was that if they each ate the same amount, he would be short-changed.

He knew what she was doing, of course. "You're taking care of me again," he observed. "You're hell on my image, you know that? I'm supposed to be taking care of you."

"You're a lot bigger than I am. You need larger portions."

"Let me worry about the food, sweetheart. We won't starve. There's more game to catch, and tomorrow I'll look for some edible plants to round out our diet."

"Bird and bush," she said lightly. "What all the trendy people are eating these days."

Her quip made him grin. He persuaded her to eat a little more of the meat, then they finished off one of the remaining nutrition bars. Their hunger appeased, they began getting ready to turn in for the night.

He banked the fire while she got the tent ready. They

brushed their teeth and made one last nature call, just like old married folks, she thought in amusement. Their "home" wasn't much, really nothing more than a niche in the rock, but their preparations for the night struck her as very domestic—until he said, "Do you want to wear my shirt tonight? It would be more like a night-gown on you than the shirt you're wearing."

There was nothing the least bit tamed in the way he was looking at her. Her heartbeat picked up in speed, and the now familiar heat began spreading through her. That was all he had to do, she thought; one look and she was aroused. He had taught her body well during the short time she had been sprawled beneath him on the blanket. Now that she knew exactly how it felt to take his hard length inside her, she craved the sensation. She wanted that convulsive peak of pleasure, even though it had frightened her with its intensity. She hadn't realized she would feel as if she were flying apart, as if her soul was being wrenched from her body. In a blind-ing, paralyzing moment of clarity, she knew that no other man in the world would be able to do that for her, to her. He was the One for her, capital *O,* big letter, underlined and italicized. The *One.* She would never again be whole without him.

She must have looked stricken, because suddenly he was by her side, supporting her with an arm around her waist as he gently but inexorably guided her to the tent. He would be considerate, she realized, but he didn't in-tend to be refused.

She cleared her throat, searching for her equilibrium. "You'll need your shirt to keep warm—"

"You're joking, right?" He smiled down at her, the corners of his eyes crinkling. "Or did you think we were through for the night?"

She couldn't help smiling back. "That never crossed my mind. I just thought you'd need it *afterward*."

"I don't think so," he said, his hands busy unsnapping her jeans.

They were both naked and inside the tent in record time. He switched off the flashlight to save the batteries, and the total darkness closed around them, just as it had the night before. Making love when one was going totally by feel somehow heightened the other senses, she found. She was aware of the calluses on his hands as he stroked her, of the heady male scent of his skin, of the powerful muscles that bunched under her own exploring hands. His taste filled her; his kisses were a feast. She reveled in the smooth firmness of his lips, the sharp edges of his teeth; she rubbed his nipples and felt them contract under her fingers. She loved the harsh groan he gave when she cupped the soft, heavy sacs between his legs, and the way they tightened even as she held them.

She was shocked when she closed her hand around his pulsing erection. How on earth had she ever taken him inside her? The long, thick column ended in a smooth, bulbous flare, the tip of which was wet with fluid. Entranced, she curled down until she could take the tip in her mouth and lick the fluid away.

He let out an explosive curse and tumbled her on her back, reversing their positions. The confines of the small tent restricted their movement, but he managed the shift with his usual powerful grace.

She laughed, full of wonder at the magic between them, and draped her arms around his neck as he settled on top of her. "Didn't you like it?"

"I almost came," he growled. "What do you think?"

"I think I'll have my way with you yet. I may have

to overpower you and tie you up, but I think I can handle the job.''

''I'm positive of it. Let me know when you're going to overpower me, so I can have my clothes off.''

That afternoon, caught in the whirlpool of his love-making, she wouldn't have believed she would be so at ease with him now, that they could indulge in this sensual teasing. She wouldn't have believed how naturally her thighs parted to accommodate his hips, or how comfortable it was, as if nature had designed them to fit together just so. Actually nature had; she just hadn't realized it until now.

He gave her a taste of her own medicine, kissing his way down her body until his hair brushed the insides of her thighs and she discovered a torture so sweet she shattered. When she could breathe again, when the colored pinpoints of light stopped flashing against her closed eyelids, he kissed her belly and laid his head on the pillowing softness. ''My God, you're easy,'' he whispered.

She managed a strangled sound that was almost a laugh. ''I guess I am. For you, anyway.''

''Just for me.'' The dark tones of masculine possessiveness and triumph underlaid the words.

''Just for you,'' she whispered in agreement.

He put on a condom and slid into place between her thighs. She fought back a cry; she was sore and swollen, and he was big. He moved gently back and forth until she accepted him more easily and the discomfort faded, but gradually his thrusts quickened, became harder. Even then she sensed he was holding himself back to keep from hurting her. When he climaxed, he pulled back so only half his length was inside her, and held himself there while shudders racked his strong body.

Afterward, he tugged his T-shirt on over her head, immediately enveloping her in his scent. The roomy garment came halfway to her knees—or it would have if he hadn't bunched it around her waist. He cradled her in his arms, one big hand on her bare bottom to keep her firmly against him. He used her rolled-up cardigan for a pillow, and she used him. Oh, this was wonderful.

"Is Sunny your real name, or is it a nickname?" he asked sleepily, his lips brushing her hair.

Even as relaxed as she was, as sated, a twinge of caution made her hesitate. She never told anyone her real name. It took her a moment to remember that none of that made any difference here now. "It's a nickname," she murmured. "My real name is Sonia, but I've never used it. Sonia Ophelia Gabrielle."

"Good God." He kissed her. "Sunny suits you. So you're saddled with four names, huh?"

"Yep. I never use the middle ones, though. What about you? What's your middle name?"

"I don't have one. It's just Chance."

"Really? You aren't lying to me because it's something awful, like Eustace?"

"Cross my heart."

She settled herself more comfortably against him. "I suppose it balances out. I have four names, you have two—together, we average three."

"How about that."

She could hear a smile in his voice now. She rewarded him with a small, sneaky pinch that made him jump. His retaliation ended, a long time later, in the use of another condom.

Sunny went to sleep to the knowledge that she was happier now, with Chance, than she had ever before been in her life.

Chapter 9

The next morning the traps were empty. Sunny struggled with her disappointment. After such an idyllic, pleasure-filled night, the day should have been just as wonderful. A nice hot, filling breakfast would have been perfect.

"Could you shoot something?" she asked as she chewed half of one of the tasteless nutrition bars. "We have eight of these bars left." If they each ate a bar a day, that meant they would be out of food in four days.

In three days, Margreta would call.

Sunny pushed that thought away. Whether or not they got out of here in time for her to answer Margreta's call was something she couldn't control. Food was a more immediate problem.

Chance narrowed his eyes as he scanned the rim of the canyon, as if looking for a way out. "I have fifteen rounds in the pistol, and no extra cartridges. I'd rather save them for emergencies, since there's no telling how long we'll be here. Besides, a 9mm bullet would tear a rabbit to pieces and wouldn't leave enough left of a bird for us to eat. Assuming I could hit a bird with a pistol shot, that is.''

She wasn't worried about his marksmanship. He was probably much better with a rifle, but with his military background, he would be more than competent with the pistol. She looked down at her hands. ''Would a .38 be better?''

''It isn't as powerful, so for small game, yeah, it would be better. Not great, but better—but I have a 9mm, so it's a moot point.''

''I have one,'' she said softly.

His head whipped around. Something dangerous flashed in his eyes. ''What did you say?''

She nodded toward her bag. ''I have a .38.''

He looked in the direction of her gaze, then back at her. His expression was like flint. ''Would you like to tell me,'' he said very deliberately, ''just how you happen to have a pistol of any kind with you? You were on a commercial flight. How did you get past the scanners?''

She didn't like giving away all her secrets, not even to Chance. A lifetime on the run had ingrained caution into her very bones, and she had already given him more of herself than she ever had anyone else. Still, they were in this together. ''I have some special containers.''

''Where?'' he snapped. ''I saw you unpack everything in your bag and there weren't any—ah, hell. The hair spray can, right?''

Unease skittered along her spine. Why was he angry? Even if he was a stickler for rules and regulations, which she doubted, he should be glad they had an extra weapon, no matter how they came by it. She straightened her shoulders. "And the blow-dryer."

He stood over her like an avenging angel, his jaw set. "How long have you been smuggling weapons on board airplanes?"

"Every time I've flown," she said coolly, standing up. She was damned if she would let him tower over her as if she was a recalcitrant child. He still towered over, just not as much. "I was sixteen the first time."

She walked over to the bag and removed the pertinent items. Chance leaned down and snagged the can of spray from her hands. He took the cap off and examined the nozzle, then pointed it away from him and depressed it. A powder-fine mist of spray shot out.

"It's really hair spray," she said. "Just not much of it." She took the can and deftly unscrewed the bottom. A short barrel slid out of the can into her hands. Putting it aside, she lifted the hair-dryer and took it apart with the same deft twist, yielding the remaining parts of the pistol. She assembled it with the ease of someone who had done the task so often she could do it in her sleep, then fed the cartridges into the magazine, snapped it into place, reversed the pistol and presented it to him butt-first.

He took it, his big hand almost swallowing the small weapon. "What in *hell* are you doing with a weapon?" he bit out.

"The same thing you are, I imagine." She walked away from him and missed the look of shock that crossed his face. With her back to him she said, "I carry it for self-protection. Why do you carry yours?"

"I charter my plane to a lot of different people, most of whom I don't know. I fly into some isolated areas sometimes. And my weapon is licensed.'' He hurled the words at her like rocks. ''Is yours?''

''No,'' she said, unwilling to lie. ''But I'm a single woman who travels alone, carrying packages valuable enough that a courier service is hired to deliver them. The people I deliver the packages to are strangers. Think about it. I'd have to be a fool not to carry some means of protection.'' That was the truth, as far as it went.

''If your reason for carrying is legitimate, then why don't you have a license?''

She felt as if she were being interrogated, and she didn't like it. The tender, teasing lover of the night was gone, and in his place was someone who sounded like a prosecutor.

She had never applied for a license to carry a concealed weapon because she didn't want any background checks in the national data system, didn't want to bring herself to the notice of anyone in officialdom.

''I have my reasons,'' she retorted, keeping her tone very deliberate.

''And you aren't going to tell me what they are, right?'' He threw her a look that was almost sulfuric in its fury and stalked off in the direction of the traps. His stalking, like everything else he did, was utterly graceful—and completely silent.

''Good riddance, Mr. Sunshine,'' she hurled at his back. It was a childish jab, but she felt better afterward. Sometimes a little childishness was just what the doctor ordered.

With nothing better to do, she set off in the opposite direction, toward the plane, to gather more sticks and twigs for the all-important fire. If he tried to keep her pistol when they got out of here—and they *would* get out, she had to keep hoping—then it would be war.

*   *   *

Chance examined the compact pistol in his hand. It was unlike any he had ever seen before, for the simple reason that it hadn't come from any manufacturer. A gunsmith, a skilled one, had made this weapon. It bore no serial number, no name, no indication of where or when it was made. It was completely untraceable.

He couldn't think of any good reason for Sunny to have it, but he could think of several bad ones.

After yesterday, he had been more than halfway convinced she was innocent, that she was in no way involved with her father. Stupid of him, but he had equated chastity with honor. Just because a woman didn't sleep around didn't mean she was a fine, upstanding citizen. All it meant was that, for whatever reason, she hadn't had sex.

He knew better. He was far better acquainted with the blackness of the human soul than with its goodness, because he had chosen to live in the sewers. Hell, he came from the sewers; he should be right at home there, and most of the time he was. The blackness of his own soul was always there, hidden just a few layers deep, and he was always aware of it. He used to make his way in the dangerous world he had chosen, shaped it into a weapon to be used in defense of his country and, ultimately, his family. And being on such intimate terms with hell, with the twisted evil humans could visit on one another, he should know that golden hair and bright, sparkling eyes didn't necessarily belong on an angel. Shakespeare had hit the nail on the head when he warned the world against smiling villains.

It was just—*damn* it, Sunny got to him. She had slipped right past defenses he would have sworn were impregnable, and she had done it so easily they might as well not have been there at all. He wanted her, and so he had almost convinced himself that she was innocent.

Almost. There was just too much about her that didn't add up, and now there was this untraceable pistol that she smuggled on board airplanes, concealed in some very effective but simple containers. Airport scanners would show metal, but if a security guard was suspicious enough to check, he or she would find only the normal female styling aids. The hair spray can actually sprayed, and he didn't doubt the blow-dryer would work, too.

If Sunny could get a pistol on board a plane, then others could, too. He went cold at the thought of how many weapons must be flying around at any given time. Airport security wasn't his line of work, but damn if he wasn't going to make it a point to kick some asses over this.

He shoved his anger aside so he could concentrate on this assignment. He hoped he hadn't blown it by losing his temper with her, but his disillusionment had been too sharp for him to contain. The pleasure of the night they had just spent together should more than outweigh their first argument. Her inexperience with men worked against her; she would be easy to manipulate, where a seasoned veteran of the mattress wars would be more wary and blasé about their lovemaking. He still held all the trump cards, and soon he would be playing them.

He reached a particular point in the canyon and positioned himself so he was in the deepest morning shadows. Sunny couldn't catch him unawares here, and he had a clear line of sight to a certain rock on the rim of the canyon. He took a laser light from his pocket, a pencil-thin tube about two inches long that, when clicked, emitted an extraordinarily bright finger of light.

He aimed it at the rock on the rim and began clicking, sending dashes of light in the code he and Zane had agreed on at the beginning of the plan. Every day he signalled Zane, both to let him know that everything was all right and that they shouldn't be rescued yet.

There was an answering flash, message received. No matter how closely he watched that rock, he never saw any movement, though he knew Zane would have immediately pulled back. He himself was damn good at moving around undetected, but Zane was extraordinary even for a SEAL. There was no one else on this earth Chance would rather have beside him in a fight than Zane.

That mission accomplished, Chance settled down in some cover where he could watch the trickle of water. Since the traps hadn't been productive overnight, he really did need to shoot something for supper. He was willing to starve to achieve his ends—but only if he had to. If a bunny rabbit showed its face, it was history.

As Sunny walked the canyon floor, picking up what sticks she could find, she studied the rock walls, looking for a fissure that might have escaped notice, an animal trail, anything that might point the way to freedom. If they only had some rock-climbing gear, she thought wistfully. A rope, cleats, anything. She had tried to anticipate any possible need when she packed her bag, but somehow being trapped in a box canyon hadn't occurred to her.

For the most part, the walls were perpendicular. Even when they slanted a little, the angle wasn't much off ninety degrees. Erosion from wind and rain had, over millions of years, cut grooves in the rock that looked like ripples in water. The only sign the canyon wasn't impregnable was the occasional little heap of rubble where smaller rocks had crumbled and fallen.

She had passed several of those small heaps before the light went on.

A fragile stirring of hope made her stomach tighten as she investigated one scattered pile of rock. It looked as if a larger boulder had fallen from the rim and shattered on impact. She picked up a fist-sized rock and rubbed her thumb over the surface, finding it gritty, the texture of sandpaper. Sandstone, she thought. It was a lovely pink color. It was also soft.

Just to be certain, she banged the rock down on a larger rock, and it broke into several pieces.

This site was no good; it was too steep. She walked along the wall, looking up at the rim and trying to find a place where the wall slanted back just a little. That was all she asked; just a little slant, enough that the angle wasn't so extreme.

There. One of the ripples curved backward, and when she picked her way through rocks and bushes to investigate she saw the opportunity for which she had been looking. She ran her hand over the rock, exulting in the sandpaper texture of it under her palm. Maybe, just maybe…

She ran back to the camp and grabbed the curling iron out of the bag. Chance hadn't asked, but the pistol wasn't the only weapon she carried. Quickly she unscrewed the metal barrel from the handle and removed a knife from the interior. It was a slender blade, made for slicing rather than hacking, but sharp and almost indestructible.

Her idea registered somewhere between being a long shot and just plain crazy, but it was the only idea she'd had that was even remotely possible. At least she would be doing *something,* rather than just waiting around for a rescue that might never happen.

She needed gloves to protect her hands, but she didn't have any. Hastily she opened the first-aid box and took out the roll of gauze. She wrapped the gauze around her palms and wove it in and around her fingers, then taped the loose ends. The result was crude but workable, she thought. She had seen the gloves rock climbers wore, with their fingers and thumbs left free; this makeshift approximation would have to do. She might wear blisters on her hands, anyway, but that was a small price to pay if they could get out of here.

Knife in hand, she went back to her chosen point of attack and tried to figure out the best way to do this. She needed another rock, she realized, one that wasn't soft. Anything that crumbled would be useless. She scouted around and finally found a pitted, dark gray rock that was about the size of a grapefruit, heavy enough to do the job.

Digging the point of the knife into the soft sandstone of the wall, she gripped the rock with her right hand and pounded it against the knife, driving the blade deeper. She jerked the blade out, moved it a little to the right, and pounded it in again. The next time she drove the knife in at a right angle to the original gouge, and hammered it downward. A chunk of sandstone broke loose, leaving a nice little gouge in the rock.

"This just might work," Sunny said aloud, and set herself to the task. She didn't let herself think how long it would take to carve handholds out of the rock all the way to the top, or if it was even possible. She was going to try; she owed it to Margreta, and to herself, to do everything she could to get out of this canyon.

Almost two hours later, the sharp crack of a pistol

shot reverberated through the canyon, startling her so much that she nearly fell. She clung to the rock, her cheek pressed against the rough surface. Her heart pounded from the close call. She wasn't that high, only about ten feet, but the canyon floor was jagged with rock, and any fall was certain to cause injuries.

She wiped the sweat from her face. The temperature was rising by the minute, and the rock was getting hotter and hotter. Standing with her toes wedged into the gouges she had hammered out of the rock, she had to lean inward against the rock to brace herself, because she had to have both hands free to wield the knife and the rock. She couldn't put nearly as much effort into it now, or the impact would jar her from her perch.

Panting, she reached over her head and blindly swung the rock. Because she had to press herself to the rock to keep her balance, she couldn't see to aim. Sometimes she hit the target and the knife bit into the rock; sometimes she hit her own hand. There had to be a better way to do this, but she couldn't think of one. She was an expert at working with what she had; she could do it this time, too. All she had to do was be careful, and patient.

"I can do this," she whispered.

Chance carried the skinned and cleaned rabbit back to the camp. He had also found a prickly pear cactus and cut off two of the stems, sticking himself several times as he removed the spines. The prickle pear was both edible and nutritious; it was usually fried, but he figured roasting would do just as well.

His temper had cooled. All right, so she had taken him in. He hadn't blown the plan; everything was still on track. All he had to do was remember not to be fooled by that oh-so-charming face she presented to the world and the plan would work just as he had expected. Maybe he couldn't make her love him, but he could make her think she did, and that was all he needed. A little trust, a little information, and he was in business.

He stepped beneath the overhang, grateful for the relief the shade afforded, and took off his sunglasses. Sunny wasn't here. He turned around and surveyed what he could see of the canyon but couldn't spot her. Her green T-shirt and beige jeans didn't exactly stand out in the terrain, he thought, and abruptly realized what effective camouflage her clothing was. Had she chosen it for that exact purpose? She must have; everything she carried in that bag had been geared toward survival, so why should her clothing be any different?

"Sunny!" he called. His voice echoed, then died. He listened, but there was no answer.

Damn it, where was she?

The fire had died down, which meant she hadn't tended it in quite a while. He bent down and added more sticks, then skewered the rabbit and set it on the spit, more to keep it away from insects than anything else. The fire was too low to cook it, but the smoke wafting over the meat would give it a good flavor. He wrapped the prickly pear stems in his handkerchief and walked back under the overhang to keep them out of the sun until he was ready to cook them.

The first thing he saw was the open first aid kit.

Alarm punched him in the gut. The paper wrapping had been torn off the roll of gauze; the tape was lying in the lid of the box, and it had also been used, because the end had been left free rather than stuck back to the roll.

Another detail caught his eyes. The curling iron had been taken apart; the two halves of it lay in the sand.

He swore viciously. Damn it, he should have remembered the curling iron and not assumed the pistol was the only weapon she had. She couldn't have hidden another pistol in the curling iron, but a knife would fit.

He didn't see any blood, but she must have injured herself somehow. Where in the hell was she?

"Sunny!" he roared as he stepped back out into the sun. Only silence answered him.

He studied the ground. Her footprints were everywhere, of course, but he saw where she had walked to her bag, presumably to get the first aid kit; then the prints led back out into the canyon. She was headed toward the plane.

He wasn't aware of reaching for his pistol. He was so accustomed to it that he didn't notice the weight of it in his hand as he followed her tracks, everything in him focusing on finding her.

If it hadn't been for the tracks, he would have missed her. She was almost at the far end of the canyon, past where the plane sat baking in the sun. The rock walls were scored with hundreds of cuts, and she was tucked inside one of them, clinging to the rock about a dozen feet off the ground.

Astonishment, anxiety, relief and anger all balled together in his gut. In speechless fury he watched her reach over her head and stab a wicked-looking blade into the soft rock, then, still keeping her face pressed against the hot stone, use another rock to try to pound the knife deeper. She hit her hand instead of the knife handle, and the curse she muttered made his eyebrows rise.

Strips of gauze were wound around her hands. He didn't know if she had wrapped her hands because she had hurt them, or if the gauze was an effort to keep them from being hurt. All he knew was that if she fell she would likely maim herself on the rocks, and that he really, *really* wanted to spank her.

He ruthlessly restrained the urge to yell at her. The last thing he wanted to do was startle her off her precarious perch. Instead, he stuck the pistol in his waistband at the small of his back and worked his way over until he was standing beneath her, so he could catch her if she fell.

He forced himself to sound calm. "Sunny, I'm right beneath you. Can you get down?"

She stopped with her right hand drawn back to deliver another blow with the rock. She didn't look down at him. "Probably," she said. "It has to be easier than getting up here."

He was fairly certain what she was doing, but the sheer magnitude of the task, the physical impossibility of it, left him stunned. Just for confirmation he asked, "What are you doing?"

"I'm cutting handholds in the rock, so we can climb out of here." She sounded grim, as if she also realized the odds against success.

His hands clenched into fists as he fought for control. He looked up at the towering wall, at the expanse stretching above her. The dozen feet she had climbed was only about one tenth of the distance needed—and it was the easiest tenth.

He put his hand on the rock and almost jerked back at the heat radiating from it. A new concern gnawed at him. He didn't yell at her that this was the stupidest idea he'd ever heard of, the way he wanted. Instead, he said, "Sweetheart, the rock's too hot. Come down before you're burned."

She laughed, but without her usual humor. "It's too late."

To hell with cajoling. "Throw the knife down and get off that damn rock," he barked in sharp command.

To his surprise, she dropped the knife, then the rock she held in her right hand, tossing both to the side so they wouldn't land near him. Every muscle in her body was taut with strain as she reached for the handholds she had cut and began to work her way down, feeling with her toes for the gouges. He stood directly beneath her, reaching up for her in case she fell. The muscles in her slender arms flexed, and he realized anew just how strong she was. One didn't get that kind of strength with a once-in-a-while jog or the occasional workout in a gym. It took dedication and time; he knew, because he kept himself in top physical condition. Her normal routine would be at least an hour of work, maybe two, every day. For all he knew, while he had been checking the traps she had been doing pushups.

For all the gut-deep burn of his anger, it was overridden by his concern as he watched her inch her way down the face of the rock. She was careful and took her time, despite the fact that he knew the rock was scorching her fingers. He didn't speak again, not wanting to distract her; he simply waited, not very patiently, for her to get within his reach.

When she did, he caught her feet and guided them to the next gouges. "Thanks," she panted, and worked her way down another foot.

That was enough. He caught her around the knees and scooped her off the rock. She shrieked, fighting for her balance, but now that he had her in his grip he wasn't about to let her go. Before she could catch her breath, he turned her and tossed her face down over his shoulder.

"Hey!" The indignant protest was muffled against his back.

"Just shut up," he said between his teeth as he dipped down to pick up her knife, then set off for the camp. "You scared the hell out of me."

"Good. You had too much hell in you, anyway." She clutched him around the waist to steady herself. He just hoped she didn't grab the pistol out of his waistband and shoot him, since it was so close to hand.

"Damn it, don't you dare joke about it!" Her upturned bottom was very close to his hand. Temptation gnawed at him. Now that he had her down, he was shaking, and he wanted some retribution for having been put through that kind of anxiety. He put his hand on her butt and indulged in a few moments of fantasy, which involved her jeans around her knees and her bent over his lap.

He realized he was stroking his palm over the round curves of her buttocks and regretfully gave up on his fantasy. Some things weren't going to happen. After he tended her hands and got through raising hell with her for taking such a risk, he fully intended to burn off his fright and anger with an hour or two on the blanket with her.

How could he still want her so much? This wasn't part of the job; he could live with it, if it had been. This was obsession, deep and burning and gut-twisting. He had tried to put a light face on it, for her benefit, but if she had been more experienced, she would have known a man didn't make love to a woman five times during the night just because she was available. At this rate, those three dozen condoms wouldn't last even a week.

He had already used six, and it might take two or three more to get him settled down after the scare she had given him.

The hard fact of it was, a man didn't make love to a woman that often unless he was putting his brand on her.

This wouldn't work. Couldn't work. He had to get himself under control, stay focused on the job.

He heard her sniffing as they neared the camp. "Are you *crying?*" he demanded incredulously.

She sniffed again. "Don't be silly. What's that smell?" She inhaled deeply. "It smells like...food."

Despite himself, a smile quirked the corners of his mouth. "I shot a rabbit."

There was a small disruption on his shoulder as she twisted around so she could see the fire. Her squeal of delight almost punctured his eardrums, and his smile grew. He couldn't stop himself from enjoying her; he had never before met anyone who took such joy in life, who was so vibrantly alive herself. How she could be a part of a network devoted to taking lives was beyond his understanding.

He dumped her on the ground under the overhang and squatted beside her, taking both her hands in his and turning them up for his inspection. He barely controlled a wince. Her fingers were not only scorched from the hot rock, they were scraped raw and bleeding.

Fury erupted in him again, a flash fire of temper at seeing the damage she had done to herself. He surged to his feet. "Of all the stupid, lame-brained...! What in hell were you thinking? You weren't thinking at all, from the looks of it! Damn it, Sunny, you risked your life pulling this stupid stunt—"

"It wasn't stupid," she shouted, shooting to her feet

to face him, her brilliant eyes narrowed. She clenched her bleeding hands into fists. "I know the risks. I also know it's my only hope of getting out of this damn canyon before it's too late!"

"Too late for what?" he yelled back. "Do you have a date this weekend or something?" The words were heavy with sarcasm.

"Yeah! It just so happens I do!" Breathing hard, she glared at him. "My sister is supposed to call."

Chapter 10

A sister? Chance stared at her. His investigation hadn't turned up any information about a sister. The Millers hadn't had any children of their own, and he had found adoption papers only on Sunny. His mind raced. "You said you didn't have any family."

She gave him a stony look. "Well, I have a sister."

Yeah, right. "You'd risk your life for a phone call?" Some terrorist act was being planned after all, he thought with a cold feeling in the pit of his stomach. That was why she'd been lugging the tent around. He didn't know how the tent fit into the scheme, but evidently she had been planning to drop out of sight.

"I would for this one." She wheeled away, every line of her body tense. "I have to try. Margreta calls my cell phone every week at the same time. It's how we know the other is still alive." She turned back to him and shouted, "If I don't answer that call, she'll think I'm dead!"

Whoa. Once again, the pieces of the puzzle that was Sunny had been scattered. Margreta? Was that a code name? He searched his memory, which was extensive, but couldn't find anything or anyone named Margreta. Sunny was so damned convincing....

"Why would she think you're dead?" he demanded. "You might just be in a place that doesn't have a signal—like here. What is she, some kind of nutcase?"

"I make certain I'm always somewhere that has a signal. And, no, she isn't a *nutcase!*" She threw the words back at him like bullets, her mouth twisted with fury at him, at the situation, at her own helplessness. "Her problem is the same as mine—we're our father's daughters!"

His pulse leaped. There it was, out in the open, just like that. He hadn't needed seduction; anger had done the job. "Your father?" he asked carefully.

Tears glittered in her eyes, dripped down her cheeks. She dashed them away with a furious gesture. "Our father," she said bitterly. "We've been running from him all our lives."

The pieces of the puzzle jumped about a little more, as if a fist had slammed down and jarred them. Easy, he cautioned himself. Don't seem too interested. Find out exactly what she means; she could be referring to his influence. "What do you mean, running?"

"I mean running. Hiding." She wiped away more tears. "Father dear is a terrorist. He'll kill us if he ever finds us."

Chance gently cleaned her hands with the alcohol wipes from the first aid kit, soothed the red places with burn ointment and the raw spots with antibiotic cream. The gauze she'd wrapped around her hands had protected her palms, but her fingers were a mess. Sunny felt a little bewildered. One minute they had been yelling at each other, the next she had been locked against him, his arms like a vise around her. His heart had been pounding like a runaway horse.

Since then he had been as tender as a mother with a child, rocking her in comfort, cuddling her, drying her tears. The emotional firestorm that had burned through her had left her feeling numb and disoriented; she let him do whatever he wanted without offering a protest, not that she had any reason to protest. It felt good to lean on him.

Satisfied with the care he had given her hands, he left her sitting on the rock while he added some fuel to the fire and turned the rabbit on the spit. Coming back under the overhang, he spread the blanket against the wall, scooped her into his arms, and settled on the blanket with her cradled against him. He propped his back against the wall, arranged her so she was draped half across his lap and lifted her face for a light kiss.

She managed a shaky smile. "What was that? A kiss to make it better?"

He rubbed his thumb over her bottom lip, his expression strangely intent as if studying her. "Something like that."

"I'm sorry for crying all over you. I usually handle things better than this."

"Tell me what's going on," he said quietly. "What's this about your father?"

She leaned her head on his shoulder, grateful for his strength. "Hard to believe, isn't it? But he's the leader of a terrorist group that has done some awful things. His name is Crispin Hauer."

"I've never heard of him," Chance lied.

"He operates mostly in Europe, but his network extends to the States. He even has someone planted in the FBI." She was unable to keep the raw bitterness out of her voice. "Why do you think I don't have a license for that pistol? I don't know who the plant is, how high he ranks, but I do know he's in a position to learn if the FBI gets any information Hauer wants. I didn't want to be in any database, in case he found out who adopted me and what name I'm using."

"So he doesn't know who you are?"

She shook her head. She had spent a lifetime keeping all her fear and worry bottled up inside her, and now she couldn't seem to stop it from spewing out. "My mother took Margreta and left him before I was born. I've never met him. She was five months pregnant with me when she ran."

"What did she do?"

"She managed to lose herself. America's a big place. She stayed on the move, changing her name, paying with cash she had taken from his safe. When I was born, she intended to have me by herself, in the motel room she'd taken for the night. But I wouldn't come, the labor just kept on and on, and she knew something was wrong. Margreta was hungry and scared, crying. So she called 911."

He wound a strand of golden hair around his finger. "And was there something wrong?"

"I was breech. She had a C-section. While she was groggy from the drugs, they asked her the father's name and she didn't think to make up a name, just blurted out *his.* So that's how I got into the system, and how he knows about me."

"How do you know he knows?"

"I was almost caught, once." She shivered against

him, and he held her closer. "He sent three men. We were in…Indianapolis, I think. I was five. Mom had bought an old car and we were going somewhere. We were always on the move. We got boxed in, in traffic. She saw them get out of their cars. She had taught us what to do if she ever told us to run. She dragged us out of the car and screamed 'Run!' I did, but Margreta started crying and grabbed Mom. So Mom took off running with Margreta. Two men went after them, and one came after me." She began shuddering. "I hid in an alley, under some garbage. I could hear him calling me, his voice soft like he was singing. 'Sonia, Sonia.' Over and over. They knew my name. I waited forever, and finally he went away."

"How did your mother find you again? Or was she caught?"

"No, she and Margreta got away, too. Mom taught herself street smarts, and she never went anywhere that she wasn't always checking out ways to escape."

He knew what that was like, Chance thought.

"I stayed in my hiding place. Mom had told us that sometimes, after we thought they were gone, the bad men would still be there watching, waiting to see if we came out. So I thought the bad men might be watching, and I stayed as still as I could. I don't think it was winter, because I wasn't wearing a coat, but when night fell I got cold. I was scared and hungry and didn't know if I'd ever see Mom again. I didn't leave, though, and finally I heard her calling me. She must have noticed where I ran and worked her way back when she thought it was safe. All I knew was that she'd found me. After that was when she decided it wasn't safe to keep us with her anymore, so she began looking for someone to adopt us."

Chance frowned. He hadn't found a record of any adoption but hers. "The same family took both of you?"

"Yes, but I was the only one adopted. Margreta wouldn't." Her voice was soft. "Margreta...remembers things. She had lost everything except Mom, so I guess she clung more than I did. She had a hard time adapting." She shrugged. "Having grown up the way I did, I can adjust to pretty much anything."

Meaning she had taught herself not to cling. Instead, with her sunny personality, she had found joy and beauty wherever she could. He held her closer, letting her cling to him. "But...you said he was trying to kill you. It sounds as if he was trying very hard to get you back."

She shook her head. "He was trying to get *Margreta* back. He didn't know me. I was just a means he could have used to force Mom to give Margreta back to him. That's all he would want with me now, to find Margreta. If I was caught, when he found out I don't know where she is, I'd be worthless to him."

"You don't know?" he asked, startled.

"It's safer that way. I haven't seen her in years." Unconscious longing for her sister was in her voice. "She has my cell phone number, and she calls me once a week. So long as I answer the call, she knows everything is all right."

"But you don't know how to get in touch with her?"

"No. I can't tell them what I don't know. I move around a lot, so a cell phone was the best way for us. I keep an apartment in Chicago, the tiniest, cheapest place I could find, but I don't live there. It's more of a decoy than anything else. I suppose if I live anywhere it's in Atlanta, but I take all the assignments I can get. I seldom spend more than one night at a time in one place."

"How would he find you now, since your name has

been changed? Unless he knows who adopted you, but how could he find that out?'' Chance himself had found her only because of the incident in Chicago, when her courier package was stolen and he checked her out. As soon as he said it, though, he knew that the mole in the FBI—and he would damn sure find out who *that* was— had probably done the same checking. Had he gone as deep in the layers of bureaucracy as Chance had, to the point of hacking into those sealed adoption records? Sunny's cover might have been blown. He wondered if she realized it yet.

"I don't know. I just know I can't afford to assume I'm safe until I hear he's dead."

"What about your mom? And Margreta?"

"Mom's dead." Sunny paused, and he felt her inhale as if bracing herself. "They caught her. She committed suicide rather than give up any information on us. She had told us she would—and she did."

She stopped, and Chance gave her time to deal with the bleakness he heard in her voice. Finally she said, "Margreta is using another name, I just don't know what it is. She has a heart condition, so it's better if she stays in one location."

Margreta was living a fairly normal life, he thought, while Sunny was on the move, always looking over her shoulder. That was what she had known since birth, the way she had been taught to handle the situation. But what about the years they had spent with the Millers? Had her life been normal then?

She answered those questions herself. "I miss having a home," she said wistfully. "But if you stay in one place you get to know people, form relationships. I couldn't risk someone else's life that way. God forbid I should get married, have children. If Hauer ever found

me—'' She broke off, shuddering at the thought of what
Hauer was capable of doing to someone she loved in
order to get the answers he wanted.

One thing didn't make sense, Chance thought. Hauer
was vicious and crazy and cunning, and would go to any
lengths to recover his daughter. But why Margreta, and
not Sunny, too? ''Why is he so fixated on your sister?''

''Can't you guess?'' she asked rawly, and began shuddering again. ''That's why Mom took Margreta and ran.
She found him with her, doing…things. Margreta was
only four. He had evidently been abusing her for quite
a while, maybe even most of her life. By then Mom had
already found out some of what he was, but she hadn't
worked up the nerve to leave. After she found him with
Margreta, she didn't have a choice.'' Her voice dropped
to an agonized whisper. ''Margreta remembers.''

Chance felt sick to his stomach. So in addition to being a vicious, murdering bastard, Hauer was also a per-
vert, a child molester. Killing was too good for him; he
deserved to be dismembered—slowly.

Worn out by both physical labor and her emotional
storm, Sunny drifted to sleep. Chance held her, content
to let her rest. The fire needed more fuel, but so what?
Holding her was more important. Thinking his way
through this was more important.

First and foremost, he believed every word she'd said.
Her emotions had been too raw and honest for any of it
to have been faked. For the first time, all the pieces of
the puzzle fit together, and his relief was staggering.
Sunny was innocent. She had nothing to do with her
father, had never seen him, had spent her entire life running from him. That was why she lugged around a tent,
with basic survival provisions; she was ready to disappear at any given moment, to literally go to ground and

live out in the forest somewhere until she thought it was safe to surface and rebuild her life yet again.

She had no way of contacting Hauer. The only way to get to him, then, was to use her as bait. And considering how she felt about her father, she would never, under any circumstances, agree to any plan that brought her to his attention.

He would have to do it without her agreement, Chance thought grimly. He didn't like using her, but the stakes were too high to abandon. Hauer couldn't be left free to continue wreaking his destruction on the world. How many innocent people would die this year alone if he wasn't caught?

There was no point in staying here any longer; he'd found out what he needed to know. Zane wouldn't check in again, though, until tomorrow morning, so they were stuck until then. He adjusted Sunny in his arms and rested his face against the top of her head. He would use the time to formulate his game plan—and to use as many of those condoms as possible.

"Get away from me," Sunny grumbled the next morning, turning her head away from his kiss. She pried his hand off her breast. "Don't touch me, you—you *mink.*"

Chance snorted with laughter.

She pulled his chest hair.

"Ouch!" He drew back as far as he could in the small confines of the tent. "That hurt."

"Good! I don't think I can walk." Quick as a snake, her hand darted out and pulled his chest hair again. "This way, you can have as much fun as I'm having."

"Sunny," he said in a cajoling tone.

"Don't 'Sunny' me," she warned, fighting her way

into her clothes. Since they barely had room to move, he began dodging elbows and knees, and his hands slipped over some very interesting places. "Stop it! I mean it, Chance! I'm too sore for any more monkey business."

More to tease her than anything else, he zeroed in on an interesting place that had her squealing. She shot out of the tent, and he collapsed on his back, laughing—until she raised the tent flap and dashed some cold water on him.

"There," she said, hugely satisfied by his yelp. "One cold shower, just what you needed." Then she ran.

If she thought the fact that he was naked would hamper his pursuit, she found out differently. He snatched up a bottle of water as he passed by their cache of supplies and caught her before she had gone fifty yards. She was laughing like a maniac, otherwise she might have gotten away. He held her with one arm and poured the water over her head. It was ice-cold from having been left out all night, and she shrieked and sputtered and giggled, clinging to him when her legs went weak from so much laughter.

"Too sore to walk, huh?" he demanded.

"I w-wasn't walking," she said, giggling as she pushed her wet hair out of her face. Cold droplets splattered on him, and he shivered.

"Damn, it's cold," he said. The sun was barely up, so the temperature was probably in the forties.

She slapped his butt. "Then get some clothes on. What do you think this is, a nudist colony?"

He draped his arm around her shoulders, and they walked back to the camp. Her playfulness delighted him; hell, everything about her delighted him, from her wit to her willingness to laugh. And the sex—God, the sex was unbelievable. He didn't doubt she was sore, because *he* was. Last night had been a night to remember.

When she awakened yesterday afternoon she had been naturally melancholy, the normal aftermath of intense emotions. He hadn't talked much, letting her relax. She went with him to check the traps, which were still empty, and they had bathed together. After a quiet supper of rabbit and cactus they went to bed, and he had devoted the rest of the night to raising her spirits. His efforts had worked.

"How are your hands?" he asked. If she could pull his chest hairs and slap his butt, the antibiotic cream must have worked wonders.

She held them out, palms up, so he could see. The redness from the burns was gone, and her raw fingertips looked slick and shiny. "I'll wrap Band-Aids around them before I get started," she said.

"Get started doing what?"

She gave him a startled look. "Cutting handholds in the rock, of course."

He was stunned. He stared at her, unable to believe what he was hearing. "You're not climbing back on that damn wall!" he snapped.

Her eyebrows rose in what he now recognized as her "the-hell-you-say" look. "Yes, I am."

He ground his teeth. He couldn't tell her they would be "rescued" today, but no way was he letting her wear herself out hacking holes in rock or put herself at that kind of risk.

"I'll do it," he growled.

"I'm smaller," she immediately objected. "It's safer for me."

She was trying to protect him again. He felt like beating his head against a rock in frustration.

''No, it isn't,'' he barked. ''Look, there's no way you can cut enough handholds for us to climb out of here in the next two days. You got, what, twelve feet yesterday? If you managed twelve feet a day—and you wouldn't get that much done today, with your hands the way they are—it would take you over a week to reach the top. That's if—*if*— you didn't fall and kill yourself.''

''So what am I supposed to do?'' she shot back. ''Just give up?''

''Today you aren't going to do a damn thing. You're going to let your hands heal if I have to tie you to a rock, is that clear?''

She looked as if she wanted to argue, but he was a lot bigger than she was, and maybe she could tell by his expression that he meant exactly what he said. ''All right,'' she muttered. ''Just for today.''

He hoped she would keep her word, because he would have to leave her alone while he went to the spot where he signaled Zane. He would just have to risk it, but there would be hell to pay if he came back to find her on that rock.

He quickly dressed, shivering, and they ate another cold breakfast of water and nutrition bar, since there wasn't anything left of the rabbit from the night before. Tomorrow morning, he promised himself, breakfast would be bacon and eggs, with a mountain of hash browns and a pot of hot coffee.

''I'm going to check the traps,'' he said, though he knew there wouldn't be anything in them. When he'd checked them the afternoon before, knowing they would be leaving here today, he had quietly released them so they couldn't be sprung. ''Just tend to the fire and keep it smoking. You take it easy today, and I'll wash our clothes this afternoon.'' That was a safe promise to make.

"It's a deal,'' she said, but he could tell she was thinking about Margreta.

He left her sitting by the fire. It was a good ten-minute walk to the designated spot, but he hurried, unwilling to leave her to her own devices for so long. Taking the laser light from his pocket, he aimed it toward the rock on the rim and began flashing the pickup signal. Immediately Zane flashed back asking for confirmation, to make certain there wasn't an error. After all, they hadn't expected this to happen so fast. Chance flashed the signal again and this time received an okay.

He dropped the light back in his pocket. He didn't know how long it would take for Zane to arrange the pickup, but probably not long. Knowing Zane, everything was already in place.

He was walking back to the camp when the small twin-engine plane flew over. A grin spread across his face. That was Zane for you!

He began running, knowing Sunny would be beside herself. He heard her shrieking before he could see her; then she came into view, jumping in her glee as she came to meet him. "He saw me!'' she screamed, laughing and crying at the same time. "He waggled the wings! He'll come back for us, won't he?''

He caught her as she hurled herself into his arms and couldn't stop himself from planting a long, hard kiss on that laughing mouth. "He'll come back,'' he said. "Unless he thought you were just waving hello at him.'' The opportunity to tease her was too great to resist, considering she had pulled his chest hair and poured cold water on him. He'd retaliated for the cold water; this was for the hair-pulling.

She looked stricken, the laughter wiped from her face as if it had never been. "Oh, no," she whispered.

He didn't have the heart to keep up the pretense. "Of course he'll come back," he chided. "Waggling the wings was the signal that he saw you and would send help."

"Are you sure?" she asked, blinking back tears.

"I promise."

"I'll get you for this."

He had to kiss her again, and he didn't stop until she had melted against him, her arms locked around his neck. He hadn't thought he would be interested in sex for quite a while, not after last night, but she proved him wrong.

He huffed out a breath and released her. "Stop manhandling me, you hussy. We have to get packed."

The smile she gave him was brilliant, like the sun rising, and it warmed him all the way through.

They gathered their belongings. Chance returned her pistol to her, and watched her break it down and store the pieces in their hiding places. Then they walked back to the plane and waited.

Rescue came in the form of a helicopter, the blades beating a thumping rhythm in the desert air, the canyon echoing with the sound. It hovered briefly over them, then lowered itself like a giant mosquito. Sand whipped into their air, stinging them, and Sunny hid her face against his shirt.

A sixtyish man with a friendly face and graying beard hopped out of the bird. "You folks need some help?" he called.

"Sure do," Chance answered.

When he was closer, the man stuck out his hand. "Charlie Jones, Civil Air Patrol. We've been looking for you for a couple of days. Didn't expect to find you this far south.''

''I veered off course looking for a place to land. Fuel pump went out.''

''In that case, you're mighty lucky. That's rough territory out there. This might be the only spot in a hundred miles when you could have landed. Come on. I expect you folks are ready for a shower and some food.''

Chance held out his hand to Sunny, and she gave him that brilliant smile again as she put her hand in his and they walked to the helicopter.

Chapter 11

Sunny was almost dizzy with mingled relief and regret; relief because she wouldn't miss Margreta's call, regret because this time with Chance, even under such trying conditions, had been the happiest, most fulfilling few days of her life and they were now over. She had known from the beginning that their time together was limited; once they were back in the regular world, all the old rules came back into play.

She couldn't, wouldn't risk his life by letting him be a part of hers. He had given her two nights of bliss, and a lifetime of memories. That would have to be enough, no matter how much she was already aching at the thought of walking away from him and never seeing him again. At least now she knew what it was to love a man, to revel in his existence, and she was richer for it. She wouldn't have traded these few days with him for any amount of money, no matter the price in loneliness she would have to pay.

So she held his hand all during the helicopter flight to a small, ramshackle air field. The only building was made of corrugated metal, rounded at the top like a Quonset hut, with a wooden addition, housing the office, added to one side. If the addition had ever seen a coat of paint, the evidence of it had long since been blasted off by the wind-driven sand. After living under a rock for three days, Sunny thought the little field looked like heaven.

Seven airplanes, of various makes and vintage, were parked with almost military precision along one side of the air strip. Charlie Jones landed his helicopter on a concrete pad behind the corrugated building. Three men, one wiping his greasy hands on a stained red rag, left the building by the back door and walked toward them, ducking their heads against the turbulence of the rotor blades.

Charlie took off his headset and hopped out of the chopper, smiling. "Found 'em," he called cheerfully to the approaching trio. To Chance and Sunny he said, "The two on the left fly CAP with me. Saul Osgood, far left, is the one who spotted your smoke this morning and radioed in your position. Ed Lynch is the one in the middle. The one with the greasy hands is Rabbit Warren, the mechanic here. His real name's Jerome, but he'll fight you if you call him that."

Sunny almost laughed aloud. She controlled the urge, but she was careful not to look at Chance as they shook hands with the three men and introduced themselves.

"I couldn't believe it when I saw your bird in that little bitty narrow canyon," Saul Osgood said, shaking his head after Chance told them what had happened. "How you ever found it is a miracle. And to make a

dead stick landing—'' He shook his head again. ''Someone was sure looking out for you, is all I can say.''

''So you think it was your fuel pump went out, huh?''
Rabbit Warren asked as they walked into the hangar.

''Everything else checked out.''

''It's a Skylane, right?''

''Yeah.'' Chance told him the model, and Rabbit
stroked his lean jaw.

''I might have a pump for that. There was a feller in
here last year flying a Skylane. He ordered some parts
for it, then left and never did come back for 'em. I'll
check while you folks are refreshing yourselves.''

If ''refreshing'' themselves had anything to do with a
bathroom, Sunny was more than ready. Chance gave her
the first turn, and she almost crooned with delight at the
copious water that gushed from the faucet at a turn of
the handle. And a flush toilet! She was in heaven.

After Chance had his turn, they indulged in ice-cold
soft drinks from a battered vending machine. A snack
machine stood beside it, and Sunny surveyed the offer-
ings with an eager eye. ''How much change do you
have?'' she asked Chance.

He delved his hand into his front pocket and pulled
out his change, holding it out for Sunny to see. She
picked out two quarters and fed them into the machine,
punched a button, and a pack of cheese and crackers fell
to the tray.

''I thought you'd go for a candy bar,'' Chance said
as he fed more quarters into the machine and got a pack
of peanuts.

''That's next.'' She raised her eyebrows. ''You didn't
think I was going to stop with cheese and crackers, did
you?''

Ed Lynch opened the door to the office. ''Is there

anyone you need to call? We've notified the FAA and called off the search, but if you have family you want to talk to, feel free to use the phone.''

''I need to call the office,'' Sunny said, pulling a wry face. She had a good excuse—a very good one—for not making her delivery, but the bottom line was that a customer was unhappy.

Chance waited until she was on the phone, then strolled over to where Rabbit was making a show of looking for a fuel pump. His men were good, Chance thought; they had played this so naturally they should have been on the stage. Of course, subterfuge was their lives, just as it was his.

''Everything's good,'' Chance said quietly. ''You guys can clear out after Charlie takes us back to the canyon with the fuel pump.''

Rabbit pulled a greasy box from a makeshift shelf that was piled with an assortment of parts and tools. Over Chance's shoulder he eyed Sunny through the windowed door to the office. ''You pulled a real hardship assignment this time, boss,'' he said admiringly. ''That's the sweetest face I've seen in a while.''

''There's a sweet person behind it, too,'' Chance said as he took the box. ''She's not part of the organization.''

Rabbit's eyebrows went up. ''So all this was for nothing.''

''No, everything is still a go. The only thing that's changed is her role. Instead of being the key, she's the bait. She's been on the run from Hauer her entire life. If he knows where she is, he'll come out of hiding.'' He glanced around to make certain she was still on the phone. ''Spread the word that we're going to be extra careful with her, make sure she doesn't get hurt. Hauer has already caused enough damage in her life.''

And he himself was going to cause more, Chance thought bleakly. As terrified as she was of Hauer, when she learned Chance had deliberately leaked her location to the man she was going to go ballistic. That would definitely be the end of *this* relationship, but he'd known from the beginning this was only temporary. Like her, he wasn't in any position for permanent ties. Sunny's circumstances would change when her father was gone, but Chance's wouldn't; he would move on to another crisis, another security threat.

Just because he was her first lover didn't mean he would be her last.

The idea shot a bolt of pure rage through him. Damn it, she was *his*—he caught the possessive thought and strangled it. Sunny wasn't his; she was her own person, and if she found happiness in her life with some other man, he should be happy for her. She more than deserved anything good that came her way.

He wasn't happy. Her laughter, her passion—he wanted it all for himself. Knowing he couldn't have her was already eating a huge hole out of his insides, but she deserved far better than a mongrel with blood on his hands. He had chosen his world, and he was well-suited for it. He was accustomed to living a lie, to pretending to be someone he wasn't, to always staying in the shadows. Sunny was…sunny, both by name and by nature. He would enjoy her while he had her—by God, he'd enjoy her—but in the end he knew he would have to walk away.

Sunny ended the call and left the office. Hearing the door close, he turned to watch her approach, and he let himself savor the pleasure of just watching her.

She wrinkled her nose. "Everyone's glad the plane didn't crash, that I'm alive—but the fact that I didn't die makes it a little less forgivable that I didn't deliver the package on time. The customer still wants it, though, so I still have to go to Seattle.''

She came to him as naturally as if they had been together for years, and just as naturally he found himself slipping his arm around her slender waist. "Screw 'em," he said dismissively. He lifted the box. "Guess what I have.''

She beamed. "The keys to the kingdom."

"Close enough. Charlie's going to take me back to the plane so I can swap out the fuel pump. Do you want to go with me, or stay here and rest until I get back?''

"Go with you," she said promptly. "I don't know anything about airplanes, but I can keep you company while you work. Are we coming back here, anyway?''

"Sure. This is as good a place to refuel as any." Plus she wouldn't find out they weren't in Oregon as he'd told her.

"Then I'll leave my bag here, if that's all right with Rabbit.'' She looked inquiringly at Rabbit, who nodded his head.

"That'll be just fine, ma'am. Put it in the office and it'll be as safe as a baby in the womb.''

Sunny walked away to get the bag. She felt safe, Chance realized, otherwise she would never let the bag out of her possession. Except for her worry for Margreta, these last few days she must have felt free, unburdened by the need to constantly look over her shoulder.

He had enjoyed their little adventure, too, every minute of it, because he had known they weren't in any danger. Sunny made him feel more alive than he ever had before, even when he was angry at her because she had just scared him half to death. And when he was inside her—then he was as close to heaven as he was ever likely to get. The pleasure of making love to her was so intense it was almost blinding.

He grinned to himself as he hefted his own overnight bag. No way was he leaving it here; after all, the condoms were in it. No telling what might happen when he and Sunny were alone.

The afternoon was wearing on when Charlie set the helicopter down in the canyon again. He looked up at the light with an experienced pilot's eye. "You think you have enough time to get that fuel pump put on before dark?"

"No problem," Chance said. After all, as he and Charlie both knew, there was nothing wrong with the fuel pump, anyway. He would tinker around for a while, make it look realistic. Sunny wasn't likely to stand at his elbow the entire time, and if she did he would distract her.

He and Sunny jumped out of the helicopter, and he leaned in to get his bag. "See you in a few hours."

"If you don't make it back to the airfield, we know where you are," Charlie said, saluting.

They ducked away from the turbulence as the helicopter lifted away. Sunny pushed her hair away from her face and looked around the canyon, smiling. "Home again," she said, and laughed. "Funny how it looks a lot more inviting now that I know we aren't stuck here."

"I'm going to miss it," he said, winking at her. He carried his bag and the box containing the fuel pump over to the plane. "But we'll find out tonight if a bed is more fun than a tent."

To his surprise, sadness flashed in her eyes. "Chance...once we're away from here..." She shook her head. "It won't be safe."

He checked for a moment, then very deliberately put

down the bag and box. Turning back to her, he put his hands on his hips. "If you're saying what I think you're saying, you can just forget about it. You aren't dumping me."

"You know what the situation is! I don't have a choice."

"*I* do. You're not just a fun screw who was available while we were here. I care about you, Sunny," he said softly. "When you look over your shoulder, you're going to see my face. Get used to it."

Tears welled in her brilliant eyes, filling them with diamonds. "I can't," she whispered. "Because I love you. Don't ask me to risk your life, because I can't handle it."

His stomach muscles tightened. He had set out to make her love him, or at least get involved in a torrid affair with him. He had succeeded at doing both. He felt humbled, and exhilarated—and sick, because he was going to betray her.

He had her in his arms before he was aware of moving, and his mouth was on hers. He felt desperate for the taste of her, as if it had been days since he'd kissed her instead of just hours. Her response was immediate and wholehearted, as she rose on her tiptoes to fit her hips more intimately to his. He tasted the salt of her tears and drew back, rubbing his thumbs across her wet cheeks.

He rested his forehead against hers. "You're forgetting something," he murmured.

She sniffed. "What?"

"I was a ranger, sweetheart. I'm a little harder to kill than your average guy. You need someone watching your back, and I can do it. Think about it. We probably made the news. When we get to Seattle, don't be surprised if there's a television camera crew there. Both our faces will be on television. Besides that, we were reported missing to the FAA, which is federal. Information would have been dug up on both of us. Our names our linked. If the mole in the FBI tumbles to who you are, your father's goons will be after me, anyway—especially if they can't find you.''

She went white. "Television?" She looked a lot like her mother; Chance had seen old photos of Pamela Vickery Hauer. Anyone familiar with Pamela would immediately notice the resemblance. As sharp as she was, Sunny also knew the danger of being on television, even a local newscast.

"We're in this together." He lifted her hand to his mouth and kissed her knuckles, then grinned down at her. "Lucky for you, I'm one mean son of a bitch when I need to be—lucky for you, unlucky for them."

Nothing she said would sway him, Sunny thought with despair late that night as she showered in the hotel suite he had booked them into for the night—a suite because it had more than one exit. He had been exactly right about the television news crew. Crews, she corrected herself. News had been slow that day, so every station in Seattle had jumped on the human-interest story. The problem was, so had both national news channels.

She had evaded the cameras as much as possible, but the reporters had seemed fixated on her, shouting questions at her instead of Chance. She would have thought the female reporters, at least, would be all over Chance, but he'd worn such a forbidding expression that no one had approached him. She hadn't answered any questions on camera, though at Chance's whispered suggestion she had given them a quick comment off-camera, for them to use as a filler on their broadcast.

Her one break was that, since it had been so late when they landed, the story didn't make even the late news. But unless something more newsworthy happened soon, the story would air in just a few hours over millions of breakfast tables countrywide.

She had to assume her cover had been blown. That meant leaving the courier service, moving—not that she had much to move; she had never accumulated many possessions—even changing her name. She would have to build a new identity.

She had always known it could happen, and she had prepared for it, both mentally and with actual paperwork. Changing her name wouldn't change who she was; it was just a tool to use to escape her father.

The real problem was Chance. She couldn't shake him, no matter how she tried, and she knew she was good at that kind of thing. She had tried to lose him at the airport, ducking into a cab when his back was turned. But he seemed to have a sixth sense where she was concerned, and he was sliding in the other door before she could give the driver the address where she had to deliver the courier package. He had remained within touching distance of her until they walked into the hotel room, and she had no doubt that, if she opened the bathroom door, she would find him sprawled across the bed, watching her.

In that, she underestimated him. Just as she began lathering her hair, the shower curtain slid back and he stepped naked into the tub with her. "I thought I'd conserve water and shower with you," he said easily.

"Hah! You're just afraid I'll leave if you shower by yourself," she said, turning her back on him.

A big hand patted her bottom. "You know me so well."

She fought a smile. Damn him, why did he have to be so well-matched to her in every way? She could, and had, run rings around most people, but not Chance.

She hogged the spray, turning the nozzle down to rinse her hair. He waited until she was finished with that, at least, then adjusted the nozzle upward so the water hit him in the chest. It also hit her full in the face. She sputtered and elbowed him. "This is *my* shower, and I didn't invite you. I get control of the nozzle, not you."

She knew challenging him was a mistake. He said, "Oh, yeah?" and the tussle was on. Before she knew it she was giggling, he was laughing, and the bathroom was splattered with water. She had played more with Chance than she had since she'd been a little girl; she felt lighthearted with him, despite her problems. Their wet, naked bodies slid against each other, and neither of them could get a good grasp on any body part. At least, she couldn't. She suspected he could have won the tussle at any time simply by using his size and strength and wrapping his arms around her, but he held back and played at her level, as if he were used to restraining his strength to accommodate someone weaker than himself.

His hands were everywhere: on her breasts, her bottom, sliding between her legs while she laughed and batted them away. One long finger worked its way inside her and she squealed, trying to twist away while excitement spiraled wildly through her veins. Their naked wrestling match was having a predictable effect on both of them. She grabbed for the nozzle and aimed the blast of water at his face, and while he was trying to deflect the spray she made her escape, hopping out of the tub and snatching up a towel to wrap around her.

He vaulted out of the tub and slammed the door shut just as she reached for it. "You left the shower running," she accused, trying to sidetrack him.

"I'm not the one who turned it on." He grinned and hooked the towel away from her.

"Water's getting all over the floor." She tried to sound disapproving.

"It needed mopping, anyway."

"It did not!" She pushed a strand of dripping wet hair out of her eyes. "We're going to be kicked out. Water will drip through the floor into the room below and we'll be kicked out."

He grabbed her and swung her around so she was facing the shower. "Turn it off, then, if you're worried."

She did, because she hated to waste the water, and it was making such a mess. "There, I hope you're satisfied."

"Not by a long shot." He turned her to face him, holding her lips against his and angling her torso away from him, so he could look his fill at her. "Have I told you today how damn sexy you are?"

"Today? You've never told me at all!"

"Have so."

"Have not. When?"

"Last night. Several times."

She tried not to be entranced by the way water droplets were clinging to his thick dark lashes. "That doesn't count. Everyone knows you can't believe anything a man says when he's in…uh—"

"You?" he supplied, grinning.

She managed a haughty look. "I was going to say 'extremis,' but I think that applies only to dying."

"Close enough." He looked down at her breasts, his expression altering and the laughter fading. Still holding her anchored to him with one arm, he smoothed a hand up her torso to cup her breasts, and they both watched his long brown fingers curve around the pale globes. "You're sexy," he murmured, a slow, dark note entering his voice. She knew that note well, having heard it many times over the past two nights. "And beautiful. Your breasts are all cream-and-rose colored, until I kiss your nipples. Then they pucker up and turn red like they're begging me to suck them."

Her nipples tightened at his words, the puckered tips flushing with color. He groaned and bent his dark head, water dripping from his hair onto her skin as he kissed both breasts. She was leaning far back over his arm, supported by his arm around her hips and her own desperate grasp on his shoulders. She didn't know how much longer she would be able to stand at all. Her loins throbbed, and she gasped for breath.

"And your ass," he growled. "You have the sweetest little ass." He turned her around so he could stroke the aforementioned buttocks, shaping his palms to the full, cool curves. Sunny's legs trembled, and she grabbed the edge of the vanity for support. The cultured marble slab was a good six feet long, and a mirror covered the entire wall behind it. Sunny barely recognized herself in the naked woman reflected there, a woman whose wet hair dripped water down her back and onto the floor. Her expression was etched with desire, her face flushed and her eyes heavy-lidded.

Chance looked up, and his gaze met hers in the mirror. Electricity sparked between them. "And here," he whispered, sliding one hand around her belly and between her legs. His muscled forearm looked unbelievably powerful against her pale belly, and his big hand totally covered her mound. She felt his fingers sliding between her folds, rubbing her just as she liked. She moaned and collapsed against him, her legs going limp.

"You're so soft and tight," the erotic litany continued in her ear. "I can barely get inside you. But once I do— my heart stops. And I can't breathe. I think I'm going to die, but I can't, because it feels too good to stop." His fingers slid farther, and he pressed two of them inside her.

She arched under the lash of sensation, soaring close to climax as his fingers stretched her. She heard herself cry out, a strained cry that told him exactly how near she was to fulfillment.

"Not yet, not yet," he said urgently, sliding his fingers out of her and bending her forward. He braced her hands on the vanity. "Hold on, sweetheart."

She didn't know if he meant to the vanity, or to her control. Both were impossible. "I can't," she moaned. Her hips moved, undulating, searching for relief. "Chance, I can't—please!"

"I'm here," he said, and he was, dipping down and pushing his muscled thighs between her legs, spreading them. She felt his lower belly against her buttocks, then the smooth, hard entry of his sex. Instinctively she bent forward to aid his penetration, taking all of him deep within her. He began driving, and on the second hard thrust she convulsed, crying out her pleasure. His climax erupted a moment later, and he collapsed over her back, holding himself as deep as he could while he groaned and shook.

Sunny closed her eyes, fighting for breath. Oh God, she loved him so much she ached with it. She wasn't strong enough to send him away, not even for his own protection. If she had been really trying, she could have gotten away from him, but deep down she knew she couldn't give him up. Not yet. Soon. She would have to, to keep him safe.

Just one more day, she thought as tears welled. One more. Then she would go.

Chapter 12

Ten days later, Sunny still hadn't managed to shake him. She didn't know if she was losing her touch or if army rangers, even ex ones, were very, very good at not being shaken.

They had left Seattle early the next morning. Sunny was too cautious to fly back to Atlanta; as she had feared, the morning newscasts had been splashed with the ''real-life romantic adventure'' she and Chance had shared. His name was mentioned, but by some perverse quirk his face was never clearly shown; the camera would catch the back of his head, or while he was in a quarter profile, while hers was broadcast from coast to coast.

One of the a.m. news shows even tracked them down at the hotel, awakening them at three in the morning to ask if they would go to the local affiliate studios for a live interview.

''Hell, no,'' Chance had growled into the phone before he slammed it down into the cradle.

After that, it had seemed best they remove themselves from the reach of the media. They checked out of the hotel and took a taxi to the airport before dawn. The plane was refueled and ready to go. By the time the sun peeked over the Cascades they were in the air. Chance didn't file a flight plan, so no one had any way of finding out where they were going. Sunny didn't know herself until they landed in Boise, Idaho, where they refurbished their wardrobes. She always carried a lot of cash, for just such a situation, and Chance seemed to have plenty, too. He still had to use his credit card for refueling, so she knew they were leaving a trail, but those records would show only where they had last been, not where they were going.

Chance's presence threw her off her plan. She knew how to disappear by herself; Chance and his airplane complicated things.

From a pay phone in Boise, she called Atlanta and resigned her job, with instructions to deposit her last paycheck into her bank. She would have the money wired to her when she needed it. Sometimes, adrift from the familiar life she had fashioned for herself, she wondered if she was overreacting to the possibility anyone would recognize her. Her mother had been dead for over ten years; there were few people in the world able to see the resemblance. The odds had to be astronomical against one of those few people seeing that brief human-interest story that had been shown for only one day.

But she was still alive because her mother had taught her that any odds at all were unacceptable. So she ran, as she had learned how to do in the first five years of her life. After all, the odds were also against her getting pregnant, yet here she was, waiting for a period that hadn't materialized. They had slipped up twice, only twice: once in the canyon, and in the hotel bathroom in Seattle. The timing hadn't been great for her to get pregnant even if they hadn't used protection at all, so why hadn't her period started? It was due two days ago, and her cycle was relentlessly regular.

She didn't mention it to Chance. She might just be late, for one of the few times in her life since she'd starting having menstrual periods. She had been terrified when she thought they were going to crash; maybe her emotions had disrupted her hormones. It happened.

She might sprout wings and fly, too, she thought in quiet desperation. She was pregnant. There were no signs other than a late period, but she knew it deep down in her bones, as if on some level her body was communicating with the microscopic embryo it harbored.

It would be so easy just to let Chance handle everything. He was good at this, and she had too much on her mind to be effective. She didn't think he'd noticed how easily distracted she'd been these past few days, but then, he didn't know when her period had been due, either.

She had talked to Margreta twice, and told her she was going underground. She would have to arrange for a new cellular account under a different name, with a new number, and do it before the service she now had was disconnected. She had tried to tell Margreta everything that was going on, but her sister, as usual, kept the calls short. Sunny understood. It was difficult for Margreta to handle anything having to do with their father. Maybe one day they would be able to live normal lives, have a normal sisterly relationship; maybe one day Margreta would be able to get past what he had done to her and find some happiness despite him.

Then there was Chance. He had brought sunshine into her life when she hadn't even known she was living in shadows. She had thought she managed quite well, but it was as if B.C., Before Chance, had been in monochrome. Now, A.C., was in vivid technicolor. She slept in his arms every night. She ate her meals with him, quarreled with him, joked with him, made plans with him—nothing long term, but plans nevertheless. Every day she fell more and more in love with him, when she hadn't thought it possible.

Sometimes she actually pinched herself, because he was too good to be true. Men like him didn't come along every day; most women lived their entire lives without meeting a man who could turn their worlds upside down with a glance.

This state of affairs couldn't last much longer, this aimless drifting. For one thing, it was expensive. Chance wasn't earning any money while they were flying from one remote airfield in the country to another, and neither was she. She needed to get the paperwork for her new name, get a job, get a new cellular number—and get an obstetrician, which would cost money. She wondered how her mother had managed, with one frightened, traumatized child in tow, pregnant with another, and without any of the survival skills Sunny possessed. Pamela must have spent years in a state of terror, yet Sunny remembered her mother laughing, playing games with them, and making life fun even while she taught them how to survive. She only hoped she could be half as strong as her mother had been.

She was full of wild hopes these days. She hoped she hadn't been recognized. She hoped her baby would be healthy and happy. Most of all, she hoped she and Chance could build a life together, that he would be thrilled about the baby even though it was unplanned, that he truly cared about her as much as he appeared to. He never actually said he loved her, but it was there in his voice, in his actions, in his eyes and his touch as he made love to her.

Everything had to be all right. It had to. There was too much at stake now.

Sunny slept through the landing as Chance set the plane down in Des Moines. He glanced at her, but she was soundly asleep, like a child, her breathing deep and her cheeks flushed. He let her sleep, knowing what was coming to a head.

The plan was working beautifully. He had arranged for Sunny's face to be broadcast worldwide, and the bait had been taken immediately. His people had tracked two of Hauer's men into the country and maintained discreet but constant surveillance on them. Chance hadn't made it easy for anyone to follow him and Sunny; that would have been too obvious. But he had left a faint trail that, if the bloodhounds were good, they would be able to follow. Hauer's bloodhounds were good. They had been about a day behind them for about a week now, but until Hauer himself showed up, Chance made sure the hounds never caught up with him.

The news he'd been waiting for had finally come yesterday. Word in the underground of terrorist organizations was that Hauer had disappeared. He hadn't been seen in a few days, and there was a rumor he was in the States planning something big.

Somehow Hauer had slipped out of Europe and into America without being spotted, but now that Chance knew there was a mole in the FBI helping Hauer, he wasn't surprised.

Hauer was too smart to openly join his men, but he would be nearby. He was the type who, when Sunny was captured, would want to interrogate this rebellious daughter himself.

Chance would take him apart with his bare hands before he let that happen.

But he would have to let them think they had her, not knowing they were surrounded at all times, at a distance, by his men. Chance just hoped he himself wasn't shot at the beginning, to get him out of the way. If Hauer's men were smart, they would realize they could use threats to Chance to keep Sunny in line, and they had proven they were smart. This was the risky part, but he had taken all the safeguards he could without tipping his hand.

His interlude with Sunny would end tonight, one way or another. If all went well, they would both live through it, and she would be free to live her life out in the open. He just hoped that one day she wouldn't hate him, that she would realize he had done what he had to do in order to capture Hauer. Who knows? Maybe one day he would meet her again.

He guided the Cessna to a stop in its designated spot and killed the engine. Sunny slept on, despite the sudden silence. Maybe he'd cost her too much sleep and it had finally caught up with her, he thought, smiling despite his inner tension. He had glutted himself with sex for the past two weeks, as if subconsciously he had been trying to stockpile memories and sensations for the time when she was no longer there. But as often as he'd had her, he still wanted her. Again. More. He was half hard right now, just thinking about her.

Gently he shook her, and she opened her sleepy eyes with a look of such trust and love that his heart leaped. She sat up, stretching and looking around. "Where are we?"

"Des Moines." Puzzled, he said, "I told you where we were going."

"I remember," she said around a yawn. "I'm just groggy. Wow! That was some nap. I don't usually sleep during the daytime. I must not be getting enough sleep at night." She batted her eyelashes at him. "I wonder why."

"I have no idea," he said, all innocence. He opened the door and climbed out, turning around to hold his hands up for her. She clambered out, and he lifted her to the ground. Looking up at the wide, cerulean-blue sky, he stretched, too, twisting his back to get out the kinks. "It's a pretty day. Want to have a picnic?"

"A what?" She looked at him as if he were speaking a foreign language.

"A picnic. You know, where you sit on the ground and eat with your hands, and fight wild animals for your food."

"Sounds like fun. But haven't we already done that?"

He laughed. "This time we'll do it right—checkered tablecloth, fried chicken, the works."

"All right, I'm game. Where are we going to have this picnic? Beside the runway?"

"Smart-ass. We'll rent a car and go for a drive."

Her eyes began to sparkle as she realized he meant it. That was what he loved best about Sunny, her ability to have fun. "How much time do we have? What time are we leaving?"

"Let's stay for a couple of days. Iowa's a nice place,

and my tail could use some time away from that airplane seat.''

He handled his business with the airport, then went to a rental car desk and walked away with the keys to a sport utility.

"You rented a *truck?*" Sunny teased when she saw the green Ford Explorer. "Why didn't you get something with style, like a red sports car?"

"Because I'm six-three," he retorted. "My legs don't fit in sports cars."

She had bought a small backpack that she carried instead of the bulky carry-on she had been lugging around. She could get her toiletries and a change of clothes into the backpack, and that was enough for the single night they usually spent in a place. That meant her pistol was always with her, fully assembled when they weren't having to go through x-ray scanners, and he didn't protest. He always carried his own pistol with him, too, tucked into his waistband under his loose shirt. She put the backpack on the floorboard and climbed into the passenger seat, and began pushing buttons and turning knobs, every one she could reach.

Chance got behind the wheel. "I'm afraid to start this thing now. There's no telling what's going to happen."

"Chicken," she said. "What's the worst that could happen?"

"I'm just thankful Explorers don't have ejection seats," he muttered as he turned the key in the ignition. The engine caught immediately. The radio blared, the windshield wipers flopped back and forth at high speed, and the emergency lights began blinking. Sunny laughed as Chance dived for the radio controls and turned the volume down to an acceptable level. She buckled herself into the seat, smiling a very self-satisfied smile.

He had a map from the rental car company, though he already knew exactly where he was going. He had gotten very specific directions from the clerk at the rental agency, so the clerk would remember where they had gone when Hauer's men asked. He had personally scouted out the location before putting the plan into motion. It was in the country, to cut the risk of collateral damage to innocent civilians. There was cover for his men, who would be in place before he and Sunny arrived. And, most important, Hauer and his men couldn't move in without being observed. Chance had enough men in place that an ant couldn't attend this picnic unless he wanted it there. Best of all, he knew Zane was out there somewhere. Zane didn't usually do fieldwork, but in this instance he was here guarding his brother's back. Chance would rather have Zane looking out for him than an entire army; the man was unbelievable, he was so good.

They stopped at a supermarket deli for their picnic supplies. There was even a red-checkered plastic cloth to go on the ground. They bought fried chicken, potato salad, rolls, cole slaw, an apple pie, and some green stuff Sunny called pistachio salad. He knew he wasn't about to touch it. Then he had to buy a small cooler and ice, and some soft drinks to go in it. By the time he got Sunny out of the supermarket, over an hour had passed and he was almost seventy bucks lighter in the wallet.

"We have apple pie," he complained. "Why do we need apples?"

"I'm going to throw them at you," she said. "Or better yet, shoot them off your head."

"If you come near me with an apple, I'll scream," he warned. "And pickled beets? Excuse me, but who eats pickled beets?"

She shrugged. "Someone does, or they wouldn't be on the shelves."

"Have *you* ever eaten pickled beets?" he asked suspiciously.

"Once. They were nasty." She wrinkled her nose at him.

"Then why in hell did you buy them?" he shouted.

"I wanted you to try them."

He should be used to it by now, he thought, but sometimes she still left him speechless. Muttering to himself, he stowed the groceries—including the pickled beets—in the back of the Explorer.

God, he was going to miss her.

She rolled down the window and let the wind blow through her bright hair. She had a happy smile on her face as she looked at everything they passed. Even service stations seemed to interest her, as did the old lady walking a Chihuahua that was so fat its belly almost kept its feet from touching the ground. Sunny giggled about the fat little dog for five minutes.

If it made her laugh like that, he thought, he would eat the damn pickled beets. But he'd damn sure eat something else afterward, because if he got shot, he didn't want pickled beets to be the last thing he tasted.

The late August afternoon was hot when he pulled off the road. A tree-studded field stretched before them. "Let's walk to those trees over there," he said, nodding to a line of trees about a hundred yards away. "See how they're growing, in a line like that? There might be a little creek there."

She looked around. "Shouldn't we ask permission?"

He raised his eyebrows. "Do you see a house anywhere? Who do we ask?"

"Well, all right, but if we get in trouble, it's your fault."

He carried the cooler and most of the food. Sunny slung her backpack on her shoulders, then took charge of the ground cloth and the jar of pickled beets. "I'd better carry these," she said. "You might drop them."

"You could take something else, too," he grunted. This stuff was heavy.

She stretched up to peek in the grocery bag. The apple pie was perched on top of the other stuff. "Nah, you won't drop the pie."

He grumbled all the way to their picnic site, more because she enjoyed it than any other reason. This was the last day she would ever tease him, or he would see that smile, hear that laugh.

"Oh, there *is* a creek!" she exclaimed when they reached the trees. She carefully set the jar of beets down and unfolded the ground cloth, snapping it open in that brisk, economical movement all women seemed to have, and letting it settle on the thick, overgrown grass. A light breeze was blowing, so she anchored the cloth with her backpack on one corner and the jar of beets on the another.

Chance set the cooler and food down and sprawled out on the cloth. "I'm too tired now to enjoy myself," he complained.

She leaned over and kissed him. "You think I don't know what you're up to? Next thing I know you'll get something in your eye, and I'll have to get really, really close to see it. Then your back will need scratching, and you'll have to take off your shirt. Before I know it, we'll both be naked and it'll be time to leave, and we won't have had a bite to eat."

He gave her a quizzical look. "You have this all planned out, don't you?"

"Down to the last detail."

"Suits me." He reached for her, but with a spurt of laughter she scooted out of reach. She picked up the jar of beets and looked at him expectantly.

He flopped back with a groan. "Oh, man. Don't tell me you expect me to try them *now*."

"No, I want you to open the jar so *I* can eat them."

"I thought you said they were nasty."

"They are. I want to see if they're as nasty as I remember." She handed him the jar. "If you'll open them for me, I'll let you eat fried chicken and potato salad to build up your strength before I wring you out and hang you up to dry."

He sat up and took the jar. "In your dreams, little miss 'don't-touch-me-again-you-lech.'" He put some muscle behind the effort, twisting the lid free.

"I've been sandbagging," she said. "This time, don't even bother begging for mercy."

She reached for the jar. The loosened lid came off, and the jar slipped from her hands. He dived for it, not wanting beets all over everything. Just as he moved, the tree beside him exploded, and a millisecond later he heard the blast of the shot.

He twisted in midair, throwing himself on top of Sunny and rolling with her behind the cover of the tree.

Chapter 13

"**S**tay down!" Chance barked, shoving her face into the grass.

Sunny couldn't have moved even if she had wanted to, even if his two hundred-plus pounds hadn't been lying on top of her. She was paralyzed, terror freezing in her veins as she realized her worst nightmare had come true; her father had found them, and Chance was nothing more than an obstacle to be destroyed. That bullet hadn't been aimed at *her*. If she hadn't dropped the jar of beets, if Chance hadn't lunged for it, the slug that blew chunks of wood out of the tree would have blown off half his head.

"Son of a bitch," he muttered above her, his breath stirring her hair. "Sniper."

The earth exploded two inches from her head, clods of dirt flying in her face, tiny pieces of gravel stinging her like bees. Chance literally threw her to the side, rolling with her again; the ground dropped out from beneath her, and her stomach gave a sickening lurch. As suddenly as the fall began, it stopped. She landed hard in three inches of sluggish water.

He had rolled them into the creek, where the banks afforded them more cover. A twist of his powerful body and he was off her, his big pistol in his hand as he flattened himself against the shallow bank. Sunny managed to get to her knees, slipped on the slimy creek bottom, and clambered on her hands and knees to a spot beside him. She felt numb, as if her arms and legs didn't belong to her, yet they were working, moving.

This wasn't real. It couldn't be. How had he found them?

She closed her eyes, fighting the terror. She was a liability to Chance unless she got herself under control. She'd had close calls before and handled herself just fine, but she had never before seen the man she loved almost get killed in front of her. She had never before been pregnant, with so much to lose.

Her teeth were chattering. She clamped her jaw together.

Silence fell over the field. She heard a car drive by on the road, and for a wild moment she wondered why it didn't stop. But why would it? There was nothing the average passerby would notice, no bodies lying around on the highway, no haze of gun smoke hanging over the green grass. There was only silence, as if even the insects had frozen in place, the birds stopped singing; even the breeze had stopped rustling the leaves. It was as if nature held its breath, shocked by the sudden violence.

The shot had come from the direction of the road, but she hadn't seen anyone drive up. They had only just arrived themselves; it was as if whoever had shot at them had already been here, waiting. But that was impossible, wasn't it? The picnic was an impulse, and the location sheer chance; they could just as well have stopped at a park.

The only other explanation that occurred to her was if the shooter had nothing to do with her father. Maybe it was a crazy landowner who shot at trespassers.

If only she had brought her cell phone! But Margreta wasn't due to call her for several more days, and even if she had brought the phone, it would be in her backpack, which was still lying on the ground cloth. The distance of a few yards might as well be a mile. Her pistol was also in the pack; though a pistol was useless against a sniper, she would feel better if she had some means of protection.

Chance hadn't fired; he knew the futility of it even more than she did. His dark gold eyes were scanning the countryside, looking for anything that would give away the assailant's position: a glint of sunlight on the barrel, the color of his clothing, a movement. The extreme angle of the late afternoon sun picked out incredible detail in the trees and bushes, but nothing that would help them.

Only nightfall would help, she thought. If they could just hold out for…how long? Another hour? Two hours, at most. When it was dark, then they could belly down in the little creek and work their way to safety, either upstream or down, it didn't matter.

If they lived that long. The sniper had the advantage. All they had was the cover of a shallow creek bank.

She became aware that her teeth were chattering again. Again she clamped her jaw together to still the movement. Chance spared a glance at her, a split-second assessment before he returned to once again scanning the trees for the sniper. "Are you all right?" he asked, though he obviously knew she was all in one piece. He wasn't asking about her physical condition.

"S-scared spitless," she managed to say.

"Yeah. Me, too."

He didn't look scared, she thought. He looked coldly furious.

He reached out and rubbed her arm, a brief gesture of comfort. "Thank God for those beets," he said.

She almost cried. The beets. She had thoroughly enjoyed teasing him about the beets, but the truth was, when she saw them in the supermarket she had been overcome by an almost violent craving for them. She wanted those beets. She felt as if she could eat the entire jar of them. Could cravings start this early in a pregnancy? If so, then he should thank God not for the beets, but for the beginnings of life forming inside her.

She wished she had told him immediately when her period didn't come. She couldn't tell him now; the news would be too distracting.

If they lived through this, she thought fervently, she wouldn't keep the secret to herself a minute longer.

"It can't be Hauer's men," she blurted. "It's impossible. They couldn't be here ahead of us, because we didn't know we were coming here. It has to be a crazy farmer, or a—a jerk who thought it would be funny to shoot at someone."

"Sweetheart." He touched her arm again, and she realized she was babbling. "It isn't a crazy farmer, or a trigger-happy jerk."

"How do you know? It could be!"

"The sniper's too professional."

Just four words, but they made her heart sink. Chance would know; he had training in this sort of thing.

She pressed her forehead against the grassy bank,

fighting for the courage to do what she had to do. Her mother had died protecting her and Margreta; surely she could be as brave? She couldn't tell Hauer anything about Margreta, so her sister was safe, and if she could save Chance, then dying would be worth it....

Her child would die with her.

Don't make me choose, she silently prayed. *The child or the father.*

If it were just her, she wouldn't hesitate. In the short time she had known Chance—was it really just two weeks?—he had given her a lifetime of happiness and the richness of love. She would gladly give her life in exchange for his.

The life inside her wasn't really a child yet; it was still just a rapidly dividing cluster of cells. No organs or bones had formed, nothing recognizable as a human. It was maybe the size of a pin head. But the potential...oh, the potential. She loved that tiny ball of cells with a fierceness that burned through every fiber of her being, had loved it from the first startled awareness that her period was late. It was as if she had blinked and said, "Oh. Hello," because one second she had been totally unaware of its existence, and the next she had somehow known.

The child or the father. The father or the child.

The words writhed in her brain, echoing, bouncing. She loved them both. How could she choose? She couldn't choose; no woman should have to make such a decision. She hated her father even more for forcing her into this situation. She hated the chromosomes, the DNA, that he had contributed to her existence. He wasn't a father, he had never been a father. He was a monster.

"Give me your pistol." She heard the words, but the voice didn't sound at all like hers.

His head snapped around. "What?" He stared at her as if she had lost her mind.

"Give me the pistol," she repeated. "He—they—don't know we have it. You haven't fired back. I'll tuck it in the back of my jeans and walk out there—"

"The hell you will!" He glared at her. "If you think I—"

"No, listen!" she said urgently. "They won't shoot me. He wants me alive. When they get close enough for me to use the pistol I—"

"No!" He grabbed her by the shirt and hauled her close so they were almost nose to nose. His eyes were almost shooting sparks. "If you make one move to stand up, I swear I'll knock you out. Do you understand me? *I will not let you walk out there.*"

He released her, and Sunny sank back against the creek bank. She couldn't overpower him, she thought bleakly. He was too strong, and too alert to be taken by surprise.

"We have to do something," she whispered.

He didn't look at her again. "We wait," he said flatly. "That's what we do. Sooner or later, the bastard will show himself."

Wait. That was the first idea she'd had, to wait until dark and slip away. But if Hauer had more than one man here, the sniper could keep them pinned down while the other worked his way around behind them—

"Can we move?" she asked. "Up the creek, down the creek—it doesn't matter."

He shook his head. "It's too risky. The creek's shallow. The only place we have enough cover is flat against the bank on this side. If we try to move, we expose ourselves to fire.''

''What if there's more than one?''

''There is.'' He sounded positive. A feral grin moved his lips in a frightening expression. ''At least four, maybe five. I hope it's five.''

She shook her head, trying to understand. Five to two were deadly odds. ''That makes you happy?''

''Very happy. The more the merrier.''

Nausea hit the back of her throat, and she closed her eyes, fighting the urge to vomit. Did he think sheer guts and fighting spirit would keep them alive?

His lean, powerful hand touched her face in a gentle caress. ''Chin up, sweetheart. Time's on our side.''

Now wasn't the time for explanations, Chance thought. The questions would be too angry, the answers too long and complicated. Their situation was delicately balanced between success and catastrophe; he couldn't relax his guard. If he was correct and there were five men out there hunting them—and that was the only explanation, that one of his own men was a traitor and had given Hauer the location of their supposedly impromptu picnic—then they could, at any time, decide to catch him in a pincer movement. With only one pistol, and Sunny to one side of him, he couldn't handle an attack from more than two directions. The third one would get him— and probably Sunny, too. In a fire fight, bullets flew like angry hornets, and most of them didn't hit their target. If a bullet didn't hit its target, that meant it hit something—or someone—else.

His own men would have been stood down, or sent to a bogus location. That was why there hadn't been any return fire when he and Sunny were fired on—no one was there. For that to have happened, the traitor had to be someone in a position of authority, a team leader or higher. He would find out. Oh, yeah, he'd find out. There had been several betrayals over the years, but they hadn't been traceable. One such breach had almost cost Barrie, Zane's wife, her life. Chance had been trying to identify the bastard for four years now, but he'd been too smart. But this time it was traceable. This time, his men would know who had changed their orders.

The traitor must have thought it was worth blowing his cover, to have this opportunity to kill Chance Mackenzie himself. And he should be here in person, to see the job done. Hauer's two men would bring the count to three. Hauer made it four. The only way Hauer could have gotten into the country and moved about as freely and undetected as he had was with inside help—the FBI mole. If Chance were really lucky, the mole was here, too, bringing the count to five.

But they'd made a big mistake. They didn't know about his ace in the hole: Zane. They didn't know he was out there; that was an arrangement Chance had made totally off the record. If Zane wasn't needed, no one would ever know he was there. Chance's men were damn good, world class, but they weren't in Zane's class. No one was.

Zane was a superb strategist; he always had a plan, and a plan to back up his plan. He would have seen in an instant what was going down and been on the phone calling the men back into position from wherever they'd been sent. How long it took them to get here depended on how far away they were, assuming they could get here at all. And after the call Zane would have started moving, ghosting around, searching out Hauer and his men. Every minute that passed increased the odds in Chance's favor.

He couldn't explain any of that to Sunny, not now, not even to ease the white, pinched expression that made him ache to hold her close and reassure her. Her eyes were haunted, their sparkle gone. She had worked her entire life to make certain she was never caught off guard, and yet she had been; he himself had seen to it.

The knowledge was bitter in his mouth. She was terrified of the monster who had relentlessly hunted her all her life, yet she had been willing to walk out there and offer herself as a sacrifice. How many times in the short two weeks he'd known her had she put herself on the line for him? The first time had been when she barely knew him, when she swooped down to grab the snake coiled so close to his feet. She was terrified of snakes, but she'd done it. She was shaking with fear now, but he knew that if he let her, she would do exactly what she'd offered. That kind of courage amazed him, and humbled him.

His head swiveled restlessly as he tried to keep watch in all directions. The minutes trickled past. The sun slid below the horizon, but there was still plenty of light; twilight wouldn't begin deepening for another fifteen, twenty minutes. The darker it was, the more Zane was in his element. By now, he should have taken out at least one, maybe two—

A man stepped out from behind the tree under which Chance and Sunny had intended to have their picnic and aimed a black 9mm automatic at Sunny's head. He didn't say "Drop it" or anything else. He just smiled, his gaze locked with Chance's.

Carefully Chance placed his pistol on the grass. If the gun had been aimed at his own head, he would have taken the risk that his reflexes were faster. He wouldn't risk Sunny's life. As soon as he moved his hand away from the pistol, the black hole in the man's weapon centered between his eyes.

"Surprised?" the man asked softly. At his voice Sunny gasped and whirled, her feet sliding on the slippery creek bottom. Chance reached out and steadied her without taking his gaze from a man he knew very well.

"Not really," he said. "I knew there was someone."

Sunny looked back and forth between them. "Do you *know* him?" she asked faintly.

"Yeah." He should have been prepared for this, he thought. Knowing one of his own men was involved, he should have realized the traitor would have the skill to approach silently, using the same tree that helped shield them as his own cover. Doing so took patience and nerve, because if Chance had happened to move even a few inches to one side, he would have seen the man's approach.

"H-how?" she stammered.

"We've worked together for years," Melvin Darnell said, still smiling. Mel the Man. That was what the others called him, because he would volunteer for any mission, no matter how dangerous. What better way to get inside information? Chance thought.

"You sold out to Hauer," Chance said, shaking his head. "That's low."

"No, that's lucrative. He has men everywhere. The FBI, the Justice Department, the CIA...even here, right under your nose." Mel shrugged. "What can I say? He pays well."

"I misjudged you. I never thought you'd be the type to get a kick out of torture. Or are you chickening out

and leaving as soon as he gets his hands on her?''
Chance nodded his head toward Sunny.

''Nice try, Mackenzie, but it won't work. He's her
father. All he wants is his little girl.'' Mel smirked at
Sunny.

Chance snorted. ''Get a clue. Do you think she'd be
so terrified if all he wanted was to get to know her?''

Mel spared another brief glance in her direction. She
was absolutely colorless, even her lips. There was no
mistaking her fear. He shrugged. ''So I was wrong. I
don't care what he does with her.''

''Do you care that he's a child molester?'' Keep him
talking. Buy time. Give Zane time to work.

''Give it up,'' Mel said cheerfully. ''He could be Hit-
ler's reincarnation and it still wouldn't change the color
of his money. If you think I'm going to develop a conscience—well, you're the one who needs to get a clue.''

There was movement behind Mel. Three men approaching, walking openly now, as if they had nothing
to fear. Two were dressed in suits, one in slacks and an
open-necked shirt. The one in slacks and one of the suits
carried hand guns. The suit would be the FBI informant,
the one in slacks one of Hauer's bloodhounds. The man
in the middle, the one wearing the double-breasted Ital-
ian silk suit, his skin tanned, his light brown hair brushed
straight back—that was Hauer. He was smiling.

''My dear,'' he said jovially when he reached them.
He stepped carefully around the spilled beets, his nose
wrinkling in distaste. ''It is so good to finally meet you.
A father should know his children, don't you think?''

Sunny didn't speak for a moment. She stared at her
father with unconcealed horror and loathing. Beside her,
Chance felt the fear drain out of her, felt her subtly relax.
Extreme terror was like that, sometimes. When one

feared that something would happen, it was the dread and anxiety, the anticipation, that was so crippling. Once the thing actually happened, there was nothing left to fear. He took a firm grip on her arm, wishing she had remained petrified. Sunny was valiant enough when she was frightened; when she thought she had nothing left to lose, there was no telling what she would do.

"I thought you'd be taller," she finally said, looking at him rather dismissively.

Crispin Hauer flushed angrily. He wasn't a large man, about five-eight, and slender. The two men flanking him were both taller. Chance wondered how Sunny had known unerringly how to prick his ego. "Please get out of the mud—if you can bring yourself to leave your lover's side, that is. I recommend it. Head shots can be nasty. You wouldn't want his brains on you, would you? I hear the stain never comes out of one's clothes."

Sunny didn't move. "I don't know where Margreta is," she said. "You might as well kill me now, because I can't tell you anything."

He shook his head in mock sympathy. "As if I believe that." He held out his hand. "You may climb out by yourself, or my men will assist you."

There wasn't much light left, Chance thought. If Sunny could keep delaying her father without provoking him into violence, Zane should be here soon. With Hauer out in the open, Zane must be positioning himself so he could get all four men in his sights.

"Where's the other guy?" he asked, to distract them. "There *are* five of you, aren't there?"

The FBI man and the bloodhound looked around, in the direction of the trees on the opposite side of the road. They seemed vaguely surprised that no one was behind them.

Mel didn't take his attention from Chance. "Don't let him spook you," he said sharply. "Keep your mind on business."

"Don't you wonder where he is?" Chance asked softly.

"I don't give a damn. He's nothing to me. Maybe he fell out of the tree and broke his neck," Mel said.

"Enough," Hauer said, distaste for this squabbling evident in his tone. "Sonia, come out now. I promise you won't like it if my men have to fetch you."

Sunny's contemptuous gaze swept him from head to foot. Unbelievably, she began singing. And the ditty she sang was a cruel little song of the sort gradeschoolers sang to make fun of a classmate they didn't like. "Monkey man, monkey man, itty bitty monkey man. He's so ugly, he's so short, he needs a ladder to reach his butt."

It didn't rhyme, Chance thought in stunned bemusement. Children, crude little beasts that they were, didn't care about niceties such as that. All they cared about was the effectiveness of their taunt.

It was effective beyond his wildest expectation.

Mel Darnell smothered a laugh. The two other men froze, their expressions going carefully blank. Crispin Hauer flushed a dark, purplish red and his eyes bulged until white showed all around the irises. "You bitch!" he screamed, spittle flying, and he grabbed for the gun in the FBI mole's hand.

A giant red flower bloomed on Hauer's chest, accompanied by a strange, dull splat. Hauer stopped as if he had run into a glass wall, his expression going blank.

Mel had excellent reflexes, and excellent training. In that nanosecond before the sound of the shot reached them, Chance saw Mel's finger begin tightening on the trigger, and he grabbed for his own weapon, knowing he wouldn't be fast enough. Then Sunny hit him full force, her entire body crashing into him and knocking him sideways, her scream almost drowning out the thunderous boom of Mel's big-caliber pistol. She clambered off him almost as fast as she had hit him, trying to scramble up the grassy bank to get to Mel before he could fire another round, but Mel never had another opportunity to pull the trigger. Mel never had anything else, not even a second, because Zane's second shot took him dead center of the chest just as his first had taken Hauer.

Then all hell broke loose. Chance's men, finally back in position and with the threat to Chance and Sunny taken care of, opened fire on the remaining two men. Chance grabbed Sunny and flattened her in the creek again, covering her with his own body, holding her there until Zane roared a cease fire and the night was silent.

Sunny sat off to the side of the nightmarish scene, brightly lit now with battery-operated spotlights that picked out garish detail and left stark black shadows. From somewhere, one of the small army of men who suddenly swarmed the field had produced a bucket that he turned upside down for her, providing her with a seat. She was wet and almost unbearably cold, despite the warmth of the late August night. Her muddy clothes were clammy, so the blanket she clutched around her with nerveless fingers didn't do much to help, but she didn't release it.

She hurt, with an all-consuming agony that threatened to topple her off the bucket, but she grimly forced herself to stay upright. Sheer willpower kept her on that bucket.

The men around her were professionals. They were quiet and competent as they dealt with the five bodies that were laid out on the ground in a neat row. They were courteous with the local law enforcement officers who arrived *en force,* sirens blasting, blue lights strobing the night, though there was never any doubt who held jurisdiction.

And Chance was their leader.

That man, the one who had first held a gun on them, had called him "Mackenzie." And several times one or another of the locals had referred to him as Mr. Mackenzie; he had answered, so she knew there was no mistake in the name.

The events of the night were a chaotic blur in her mind, but one fact stood out: this entire scene was a setup, a trap—and she had been the bait.

She didn't want to believe it, but logic wouldn't let her deny it. He was obviously in charge here. He had a lot of men on site, men he commanded, men who could be here only if he had arranged it in advance.

Viewed in the light of that knowledge, everything that had happened since she met him took on a different meaning. She even thought she recognized the cretin who had stolen her briefcase in the Salt Lake City airport. He was cleaned up now, with the same quiet, competent air as the others, but she was fairly certain he was the same man.

Everything had been a setup. Everything. She didn't know how he'd done it, her mind couldn't quite grasp the sphere of influence needed to bring all of this off, but somehow he had manipulated her flights so that she was in the Salt Lake City airport at a certain time, for the cretin to grab her briefcase and Chance to intercept him. It was a hugely elaborate play, one that took skill and money and more resources than she could imagine.

He must have thought she was in cahoots with her

father, she thought with a flash of intuition. This had all
happened after the incident in Chicago, which was un-
doubtedly what had brought her to Chance's notice.
What had his plan been? To make her fall in love with
him and use her to infiltrate her father's organization?
Only it hadn't worked out that way. Not only was she
not involved with her father, she desperately feared and
hated him. So Chance, knowing why Hauer really
wanted her, had adjusted his plan and used her as bait.

What a masterful strategy. And what a superb actor
he was; he should get an Oscar.

There hadn't been anything wrong with the plane at
all. She didn't miss the significance of the timing of their
"rescue." Charlie Jones had just happened to find them
first thing in the morning after she spilled her guts about
her father to Chance the night before. He must have
signaled Charlie somehow.

How easy she had been for him. She had been completely duped, completely taken in by his lovemaking
and charm. He had been a bright light to her, a comet
blazing into her lonely world, and she had fallen for him
with scarcely a whisper of resistance. He must think her
the most gullible fool in the world. The worst of it was,
she was an even bigger fool than he knew, because she
was pregnant with his child.

She looked across the field at him, standing tall in the
glaring spotlights as he talked with another tall, powerful
man who exuded the deadliest air she had ever seen, and
the pain inside her spread until she could barely contain
it.

Her bright light had gone out.

Chance looked around at Sunny, as he had been doing
periodically since the moment she sank down on the

overturned bucket and huddled deep in the blanket someone had draped around her. She was frighteningly white, her face drawn and stark. He couldn't take the time to comfort her, not now. There was too much to do, local authorities to soothe at the same time that he let them know he was the one in control, not they, the bodies to be handled, sweeps initiated at the agencies Mel had listed as having Hauer's moles employed there.

She wasn't stupid; far from it. He had watched her watching the activity around her, watched her expression become even more drawn as she inevitably reached the only conclusion she *could* reach. She had noticed when people called him Mackenzie instead of McCall.

Their gazes met, and locked. She stared at him across the ten yards that separated them, thirty feet of unbridgeable gulf. He kept his face impassive. There was no excuse he could give her that she wouldn't already have considered. His reasons were good; he knew that. But he had used her and risked her life. Being the person she was, she would easily forgive him for risking her life; it was the rest of it, the way he had used her, that would strike her to the core.

As he watched, he saw the light die in her eyes, draining away as if it had never been. She turned her head away from him—

And gutted him with the gesture.

Shaken, pierced through with regret, he turned back to Zane and found his brother watching him with a world of knowledge in those pale eyes. "If you want her," Zane said, "then don't let her go."

It was that simple, and that difficult. Don't let her go. How could he not, when she deserved so much better than what he was?

But the idea was there now. Don't let her go. He

couldn't resist looking at her again, to see if she was still watching him.

She wasn't there. The bucket still sat there, but Sunny was gone.

Chance strode rapidly across to where she had been, scanning the knots of men who stood about, some working, some just observing. He didn't see that bright hair. Damn it, she was just here; how could she disappear so fast?

Easily, he thought. She had spent a lifetime practicing.

Zane was beside him, his head up, alert. The damn spotlights blinded them to whatever was behind them. She could have gone in any direction, and they wouldn't be able to see her.

He looked down to see if he could pick up any tracks, though the grass was so trampled by now that he doubted he would find anything. The bucket gleamed dark and wet in the spotlight.

Wet?

Chance leaned down and swiped his hand over the bucket. He stared at the dark red stain on his fingers and palm. Blood. Sunny's blood.

He felt as if his own blood was draining from his body. My God, she'd been shot, and she hadn't said a word. In the darkness, the blood hadn't been noticeable on her wet clothing. But that had been...how long ago? She had sat there all that time, bleeding, and not told anyone.

Why?

Because she wanted to get away from him. If they had known she was wounded, she would have to be bundled up and taken to a hospital, and she wouldn't be able to escape without having to see him again. When

Sunny walked, she did it clean. No scenes, no excuses, no explanations. She just disappeared.

If he had thought it hurt when she turned away from him, that was nothing to the way he felt now. Desperate fear seized his heart, froze his blood in his veins. "Listen up!" he boomed, and a score of faces, trained to obey his every command, turned his way. "Did anyone see where Sunny went?"

Heads shook, and men began looking around. She was nowhere in sight.

Chance began spitting out orders. "Everyone drop what you're doing and fan out. Find her. She's bleeding. She was shot and didn't tell anyone." As he talked, he was striding out of the glare of the spotlights, his heart in his mouth. She couldn't have gone far, not in that length of time. He would find her. He couldn't bear the alternative.

Chapter 14

Chance blindly paced the corridor outside the surgical waiting room. He couldn't sit down, though the room was empty and he could have had any chair he wanted. If he stopped walking, he thought, he might very well fall down and not be able to stand again. He hadn't known such crippling fear existed. He had never felt it for himself, not even when he looked down the barrel of a weapon pointed at his face—and Mel's hadn't been the first—but he felt it for Sunny. He'd been gripped by it since he found her lying facedown in the grassy field, unconscious, her pulse thready from blood loss.

Thank God there were medics on hand in the field, or she would have died before he could get her to a hospital. They hadn't managed to stop the bleeding, but they had slowed it, started an IV saline push to pump fluid back into her body and raise her plummeting blood pressure, and gotten her to the hospital still alive.

He had been shouldered aside then, by a whole team

of gowned emergency personnel. "Are you any relation to her, sir?" a nurse had asked briskly as she all but manhandled him out of the treatment room.

"I'm her husband," he'd heard himself say. There was no way he was going to allow the decisions for her care to be taken out of his hands. Zane, who had been beside him the entire time, hadn't revealed even a flicker of surprise.

"Do you know her blood type, sir?"

Of course he didn't. Nor did he know the answers to any of the other questions posed by the woman they handed him off to, but he was so numb, his attention so focused on the cubicle where about ten people were working on her, that he barely knew anyone was asking the questions, and the woman hadn't pushed it. Instead, she had patted his hand and said she would come back in a little while when his wife was stabilized. He had been grateful for her optimism. In the meantime, Zane, as ruthlessly competent as usual, had requested that a copy of their file on Sunny be downloaded to his wireless Pocket Pro, so Chance would have all the necessary information when the woman returned with her million and one questions. He was indifferent to the bureaucratic snafu he was causing; the organization would pay for everything.

But the shocks had kept arriving, one piling on top of the other. The surgeon came out of the cubicle, his green paper gown stained red with her blood. "Your wife regained consciousness briefly," he'd said. "She wasn't completely lucid, but she asked about the baby. Do you know how far along she is?"

Chance had literally staggered and braced his hand against the wall for support. "She's pregnant?" he asked hoarsely.

"I see." The surgeon immediately switched gears. "I think she must have just found out. We'll do some tests and take all the precautions we can. We're taking her up to surgery now. A nurse will show you where to wait." He strode away, paper gown flapping.

Zane had turned to Chance, his pale blue eyes laser sharp. "Yours?" he asked briefly.

"Yes."

Zane didn't ask if he was certain, for which Chance was grateful. Zane took it for granted Chance wouldn't be mistaken about something that important.

Pregnant? How? He pinched the bridge of his nose, between his eyes. He knew how. He remembered with excruciating clarity how it felt to climax inside her without the protective sheath of a condom dulling the sensation. It had happened twice—just twice—but once was enough.

A couple of little details clicked into place. He'd been around pregnant women most of his life, with first one sister-in-law and then another producing a little Mackenzie. He knew the symptoms well. He remembered Sunny's sleepiness this afternoon, and her insistence on buying the beets. Those damn pickled beets, he thought; her craving for them—for he was certain now that was why she'd wanted them—had saved his life. Sometimes the weird cravings started almost immediately. He could remember when Shea, Michael's wife, had practically wiped that section of Wyoming clean of canned tuna, a full week before she missed her first period. The sleepiness began soon in a pregnancy, too.

He knew the exact day when he'd gotten her pregnant. It had been the second time he'd made love to her, lying on the blanket in the late afternoon heat. The baby would be born about the middle of May…if Sunny lived.

She had to live. He couldn't face the alternative. He loved her too damn much to even think it. But he had seen the bullet wound in her right side, and he was terrified.

"Do you want me to call Mom and Dad?" Zane asked.

They would drop everything and come immediately if he said yes, Chance knew. The whole family would; the hospital would be inundated with Mackenzies. Their support was total, and unquestioning.

He shook his head. "No. Not yet." His voice was raw, as if he had been screaming, though he would have sworn all his screams had been held inside. If Sunny...if the worst happened, he would need them then. Right now he was still holding together. Just.

So he walked, and Zane walked with him. Zane had seen a lot of bullet wounds, too; he'd taken his share. Chance was the lucky one; he'd been cut a few times, but never shot.

God, there had been so much blood. How had she stayed upright for so long? She had answered questions, said she was all right, even walked around a little before one of the men had found that bucket for her to sit on. It was dark, she had a blanket wrapped around her—that was why no one had noticed. But she should have been on the ground, screaming in pain.

Zane's thoughts were running along the same path. "I'm always amazed," he said, "at what some people can do after being shot."

Contrary to what most people thought, a bullet wound, even a fatal one, didn't necessarily knock the victim down. All cops knew that even someone whose heart had been virtually destroyed by a bullet could still attack and kill *them,* and die only when his oxygen-starved brain died. Someone crazed on drugs could absorb a truly astonishing amount of damage and keep on fighting. On the other side of the spectrum were those who suffered relatively minor wounds and went down as if they had been poleaxed, then screamed unceasingly until they reached the hospital and were given enough drugs to quiet them. It was pure mind over matter, and Sunny had a will like titanium. He only hoped she applied that will to surviving.

It was almost six hours before the tired surgeon approached, the six longest hours of Chance's life. The surgeon looked haggard, and Chance felt the icy claw of dread. No. No—

"I think she's going to make it," the surgeon said, and smiled a smile of such pure personal triumph that Chance knew there had been a real battle in the O.R. "I had to remove part of the liver and resection her small intestine. The wound to the liver is what caused the extensive hemorrhage. We had to replace almost her complete blood volume before we got things under control." He rubbed his hand over his face. "It was touch and go for a while. Her blood pressure bottomed out and she went into cardiac arrest, but we got her right back. Her pupil response is normal, and her vitals are satisfactory. She was lucky."

"Lucky," Chance echoed, still dazed by the combination of good news and the litany of damage.

"It was only a fragment of a bullet that hit her. There must have been a ricochet."

Chance knew she hadn't been hit while he'd had her flattened in the creek. It had to have happened when she knocked him aside and Darnell fired. Evidently Darnell had missed, and the bullet must have struck a rock in the creek and fragmented.

She had been protecting him. Again.

"She'll be in ICU for at least twenty-four hours, maybe forty-eight, until we see if there's a secondary infection. I really think we have things under control, though." He grinned. "She'll be out of here in a week."

Chance sagged against the wall, bending over to clasp his knees. His head swam. Zane's hard hand gripped his shoulder, lending his support. "Thank you," Chance said to the doctor, angling his head so he could see him.

"Do you need to lie down?" the doctor asked.

"No, I'm all right. God! I'm great. She's going to be okay!"

"Yeah," said the doctor, and grinned again.

Sunny kept surfacing to consciousness, like a float bobbing up and down in the water. At first her awareness was fragmented. She could hear voices in the distance, though she couldn't make out any words, and a soft beeping noise. She was also aware of something in her throat, though she didn't realize it was a tube. She had no concept of where she was, or even that she was lying down.

The next time she bobbed up, she could feel smooth cotton beneath her and recognized the fabric as sheets.

The next time she managed to open her eyes a slit, but her vision was blurry and what seemed like a mountain of machinery made no sense to her.

At some point she realized she was in a hospital. There was pain, but it was at a distance. The tube was gone from her throat now. She vaguely remembered it being removed, which hadn't been pleasant, but her sense of time was so confused that she thought she remembered the tube being there after it was removed. People kept coming into the small space that was hers, turning on bright lights, talking and touching her and doing intimate things to her.

Gradually her dominion over her body began to return, as she fought off the effects of anesthesia and drugs. She managed to make a weak gesture toward her belly, and croak out a single word. ''Baby?''

The intensive care nurse understood. ''Your baby's fine,'' he said, giving her a comforting pat, and she was content.

She was horribly thirsty. Her next word was ''Water,'' and slivers of ice were put in her mouth.

With the return of consciousness, though, came the pain. It crept ever nearer as the fog of drugs receded. The pain was bad, but Sunny almost welcomed it, because it meant she was alive, and for a while she had thought she might not be.

She saw the nurse named Jerry the most often. He came into the cubicle, smiling as usual, and said, ''There's someone here to see you.''

Sunny violently shook her head, which was a mistake. It set off waves of agony that swamped the drugs holding them at bay. ''No visitors,'' she managed to say.

It seemed as if she spent days, eons, in the intensive care unit, but when she asked Jerry he said, ''Oh, about thirty-six hours. We'll be moving you to a private room soon. It's being readied now.''

When they moved her, she was clearheaded enough to watch the ceiling tiles and lights pass by overhead. She caught a glimpse of a tall, black-haired man and quickly looked away.

Settling her into a private room was quite an operation, requiring two orderlies, three nurses and half an hour. She was exhausted when everything, including herself, had been transferred and arranged. The fresh bed was nice and cool; the head had been elevated and a pillow tucked under her head. Sitting up even that much made her feel a hundred percent more normal and in control.

There were flowers in the room. Roses, peach ones, with a hint of blush along the edges of their petals, dispensed a spicy, peppery scent that overcame the hospital scents of antiseptics and cleaning fluids. Sunny stared at them but didn't ask who they were from.

"I don't want any visitors," she told the nurses. "I just want to rest."

She was allowed to eat Jell-O, and drink weak tea. On the second day in the private room she drank some broth, and she was placed in the bedside chair for fifteen minutes. It felt good to stand on her own two feet, even for the few seconds it took them to move her from bed to chair. It felt even better when they moved her back to the bed.

That night, she got out of bed herself, though the process was slow and unhappy, and walked the length of the bed. She had to hold on to the bed for support, but her legs remained under her.

The third day, there was another delivery from a florist. This was a bromeliad, with thick, grayish green leaves and a beautiful pink flower blooming in its center. She had never had houseplants for the same reason she had never had a pet, because she was constantly on the move and couldn't take care of them. She stared at the bromeliad, trying to come to grips with the fact that she could have all the houseplants she wanted now. Everything was changed. Crispin Hauer was dead, and she and Margreta were free.

The thought of her sister sent alarm racing through

her. What day was it? When was Margreta due to call? For that matter, where was her cell phone?

On the afternoon of the fourth day, the door opened and Chance walked in.

She turned her head to look out the window. In truth, she was surprised he had given her this long to recover. She had held him off as long as she could, but she supposed there had to be a closing act before the curtain could fall.

She had held her inner pain at bay by focusing on her physical pain, but now it rushed to the forefront. She fought it down, reaching for control. There was nothing to be gained by causing a scene, only her self-respect to lose.

"I've kept your cell phone with me," he said, walking around to place himself between her and the windows, so she had to either look at him or turn her head away again. His conversational opening had guaranteed she wouldn't turn away. "Margreta called yesterday."

Sunny clenched her fists, then quickly relaxed her right hand as the motion flexed the IV needle taped to the back of it. Margreta would have panicked when she heard a man's voice answer instead of Sunny's.

"I talked fast," Chance said. "I told her you'd been shot but would be okay, and that Hauer was dead. I told her I'd bring the phone to you today, and she could call again tonight to verify everything I said. She didn't say anything, but she didn't hang up on me, either."

"Thank you," Sunny said. He had handled the situation in the best possible way.

He was subtly different, she realized. It wasn't just his clothing, though he was now dressed in black slacks and a white silk shirt, while he had worn only jeans, boots, and casual shirts and T-shirts before. His whole demeanor was different. Of course, he wasn't playing a raffish, charming charter pilot any longer. He was himself now, and the reality was what she had always sensed beneath the surface of his charm. He was the man who led some sort of commando team, who exerted enormous influence in getting things done his way. The dangerous edge she had only glimpsed before was in full view now, in his eyes and the authority with which he spoke.

He moved closer to the side of the bed, so close he was leaning against the rail. Very gently, the touch as light as gossamer, he placed his fingertips on her belly. "Our baby is all right," he said.

He knew. Shocked, she stared at him, though she realized she should have known the doctor would tell him.

"Were you going to tell me?" he asked, his golden-brown eyes intent on her face, as if he wanted to catch every nuance of expression.

"I hadn't thought about it one way or the other," she said honestly. She had just been coming to terms with the knowledge herself; she hadn't gotten around to forming any plans.

"This changes things."

"Does it really," she said, and it wasn't a question. "Was *anything* you told me the truth?"

He hesitated. "No."

"There was nothing wrong with the fuel pump."

"No."

"You could have flown us out of the canyon at any time."

"Yes."

"Your name isn't Chance McCall."

"Mackenzie," he said. "Chance Mackenzie."

"Well, that's one thing," she said bitterly. "At least your first name was really your own."

"Sunny…don't."

"Don't what? Don't try to find out how big a fool I am? Were you really an army ranger?"

He sighed, his expression grim. "Navy. Naval Intelligence."

"You arranged for all of my flights to be fouled up that day."

He shrugged an admittance.

"The cretin was really one of your men."

"A good one. The airport security people were mine, too."

She creased the sheet with her left hand. "You knew my father would be there. You had it set up."

"We knew two of his men were trailing us, had been since the television newscast about you aired."

"You arranged that, too."

He didn't say anything.

"Why did we fly all over the country? Why didn't we just stay in Seattle? That would have been less wear and tear on the plane."

"I had to make it look good."

She swallowed. "That day…the picnic. Would you have made love—I mean, had sex—with me with your men watching? Just to make it look good?"

"No. Having an affair with you was necessary, but…private."

"I suppose I should thank you for that, at least. Thank you. Now get out."

"I'm not going anywhere." He sat down in the bedside chair. "If you've finished with the dissection, we need to make some decisions."

"I've already made one. I don't want to see you again."

"Sorry about that, but you aren't getting your wish. You're stuck with me, sweetheart, because that baby inside you is mine."

Chapter 15

Sunny was released from the hospital eight days after the shooting. She could walk, gingerly, but her strength was almost negligible, and she had to wear the night-gown and robe Chance had bought her, because she couldn't stand any clothing around her middle. She had no idea what she was going to do. She wasn't in any condition to catch a flight to Atlanta, not to mention that she would have to travel in her nightgown, but she had to find somewhere to stay. Once she knew she was being released, she got the phone book and called a hotel, made certain the hotel had room service, and booked herself a room there. The hotel had room service; until she was able to take care of herself again, a hotel was the best she could do.

In the hospital she had, at first, entertained a fragile hope that Margreta would come to stay with her and help her until she was recovered. With their father dead, they didn't have to hide any longer. But though Margreta had sounded happy and relieved, she had resisted Sunny's suggestion that she come to Des Moines. They had exchanged telephone numbers, but that was all—and Margreta hadn't called back.

Sunny understood. Margreta would always have problems relating to people, forming relationships with them. She was probably very comfortable with the long-distance contact she had with Sunny, and wanted nothing more. Sunny tried to fight her sadness as she realized she would never have the sister she had wanted, but melancholy too easily overwhelmed her these days.

Part of it was the hormonal chaos of early pregnancy, she knew. She found herself tearing up at the most ridiculous things, such as a gardening show she watched on television one day. She lay in her hospital bed and began thinking how she had always wanted a flower garden but had never been able to have one, and presto, all of a sudden she was feeling sorry for herself and sitting there like an idiot with tears rolling down her face.

Depression went hand in glove with physical recovery, too, one of the nurses told her. It would pass as she got stronger and could do more.

But the biggest part of her depression was Chance. He visited every day, and once even brought along the tall, lethal-looking man she had noticed him talking to the night she was injured. To her surprise, Chance introduced the man as his brother, Zane. Zane had shaken her hand with exquisite gentleness, shown her photos of his pretty wife and three adorable children, and spent half an hour telling her yarns about the exploits of his daughter, Nick. If even half of what he said about the child was true, the world had better brace itself for when she was older.

After Zane left, Sunny was even more depressed. Zane

had what she had always wanted: a family he loved, and who loved him in return.

When he visited, Chance always avoided the subject that lay between them like a coiled snake. He had done what he had done, and no amount of talking would change reality. She had to respect, reluctantly, his lack of any attempt to make excuses. Instead, he talked about his family in Wyoming, and the mountain they all still called home, even though only his parents lived there now. He had four brothers and one sister, a dozen nephews—and one niece, the notorious Nick, whom he obviously adored. His sister was a horse trainer who was married to one of his agents; one brother was a rancher who had married the granddaughter of an old family enemy; another brother was an ex-fighter pilot who was married to an orthopedic surgeon; Zane was married to the daughter of an ambassador; and Joe, his oldest brother, was General Joseph Mackenzie, chairman of the Joint Chiefs of Staff.

That couldn't all be true, she thought, yet the tales had a ring of truth to them. Then she remembered that Chance was a consummate actor, and bitterness would swamp her again.

She couldn't seem to pull herself out of the dismals. She had always been able to laugh, but now she found it difficult to even smile. No matter how she tried to distract herself, the knowledge was always there, engraved on her heart like a curse that robbed her life of joy: Chance didn't love her. It had all been an act.

It was as if part of her had died. She felt cold inside, and empty. She tried to hide it, tried to tell herself the depression would go away if she just ignored it and concentrated on getting better, but every day the grayness inside her seemed to spread and deepen.

The day she was released, the escort finally arrived with a wheelchair and Sunny called a taxi to meet them at the entrance in fifteen minutes. She gingerly lowered herself into the wheelchair, and the escort obligingly placed the small bag containing her few articles of clothing and her backpack on her lap, then balanced the bromeliad on top.

"I'm sure I have to sign some papers before I'm released," Sunny said.

"No, I don't think so," the woman said, checking her orders. "According to this, you're all ready to go. Your husband probably handled it for you."

Sunny bit back the urge to snap that she wasn't married. He hadn't mentioned it, and in truth she hadn't given a thought to how she would pay for her hospital care, but now that she thought about it, she realized Chance had indeed handled all of that. Maybe he thought the least he could do was pick up her tab.

She was surprised he wasn't here, since he'd been so adamant about being a part of the baby's life, and persistent in visiting. For all she knew, she thought, he had been called away on some mysterious spy stuff.

She underestimated him. When the escort rolled her to the doors of the patient discharge area, she saw a familiar dark green Ford Explorer parked under the covered entrance. Chance unfolded his long length from behind the steering wheel and came to meet her.

"I've already called a taxi," she said, though she knew it was a waste of breath.

"Tough," he said succinctly. He took her clothes and the bromeliad and put them in the back of the Explorer, then opened the passenger door.

Sunny began to inch herself forward in the wheelchair seat, preparatory to standing; she had mastered the art when seated in a regular chair, but a wheelchair was trickier. Chance gave her an exasperated look, then leaned down and scooped her up in his powerful arms, handling her weight with ease as he deposited her in the Explorer.

"Thank you," she said politely. She would at least be civil, and his method had been much less painful and time-consuming than hers.

"You're welcome." He buckled the seat belt around her, making certain the straps didn't rub against the surgical incision, then closed the door and walked around to slide under the steering wheel.

"I've booked a room in a hotel," she said. "But I don't know where it is, so I can't give you directions."

"You aren't going to a hotel," he growled.

"I have to go somewhere," she pointed out. "I'm not able to drive, and I can't handle negotiating an airport, so a hotel with room service is the only logical solution."

"No it isn't. I'm taking you home with me."

"No!" she said violently, everything in her rejecting the idea of spending days in his company.

His jaw set. "You don't have a choice," he said grimly. "You're going—even if you kick and scream the whole way."

It was tempting. Oh, it was tempting. Only the thought of how badly kicking would pull at the incision made her resist the idea.

The dime didn't drop until she noticed he was driving to the airport. "Where are we going?"

He gave her an impatient glance. "I told you. Hell, Sunny, you know I don't live in Des Moines."

"All right, so I know where you *don't* live. But I *don't* know where you *do* live." She couldn't resist adding, "And even if you had told me, it would probably be a lie."

This time his glance was sulfuric. "Wyoming," he said through gritted teeth. "I'm taking you home to Wyoming."

She was silent during the flight, speaking only when necessary and then only in monosyllables. Chance studied her when her attention was on the landscape below, his sunglasses hiding his eyes. They had flown around so much during the time they'd been together that it felt natural to once again be in the plane with her, as if they were where they belonged. She had settled in with a minimum of fussing and no complaints, though he knew she had to be exhausted and uncomfortable.

She looked so frail, as if a good wind would blow her away. There wasn't any color in her cheeks or lips, and she had dropped a good ten pounds that she didn't need to lose. The doctor had assured him that she was recovering nicely, right on schedule, and that while her pregnancy was still too new for any test to tell them anything about the baby's condition, they had taken all precautions and he had every confidence the baby would be fine.

As thrilled as he was about the baby, Chance was more worried that the pregnancy would sap her strength and slow her recovery. She needed all the resources she could muster now, but nature would ensure that the developing child got what it needed first. The only way he could be confident she was getting what *she* needed was if he arranged for her to be watched every minute, and coddled and spoiled within an inch of her life. The best place for that was Mackenzie's Mountain.

He had called and told them he was bringing Sunny

there, of course. He had told them the entire situation, that she was pregnant and he intended to marry her, but that she was still mad as hell at him and hadn't forgiven him. He had set quite a task for himself, getting back in Sunny's good graces. But once he had her on the Mountain, he thought, he could take his time wearing her down.

Mary, typically, was ecstatic. She took it for granted Sunny would forgive him, and since she had been prodding him about getting married and giving her more grandchildren, she probably thought she was getting everything she wanted.

Chance was going to do everything he could to see that she did, because what she wanted was exactly what he wanted. He'd always sworn he would never get married and have children, but fate had stepped in and arranged things otherwise. The prospect of getting married scared him—no, it terrified the hell out of him, so much so that he hadn't even broached the subject to Sunny. He didn't know how to tell her what she needed to know about him, and he didn't know what she would do when she found out, if she would accept his proposal or tell him to drop dead.

The only thing that gave him hope was that she'd said she loved him. She hadn't said it since she found out how he'd set her up, but Sunny wasn't a woman who loved lightly. If there was a spark of love left in her, if he hadn't totally extinguished it, he would find a way to fan it to life.

He landed at the airstrip on Zane's property, and his heart gave a hard thump when he saw what was waiting for them. Even Sunny's interest was sparked. She sat up straighter, and for the first time since she'd been shot he saw a hint of that lively interest in her face. "What's going on?" she asked.

His spirits lifting, he grinned. "Looks like a welcoming party."

The entire Mackenzie clan was gathered by the airstrip. Everyone. Josh and Loren were there from Seattle with their three sons. Mike and Shea and their two boys. Zane and Barrie, each holding one of the twins. And there was Joe, decked out in his Air Force uniform with more rows of fruit salad on it than should be allowed. How he had carved time out of his schedule to come here, Chance didn't know—but then, Joe could do damn near anything he wanted, since he was the highest ranking military officer in the nation. Caroline, standing beside him and looking positively chic in turquoise capri pants and white sandals—and also looking damn good for her age—had probably had a harder time getting free. She was one of the top-ranked physicists in the world. Their five sons were with him, and John, the oldest, wasn't the only one this time who had a girlfriend with him. Maris and Mac stood together; Mac had his arm draped protectively around Maris's slight frame. And Mom and Dad were in the middle of the whole gang, with Nick perched happily in Wolf's arms.

Every last one of them, even the babies, held a balloon.

"Oh, my," Sunny murmured. The corners of her pale mouth moved upwards in the first smile he had seen in eight days.

He cut the motor and got out, then went to the other door and carefully lifted Sunny out. She was so bemused by the gathering that she put her arm around his neck.

That must have been the signal. Wolf leaned down and set Nick on her feet. She took off toward Chance like a shot, running and skipping and shrieking his name in the usual litany. "UncaDance, UncaDance, Unca-*Dance!*" The balloon she was holding bobbed like a mad thing. The whole crowd started forward in her wake.

In seconds they were surrounded. He tried to introduce everyone to Sunny, but there was too much of a hubbub for him to complete a sentence. His sisters-in-law, bless them, were laughing and chattering as if they had known her for years; the men were flirting; Mary was beaming; and Nick's piping voice could be heard above everyone. "Dat's a weally, weally pwetty dwess." She fingered the silk robe and beamed up at Sunny.

John leaned down and whispered something in Nick's ear. "*Dress,*" she said, emphasizing the *r.* "Dat's a weally, weally pwetty *dress.*"

Everyone cheered, and Nick glowed.

Sunny laughed.

Chance's heart jumped at the sound. His throat got tight, and he squeezed his eyes shut for a second. When he opened them, Mary had taken control.

"You must be exhausted," she was saying to Sunny in her sweet, Southern-accented voice. "You don't have to worry about a thing, dear. I have a bed all ready for you at the house, and you can sleep as long as you want. Chance, carry her along to the car, and be careful with her."

"Yes, ma'am," he said.

"Wait!" Nick wailed suddenly. "I fordot de sign!"

"What sign?" Chance asked, gently shifting Sunny so he could look down at his niece.

She fished in the pocket of her little red shorts and pulled out a very crumpled piece of paper. She stretched up on her tiptoes to hand it to Sunny. "I did it all by myself," she said proudly. "Gamma helped."

Sunny unfolded the piece of paper.

"I used a wed cwayon," Nick informed her. "Because it's de pwettiest."

"It certainly is," Sunny agreed. She swallowed audibly. Chance looked down to see the paper shaking in her hand.

The letters were misshapen and wobbly and all different sizes. The little girl must have labored over them for a long time, with Mary's expert and patient aid, because the words were legible. "'Welcome home Sunny,'" Sunny read aloud. Her face began to crumple. "That's the most beautiful sign I've ever seen," she said, then buried her face against Chance's neck and burst into tears.

"Yep," Michael said. "She's pregnant, all right."

It was difficult to say who fell more in love with whom, Sunny with the Mackenzies, or the Mackenzies with her. Once Chance placed her in the middle of the king-sized bed Mary had made up for her—he didn't tell her it was his old bedroom—Sunny settled in like a queen holding court. Instead of lying down to sleep, she propped herself up on pillows, and soon all of the women and most of the younger kids were in there, sitting on the bed and on the floor, some even in chairs. The twins were working their way from one side of the bed to the other and back again, clutching the covers for support and babbling away to each other in what Barrie called their "twin talk." Shea had Benjy down on the floor, tickling him, and every time she stopped he would shriek, "More! More!" Nick sat cross-legged on the bed, her "wed cwayon" in hand as she studiously worked on another sign. Since the first one had been such a resounding success, this one was for Barrie, and she was embellishing it with lopsided stars. Loren, being a doctor, wanted the details of Sunny's wound and present condition. Caroline was doing an impromptu fashion consultation, brushing Sunny's hair and swirling it on top of her head, with some very sexy tendrils curling loose on her slender neck. Maris, her dark eyes glowing, was telling Sunny all about her own pregnancy, and Mary was overseeing it all.

Leaving his family to do what they did best, weave a magic spell of warmth and belonging, Chance walked down to the barn. He felt edgy and worried and a little panicked, and he needed some peace and quiet. When everything quieted down tonight, he had to talk to Sunny. He couldn't put it off any longer. He prayed desperately that she could forgive him, that what he had to tell her didn't completely turn her against him, because he loved her so much he wasn't certain he could live without her. When she had buried her face against him and cried, his heart had almost stopped because she had turned *to* him instead of away from him.

She had laughed again. That sound was the sweetest sound he'd ever heard, and it had almost unmanned him. He couldn't imagine living without being able to hear her laugh.

He folded his arms across the top of a stall door and rested his head on them. She had to forgive him. She had to.

"It's tough, isn't it?" Wolf said in his deep voice, coming up to stand beside Chance and rest his arms on top of the stall door, too. "Loving a woman. And it's the best thing in the world."

"I never thought it would happen," Chance said, the

words strained. "I was so careful. No marriage, no kids. It was going to end with me. But she blindsided me. I fell for her so fast I didn't have time to run."

Wolf straightened, his black eyes narrowed. "What do you mean, 'end with you'? Why don't you want kids? You love them."

"Yeah," Chance said softly. "But they're Mackenzies."

"You're a Mackenzie." There was steel in the deep voice.

Tiredly, Chance rubbed the back of his neck. "That's the problem. I'm not a real Mackenzie."

"Do you want to walk in the house and tell that little woman in there that you're not her son?" Wolf demanded sharply.

"*Hell*, no!" No way would he hurt her like that.

"You're my son. In all the ways that matter, you're mine."

The truth of that humbled Chance. He rested his head on his arms again. "I never could understand how you could take me in as easily as you did. You know what kind of life I led. You may not know the details, but you have a good general idea. I wasn't much more than a wild animal. Mom had no idea, but you did. And you still brought me into your home, trusted me to be around both Mom and Maris—"

"And that trust was justified, wasn't it?" Wolf asked.

"But it might not have been. You had no way of knowing." Chance paused, looking inward at the darkness inside him. "I killed a man when I was about ten, maybe eleven," he said flatly. "That's the wild kid you brought home with you. I stole, I lied, I attacked other kids and beat them up, then took whatever it was they had that I wanted. That's the kind of person I am. That kid will always live inside me.''

Wolf gave him a sharp look. ''If you had to kill a man when you were ten, I suspect the bastard deserved killing.''

''Yeah, he deserved it. Kids who live in the street are fair game to perverts like that.'' He clenched his hands. ''I have to tell Sunny. I can't ask her to marry me without her knowing what she'll be getting, what kind of genes I'll be passing on to her children.'' He gave a harsh laugh. ''Except I don't know what kind of genes they are. I don't know what's in my background. For all I know my mother was a drugged-out whore and—''

''Stop right there,'' Wolf said, steel in his voice.

Chance looked up at him, the only father he had ever known, and the man he respected most in the world.

''I don't know who gave birth to you,'' Wolf said. ''But I do know bloodlines, son, and you're a thoroughbred. Do you know what I regret most in my life? Not finding you until you were fourteen. Not feeling your hand holding my finger when you took your first step. Not getting up with you in the night when you were teething, or when you were sick. Not being able to hold you the way you needed holding, the way all kids need holding. By the time we got you I couldn't do any of that, because you were as skittish as a wild colt. You didn't like for us to touch you, and I tried to respect that.

''But one thing you need to know. I'm more proud of you than I've ever been of anything in my life, because you're one of the finest men I've ever known, and you had to work a lot harder than most to get to where you are. If I could have had my pick of all the kids in the world to adopt, I still would have chosen you.''

Chance stared at his father, his eyes wet. Wolf Mackenzie put his arms around his grown son and hugged him close, the way he had wanted to do all these years. "I would have chosen you," he said again.

Chance entered the bedroom and quietly closed the door behind him. The crowd had long since dispersed, most to their respective homes, some spending the night here or at Zane's or Michael's. Sunny looked tired, but there was a little color in her cheeks.

"How do you feel?" he asked softly.

"Exhausted," she said. She looked away from him. "Better."

He sat down beside her on the bed, taking care not to jostle her. "I have some things I need to tell you," he said.

"If it's an explanation, don't bother," she shot back. "You used me. Fine. But *damn* you, you didn't have to take it as far as you did! Do you know how it makes me feel that I was such a fool to fall in love with you, when all you were doing was playing a game? Did it stroke your ego—"

He put his hand across her mouth. Above his tanned fingers, her gray eyes sparked pure rage at him. He took a deep breath. "First and most important thing is: I love you. That wasn't a game. I started falling the minute I saw you. I tried to stop it but—" He shrugged that away and got back to the important part. "I love you so much I ache inside. I'm not good enough for you, and I know it—"

She swatted his hand aside, scowling at him. "What? I mean, I agree, after what you did, but—what do you mean?"

He took her hand and was relieved when she didn't pull away from him. "I'm adopted," he said. "That part's fine. It's the best. But I don't know who my biological parents are or anything about them. They—she—tossed me into the street and forgot about me. I grew up wild in the streets, and I mean literally in the streets. I don't remember ever having a home until I was about fourteen, when I was adopted. I could come from the trashiest people on the planet, and probably do, otherwise they wouldn't have left me to starve to death in the gutter. I want to spend the rest of my life with you, but if you marry me, you have to know what you'll be getting.''

''What?'' she said again, as if she couldn't understand what he was telling her.

''I should have asked you to marry me before,'' he said, getting it all out. ''But—hell, how could I ask anyone to marry me? I'm a wild card. You don't know what you're getting with me. I was going to let you go, but then I found out about the baby and I couldn't do it. I'm selfish, Sunny. I want it all, you and our baby. If you think you can take the risk—''

She drew back, such an incredulous, outraged look on her face that he almost couldn't bear it. ''I don't believe this,'' she sputtered, and slapped him across the face.

She wasn't back to full strength, but she still packed a wallop. Chance sat there, not even rubbing his stinging jaw. His heart was shriveling inside him. If she wanted to hit him again, he figured he deserved it.

''You fool!'' she shouted. ''For God's sake, my father was a *terrorist!* That's the heritage *I'm* carrying around, and you're worried because you *don't know who your parents were?* I wish to hell I didn't know who my father was! I don't believe this! I thought you didn't love me! Everything would have been all right if I'd known you love me!''

Chance uttered a startled, profound curse, one of Nick's really, really bad words. Put in those terms, it did sound incredibly trivial. He stared at her lovely, outraged face, and the weight lifted off his chest as if it had never been. Suddenly he wanted to laugh. "I love you so much I'm half crazy with it. So, will you marry me?"

"I have to," she said grumpily. "You need a keeper. And let me tell you one thing, Chance Mackenzie, if you think you're still going to be jetting all over the world getting stabbed and shot at while you get your adrenaline high, then you'd better think again. You're going to stay home with me and this baby. Is that understood?"

"Understood," he said. After all, the Mackenzie men always did whatever it took to keep their women happy.

Epilogue

Sunny was asleep, exhausted from her long labor and then the fright and stress of having surgery when the baby wouldn't come. Her eyes were circled with fatigue, but Chance thought she had never been more beautiful. Her face, when he laid the baby in her arms, had been exalted. Until he died, he would never forget that moment. The medical personnel in the room had faded away to nothing, and it had been just him and his wife and their child.

He looked down at the wrinkled, equally exhausted little face of his son. The baby slept as if he had run a marathon, his plump hands squeezed into fierce little fists. He had downy black hair, and though it was difficult to judge a newborn's eye color, he thought they might turn the same brilliant gray as Sunny's.

Zane poked his head in the door. "Hi," he said softly. "I've been sent to reconnoiter. She's still asleep, huh?"

Chance looked at his wife, as sound asleep as the baby. "She had a rough time."

"Well, hell, he weighs ten pounds and change. No wonder she needed help." Zane came completely into the room, smiling as he examined the unconscious little face. "Here, let me hold him. He needs to start meeting the family." He took the baby from Chance, expertly cradling him to his chest. "I'm your uncle Zane. You'll see me around a lot. I have two little boys who are just itching to play with you, and your aunt Maris—you'll meet her in a minute—has one who's just a little older than you are. You'll have plenty of playmates, if you ever open your eyes and look around."

The baby's eyelids didn't flicker open, even when Zane rocked him. His pink lips moved in an unconscious sucking motion.

"You forget fast how little they are," Zane said softly as he smoothed his big hand over the baby's small round skull. He glanced up at Chance and grinned. "Looks like I'm still the only one who knows how to make a little girl."

"Yeah, well, this is just my first try."

"It'll be your last one, too, if they're all going to weigh ten pounds," came a voice from the bed. Sunny sighed and pushed her hair out of her eyes, and a smile spread across her face as she spied her son. "Let me have him," she said, holding out her arms.

There was a protocol to this sort of thing. Zane passed the baby to Chance, and Chance carried him to Sunny, settling him in her arms. No matter how often he saw it, he was always touched by the communion between mother and new baby, that absorbed look they both got as if they recognized each other on some basic, primal level.

"Are you feeling well enough for company?" Zane asked. "Mom's champing at the bit, wanting to get her hands on this little guy."

"I feel fine," Sunny said, though Chance knew she didn't. He had to kiss her, and even now there was that flash of heat between them, even though their son was only a few hours old. She pulled back, laughing a little and blushing. "Get away from me, you lech," she said, teasing him, and he laughed.

"What are you going to name him?" Zane demanded. "We've been asking for months, but you never would say. It can't stay a secret much longer."

Chance trailed his finger down the baby's downy cheek, then he put his arms around both Sunny and the baby and held them close. Life couldn't get much better than this.

"Wolf," he said. "He's little Wolf."

* * * * *

♥ SILHOUETTE®
*Super*ROMANCE™

LEAVING ENCHANTMENT by CJ Carmichael
The Birth Place

When an abandoned baby is found, paediatrician Joanna Weston is outraged when she finds out her handsome neighbour is the child's deadbeat dad. Until she sees the tender concern he shows the daughter he didn't know he had. The daughter he'll now do anything to keep.

THE GIFTS OF CHRISTMAS
Three great stories from three great authors – the perfect gift for Christmas!

Stuck with Each Other – Jan Freed
Undercover Santa – Janice Kay Johnson
Epiphany – Margot Early

A BABY IN THE HOUSE by Pamela Bauer
9 Months Later

Dr Garret Donovan had his life all mapped out, or so he thought. But that was before he and Krystal Graham got together. Now he has to put his plans aside to make room for a surprise addition to the family.

A HOME OF HER OWN by Brenda Novak

When Lucky was ten, her mother, Red, married Morri Caldwell, a wealthy and much older man. Mike Hill, his grandson, feels that Red and her kids alienated Morris from his family. Now Lucky's back, which means Mike has a new neighbour. One he doesn't want to like…

On sale from 21st October 2005

Available at most branches of WHSmith, Tesco, ASDA, Borders, Eason, Sainsbury's and most bookshops

Visit our website at www.silhouette.co.uk

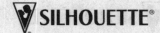

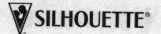 **SILHOUETTE®**

1005/23b

SPECIAL EDITION™

THE TRUTH ABOUT THE TYCOON
by Allison Leigh

Worldly tycoon Dane Rutherford was accustomed to handling billion-dollar negotiations, though one small-town girl had just got the better of him. He'd come to Montana with only one goal in mind—revenge. But his plans changed the second that Hadley Golightly crashed into his life...

THE DEVIL YOU KNOW
by Laurie Paige

Sparks sizzled from the moment beautiful computer whiz Veronica Dalton laid eyes on Adam Smith. But a year after their initial meeting, one torrid night of passion together left them with more than they bargained for: a marriage licence!

THE BRIDESMAID AND THE BEST MAN
by Victoria Pade

Northbridge Nuptials

For a guy who'd sworn off women, trying to ignore the way Kit made his libido stand up and take notice was proving impossible. And regardless of her jitters about weddings, Addison couldn't help but imagine joining her in a trip down the aisle...as her husband!

Don't miss out!
On sale from 21st October 2005

Available at most branches of WHSmith, Tesco, ASDA, Borders, Eason, Sainsbury's and most bookshops

Visit our website at www.silhouette.co.uk

SILHOUETTE®

Desire™ 2 in 1

DYNASTIES: THE DANFORTHS

TERMS OF SURRENDER by Shirley Rogers

David Taylor and amnesiac Tanya Winters were to live at Cotton Creek Plantation for one year or lose their inheritance. The bedroom became a passionate battleground, pleasure the ultimate prize. But one day Tanya's memory might return…what then?

SHOCKING THE SENATOR
by Leanne Banks

Nicola Granville was Abe Danforth's campaign manager and more. For months her affair with the charismatic senator was conducted in secret. Professionals by day and intimate lovers by night. *Until she took a home pregnancy test…*

BEST-KEPT LIES by Lisa Jackson

Kurt Striker believed Randi McCafferty would always be in danger until she revealed the identity of her child's father, so he was determined to discover her deepest secret…any way he could.

WILD IN THE MOMENT by Jennifer Greene

A fierce blizzard and a sexy stranger were exactly what Daisy Campbell needed. She'd never expected to throw caution—and her clothes—to the wind, but they had to stay warm somehow! Could one night by a fire turn into a red-hot forever?

On sale from 21st October 2005

Available at most branches of WHSmith, Tesco, ASDA, Borders, Eason, Sainsbury's and most bookshops

Visit our website at www.silhouette.co.uk

Three beautiful daughters,
three heartwarming tales.

After years in prison for a crime he didn't commit,
Major Brad Henderson is finally released. Now he's
determined to find the three beautiful daughters he was
forced to abandon – and to reunite them all for a very
special Christmas. Little does he know that his daughters
have lived very separate lives – and that each has her
own special story to tell.

By bestselling authors

Jasmine Cresswell
Tara Taylor Quinn
& Kate Hoffmann

On sale 21st October 2005

Christmas is magical – when you share it with someone special

SHENANDOAH CHRISTMAS by Lynnette Kent

After his wife dies, Ben Tremaine doesn't think the holidays will ever be festive again for his children – or him. But when Caitlyn Gregory arrives and puts smiles on their faces, he starts to wonder if Christmas wishes can come true after all.

THE CHRISTMAS WIFE by Sherryl Lewis

A single father has enough trouble juggling career, home and family – let alone the attraction he feels for a former high school classmate. But perhaps a trip down memory lane is just what he needs to make this Christmas the best – and most romantic – ever.

On sale 21st October 2005

Introducing a very special holiday collection

Inside you'll find

Roses for Christmas *by Betty Neels*

Eleanor finds herself working with the forceful Fulk van Hensum from her childhood – and sees that he hasn't changed. So why does his engagement to another woman upset her so much?

Once Burned *by Margaret Way*

Celine Langton ends her relationship with Guy Harcourt thinking he deserves someone more sophisticated. But why can't she give back his ring?

A Suitable Husband *by Jessica Steele*

When Jermaine begins working with Lukas Tavinor, she realises he's the kind of man she's always dreamed of marrying. Does it matter that her sister feels the same way?

On sale Friday 7th October 2005

COMFORT AND JOY by Margaret Moore
1860 Llanwyllan, Wales

After a terrible accident, Griffin Branwynne gives up on the joys of Christmas—until the indomitable Gwendolyn Davies arrives on his doorstep and turns his world upside-down. Can the earl resist a woman who won't take no for an answer?

LOVE AT FIRST STEP by Terri Brisbin
1199 England

While visiting friends in England for the holidays, Lord Gavin MacLeod casts his eye upon the mysterious Elizabeth. She is more noble beauty than serving wench, and Gavin vows to uncover her past—at any cost!

A CHRISTMAS SECRET by Gail Ranstrom
1819 Oxfordshire, England

Miss Charity Wardlow expects a marriage proposal from her intended while attending a Christmas wedding. But when Sir Andrew MacGregor arrives at the manor, Charity realises that she prefers this Scotsman with the sensual smile…

On sale 2nd December 2005